Three Days of the Animal Olympians

Fight WITH *Nature*
by **Drats**

PAPERBACK EDITION
* * * * *
PUBLISHED BY:
Exaggerist Edutainment, USA
Copyright © 2015 by Jaya Drats
JayaDrats@Hotmail.com

= Suggestion =
The author suggests that readers enjoy this novel in three consecutive days; adhering to completing Day 1, Day 2, and Day 3 respectively on each day in a row, to experience the adventure, sheer terror, and undying hope over the same duration of time as the animals and the athletes do.

= Disclaimer =
The author created most of these characters from fictitious imagination.

=WARNING =
Adult Reading Material for Mature Humans Only

= Dedication =
To the smallest, weakest, and most frail of Earth's creatures; and to those who will fight with their all to protect them.

3DAO
Fight WITH *Nature!*

Three Days of the Animal Olympians
Fight WITH *Nature*
by Drats

Table of Contents

The Humans
Shrike == Manager
Sara == Psychologist
Cruise == Commander
Lohan == 2nd in Command
Joaquin == 3rd in Command
Gwen == Holder of Stocks
James == Hurdler
Daniel == Diver
Colt == Equestrian
Tara == One of many Athletes mentioned
Dumpy == One of many Commandos mentioned
and Jay == … just an innocent Hiker

The Animals
Western Screech-owl
American Marten
Cougar
and the rest of the Animal Kingdom

Cover art and editing by Stingray, Edmonton, Alberta; and Jaya Drats, Auckland, NZ
Shrike Model: The actual Chelonia from *Humans Need Three Hands*

Chapter 1

Crash!

Bright puffy-white clouds streak across the Rocky
Mountain sky. A lone hiker summits a ridge and looks far below
upon the golden majesty that is Yellowstone National Park. He
runs his tongue over his teeth, takes a swig of water and a deep
breath, and then stretches. A shiny reflection captures his
attention. It's so far away -- miles and miles away, but there it is
again… and again. Curiosity gets the better of Jay the hiker, so
he slides his heavy pack down his body, resting it on a boulder.
He takes out his binoculars as a hawk darts by. He focuses the
lens to see what looks like little teeny mites far below ---- a crew
of about 100 colorfully uniformed teammates load a heavy gray
cargo plane on a tarmac.

Down on the sun-drenched airstrip, a petite, beautiful
woman comes marching through the buzzing crowd giving
concise, direct, pragmatic orders. U.S. Olympic medalists in
smartly designed sweat suits clutch their competition gear,
reacting and moving quickly to load the gaping maw of the
massive C-17 military transport jet.

A hurdler with two golds dangling low from his neck says,
"Wow Shrike, you really got the hang of this. You former GI?"
The stunning brunette, with piercing eyes glimmering in the
sunshine, responds as a group of athletes spontaneously
assemble for attendance before her on the breezy airfield.

Shrike answers the hurdler, "There has never been a just
war. The only war I could ever justify would be a war to save
nature, to protect wildlife. I would fight and die for that, but we
don't fight those kind of battles in the U.S., so no, never been
in."

"Me too." a couple of the athletes agree, "They're
innocents."

The lanky hurdler, James, retorts, "I'd defend all innocents,
animal or people."

Shrike counters, "That's what's tricky: Animals are always innocent; adult people rarely are."

A tall handsome diver concurs, "Only the young, to a certain age, are innocent. The rest of us, including the old, need to take responsibility for wars and why we let them happen."

James, and a few of the other athletes shake their heads in disagreement with Daniel. Shrike throws her hands up in the air in exasperation, realizing that she should be ejecting orders from her mouth, not engaging in philosophical debates. Nearby, Shrike's computer sits on a steamer trunk full of badminton and table tennis racquets. Sara, the team counselor (technically a psychologist with her PhD from Harvard), hears Skype chime on.

"Shrike. You're being Skyped," she reports.

Shrike hands her clipboard off to one of the athletes and goes over to find her current boyfriend onscreen, wearing a sun hat and sweating profusely.

"How's it going honey?" Shrike asks over the wind and noise all around the open airfield.

He answers with a slight whine, "Okay, but I still can't track down that lifer."

Shrike replies supportively, "Stiff upper lip, and you won't get gripped."

He doesn't crack a smile nor does he condone or enable her supportive 'loving' behavior.

Shrike continues, "We are loading right now so I have to crank. The entire group of U.S. medalists from the last Olympics and I are heading for a photo op with the President. Be safe."

He replies "You too" in a dry, glum, and emotionless way, like most hardcore bird tickers.
Shrike signs off of Skype and turns to get back to work, almost running into the observant shrink.

Languid and delicate, Sara says, "Where is he and is he going after criminals?"

Shrike laughs heartily, "No, he's in Peru looking for some bird he has never seen before, so that's what a 'lifer' is … in this context."

The arresting and thin Adonis of a diver butts in, "Wow, and I thought I wasted a lot of my life diving."

Several of the other athletes laugh under the cerulean sky, as they file by with gear and equipment, in a quick and orderly manner. Shrike lets it roll off her shoulders, and starts moving around at full speed. It is amazing how much work she can get done.

The crew moves around in the cockpit and about the outside of the aircraft for final inspection; like miniature worker insects grooming a bloated, over-sized queen.
Shrike bats her eyes at the diver as he gives her a second look. By her own bias she had presumed him to be gay, being a diver after all, but the diver's mouth waters as he looks into her eyes. Daniel can't help but notice Shrike; A real and total knockout in any circle. Not one for oblivion, she locks on to him for an instant. She can feel it.

Sara observes aloofly, then prods "Hunk of a boy there, huh?"

Shrike reacts to Sara with surprise, unaware of being noticed. She pries her eyes off of the diver's butt, then slowly turns and looks deeply into Sara's scarab beetle eyes.

Shrike admits, "The last four guys I've dated have been the top four birders in America."

Sara says softly, "What? You?"

Shrike fires, "I shit you not!" then nods her head with a bit of embarrassment. She turns and yells to the group, "Caps on all pointed objects. Everything! Safety first! No pokey!"

Sara says, "Why?"
Shrike thinks for a second. She doesn't know.

Sara queries, "Because you feel like they are ultra nerds and you have complete control and power?"

Shrike laughs really loud, and then her face goes flame red. "I also like the fact that I am much prettier than any of the birder girls and the tickers' wives."

Sara says, "I bet you are. They don't like you one bit . . . hanging around their weak and susceptible bird experts. It's like Ginger Grant dating The Professor; or Marilyn married to Salinger, or Steinbeck, or whoever that *Tropic of* whatever guy was."

They laugh together like old chums, this conversation completely devoid of any hint of animosity or aggression.

Shrike gives a few more verbal commands and some hand signals to the hustling athletes, then takes a swig of her iced tea from the bottle and wipes her moist brow with her soft forearm and wrist.

Perceptive Sara pauses, instantly picking up on Shrike's insecurity and wondering "Not to pry but even though you work as the Athletic Coordinator of the Olympic Team, you date only birders? I thought you might be into athletes, ya know?"

Shrike doesn't respond, but instead thinks for a second. Though Sara feels like she's starting to bond with Shrike, she already hatches her own doubts about the Olympic Team Manager's stability.

Sara suggests clinically, under her breath, "You need to take lithium and balance out your brain."
Shrike gives her a dismissive glare.

Sara continues, "Seriously, all of these hot and available athletes about?"

Shrike looks scared, like she just saw a freaky clown. Sara immediately realizes how insecure Shrike is about that idea. She has an internal nervousness, masked by her external power and looks.

Shrike says pensively, in a very soft, vulnerable whisper "What's that diver's name?"
She follows him with her eyes, but doesn't move her head. Shrike's cell rings.

Sara spits the name out, "It's Daniel," before Shrike can get the phone to her ear.

Shrike acknowledges Sara, then answers the call, "Hello . . . Yes, . . . I understand . . . We are boarding now. We left Colorado Springs eleven hours ago and now we are just loading the last of the equipment in Jackson Hole. Shrike Tomial. Correct. Shrike, Tomial. Everything is set and on time. Thank you sir," and hangs up.

Shrike yells, "Don't forget; all the excess equipment comes not only for the photo shoot, but also to give away ceremonially to the world of Olympic Teams that will be represented there at the ceremony. Stack your gear by your seat so you can autograph with the provided markers while we are en route to D.C. I for one am excited about being in The White House."

Now laden with everything from an equestrian horse to a sailboat, the C-17 cargo plane, bathed in sunlight, finally looks packed. Athletes scramble around to drag their equipment bags to their seats and between their legs as the first engine winds on.

From the black shadows, an inconspicuous fire team of three commandos sneaks out of the thick trees near the edge of the tarmac and onto the plane. Their uniforms lack any contrast against the pitch blackness of the deep shadows and pavement, and the crew squint in the blinding, reflected daytime glare, unable to see much out of the windows. The horse neighs, but none of the 117 athletes, nor Shrike or Sara, notice the sneaky commandos scurrying low along the ground. They slip in like Vaselined ninjas, tightly wedge into the fuselage, and freeze in silence as the final automated hatches close and lock. The plane steeply takes off and up over the magnificent Rocky Mountains. On the ground, the Air Force cadet assigned to monitor the activities, watches the plane take off with a broad smile of satisfaction, unaware of the stowaways. He gets into his patrol vehicle and drives away past the glowing greenish yellow grasses and runway lights.

Hiking his way steadily along the mountaintop, Jay pauses to see the heaping hulk lumber into the air. He pulls out a small, shiny piece of hardened purple aluminum, shaped like a tiny baseball bat. He pulls up his lighter. It's a pipe. Jay takes in a long relaxing hit, and blows a globular cloud of smoke up into the sky like an Apache medicine man.

Back up in the cockpit, the copilot reports efficiently "We are off by like well over 400-pounds sir," unknowingly accounting for the sneaky fire team's additional weight.

The captain says, "I'm not surprised. With everything on board here, I didn't expect the weight prediction to be that accurate."

The copilot concurs, "Yeh. How much do you think the horse weighs? It's probably the friggin'' horse."

The captain says, "That's too bad, cause I thought that Shrike character appeared to have a really good head on her shoulders. I'm kinda surprised she would miss such a detail."

In flight, with all of the passengers settling in, relaxing, and softly chatting, the hidden commandos stir from the inky blackness, peeking about. For mostly young and energetic athletes, one would expect a locker-room joviality and exuberance; yet, these people work so hard and so long every day that a few hours on a plane means shut down and veg out, undisturbed.

Shrike wakes from a half daze and lifts her resting lids. She can hear two of the athletes arguing, but she can't see them from her position or make out their voices, so she rests her hard-working eyes again and unwillingly listens to the disembodied voices.

James says, "We are evolving at a breakneck pace!"

Daniel says, "No we aren't. If anything, we are going backwards."

James ponders, "How do you get that?"

Daniel explains matter-of-factly, "Look at how fucked up everything is. Give me proof that we are evolving at this exponential rate so you say."

In the meantime, the commandos make their way up to the door of the cockpit and give each other a series of cryptic, semi-laughable hand signals. Sweat bubbles up through the pores on their faces in the cramped, closet-like space.

James continues, "Just look at music for example. If you or I listen to a song right now that came out 12 years ago, no big whoop. Totally fits in without notice."
Daniel agrees, "Yeah, a song that came out in '03, that would sound fine."
James says, "Right, but in 1977, would you listen to a song that came out 12 years ago? Rock music from 1965 to '77 was completely different. Listing to The Sex Pistols, Blondie, The Ramones, I couldn't really go back and groove to early Dylan and The Everly Brothers and junk like that. Huge difference."
Daniel says, "Ahh, I catch your drift. Hmm, technology has a hand in that, but I think ultimately that proves my point about how we are not evolving. Music isn't changing as quickly as it did in the 1900s."
James postulates, "This is all more a matter of perception, is it not?"
Shrike pops her eyes open. They dart around.
Not bitchy at all, but in a tone that sounds sharp and smart, Shrike says to Sara, "Ah, you're wearing my shades."
Sara replies, "What?"
Shrike says, "Those are my sunglasses."
Sara denies, "They are not."
Shrike says, "Yes they are."
Unafraid, Sara says "No, you are mistaken."
Shrike defends, "I bought those for six bucks at the CVS near Boulder."

Sara says, "No. I bought them a week ago near the Vegas strip."

Shrike says, "No you didn't."

With powerful self-righteousness Sara says, "I certainly most did."

Shrike gasps, "Oh my god. Check your pockets please. I'm sure those are mine."

Sara counters with indignant mortification, "*You* check *your* pockets."

Neither of them moves a muscle or checks any pockets.

The commandos silently turn the knob and enter the cockpit.

Shrike says, "Okay, if you like them, keep the glasses."

Sara says, "No, if you think these are yours then here… you should have my glasses."

Sara tries to hand the glasses to Shrike, but she won't take them. They gaze at each other with anger, like tween sisters. It's kind of like alpha cheerleader high school crap. Sara tries to throw the glasses onto Shrike's lap, but she bats them away like a fiddler crab.

Shrike says, "Well I guess we know who will be the bigger person in this relationship."

Sara snorts clumsily, "Pff, I didn't know you were so self-conscious."

Daggers fly from their stunning irises.

The enormous aircraft climbs and levels at altitude over spectacular Yellowstone National Park.

Meanwhile, at this very moment a flash drive arrives at the Orange County Fox affiliate near Irvine, California; a thousand miles away. The news director quickly contacts the FBI, who in an explosive chain reaction contacts 17 of the most appropriately connected authorities, from SWAT to NASA, in under a minute and thirty-nine seconds. The FBI instructs the affiliate to broadcast the clip nationally. Everyone hustles and bustles in a panic. In the White House, the president's meeting is interrupted when a laptop is placed in front of him and an attractive young intern, with huge lips, flicks on a large-screen TV in the corner. People everywhere across the country and beyond involuntarily watch the invasive news bulletin.

As the image on the screen fades into focus, they see an older heavy-set woman standing in a statue-esque pose. Wearing a shiny diamond encrusted America flag pin on her snow leopard fur coat, and nodding her head to *Sweet Home Alabama*, Gwendolyn Von Snifferhogan appears on the dark, gloomy, underexposed-looking screen, bigger than life. Maybe not really an older woman, but just rough and worn looking from flaunting extreme wealth; she strives to emulate the Bush family; --- kind of super-wealthy and evil. In a luxurious display case behind her, barely visible in the cavernous background, shines an array of pristine, modern assault rifles; many of which reside upon the FBI's contraband list.

To her right is some kind of cannon on wheels that looks like it could be a WWII era anti-tank gun. She obviously loves firepower and seems to thrive on a funny kind of a neo-fascist American lifestyle of the uber rich, screaming *IMAGE IS EVERYTHING!*

She reveals in a low, raspy voice with a choke "Many of you know who I am ... Kuk! ... Atch! ... but I don't want to focus all of the attention on me and my celebrity and well-known notoriety, but on my ultimate plan to raise a billion dollars, not for myself, but to save America!"

Back in sunny D.C., The President looks about in confusion. "Do I know her? Am I supposed to know who she is?"

The intern bubbles, "She's one of those well-known Republican donors. That's all I know her for."

An aid yells from the peanut gallery "She's in tobacco." The President's other aids all shrug their shoulders at what they think of as simply an over-the-top wacko.

People all over America, including Mexico and Canada, feel compelled to watch their hijacked televisions in confusion and with concern:

In a sweltering cantina down on the west coast, near the border of Guatemala, three Mexican businessmen drink Tecate, their armpits sweating profusely.

One loosens his tie and says, "Quien es la loca?"

In a bar near Edmonton, a dirty 'rig pig' oil worker and a lumberjack, unshaven and filthy, watch as well. From their wooden stools, they chug their mugs of Moosehead in the filtered sunlight.

One says, "Heck of a hoser, eh?"

The other says, "Yeah, you said it eh."

They refocus their attention on the screen.

Her dramatic message includes tornado clouds shuffling past the window like the gray ghosts of tumbleweeds, as Gwen spews, "Many of you probably already know who I am and you know I'm untouchable, or as law enforcement must put it, 'above the law', and yet, even with all of the money I've made off of my fast food and cigarette empires, I just don't have enough to pull off what some may consider a risky wager, but what most true American freedom lovers would see as the only good idea so far to break the stalemate. I've already spent well over half of my fortune to get this far, so there won't be any turning back."

Snooty Gwen pauses for dramatic effect, as millions of viewers collectively scratch their befuddled heads. Lightning and thunder crack outside her window, on cue. She takes a long, slow, sexual drag off of her cigarette and blows the smoke theatrically into a dirty cloud above her stacked hair.

All over America, people unconsciously grab for their smokes, like Pavlov's zombies; completely programmed.

She harps, "One billion dollars or the death of the American hero athletes. Pay right away and I have every intent to return the athletes alive."
Words like 'kidnapper' and 'hijacking' spill out over the Internet in viral fashion.

Air defense units across the U.S. instantly verify that the C-17 aircraft appears to be on course and in communication with ground personnel. Whitehouse staff, media pundits, and basically everyone involved become convinced that Gwen lies about the hijacking, and quickly hold brief high-level meetings to conclude as much.

The President holds a quick press briefing on the brilliantly glowing White House lawn. "Look, if the U.S. Air Force tells me they are in contact with the plane, and everything is okay, then, I believe them. I'm putting this situation on hold until a viable threat presents itself, but we're not treating this as a hoax, yet."

Meanwhile… Back in her lair, Gwen smugly sits laughing to herself. Alpha male Cruise, the head commando in Gwen's para-military unit of mercenaries, marches into her chamber with his second, Lohan (a strong, young, attractive, powerful, and harsh woman from LA), and his third, Joaquin (a conniving, smarmy, yes man from Arizona).

Cruise looks at Gwen, serious as a heart attack, and asks bluntly "Gwen, we just heard your demands on national television. What is the EXTRA BILLION DOLLARS for?"

Gwen laughs as she drools, "A devious, deviant plan. As you know, I have no intent to return the athletes, alive or dead, but instead, intend to make a cool billion on the Asian black market selling the Olympic Athletes' organs for transplants. And also, as I mentioned before, I plan to keep a number of organs for myself."

Cruise corrects for verification, "…and also for your commando team."

Gwen's belch echoes in her raw castle, "Yes, yes, of course. You bunch of disgruntled and psychotic armed forces outlaws, rapists, and rejects; you too will be made into super, long-lasting men! My tools. My marvelous tools."

Cruise looks at her as if he'd like to off her right now, but he's such a whore that he will do anything to get rich and be done with all aspects of the military and Gwen, once and for all after this his last, final, major mission.

He says with frustration, "Right, that's the first billion from the organs. Why would you announce the hijacking and what is the second billion for?"

Gwen says, "I can't see how it can hurt to tell you and your dweebs. You will probably just find it another bizarre reason. This additional money gives me just enough to complete the arms deal with my contacts in the weapons underground. You know, former top American Pentagon chiefs, so I can tip five missiles with neutron warheads, and hit the five largest prisons in California, instantly killing over 83,956 prisoners, 8,234 guards and staff, and 2,348 non-targeted civilians."
Gwen's brain, like a steel trap, is sharp, tense, and ready to spring!

The commandos look at each other. The chill of death fills Gwen's uncomfortable and unwelcoming abode. Now they know she is really crazy. Crazier than them! Neutron bombs not only kill people; they kill life! They disrupt cells in animate objects. It is not a bomb as much as it is a "life killer". Gwen, and most other humans, could care less, but thousands of birds, mammals, herps, plants, and other creatures that live around these prisons in Mule Creek, Solano, Salinas, Chuckwalla, and other insanely overcrowded facilities, will also die immediately.

Back over the immaculate Rockies, approaching 20,233 feet, all 111 pounds of Shrike gets a text.

Over the glistening snowcapped mountain peaks, Shrike mumbles, "Who the hell is texting me? Everyone who knows me knows I hate texts. What a stupid-ass waste of time and an insult."

16

Shrike looks at the text. "If they want to talk to me, call me," she spurts to Sara with frustration over the hum of the massive aircraft.

Sara thinks, then says "Shrike, you're too uptight, and the one acting like a stupid ass. I use texts all the time so I can send one-way messages, assert what I want, and shut everyone else up."

Shrike resentfully looks down at the text, then freezes like a Medusa victim.

It reads one word: HIJACKERS.

Shrike does not recognize where the call came from, but typical to form, she reacts like an ermine on acid.

"Hijackers!" she says loudly. She unbuckles her seatbelt and stands in the isle facing aft spurting "Hijackers! Hijackers!" The athletes jump to their feet and swarm about the plane aggressively like army ants.

The five-foot-one Shrike sprints forward to the cabin. When she carefully opens the door, she finds all three crewmembers dead on the floor and two of the hijackers flying the vessel. The third hijacker attempts to make radio contact with Gwen. The commando sends a code, transferring the radio and radar signals to a control center in Gwen's lair.

He says, "We're patched through to Gwen. They have control now."

Back in the darkness of Gwen's castle, with a storm raging outside, Gwen's pet hacker nods in confirmation. They have managed to make the flight appear to be on course, virtually, while they remotely pilot the plane from miles away.

Gwen says with jubilation, "Excellent! Praise be to the All Mighty Lord. My plan is working."

Back in the cockpit, one of the commandos adjusts his headset and tries to reconfirm operations with Gwen, when he looks up to see Shrike.

"Hey!" the commando yells.

A second commando jumps to his feet while the third one continues to fly the plane.

Suddenly the commandos find themselves in an unexpected battle with Shrike and the athletes, who crowd into the cockpit before the commandos can even raise a gun. Though not an athlete, Shrike tenaciously puts up an incredible Jason Borne-type fight, clawing at one of the commando's eyes repeatedly and pulling out wicked fast moves that make James Bond look like Pee-wee Herman. The shot putter pushes past everyone and chokes the commando flying the plane, who passes out instantly. The auto-pilot system gets jerked off in the commotion and the aircraft violently turns northwest and into a massive anvil-shaped thunderhead. One of the commandos hurls Shrike's body back against the control panel in the crowded cockpit, now almost dark from the black clouds engulfing the raging behemoth. One of the commandos raises his knife to kill Shrike just as a bolt of lightning hits the plane. The electrical charge shorts out the controls. All of the lights in the entire aircraft blink once and go out. The plane bounces and jumps like a low rider in Los Angeles.

The bolt jolts through Shrike's deliciously petite body and she shakes violently like a molested blow-up doll on the verge of exploding. The lightning transfers through her and channels directly into the knife-wielding commando, fusing the knife to the skin and bones of his hand forever. His crispy corpse collapses like the remnants of a bonfire. The lightning bolt then deflects and radiates down to the ground, thousands of feet below; spreading and sending a bizarre charge from Shrike's body through all of the living animals within a radius in Yellowstone National Park. With the exception of the few humans in the area, all of the stimulated animals in the park stand frozen as the magical electricity pulses through them. The creatures pause, sensing this strange new mental signal, then return to their activities like nothing happened.

Shrike feels the electrification zip around her synapses. The blow of the bolt resonates, and she sees flashing images of thousands of animals in the matter of a millisecond. She then collapses unconscious as the turbulence bounces the athletes out of the cockpit and onto the floor. More athletes crowd forward toward the cramped cockpit, climbing over each other like salmon fighting up stream. They struggle to pummel the commandos so competitively that it looks like a tangled race to see who can get into the cockpit first. Overcome, the stunned commando who had been choked so crushingly gets dragged into the isle and additional punched to assure unconsciousness. The third commando; dazed, injured, and confused by the beating he has received so far; struggles to keep the plane aloft. He keeps flipping switches and inputting nav. data, not realizing that he has no controls operating whatsoever. He can't get the plane level. All of the buttons and toggles and bells and whistles do nothing, but he keeps working like a panicked banshee.

When the plane falls out of the black storm cloud and into the light, everyone's eyes spring wide open, wildly. A massive mountain stands right in front of them. James strides over with his long hurdler legs and lifts up Shrike, carrying her limp body back to the seats where he buckles her and himself in. He sprawls his long black limbs across her to protect her from the impact, and feels a strong electrical charge coming off of her furnace-like body.

Another athlete screams, "We are going to crash!"

The athletes rush back to their seats and buckle themselves in for the crash. Daniel dives into the empty copilot's chair next to the despondent commando, and takes over piloting the plane. He pulls back hard on the stick manually. The flaps respond, sending the nose of the heavy craft upwards at a 41-degree angle and causing the tail to start clipping off treetops. Daniel steps adeptly out of the cockpit and rides out the crash by gripping the cargo straps like a gibbons stretched out between tree limbs.

Back on the high mountain ridge, Jay, the lone hiker, sees the cargo plane drop out of the clouds, and head straight for the mountain peaks. He checks his cell to see if he can get a signal so he can call for help. No signal. He puts the phone away, then looks around hopelessly for an idea. It's only one mountain over, so he decides going to the crash site would be his most helpful course of action.

The C-17 crashes high in the mountains of Yellowstone National Park. Though the tail hits first, the impact crushes the cockpit, killing two of the commandos; jettisoning one 13 meters from the plane and against some icy rocks. The only surviving commando, lying prone in the isle, slides forward like a bobsledder and hits the cockpit door, braking his left ankle and right knee. That's going to hurt when he comes to.

Complete white. Complete silence.

The aircraft sits on the mountain; still, quiet, smashed but intact.

After about three minutes, Sara and the athletes stir to the whinnies of the horse. No one can believe they are alive and still buckled in their seats. Due to the heavy powdery snow pack, none of the athletes suffer serious injury, but the horse, though harnessed correctly, suffers a broken leg. The athletes check on each other.

Above the veil of sparkling snow blowing like infinitesimal angels, Sara's soft voice can be heard like a calming comforter blanketing the scene, "Is anyone seriously hurt? Stay calm and in control. You are heroes."
More shuffling ensues, as the rest of the athletes spring into action; slipping through the gaping scars in the fuselage and out into the blinding snow. They know that plane crash or not, they have to save themselves.

Daniel and James try to bring Shrike to in the shelter of the damaged fuselage. They pet her face, and whisper to her. Sara brings over a handful of snow. When they put a little snow on her forehead it evaporates into steam instantly with a sizzle. Shrike slowly opens her eyes into slender salamander slits, narrow and wriggly.

James asks, "Can you talk Shrike?"

Daniel gives her the slightest taste of water. A number of athletes hustle about, giving orders, shutting off fuel lines and other potentially hazardous valves, displaying the best in cool-headed problem-solving teamwork.

Shrike offers constipated groans, "Aaaaahhhhhhhhh. Status?"

James says, "Well …"

Daniel says, "Ah, how much do you remember?"

Shrike says, more clearly, "Status?"

The men look at each other.

James says, "The plane crashed into a mountain. There doesn't appear to be any fire. Two of the commandos are dead and the other is knocked-out. None of the athletes appear to be hurt, but the commandos killed the crew, so that's a horrible tragedy in itself."

Shrike says, "When the surviving commando regains consciousness, perform first aid on him. Take and use everything from the commandos, including their weapons and mess kits, and most importantly, a working headset radio."

A group of athletes come together and stand over Shrike, looking down at her.

With expressions of critical concern across their faces as they stand over Shrike, Daniel and James listen intently.

Shrike says, "Continue."

James says, "I guess we have got to figure out the next step. How are you feeling?"

Sara suddenly butts in with, "Lousy. Let's let her rest for a while. Her vital signs are fine."

Moments after Sara shoos them away, Shrike slowly begins tossing and turning with hallucinations. She can hear the thoughts of animals all through the park. She can sense a cow moose keeping an eye on a bear, and a flicker watching the movements of a goshawk from a cavity in a fir. She feels as if she is underground, with thousands of other like-organisms moving at a frenetic pace. She vibrates with the sensation of

flight, then swimming, then digging in packed soil, then leaping over logs. There's no language, just unspoken understanding. Feelings. Smells. Chills. Adrenaline rushes. Breezes.
Sara reenters the area to observe Shrike.

When Sara's arm brushes by Shrike, she grabs it and pulls Sara down to her face, "Why are the animals talking to me?"

Sara explains her view of it, "Shrike, you got zapped. Having any sort of powerful electrical jolt like can even make ya see Jesus, or Elvis! Why do you think we use Shock Therapy? It works!"

Shrike quotes robotically, "In final analysis, no two species well established in a region occupy precisely the same ecologic space; each has its own peculiar places for foraging, and for securing safety for itself and for its eggs or young. These ultimate units of occurrence are called 'ecologic niches.'"

Daniel wonders, "Where the hell did that come from?"

Sara says analytically, "I don't know."

Shrike answers, "Grinnell and Storer, 1924."

James says, "That ain't normal."
Raising her eyebrows, Shrike snaps out of her electro-daze and into a super-lucid state, while feeling as surprised and confused as anyone about where that tidbit of fact came from.

She questions Sara, "Everything's in my head?"

Sara curtly responds, "Where else could it be? Rest, but don't fall asleep. Don't let her fall asleep."
Sara loves to feel like she is in charge and in control at all times, so she goes off full of pride to see who else needs psych-healing.

Shrike starts to second guess herself, and tries to control - and at times shut out - the voices. She plays with it in her mind, and soon realizes that the animals communicate back with her, and, they appear to be amenable to suggestion. Shrike focuses on the crotch of an aspen tree, far off, but she only sees what's in her mind's eye. Like a strong dream, she can feel and sense movement and heat, weight and rubbing, and the overwhelming odor of skunk, which vanishes quickly without a trace. In her mind, she calls a screech owl. In reality, the owl calls, and the athletes turn and look up for it. Shrike smiles. In her mind, Shrike calls a bumblebee to land on her forehead. From far below, a bumblebee blasts up the sides of the sheer cliffs and arrives within moments to alight gently upon Shrikes practically pristinely-perfect epidermis. Shrike smiles again, with mild disbelief.

James says, "A bee."

Before James can initiate a fore swing to swipe it from Shrike's head, she mentally 'orders' it to buzz off. The bumblebee blasts away and vanishes a mile back down the slope, going right back to feeding on the poppies below the snow line. Shrike lies motionless, pretending to be at serene rest.

Far off in the gloom of her evil headquarters and with Pat Boone playing in the background, livid Gwen calls in the rest of her lead team to send them to retrieve the athletes before rescue teams can reach the wreckage.

Gwen yells, "We lost contact with the plane! They had a simple job to do. Get the plane and fly the athletes to me. Incompetence! I sent three of them for Christ's sake. There, I just took the Lord's name in vain. See what they made me do! Your unit is ready. You are in command of a full company. You have your orders. Get out of my face!"

Cruise complains, "We can't parachute in right now with the way the weather is up there."

Gwen retaliates, "We don't know where the hell they are. You can't just be dropped in on them. You will have to hijack heli'copters with pilots, spread out, and try to find the plane crash as discreetly as possible; that's why I'm giving you a hundred troops."

Cruise look at Gwen with surprise for a moment, then convinces himself again that he can pull of anything.

Cruise clumsily exposes, "I want the U.S. Military to know they made a mistake. When they see how seamless this operation goes off, and later, in the history books, when they mark down who, who did it . . . it will be my face in the textbooks. You don't cut a guy like me loose. I'm what's known as *a valuable asset*."

Gwen volleys, "I've checked out how valuable your ass . . . asset is. Nice. Hallelujah Lord."

Cruise says, "You can knock off all the 'praise the lord' shit while the cameras are off, okay?"

Gwen commands, "Shun upon me heresy against our Lord our God, The Father."

Cruise gets up in her face, gritting his teeth, "Don't forget Gwen, you still need me and I still need my money!"

A grimace squirms across Gwen's leech-like lips, "Ummmm. Maybe you'd like to take it out in trade."
Cruise stays frozen for a moment in repellant disgust, then turns and walks out with Lohan and Joaquin right behind him.

Gwen resigns, "I'll get somebody else to do it. Every whore has his price."

Standing on the large, stone porch with its parapets, in stark silence, the commander, Cruise, turns to Lohan and Joaquin privately, his second and third in command. They had watched this exhibition of Gwen with fixed concentration. Inaudible to the engrossed and titillated Gwen, he murmurs, "We don't have any morals about prisons or America."

Lohan says stoically, "Stick with the plan!"

Joaquin joins, "Don't forget about . . . We want those organs."

Lohan adds ruthlessly, almost like a begging addict, "To kill as many athletes as possible, for us."

Joaquin adds sadistically, "Rape the rhythmic gymnasts and synchronized swimmers, and harvest the athletes organs for our own bodies so as to super-charge ourselves and life spans. Since Gwen has high-tech top-secret labs, we are obligated to serve her until we get what we want."

Lohan winces, then directs toward Cruise, "Sir, some of these disgruntled commandos in this company we are taking hate America, and therefore, hate jingoistic Gwen."

Cruise says, "Yah. The last thing a lot of these discharged commandos would care about is offing prisoners or helping the world."

Joaquin counters, "Actually, I have heard a couple of them saying they got friends and know people in jail. So they won't even like this plan. They just want the money and the organs; plus, it sounds like a fun trip. Let's agree to not tell any of the commandos about the prison bombing idea."

Lohan looks at him briefly with disgust. She knows he is a serial rapist and it is that part, and that part of the mission alone, that makes him drool like a Komodo Dragon.

Cruise can see the whole picture. He ruminates on what will transpire, and how he will have to make his moves.

He says, "We are using each other, for now."

Gwen bellows from far down the stone hallway, "Well. If there isn't anything else, get on with it!"

The three commandos, and Gwen's other non-military staff, split off in all directions. After they disperse on their missions, a servant comes up to Gwen carrying a cute little piglet and a cute little bunny.

Gwen growls, "Oh, the piglet is definitely the cuter one."

"Yes madam," whines the servant, as he turns to leave hastily.

"Wait a second," she commands. "You know I like to see them slaughtered in front of me."

"Yes madam," the servant winces.

Smoke from the fireplace clouds the room. While Gwen watches without blinking, it becomes obvious that the servant would rather kill himself. He regretfully raises a meat cleaver in the dimness of the flickering firelight, and cuts off the piglet's head, squirting blood everywhere. Streams shoot up, hitting the grinning Gwen across her garishly painted lips and pointy witch chin.

Mental sickness? Emotional disturbance? All engulfing greed?

Chapter 2

Commandos!

Back on the powdery mountainside, inside the cracked fuselage, Shrike finally opens her eyes widely and tries to focus. She straightens up in her seat and sees a blurry figure in a shroud. It looks like the Virgin Mary for a second, waving a beckoning arm, but then she sees that it is the lanky hurdler James with a towel over his head to trap in the warmth. James notices a flock of bohemian waxwings erupt from a frozen willow tree and swirl across the angular slope; a unified hissing flock. He notes something almost electrifying about them, but he can't put his finger on it. His eyes linger on the dramatic markings on their wings and tails; glowing like neon in the blinding sun.

Shrike musters, "Your little getup just freaked me out."

James retorts, "First thing you say when you start getting coherent is a complaint about my attire? Ain't you ever seen a man dressed like a nun?"

Shrike is able to force out a chuckle, but feels pain everywhere and says, "What? You in drag?"

James, straightening up a little bit says, "When I sung in some experimental bands, we would dress up in all kinds of getups. What's wrong with that?"

Shrike says, "I just think you would look a lot more like RuPaul than Wendy Williams does, that's all."

James bursts into an explosive laugh. Others in the area jump up with surprise. Shrike chuckles too, and some tears roll down her kissable cheeks. A moment later, Shrike comes to her feet and begins to gain momentum, barking orders and generally organizing. She stands up high on top of the plane's fuselage, and calls the athletes to order.

She says, "We have no means of communicating with anyone. We need to start by just doing the normal survival stuff: Create fires, ration food, etc, but more importantly, we need to figure out what is going on, and as you know as world-class athletes, keep our cool."

"How?" a rhythmic gymnast asks with worry.

Shrike looks around at the blinding white picture-postcard landscape. She sees three of the athletes tending to a dead commando, prone on the ground. Nobody bothers with the one crushed in the cockpit.

Shrike says, "Listen in on one of the commando's radios. Also, when the live one comes to, we need to pluck what we can from him. Make sure his hands are tied well and that he has absolutely nothing on him that can be used as a transmitter beacon, or as a weapon." Shrike slides back down to the ground.

Athletes spring into action like choreographed water striders. Everyone darts back and forth with gliding efficiency.

With the striking composure, intensity, and focused spirit of Tom Brady, Shrike huddles up with Sara, Daniel, and James next to the shattered body of the plane.

She says, "Where the hell are we?"

Sara says, "The hell if I know."

Daniel holds up one of the comlinks. They examine it, like early *Homo habilis* scrutinizing cracked bone for marrow. Listening in on the comlink, they first believe it to be dead, or at least minus any traffic. They flick the channels, and listen back and forth between the comlink headsets, but they don't hear a sound.

Finally, a repulsive sounding voice crackles in over the comlink, "Team K. Team K. This is Matriarch, over."

There is the typical pause, then "Team K. Team K. This is Matriarch. Come in."

Another pause, then, "Team K, you missed your call in time. Status?"

Finally, Shrike and the others her Gwen say, "No contact. Matriarch out!"

In stark contrast to the pristine mountains of Yellowstone, protected by the U.S. government, the smoldering wood from the scorched, blackened forest around Gwen's dingy headquarters produces puffy carcinogenic smoke rings that linger in air. Gwen throws her comlink down in frustration, and then she's startled when her phone rings.

Gwen yells, "Yes. I told you already. Buy all five casinos. I love the idea of people coming to my facility to lose their money. I love it! Get all five and don't fuck it up."
She slams the phone down the same way she did the comlink.

"SUCKERS!" she yells up at her arched ceiling and lights another cigarette. Her phone rings again. She answers to hear the voice of the White House Chief of Staff.

He says, "Gwen, let's be reasonable. You think killing 95,000 "bad people" will make the world a better place? We can't have that. Who gets to determine who is bad, you?"

Gwen parries, "A lot of the media agree with me. A groundswell support from The Tea Party and the radical right grows as we speak."

The staffer reasons, "Republicans like your jingoistic flag waving right now, . . ."

Gwen cuts him off with defiance ". . . and many feel that cleaning the slate in all of the prisons and starting fresh would save the government and the prison system billions of dollars ... and eliminate the scum! Have you gone to my viral YouTube spot yet? Imagine the deterrent to future crime of any kind!"

The staffer and his colleagues grab for their trendiest new social media devices and watch her YouTube video in disgust as Gwen patiently listens on the phone, grinning.
As she makes her rationalizations and appeals on her professionally crafted commercial spot, a huge, ghastly portrait of Nancy and Ronald Reagan looms behind her. A noted ex-cheerleading bleach-blonde ultra-conservative commentator named Elizabreast Hustleback stands by her side rubbing her shoulders in sorority sister support.

Gwen bellows, "After the shock of the first five prisons being wiped out, they will get accustomed to the idea, and we will have money flowing in to do away with all of the current prisoners. Then, when the prisons are refilled to the brink with more disease-ridden scum, we will neutron bomb them again. Ha ha ha. Admit it. You've thought about this same idea before right, but never had the balls to carry it out? Never send a man to do a woman's job!"

Gwen clenches the phone so tightly, it's as if she could crush a battleship in her bare hand. Hustleback massages her shoulders more strongly, wearing a phony, pretentious smile that sickens even Gwen's battle-hardened servants.

Gwen softens her tone and tries to sound a little more sane and reasonable, "If we just kill all the prisoners and blow up all the refugees, end of problem; . . . for now."

He quips, "Gwen, ..."

But she cuts him off, "... How do you know about my plan?"

He says, "We know about everything, Gwen."

She thinks for a minute about who knows what. She knows they knew about the hijacking, but she didn't know that they knew about the neutron bomb plan, so she wonders, do they know about the organ-harvesting plan? Do they know the commandos are going after the athletes? Do they know that she has no intention of returning any of the athletes at all?? Gwen needs to know but knows nothing. A basic lack of intelligence is a poor way to start any campaign.

She says, "Well, if you know everything then there is no point in going on with telling me what you know. I will have my people put the plane right back on course to D.C. and end any contact with the bomb madmen. If that satisfies you, no questions asked, then we have a deal; but you can't go after my contacts, or the deal is off!"

The White House Chief of Staff stammers, "I'm going to need that agreement in some form of writing ..."

Gwen slices, "... My word is good! I will stop the neutron project and put the plane back on course. Deal?"

The Chief of Staff resigns, "Well, sure, okay then Gwen. Thank you, and may I say that ..."

Gwen hangs up on him in mid sentence and spouts, "Fuckin'' loser! All praise to The Lord on High. Our Mighty Father. Blessed are thee."

She runs to the window like an armadillo stepping on beached jellyfish and looks out at the gloomy surroundings, wringing her hands like an ancient python twisting an obese, garbage-fed rat to death.

In soliloquy, she yells again, "They don't know the plane went down. They don't know I'm sending my entire crack unit in: A full company ----- Even more than a full company. With Cruise and Lohan, and that other grunt; they'll have 128 commandos! 'More than enough to handle the job', Cruise assures me. They don't know about the harvesting of the super human body parts!! Ha ha ha. They *do* know about the prison plan. How? I must find out!"

Cruise gives his orders, assigning four commandos to each of the two fog-shrouded airports. Simultaneously, they force eight helicopter pilots to fly them off to Yellowstone. Cruise's company *are* pros! The operation goes off smoothly, with no signals being sent, alarms going off, or anything unusual reported. The eight commandos simply sneak up on the pilots and force them to fly their 'copters at gunpoint. The heli'copters land in an open field, one-by-one, and the entire company of commandos pile in. None of the pilots, even a few of the war-weary vets, dare stand up to the commandos once they see their impressive gear and professionally trained modus operandi. The eight heli'copters lift off up into the dark, think fog; crammed with sixteen commandos per aircraft, and all their gear. The heli'copters, the pilots, and the commandos all strain. Cruise establishes communications with the other choppers via the comlink.

High above the fog, on the shiny mountaintop, all 117 of the athletes, along with Sara and Shrike, jump into action: inventorying and rationing, suiting up with more layers and locating useful items, and sadly, tending to the injured horse; when they hear Cruise's commands coming into range over the comlink. Shrike and others run over to the comlink, and listen in rabidly.

They hear Cruise's satanic voice for the first time commanding, "Keep this channel open. Get above the fog and then head for the mountain we believe the plane crashed at."

Sara says, with haste, "It's a rescue party. We are saved."

Shrike doubts, "On the commando's frequency?"

Sara bubbles with relief, "You're being paranoid, again. Let me answer them."

Sara reaches for the comlink, and Shrike quickly grabs it back from her with an animalistic growl. Darting in aggressively, a Clark's nutcracker screams a raspy scold of disapproval, directly in Sara's face, who shrinks back with a startle. The nutcracker then flies off hectically into the clear blue sky, flashing epileptic black and gray strobes.

Shrike, James, and Daniel freeze in silence, holding their breath, so not to miss a word, when they hear Cruise continue with, "When we get to the base of the mountains, I want you guys to have your choppers hover there. I will go up alone to see if we can spot the wreckage. We'll be looking for a landing area from there. We don't want to spook them."

Shrike and Sara look intensely at one another. Daniel and James look at each other as well.

They pick up more transmissions, holding their breaths while they eavesdrop intently. After several minutes of monitoring, they surmise the data and then call another group meeting. All of the athletes stand strong and erect as they listen to the most extreme news they have ever heard.

Shrike says, "From the little we were able to gather from some of the commandos chatter, we are deep in the mountains of Yellowstone National Park. Daniel is an avid hiker and he said that from scanning the area, this looks like designated wilderness and we could be miles from anyone anywhere. I don't know what elevation we crashed at, but we are probably above 6,000 feet, with another 5,000 feet above us."

The shot putters spouts, "Why should we care how much we've got above us?"

Shrike says, "Because… we are heading up, not down." The athletes mumble and grumble, while some even bumble.

Shrike says with resolve, "I shit you not! We are going to make it impossible for them to find us here."
Everyone looks about with confusion.

Shrike says, "I don't want to cause panic, or even use the word, but you've got to understand that mercenaries, crack troops, are coming after us. Just like these guys that hijacked us, but it sounds like a full regiment or the like."

Daniel worries with great concern, "What, they are commandos. They are the best, and trained to do this, they are going to track us down."

"No they aren't. Do you know how huge this park ranges? I think it's like 300 square miles. We can hide in the aspens, and move up into hidden crags," Shrike says, pointing up to the ice-age scars in the steep peaks gleaming in the relentless sunshine.

James corrects, "I came here about 2 years ago. I think it's more like 3000 square miles."

Shrike says, "Either way, we are not going to wait around for them to find us. We are taking the initiative to save ourselves."
Many of the athletes bristle with belief, and faith, in Shrike.

A number of them listen in for themselves and hear Cruise caution loudly over the comlink, "Remember; our first directive is to take them alive, or their organs will be spoiled."

James mutters, "What the fuck?"

Shrike says, "We need to get to work but fast! I have to hear what's going on here, but at the same time, we don't have time for the 'let's listen in game'. Hook me up."

Shrike stands as others help her to strap on the comlink. It immediately transforms her into a futuristic warrior. The men help her climb high up onto the cracked fuselage again. She listens to the comlink with one ear, assuring that the mute button stays locked ON.

She orates, "Listen. We need to get away from this plane as fast as possible. We need to head up this slope with everything we have as fast as we can, ... NOW!"

With that, and with the precision of a Belichick football team, the athletes start blasting around. They grab every single kind of stuff you can imagine, and when completely loaded, turn and run up the steep and treacherous slope of snowy powder, ice, and rock.

One of the athletes grabs a multi-pack of condoms. Another athlete looks over at him.

She says, "Really?"

He says, "Ya never know."

He pauses, then he throws them back with the other non-essentials to be left behind. Several of the athletes laugh at his silly actions.

Hiking briskly in the alpine zone, Jay feels that if he heads straight down he should be close to the crash site. He stops to reorient his path, and then lengthens his strides downhill to make better time.

In the meantime and many miles away, Gwen rants into the phone with humid bloodhound pants, "Yes, hire a cargo plane at the local airport with heavier equipment loaded and prepped for an airdrop."

As she hangs up the phone, she grimaces and plots, "I love to use obscure vocabulary words. It makes me feel superior to the idiots who don't have as much knowledge as I do."

Her servant, more like a slave recites, "Yes ma'am."

Gwen says, "Shut up. That's the plain language peasants understand. Shut, up."

The servant repeats, "Yes ma'am."

Gwen whips her head around so fast that she hurts her neck -- her eyes afire.

The cowering servant quickly exits the room, avoiding eye contact, and ducking.

A beautiful hummingbird flies up to Gwen by the open window, unable to find any living flowers in her vicinity. Gwen swats at it with her cigarette and then tries to close the window. The hummingbird dips back in towards her.

Gwen yells, "Servant! Servant! Get in here and close this god-forsaken window now! Burhrhhhh. I hate those buzzy things. They get tangled in your hair like bats do! Ooaah. Disgusting! Proof that god really did make a devil, for sure. Praise be Almighty for working in your mysterious ways."

The servant sprints in and closes the window with ease. The hummingbird hesitates for a minute outside, looking at Gwen as she huffs and puffs, and lights another cigarette. The tiny bird doesn't understand and darts away across Gwen's burnt and naked landscape.

The servant pleads, "Are you fine now ma'am?"

Gwen blasts, "Don't ask!"

The servant sprints back out of the room for fear of death.

Among the last few people still at the crash site, Sara finds a case of champagne with some of the other food supplies, so she suggests, "We might as well take these." She starts to peel the foil off of one of the corks.

Shrike firmly puts her foot down, "Stop! Leave it behind. We need to have our wits about us if we are to survive. It's going to be hard enough at altitude, and most of these athletes have a low tolerance for drugs."

Sara knows Shrike is right. She stares at Shrike, then glimpses up at the on-looking Olympians with embarrassment.

Sara pops some kind of pill, (like Valium, or Lithium) then says, "You are one harsh girl there Shrike ----- one tough girl. What's with all the tough girl stuff? You would probably be mellower if you smoked a little weed."

Shrike knows Sara is wrong about these statements and is projecting her own bias toward crutch drugs to get through the day.

Shrike whispers under her breath to Sara, "I could see talking and counseling as beneficial, and think it should be mandatory that everyone from Congress to truck drivers see a shrink, to remove the stigma attached; but never taking drugs, for anything other than occasional recreation, makes sense to me."

Sara recoils at that statement. In her mind, she can't live without some kind of chemical balancing her out.

Sara poses to Shrike, "Sounds like you've no experience with the process of a 12 Step Program!"

Shrike laughs with utter derision and then, like being possessed, she rattles off a most articulate list that eloquently blows all of the athletes within earshot away. "I'll give you my 12 Steps:

1. Admit that we are powerless against Nature — that our lives are managed by it.

2. Believe that a power greater than ourselves can restore us to sanity, and that power is Nature.

3. Make a decision to turn our will and our lives over to the care of Nature as we understand it scientifically.

4. Make a searching and fearless moral inventory of our own relationship with Nature.

5. Admit to ourselves, and to at least one other wild being, the exact characteristics of our wrongs against plants and animals.

6. Remove all the aforementioned defects of character, and mitigate ----- especially by planting at least one geographically appropriate native tree (and preferably a rare one).

7. Humbly remove our Nature shortcomings completely from our lives in all aspects.

8. Make a list of all wildlife we have harmed, and make amends to them all, by donation, restoration, or other mitigating means.

9. Make direct amends wherever possible, except when to do so could injure Nature worse.

10. Continue to take personal environmental inventories: promptly admitting and correcting wrongs.

11. Improve our conscious contact with Nature as we understand it, studying only for knowledge and the power to carry out constructive and appropriate environmental best practices.

12. Carry this message to everyone, and practice these principles in all our affairs, without ever forcing will upon another.

Ta Da!" Shrike abruptly finishes.

Sara puzzles, "Are you like a preachy lecturer or what? How the hell do you have that memorized?"

Shrike retorts, "Ha, with you always making unsolicited prescriptions?"

Sara says, "Wow, what a nature nut. You are the craziest."

Shrike says, "Is that a diagnosis ... or intuition?"

Powerful, intelligent, engaging ---- they stare into each other's beautifully stunning eyes.

Diver Daniel captures the intimate moment when he snaps off a shot with his iPhone.

The women turn in unison, surprised, as he reels off another shot.

"What's that for?" Sara protests.

Daniel says, "Are you kidding? As soon as I get an internet connection I'm posting this with the title 'Guess who I saw up in Yellowstone? Mila Kunis and Penelope Cruz, face-to-face!' People will believe it. You two are dead ringers for them. How about a shot of you kissing?"

At first they innocently think he means kissing him, but then they realize he wants a hot shot of them kissing each other.

Shrike sounds like a mafia don when she says, "Beat it."

Daniel slips the phone back into his tight pants.

Shrike scans the clouds below but detects nothing. The choppers still a hundred miles away, she has no idea where they are. Shrike then swiftly surveys the mountain peaks above, noticing some attractive features in the rocks. She looks down and around quickly, then fixes her eyes on the rifle-shooting medalist.

Shrike yells down to her, "Quickly, give me your gun." Surprised, the shooter follows orders and tosses the rifle up to Shrike, in a spiral. Shrike catches it handily, and brings it up to her shoulder.

The shooter says, "It's not loaded."

Shrike says, "Doesn't need to be."

She focuses the scope to search the sun-drenched rocks. Now the shooter understands that Shrike seeks a defensible outcrop. The scope doesn't help her much, but she finds a great spot anyway. Just then, juncos come down and around Shrike, chirping at her. Shrike feels like she is making eye contact with them; -- like they are staring into her eyes. Shrike gets a little flustered, and the juncos fly off. Shrike tosses the rifle back down to the medalist and goes down on one knee for stability. She focuses all of her thoughts on bringing the juncos back. She chants a messy mantra in her mind, like a child's song, 'Come here juncos, come here now'. Instantly, the two juncos reappear, followed by four more, and then another 17 little birds, including a Cassin's finch and a red crossbill. Shrike smiles, then thinks, 'bail'. The petite passerines hastily vanish down to more forested elevations where they belong. As Sara watches Shrike carefully, Shrike turns to catch Sara in the act.

Shrike snipes, "Take a picture, it lasts longer."

Sara strikes back pettily, "Maybe I will. And, some video too."

Shrike grits her teeth at Sara, and climbs down off of the fuselage and into the glistening bright powder. She grabs her own backpack and belongings, and everything she can carry (like water, and one of the hammer thrower's 16-pound hammers), takes a look around, and heads up the slope behind the dozens of athletes. After less than a minute and forty-four seconds, she stops and sees that only a few athletes scour for the last items left; like vultures picking a carcass clean. Shrike looks up vigilantly for heli'copters, but instead of detecting heli'copters she feels overwhelmed by animal sensations again. She feels like they send messages straight to her brain. She comes to the immediate conclusion that it must be from the lightning strike. She shakes it off and turns up the precipitous slope with Sara and the 117 gold medal winning Olympians.

Sara starts in with, "Are you a Madonna fan?"

Shrike strikes back, "Are you kidding me? I hate Madonna."

Sara argues with antagonistic examination, "She was a huge star. Lots of people love her."

Shrike laughs, "You mean lots of people have "loved" her (she does air quotes, with added annoying-teen sauce sass on the side) and yes, I mean that in the most disgusting and non-loving of expressions. She forced herself on us just like she forced herself on so many men's promontories. I don't respect that."

Coming up on one side James states, "She forced herself onto American society just like W Bush forced himself onto America."

Shrike fires, "Real stars, real idols, don't force themselves onto people. They don't have to."

Sara gazes into Shrike's face as she cross examines perceptively, "Aren't you being a little harsh on Madonna?"

Daniel, now appearing on the other side, assists Shrike as she traverses some ice-glazed boulders, and agrees with Shrike, "No, not in the least."

Shrike prosecutes, "Her acting is atrocious. You have to have a certain cerebral capability to be a real actor."

James adds, "Her singing is shrill and flat at the same time."

Daniel says, "Her dancing is nothing above mediocre. She is really good at self-marketing, but why would I be interested in that? I'm not a sucker."

James piles on, "Why are we even wastin' our time talkin' about Madonna?"

The three of them turn in unison to look at the dumbfounded Sara.

Daniel and James snicker, both finding themselves incredibly attracting to Shrike.

Daniel mumbles to James, "Sara is beautiful, and not a slouch in any senses. She looks strikingly similar to Penelope Cruz; but that's a tribute to just how charismatic and downright stunning Shrike is."

James quickly glances at Daniel, "You too huh? I feel as if Shrike has cast a spell on me."

Daniel empathizes, "Like you feel almost forced to love Shrike," nodding his head in knowing agreement.
Chills run down their spines; like fire ants dripping in stinging hydroid goo: The kind of enticing pain that hurts so good!

Suddenly a runner catches up to Shrike and pants, "Shrike, the sailboat haulers think it's asinine that we lug this thing up the hill."

Shrike fires back, "Poppycock! What if we need to cross a river or a lake? What if we need it as a makeshift emergency shelter, or for fire wood, or as a stretcher to carry injured??"
The runner steps back, unable to argue against any of her barrage of points.

Then, Shrike makes sure she says it loud enough for practically all of the athletes on the steep slope to hear, "Suck it up pussies! This ain't no frat party! There's a war on!"

Immediately, the effect is palpable. The athletes stiffen their backs and turn to. They double their pace, and their resolve, and really start cranking up the slope. On the steeper slopes, and places where the heavily-laden athletes look like they may fall, helpers seem to appear just in time. Some examples include: A red-tailed hawk that pulls upward on the straps of the equipment bags, grasping them in its strong talons; and a couple of deer that line the edge of the trail in precarious spots, as living guardrails for the athletes to lean on safely. The athletes look at each other in confusion over and over again. Every time an animal 'apparently' helps them, they hesitate in awe of the cooperative nature of these creatures; … these beings, and then they all look over at Shrike who just pleasantly nods with a knowing smile.

Back in the flying formation of the hijacked heli'copters, Cruise yells over the engine noise as they finally fly up and above the dense fog, "What the hell? They are not on the main roads. There are no rescue vehicles in the area. Where are the athletes? Where is the crash site?"

The pilot retaliates in horror, "We are gonna die. Unless I fly high, the cloud cover down here covers everything. If we fly low enough to get below the storm-cloud level then we will be flying in the precipitation, or in the thick fog again, or ... we are going to hit a mountain!"

Cruise holds the mute button on his comlink and pulls the microphone away from his mouth. He turns to Lohan and Joaquin and says, "We must have the element of surprise. If they hear us, they may think we are rescue 'copters, but if they see us, they will probably bolt, if they can. We need to locate them fast and find a good secure landing near enough to hump it in but far enough to enter unnoticed. Keep searching."

The 'copters continue their zigzagging search. The commandos strain, and use all of the high-tech, state-of-the-art military toys and tools at their disposal. Imagine the most insane top gear you've ever seen on TV, magazines, or wherever; and they've got it. Still, some of the commandos start getting antsy that it's taking so long to find the crash site or any sign of the Olympians.

One commando leans over to another and begs, "Hey, you got a cig?"

The nervous helicopter pilot barely hears it but whips his head around to say, "No smoking in here!"

The indignant commando counters, "Screw you. We got the guns. I'll smoke when I damn well please."

The pilot bickers for his life, "It's a hazard. Dangerous. You want to complete your mission?"

The commando takes a weak swipe at him, then orders awkwardly, "Shut up and fly. Shut you up." Then the frustrated commando looks back at the other commando and says, "C'mon. I'll have a cigarette. This is taking forever. I'm ready to fight."

The other commando nonchalantly states, "I don't got any."

The first commando, livid, growls with gritted teeth, "You lie. I know you're holding. HAND ONE OVER!"

The other commando says antagonistically, "Fuck you!"

The first commando resigns himself to going cig less, redirecting his anger by bullying the pilot with a punch in the shoulder; causing the helicopter to jerk. Speaking of "jerk", the pissed-off commando slouches back in the seat to sulk.

Unable to find any sign of the crash site or the Olympians within this majestic maze of untamed mountains, the overloaded heli'copters eventually get low on gas. Cruise, forced to err on the side of caution, makes the executive decision.

He says over the comlink, with Shrike listening in carefully to every word, "Listen up all units: Everyone is low on fuel. We will land in the major clearing, half way down the mountain. We will have to find the crash site and athletes on foot while the heli'copters go back to refuel. I'm guessing we will be anywhere from 2000 to 6000 feet below the level of the estimated crash site area, and we will have to simply climb from there."
Several of the commandos groan, sounding like disappointed grizzlies who just let a salmon slip away.

Joaquin gripes, "Sir, yomping all the way up the mountain. Why can't we call some choppers in to look for them? My pack feels like it weighs a hundred pounds."

Cruise rejects, "That's impossible. Nobody's pack should be over 80 pounds. And I told you before, we need the full element of surprise so we can end this quick and get off of this god-forsaken mountain. And don't use that Brit slang on me! Yomping? I'll give you a yomp!"

The athletes continue to scramble over rocks and ice, higher and higher into the mountain peaks. Their athletic footwear, uniforms, and sweats aren't perfect, but definitely more suitable than business attire.

Sara notices a purple book hanging out of Shrike's bag.

Sara scolds with incredulity, "You're not lugging a heavy book, that's unnecessary, up with you?"

Shrike quips, "This is the last book I've really loved. **Humans Need Three Hands**."

Sara says, "I read it. Spot on!"

Shrike says enthusiastically, "I like how the author astutely comments on Kestrel's Zima-soaked 90's idealism – on the edge of self-righteousness, but never smug or intolerant."

Sara agrees, "I love **Humans Need Three Hands**, but it's hard to read."

Shrike says, "So is James Joyce."

Sara jabs, "and Steinbeck."

Shrike retaliates, "and Faulkner," each trying to intellectually out duel each other.

Sara says, "I mean Kestrel is pretty judgmental, which makes him harder to like, but I read it as an honest account of the way many people think at least."

They cross up into the sub alpine zone. Shrike stands high on a rock, overseeing the group of staunch athletes lugging huge amounts of gear over incredibly rough terrain. Even though the horse was left behind, the sailing and canoe teams were able to get their boats out of the cracked fuselage with only minor scrapes, and with the help of a wide range of other athletes, actually carry not one, but two boats up towards the bizarre sub alpine flora: twisted, gnarled, and stunted. A streamlined sailboat and a competition canoe become the first watercraft to ever reach this land elevation, but nobody's thinking about *Guinness's World Book of Records* right now.

Shrike listens in on the comlink headset for a minute, then turns and addresses Sara, Daniel, and James, "They haven't even found the plane, and they are landing way below snow line. That will buy us plenty of time to prepare."

Sara says, "Prepare for what? You think we're gonna fight? Them?"

Shrike says, "If we have to, and I think we will, then, we will."

Far below and away from the purview of Shrike and the athletes, Cruise orders the pilots to drop in sequentially and unload everyone from the tightly-packed 'copters onto a green, lush, boggy meadow; shrouded in heavy mist and ground fog. The soldiers' boots sink into the black mud, and they struggle with the massive amount of gear weighing them down. Eventually, each helicopter flies off to refuel and so that the pilot may rest. Each pilot has a commando holding a gun to his head; dropping Cruise's ground force from 128 down to 120 soldiers.

Once the last helicopter has flown off, the commandos stand in an open, silent field for a moment, motionless. It's as if they are sensing the air. Without a word, they all spring into action, checking their gear; readying their munitions; the unit, --- more than formidable: A small, compact, tough army.

Moments later, as if the commandos weren't already armed to the teeth enough, Gwen's cargo plane flies over. Cruise's communications officer signals it from the ground. The lumbering aircraft drops a parachute of heavy weapons and supplies. The soldiers sprint over to it before the parachute settles to the spongy bog, and tear into the additional gear, loading themselves up like pack animals. Lookouts stand guard in a wide perimeter with their guns drawn; but once the 'all clear' is given, they relax and whip out cigarettes, smoking like fiends. They have those most modern and up to date M16-type rifles. One guy throws huge machinegun belts over his shoulders for an M60; another crams grenades into his breast pockets.

Shrike's asymmetrical eyes go bright hazel, as she gently shuts them and draws in a slow, deep breath. She thinks about insects; the insects down below along the mountain range's lower elevations. She senses swarms of flying insects, and she pictures many more commandos, dressed similarly to those who hijacked the C-17. She thinks on it. She mediates on it. She feels everything. She can feel everything that breathes: everything that lives, for miles and miles around.

James goes to grab her by the arm and drag her along, but Sara stops him.

Sara says observantly, "Let her do this."

James shakes his head in disapproval, and watches.

Shrike comes out of it with a, "Hmmm?" She ponders what she feels.

Well above Shrike's position, Jay takes a break on a mountain peak to eat a granola bar. His ass aches from the sharp granite seat, but he toughs it out. Suddenly, Jay sees Gwen's cargo plane slip up out of the dense fog, bank hard to the left, and vanish over the distant mountains. He scratches his head in puzzlement.

Far down and well below Jay's vantage point, the commando's weapons spree continues at a feverish pace. Before the last weapon is packed, swarms of flying insects penetrate the mouths and ears and eyes and nostrils of each of the soldiers. The clouds of insects become so thick that it's hard for the troops to see each other. Most of the women and men don their goggles, while a few opt for their full gasmasks.

Back up in the snow, Shrike feels another overwhelming sensation, like she can sense the swarms of insects hampering the commandos. Shrike falls to her knees for a second. Daniel falls down by her side and puts his arm around her. He watches her intently. Shrike knows it's working. She knows it! The insects took her direction.

Shrike stands and turns to James, Sara, and a few others, and says, "The commandos are on the ground. A lot of them. They are well below snow line. We need to make serious preparations fast none-the-less … but at least we have time to furnish a wicked welcome."

The athletes are quite frankly confused. They love athletic challenges, but now, their perceptions are about to be challenged. Shrike twists like a caterpillar dangling from a silk line, and overcome by the power of one of the "telepathic messages" (for lack of a better term) in her head, she begins to groan.

"What are these messages and how is she getting them?" the athletes wonder aloud.

Shrike tries to explain, "It feels like a painful feeling. It feels like a bad memory that inflicts pain."

Shrike then realizes that what she feels is actually a single signal from one animal: One animal in overwhelming pain; the wounded equestrian horse suffering alone next to the fuselage of the C-17 cargo jet. Shrike calls the soccer and volleyball teams to drop their gear and come rushing back down the slope.

With a totally straight face Shrike orders, "As a team, with scouts and spotters, go euthanize the horse and take the meat. Right now."

Everyone looks around at each other with complete befuddlement. Did Shrike snap? They wonder, and they worry.

Colt stands like a statue. He wants to defend his horse. It is a brilliant horse. Expensive, talented, and a real unique animal; but Colt knows what needs to happen. He turns away stoically.

The combined teams however, ready for action, blast down the hillside on her orders like The Wicked Witch's flying monkeys, and with the efficiency of a Indy pit crew, dispatch the magnificent horse instantaneously and without ceremony.

Shrike feels a stabbing, sharp pain, deep in her brain when the horse is killed, and starts to rant ----- stringing incoherent words together.

Daniel grabs her by her upper arms and says, "Pull it together Shrike. Pull it together. You're blabbering."

Shrike stops for a second. She knows how this must look to them.

She straightens herself, then says, "Right, let's keep moving."

Everyone exchanges glances and rolls their eyes, as they fall in line to follow after Shrike, up the narrow path.

Shrike goes back to concentrating on projecting a biting nightmare of insects onto the commandos. Moments later, she feels feedback from many more animals. Maybe even all animals! She empathetically broadcasts back to them. They twinge with recognition: First extra-species contact!

Back down in the murky, muggy, mucky bog; the commandos swat flies and grunt with irritated complaints. Some of the flying little Kamikazes bite, while others sting. Some bite and sting! Some try to burrow their entire body into their host's fatty tissues and take out a chunk of moist flesh in the humid air.

"What's with all the firepower sir? I thought we were pickin' up a bunch of athletes?" questions Joaquin with a slap to the back of his neck.

 Cruise responds, "Yeah, but we don't know what we will be facin'." Raising his voice for the rest of the company to hear, he spits like a tough guy and scrapes biting flies off of his mouth, declaring "We know they are the fastest, the strongest, and most competitive; like we were when we gave our blood and souls to The Marines, and the other outfits you were all in. For what? Now, we get the pay we deserve, and we want to take them alive, and this firepower will assure supremacy! I don't take no chances. Cops, SWAT teams, even National Guard; we will kick their asses; whatever they throw at us. This operation is mine, and it's for real! Nobody fucks with me, and that means, NOBODY FUCKS WITH US!"

The commandos give out involuntary cheers as they binge on the last of the treasure chest of new toys. They obviously love this gun nut's paradise: the simple array of weapons insane; the shear amount of ammo ridiculous!

Moments later and satiated with weaponry, the company begins their long and arduous trek up into the vast wilderness. Two commandos nicknamed Flaca and Dumpy walk side by side up the trail and start jawin' like good ol' Carolina Tomboys; mainly to stave off the annoyance of the biting insects.

Flaca instigates, "Anyone up for some huntin'?"

Dumpy drools, "Yeh! I haven't shot anything since last Tuesday."

Flaca asks, "What was that?"

Dumpy responds with enthusiasm, "Pronghorn. Poached it just outside the park boundary."

Dumpy wrestles with a large, heavy bazooka. She's huge, so they let her carry the bazooka because it makes her feel big and bad.

Flaca says, "Nice."

Dumpy continues, "Yeh, I say we start killing shit for fun right now."

Skinny and wiry Flaca looks around with a cautious jerk. She struggles under the weight of her pack, laden with an additional 40 pounds of bazooka rounds.

Lohan turns to look back at them and says calmly, "Knock it off and stay on the mission."

"Yes Sir," they spew, dripping with sarcasm.

Joaquin, third in command after Lohan, turns to add, "Plus, this IS a National Park."

Flaca says, "Shut the fuck up pedo."

Joaquin shrinks back like the cowering Dr. Smith from *Lost in Space*.

Insects of all kinds now, even large flying beetles, crash into the commandos' faces.

Dumpy mumbles, "I love huntin'."

Flaca concurs, "Me too."

Dumpy explains the unnecessary, "Huntin' is the balls. Not that I'm ever hungry …" pausing to touch her ample paunch, "… I just do it for the kill. The duck is alive. Then, the duck is dead. I killed it. I took its life away. I played god. I have that power."

Flaca chuckles, "I like when the animal dies."

Dumpy contributes, "Yeh; kill, kill, kill. Huntin' rules."

Many of the men get to the point where they feel as if they must stop. They shed their rifles and scrub and brush bugs from their hair, gear, and necklines, with agitated fury. They spray repellent about liberally.

Lohan knows how sadistic these sick military miscreants are, so she keeps a firm hand and commands "Cut the chatter! Stop leaning on that bazooka; ... you'll mangle it you clod."

"Yes Sir!" they answer like robots.

Suddenly, the buzzy drone of insects is broken by the howls of wolves.

With an expression of fear, Dumpy says, "Wolves?"

She drops the jerky she gnaws on to put both hands on the bazooka.

Flaca says, "Holy shit."

An ant crawls up Joaquin's nose and stings his sensitive capillaries. He snorts it out with discomfort.

Joaquin says, "They are hopefully just coyotes."

Flaca argues, "No, those are wolves!"

Lohan turns again with frustration and belches, "So what. They are wolves. Big deal. Shut up and keep it movin'."

A large armored beetle flies right into her mouth. She chokes and spits it out.

Flaca and Dumpy wake to the seriousness of the potential dangers for the first time. They straighten up, and straighten up their gear, then begin to scan about with much greater focus and intensity. No more casual or moronic hunting discussions. Flying insects still overwhelm them completely. Several of the soldiers spray more DEET until it's gone, but the relentless flow of flying insects continues to plow into the soldiers' goggles, --- and to infest their equipment.

Mysteriously, a variety of animals begin to converge on the commando company, and follow their trail, from a safe distance. Like scavengers waiting for a carcass to fester, huge and tiny creatures alike, patiently monitor every action of the commandos. The shear variety of species conjures images of Noah's Ark, with a staggering array of biodiversity glinting and then fading beyond any commando's perception. A few of the most astute commandos, like Lohan and Cruise, sense they are being watched; while others like Joaquin, Dumpy, and Flaca remain oblivious.

A deer trots up the slope to come upon the jerky Dumpy had dropped. The deer sniffs it, then looks up at a raven and wags its tail vigorously. The raven blasts down to the ground, snags the jerky in its sturdy bill, and flies high up toward the mountain peak where the athletes are, accompanied by its mate.

Emotional strain? Manufactured stress? Outlandish deductions?

Chapter 3

Swarm Stampede

The phenomenal sunset is followed by the unveiling of a magnificently bright starry night. Sitting huddled together like a band of primitive apes after the long and steep climb; everyone's spirits seem remarkably high. Many of these athletes thrive on adversity.

Sara worries, "What, what is it Shrike?"

Shrike responds in agony, "Headache."

Sara looks for her instant go-to answer; "Pills! Who has got Nexpeedrin or some other headache pill?"

A number of athletes quickly go through their gear and jacket pockets. Several produce headache pills. Shrike gulps s couple down with some bottled water, under the glowing moonlight beams.

Sara hypothesizes about Shrike's bazaar brain pain, "Altitude, the crash, some other form of trauma? Who knows?"

Shrike proclaims articulately as she looks over at the Olympians who butcher up the horse and get the small, concealed fire going, "All athletes get a little bit of well-done horse meat for breakfast."

A group of athletes who fancy themselves backyard chefs go at cooking up all of the meat as quickly as possible. A few vegan athletes decline, as does the equestrian, Colt, who says in a stuffy, proper manner, "I'm glad my cheval and I were of service in some way at least."

Shrike replies with levity, "Hold your horses there partner. We are still going to need help from everyone and all of you. Each sport has its value. I shit you not!"

The athletes prick up their ears.

Shrike says, "Our first plan of action sounds very simple: Elusion! Specifically, we will elude their detection. They will exhaust everything: Their resources, their patience, ... their will, and finally ... their sanity! We will climb to the most unreachable heights in the rocks, where secondly, we will set up defenses, booby traps, and a number of other ways to strategically leverage our advantages."

Most of the athletes nod in agreement and approval of Shrike's command and leadership, even if they don't understand exactly what she means yet, ---- athletes like good coaching after all.

At that moment, the two ravens magically appear out of the black like apparitions. One drops the jerky into Shrike's lap, while the second calls to her from a nice roosting perch. Shrike interprets the signals like hearing a native tongue; knowing that the message is loud, clear, and ominous: The commandos are coming after them! Shrike shakes it off quickly, trying to appear sane to the others, and silently signals the ravens to go back down and maintain their vigil. They glide off into the darkness; the glossy moonlight shining on the iridescent wings. Shrike then rips a big chaw off of the confiscated jerky and masticates vigorously while the others watch in disbelief.

Sara wonders, "That's weird. I've seen crows take food *from* people, but never give food *to* people."

Daniel ponders, "That's what you find weird? What about them flying at night?"

James adds, "Yah!"

Shrike dodges and corrects, "Those weren't crows."

Sara silently wonders some more, her suspicions highly aroused. 'How could any of this be happening? Could Shrike be on the other side? Is their some kind of contrived hoax afoot?'

Shrike continues, a little too honestly now under the glowing Milky Way, "As I believe some of you have already ascertained by now, I somehow have powers to reach a level of communication with animals. I plan to have them help us, if they are willing."

Shrike says, "Anyone want to see a nice pair of common mergansers fly over?"

Sara, losing patience, blathers "What the hell is that?"

Shrike chuckles, then closes her eyes gently.

Blasting in, low over the horizon, come a gorgeous hen and drake merg pair. They buzz past everyone's heads; straight as arrows; then bank and fly back over for another good look. The crowd goes, "Oooooo. Aaaahhh," as if watching a fireworks show in the crystal moonlight.

Sara takes a giant gulp, choking on her shoe leather, then gags as she forces the words out, "Nice trick?"

Daniel and James address Shrike then Sara respectively, "Sorry I ever doubted you." and "Freakin' wow! You're not going to believe that?"

Shrike brags, "and … mergs don't even fly at night."

Sara does not know how to respond or react. Trying her darnedest to avoid sounding defensive, she states, "All I *know* is, I can't let myself believe what I see with my own eyes." A furry little weasel like creature, called a marten, comes up and nips Sara with a painful pinch to the inner thigh. Sara jumps in pain.

Shrike laughs, "Can't believe what you actually feel? Pinch me, I'm dreamin!"

The marten runs up Shrikes back and onto her shoulders. They can see that Sara looks like she wants to cry, but she holds it all in; and Shrike can see that she's wasting time now, so she switches gears back into work mode.

Several of the athletes rush over to Shrike and grab her. They tie her up and gag her as Daniel, James, and a few others unsuccessfully try to intervene. They are completely outnumbered.

James says, "Stop! What are you guys doing?"

Daniel says, "Have you guys gone crazy or what?" Several of the female athletes also try to help Shrike, but too many athletes crowd around Shrike now.

Sara emerges from the shadows and monotonically states, "Everyone stay calm. This is without a doubt, for her own good, and personal safety, and for the safety of this expedition."

James says, "You can't do that."

Sara says, "I'm the team psychologist. I can, and I did."

Daniel debates, "But ---- she's not on the team."

Sara rebuts, "Even more reason to protect THE TEAM, no? Insanity can be a tricky thing."

Everyone stands with their hands on their hips, contemplating their next moves. Daniel and James both look over at Shrike with despair, not fully comprehending what's going on.

Shrike knows she needs to get herself out if this if she is to save the Olympians, so she searches her mind for the nearest bird. The ravens have already plummeted miles below to their night roost above the commandos, so instead she finds a screech owl just above their location, in a bushy section of a tree. In her mind, she concentrates on having the owl fly in over the muted fire and land on her shoulder. Instantly, the small owl abides! Gagged, Shrike can't speak, but she keeps looking over at the owl on her shoulder, and then back at Sara deliberately. Her non-verbal eye language speaks volumes.
Everyone looks over at Sara for an explanation.

Sara says, "Look, I'm the team psychologist. Whether or not I'm a dead ringer for Penelope Cruz should be neither here nor there. I know my craft. When people start buying into supernatural mumbo jumbo, it's time for me to step in."

She waits, but nobody laughs. Her credibility plummets like a mussel dropped from the bill of a herring gull.

Sara stomps her foot down, "Me thinks Shrike is totally out of her mind; ... owl on the shoulder or not. Until the animals convince me, I'll stick with hard science thank you."

Most of the athletes look confused, and a few even look legitimately stressed, for the first time. They were pretty comfortable with Shrike as leader, and many lack faith in Sara.

One of Sara's cadre tries to convince James and Daniel, (but more importantly ----- himself) as he stammers, "The owl is just coincidence. Be reasonable."

Shrike's eyes grow angry, she mentally directs the owl to fly off ----- and just as quickly ------ a huge tom cougar appears with a roar. The athletes all fall backwards in shock and fear.

Colt goes for one of the M16s, but fears he will shoot Shrike. The largest cougar anyone has ever seen licks Shrike's face with its sandpaper tongue and carefully pulls the gag precisely out of Shrike's mouth with its canines.

Shrike shakes her hair out of her face like a high-end shampoo model, but still bound, says "Do you believe me now or would you like a swarm of hornets to come in and sting the hell out of your asses like a friggin'' Biblical plague?"

The cougar uses its molars to quickly gnaw through and free Shrike's bonds. Shrike stands strong and erect. The cougar sits obediently with its left shoulder tightly heeled to Shrike's diminutive hip. A marten runs up the giant cougar's back. Shrike wraps her arm around the cougar's shoulder and neck, as one would a loving Great Dane, and the American marten sits there as well with its forepaws resting on her hand, and with its hind legs on the back of the cougar's powerful neck and skull. The owl zips back in and lands on Shrike's left shoulder. Several athletes whip out their phones and snap off shots; and what a picture it makes: The four of them standing strong, together; a unified front and formidable as all hell. Next to the diminutive Shrike, the cougar looks like a freakin' Siberian tiger.

Shrike says loudly, with great force, "The western screech-owl, the cougar, and the American marten shall stay as my sidekicks wherever I go: as my eyes, ears, and bodyguards. Shoot us if you want Colt. And shoot James and Daniel while you are at it."
Colt lowers the M16 rifle.
Nobody can believe their stunned eyes.

The small owl of the night forest, the big puma of brawny outcrops, the cutely adorable marten with its ears pointed to the stars and its oversized paws, and the nothing-less-than-gorgeous Shrike turn to look directly at Sara as Shrike says matter-of-factly, "I wouldn't try tying me up again."

The cougar loudly snarls at Sara, who feels like she might pee her pants. Sara sits down right in her place. She knows when she's been licked figuratively, or could be licked literally -----

like Shrike just was moments ago. As consolation, a snowshoe hare, and then a beaver, crawl onto the lap of Sara's tightly crossed legs. They snuggle against her, instantly pushing any trepidation aside. Sara smiles, and accepts the impossible with warm embracing hugs. Tears erupt down her beautiful cheeks and onto her kissable chin. She is quite simply overwhelmed.

A bright moon now shines on everyone's glowing and radiant faces. Not only electrified Shrike, but also everybody else, including Shrike's animal buddies, seem to glow with the aura of champions. A tiny acrobatic nuthatch flies in and lands on Shrike's head. She reaches up and takes a pine nut from the inverted bird's chisel-like bill. The nuthatch darts off into the darkness again and up to a hole in a large dead limb. Shrike first smells and then wipes off the nut before chewing it with immense enjoyment, getting the most from the tangy fatty oils. The athletes spend a fun-filled 20 minutes or so, introducing themselves to more and more of the different animals that have entered the flattened sleeping area and meander around.

Shrike returns to a little nook-like cave to rest and quietly listen to the commando's comlink. She hangs on every word intently. James strains to hear, but only gets imperceptible mumbles and buzzes. After a few moments of silence on the comlink, Shrike hands the comlink off to Colt, who quickly puts it to his ear.

Shrike gets up and comes marching back out, "I need to quickly address the group ... even if you are already sleeping. Sorry. Having the benefit of the comlinks, we just learned that the commandos dropped in at an elevation well below the crash site, believing that we would be heading down the mountains in search of help, roads, food, etc. Of course, to the contrary, I have concocted an ingenious strategy (she says with a witty and sarcastic wink to the chuckling comrades), and brought you well-conditioned athletes high up into the jagged peaks; to give official authorities time to arrive, and to avoid the commandos COMPLETELY if at all possible."

Sara says with dejection, "For my PhD thesis, I ran a mock study where people could look into the future to see how they turned out, and then they had to decide whether or not they would want to live that life (low expectations, results, and all the failure that goes along with that), or to die. People made fun of *me* for being *crazy*."

The beaver rolls onto its back for a comfy belly rub on Sara's lap. She can't deny the reality right in front of her ----- lying on her thighs!

Sara challenges as she wipes the wetness from her running nose, "Are you sure you know what you are doing Shrike?"

Shrike responds defensively, "If the athletes went down slope, we would have to separate. I can see that you don't follow, but basically, going down slope as a group would be suicide because they would easily detect us. We could have a large number captured, or lost. We could lose everything and everyone."

Sara digs awkwardly, "And, we would also have to face the Yellowstone wildlife, ----- which we still are not sure how much you can control."

Shrike says assuredly, "Sara, I'm working on the wildlife as we speak. In regards to conservation, E. O. Wilson once said, *A wilderness of sorts can be reborn in the wasteland*. The commandos, in this case, is our wasteland; and the wild is being reborn, in a sense, temporarily, and refocused. Instead of foraging, procreating, or protecting territory ... they stop the commandos. That is their goal. I'm thinking of it in that way." Everyone looks at Sara for a response but for once, she's got nothing.

James jives, "Girl ... where you comin' up with this E.O. Wilson shit?"

Shrike looks off into the night sky like a zombie on acid and utters, "I don't know. I don't know where that came from. I don't know how I know that."

Concurrently and in stark contrast to the athletes' experience, the lower foothills remain moist, foggy, raw, and pitch black; and the commandos move quickly, trying to cover as much ground as possible before they bed down. More importantly, they strive to get to the right elevation to get away from the nagging, irritating insect swarms. Though some are frazzled, many of the better-disciplined commandos maintain their composure ... for now. They shoulder their guns, and most follow in a robotic line behind their commanders: Cruise, Lohan, and Joaquin.

Joaquin questions, "How far to the crash site?"

Lohan answers, "I don't know, but we are way the hell below it. It crashed above tree line but we were dropped off at about twenty-seven hundred feet."

Joaquin says, "What's up with that?"

Cruise answers like an awkward klutz, "We don't know how many, if any, of the athletes survived. None of our guys did obviously, so none of them may have neither; but their comlinks seem to still be on, so they weren't blown to bits."

Joaquin says, "So."

Cruise continues, "They could be alive, and we know they are in good shape, so they could have headed down the mountain at brake-neck speed; and now, they are probably bivouac-ed somewhere to catch some shut-eye. We don't want any of them, especially the healthiest, getting away by slipping through beneath us. By landing low, we know any survivors must be above us, and therefore have to come past us to get down. Logic!"

A commando passes by an outstretched log. Without so much as a rattle, a snake strikes him in the soft part of the calf, and then vanishes silently. He goes down with a groan. The medic runs over and treats him. A second commando stands by watching, while the others continue on. A wasp climbs onto the commando's cheek, under his goggles, and stings him on the eyeball. He screams in pain. The medic turns and starts treating him.

Cruise says over the comlink, "What is it now?"
The medic relays the wounds.

Cruise scolds with nun-like disappointment, glazed with guilt, "Geez, most of you guys survived Paris Island and yuh can't take some spiders and snakes?"
Two more distant yells ring out in the nightmarish oak woodlands, as more commandos come under stinging and biting assaults.

High above on a windswept peak, Shrike stands with her three guardians ----- like clustered gargoyles. The elements of the cold mountain air at night, and the raw chill from sweating on the ascent up the jagged, icy cliff, and still donning the damp underwear, don't faze her in the least. Daniel stands back, watching her.
She plays with her animal communication skills.
She tests her ability to control her mind, and how seamlessly and deeply she penetrates theirs.
All of the animals' thoughts appear to be basic: Id-like.
She is surprised to find that insects have a lot of thoughts going on at once.

Daniel, worried, asks her about the thoughts, "Not gonna hurt your brain now, are you?"

She says, "Thanks for asking. This is a trip. For example, if I were to translate exactly what I'm perceiving as the signals come in, like a streaming trade ticker, the carpenter ant would be like 'chem trail, intruder, no, friend, chem trail, heat, climb over other worker, get back on chem trail, go'. The monarch butterfly is like 'Left, correct color, adjust, wind gust, land on milkweed, roll out proboscis, feed, drink, good.'

Daniel says with amazement, "If I didn't actually see you control the animals with my own eyes I would totally think you were mental."

Shrike turns and pulls him in by both of his triceps. She looks around, both left and right, then plants a hot kiss on his full lips. They both look around again. Everyone sleeps quietly way too far away, and no one is watching. Shrike's three animal friends however actually need to learn how NOT to watch so much. Shrike and Daniel slide into a vaginal-like crack in the monolithic peak and just like that, emerge again about 20 minutes later, after an incredibly hot, passionate session.

Daniel whispers with life-altering afterglow, "Feels as if an animal is unleashed when you reach orgasm."

Shrike calms, "Don't worry… it's not the lightning bolt. I've always been this hot."
A lazy smile slowly creeps across his satisfied lips.

Back in civilization, everyone is scrambling. People click their remotes, quickly cutting back and forth from channel to channel, desperate for the latest "news" and pundit puns.

"Where is the plane?"
"What happened to the athletes?"
"Is Gwen for real?"
"She is a freakin' quack!"
"Analysts" banter.
News outlets spew.
Social media rattles and buzzes.

In her gloomy, smoggy lair, a wide-screen wall mounted monstrosity crackles off. Gwen stands, then moves around the room slowly. She crinkles her fingers. It is the media frenzy she expected, but the predictability of humanity makes her sick to her purely evil stomach. She restlessly opens a pack of beef jerky, then tears off a snap and chews hard, back at her molars.

Gwen says to a servant as she walks in, "What do you think about my new product? Lead Coke! It has four times the lethal dose of lead. Every kid who shares this with a friend will all be dead, and the authorities will simply track it to all the lead paint that's still around *in the environment!*" she states with sarcasm and derision.

The jaded servant emits "Yes ma'am."
Gwen cackles, "I estimate the demise of over 617,398 Coke consumers in the first month alone. I can't wait to see that

obscene crazy clown posse spray gallons of toxic lead all over their obese, inbred fans. Ha ha ha."
The servant looks away, trying to hold back tears.

Gwen doesn't like her weak reaction, then says, "Owh, contact Cruise right fuckin'' now!"

The aid gets onto the communication system, and struggles for a moment. A second aid comes over to assist. He pulls his phone out of his pocket and makes a quick call. He pins the phone between his head and neck, and flips the computer on.

Gwen taps her fingers quickly against the top of the computer, like a time bomb ticking down. She doesn't try to help in any way. Her job is to apply pressure through fear ------ manufactured stress.

"I'm not getting through," the aid says with a wince.
Gwen looks at the aid with volcanic eyes.

The aid says, "I can't get through. I can't."
Then the aid stands, slips his phone into his pocket, and runs out of the room with his hands up above his shoulders.

Gwen yells, "You're lucky you are one of the servants I like."
The other aid quickly flicks the TV back on to pacify and distract Gwen. Reporters bicker about what may have happened to the athletes.

A Fox news pundit spouts platitudinal clichés:
"Well, if Gwen has had anything to do with this, it's time for all good and the righteous…to come forward in prayer. This situation is in God's hands now."

Gwen bursts into laughter, "Did you hear that? You hear it?"
She spins around with her martini spilling from her glass, but no one is there.

She weakly glances around, almost lonely looking for a second, and definitely sad, and says, "Ppffft. God. Like *God* has anything to do with it."

She looks straight up, and strains her upper back between her shoulder blades with a screech, like she's having a heated conversation with a sibling, "What God? You know we are good. Don't listen to those hyper freaked-out newsmen you created in your image."
She sips away at her martini and draws hard on her cigarette.

High on the open, clear, calm mountain, everyone huddles in a large group on a rare spot of bare ground. Some people burp and stretch, while everyone else snuggles in; feeling quite satisfied from eating and drinking during the nocturnal picnic from earlier in the night.

Tara, one of the smallest gymnasts, goes over and delicately asks Shrike, "Ah Shrike? As you've been listening in on the headset, have you had any insights into why these people are after us?"
Shrike looks over at the surviving commando, tied and bound to a stretcher. He appears to be asleep.

With the eyes of a predator, Shrike says thoughtfully, "I don't remember who said it, but war happens for three reasons: Fear, honor, and self-interest. Obviously they don't have any fear; and they apparently have no honor whatsoever. We need to figure out what they want from us. Is their only motive money? They don't appear to be radical fundamentalists of any kind from what I've been able to ascertain."

Sara analyzes, "The only way we can do that is to get the injured commando to talk."

Sara, James, Daniel, and even Colt all gulp hard and look at each other shamefully. No one wants to be 'the torturer'. Shrike turns and marches over to the injured commando under the deep moon shadow of a snarled and long-dead oak trunk.

They wake him gently, then they say to the commando, "Tell us."

He says, "Just kill me. I'd rather be dead. If I'm going to be captured, I'd rather be dead. I'm not going to jail."

Shrike poses, "You are a big, tough survival dude, right? How about this? You tell us everything we want to know, and we let you walk. You tell us nothing, you go to jail for life." The commando knows he is severely injured, so he deeply contemplates his options.

Shrike and the others walk away and let him ruminate.

Shrike says to Sara, Tara, James, and Daniel with full confidence, "He doesn't like the idea of breaking the code and narcing on his comrades, but once he thinks about it, he will realize his best option is to cooperate with us. I know it sounds ruthless but don't give him anything. We need to break him."

Daniel says, "No. He has faith in his unit making it here and extracting him. We've got to shake that."

Hearing that, Sara suddenly recedes from the group and moments later, appears from the other side of the thick, dark oak, and over the commando. She hunkers down low, hidden in the contrasting shade from the moonlight.

She whispers seductively, "Hey, screw those guys. They're all goody-two-shoes and stuff. I want a piece of the action. If I help you win, how much will you cut me in for?"

The commando says, "Screw you lady."

Sara hushes with her delicate and sensual finger across his lip, "Shhhhh," partly with embarrassment over the epic fail, and partly by the fact that the young soldier referred to her as 'lady', insinuating oldness. She maintains her composure, then begins to exit like a slinky into the beaming golden moonlight with a serene voice, "I'll be back to help you get out of this when your mood ripens a bit, moron! You'll be needing my help when your guys don't make it here."

The commando retaliates, "They'll make it here."

Sara challenges, "Really? Just like your hijacking plan that went off without a hitch?"

The commando looks at her with anger.

Sara pushes in right to his face, "You fucked up. Look at you. You're helpless. Big strong man. Pffft. We could dispatch you at any point we decide you are too much trouble to keep alive. We could leave you for the coyotes to come scavenge, while you're still alive. The point is; you think you are all tough and superior, but you couldn't even hijack a plane with a bunch of unarmed, untrained athletes as the only obstacle. And now, you think you are going to get us outside the plane, without the element of surprise. We have your comlink you fuckin'' fuck up. We know every single move your stupid-ass commander Cruise is making."

Shock spreads across the commando's face at the sound of Cruise's name.

Sara recognizes his pitiful mental state and pushes further, "They have no chance in ever helping you in any way. They aren't even on the same mountain. They have been talking about aborting. You wanna listen?"

Sara holds the comlink up to his ear. He can hear faint crackles, then words . . . Words like: "Sir, we need help." "Medic, Medic." "This is out of control. Who has DEET?"

Sara snaps the headset back away from the commando's meaty head, and poses "And, think about this one: Why the hell would they even bother to help you now? What, they are going to risk their lives to carry you down or medivac you out, so they can make sure they get to cut you in?"

The commando closes his eyes and tries to turn his bitter head away.

Sara says, "You have to listen to me, and I've got all night and all day tomorrow."

Sara grabs him by the face and crushes his cheeks; their noses now millimeters apart.

"Don't forget. I'm your ace in the hole. You need me and I'm the only one who can and will get you out of this. The others don't care about money. They're into their gold medals and their pride! All I care about is money, and this is *finally* my *best chance* to get a lot of it fast and vanish into some gorgeous tropical jungle island paradise for my early retirement. Sound like a nice dream? You could join me. I look great in a bikini."

Sara pauses, but the commando, though looking like he could break, says nothing. Sara gives him a passionate kiss on the lips. She pulls away, and he opens his eyes and looks into hers. He does feel that she is beautiful, and warm, but he doesn't speak.

He studies Sara carefully as she slinks back over to join the huddle of the others. By the time she gets there, they break and march back over to the commando.

The moon beaming down on her magnificent mane of hair, Shrike says, "Tell us everything and walk away a free man, or stay tied up until you go to jail or rot to death."
Shrike and the rest walk away again, giving the commando no time to answer.
The commando thinks for a second, almost speaks, and then wrestles with himself.

Finally, 22 minutes later, he says, "Wait."

They are already gone; far off making defense plans. The commando looks over at the five stone-faced athletes on guard. The commando lowers his ashy, filthy head back and closes his eyes. He coughs up a little blood. One of the guards gently wipes the spittle with a rag and then shows him the red sputum, causing the commando's heart to sink further.

As Shrike and Sara discuss ways to psych out the commando, they also can't help but notice that the athletes have gradually started to bicker a bit about the moral aspects of having the commando as a hostage. The tension builds as James tries to defend Shrike's maneuvers, but the moral furor escalates. Shrike steps away from the group and out from under the semi-cave meeting area, climbing up on some boulders. She and the owl look up in the sky for heli'copters.
Nothing.

As she monitors the inconsequential comlink chatter, she feels overwhelmed by the warm rush of animal sensations. The cougar comes over and brushes up against her. Shrike gives it a big warm tight hug. She knows she reaches them mentally, because, they reach her.

Shrike feels the insects biting the shit out of the commandos' necks and hairlines.

Shrike feels birds react when they see the commandos.

When they sit in a tree and the commandos stroll by, the birds flinch, and give off alert calls.

Shrike feels those again.

Sara approaches her from behind and gently puts a loving hand on her shoulder, as the cougar snarls and keeps a close eye on Sara.

Shrike defends, "I don't believe in that super-paranormal shit whatsoever. I know lightning should kill you, not give you powers. I am simply stating facts . . . based on evidence."

Shrike turns and looks straight into Sara's spectacular and sympathetic eyes and states lucidly, firmly grasping both of her shoulders, "I can think, and the animals will do. I don't know how. I don't know why. Don't fuckin'' ask me. It's just what is happening right now."

Sara theorizes, "It's your subconscious beliefs in these things that are tricking your mind. Just because I can't explain what is happening with these animals does not automatically mean you are correct about your outlandish assumptions."

Shrike rejects, "No. No. I'm not in denial. I never believed in ghosts or gods, or voodoo, or superstition of any kind. I don't! I'm not susceptible to that at all, and if somebody wants to tell me my moon is in retrograde, I'm like 'whatever'. I shit you not."

James defends her as well, as he approaches with Daniel, "You know Sara, she says she don't. She don't."

Daniel illuminates, "Look, I'm not saying I believe in shit, but I know some friends who are Native Americans, and they truly believe in animism, like, people, ah, you know, go back as apes and early tree dwellers, and like amphibians and fish, and all the way back. We are connected to all living things evolutionarily. We are all part of them, and vice versa. I think the lightning bolt fused something --- connected you together somehow; not to other people, but other species."

James concurs, "It's like *Life/Energy Fusion*. Maybe dark matter and shit like that."

Sara protests, "Pure and utter preposterousness!"

Daniel conjectures, "She's right. It could be fission, not fusion."

James and Shrike nod with their hands on their chins, in deep thought.

Sara blurts a frustrated "Ahh."

They look at her in confusion.

Sara says, "I don't know what I'm saying. Stupid. Ridiculous. How?"

After Shrike awakens and calls a small group together for yet another typically efficient meeting, everyone disperses. Shrike switches up the guards on the commando. Instead of a bunch of strong men with a gun, Shrike has intentionally gone with the Olympians she deemed to be simultaneously the most petite, gorgeous, and sexual. Two synchronized swimmers, a voluptuous teen tennis star, and two perky-butted gymnasts play it cool and start out subtly, and then, creeping like a fog, gently warm up to the commando. First, the commando feels as if they are being reasonably friendly, but then the suggestions and innuendos begin: playing off of his ego. A couple of the girls act inappropriately friendly with each other ------ and sometimes hug each other affectionately, right in front of the commando's eyes. Though drugged on painkillers that Sara had slipped into his water, the commando is anything but catatonic as he stays transfixed on the girls; his eyes a'droolin'. The girls can see that it's working: lock, stock and barrel. The girls swing it up into *Girls Gone Wild* party mode. On an empty stomach, with the loss of blood, and at elevation, the injured commando feels extremely buzzed and lightheaded. The girls start hugging and kissing him.

A gymnast whispers in a soft hush, "Relax sweetheart. Everything's going to be alright."

Flabbergasted, the injured commando struggles to explain, "I, I, I don't know what to say. I've never been near girls like you before."

The tennis queen rubs her lips against his ear when she coaxes, "Like Us? What do you mean by that?"

The aroused commando stammers further, "Oh I don't know… like All-American. You girls are like who Tom Petty was talking about when he wrote *American Girl* and *Last Dance with Mary Jane.*"

The girls ratchet up the seduction meter, "Mmmm." "Ha ha ha." "Mmmmm."

Encouraged now, he drives forward while he tries to inhale them, "The girls I grew up with all wore tons of makeup and perfume, and high pointy heels. You girls are so fresh and clean and natural."

They rub their bombas in his face and their fingers over his pistol. One of the girls unzips him and starts fluffing him up. The commando starts to get hard, but can't afford to let himself like it, and in turn feels smothered, apprehensive, and helpless; lying bound and immovable. He is used to being the dominant attacker (technically … the rapist), and has never played the equal, let alone the submissive.

He says, "Wait girls, can't I use my arms? C'mon."

The girls continue to molest him without missing a beat. Over the sound of the girls' sexual moaning suddenly comes that of an old woman being strangled.
All of the girls raise their heads.

Shrike approaches the commando with the cougar on a makeshift leash. She uses all of her strength to pull the cougar back, but it drags her forward as she digs her heels into the powdery soil. The cougar lets out a second, even more blood-curdling old-lady scream.

The commando looks up with a start, then yells, "Hey. Mother of god. Hey. What is goin' on?"

The cougar drags Shrike right up to the commando. The five guards "on duty" all jump back in horror with high-pitched screams.

"Get back!"

"Look Out!"

"IT'S OUT OF CONTROL!"

The bound commando screams in panic, "No, don't' let it eat me! Don't let it eat me!"

The cougar drags Shrike forward, putting its heavy paw upon the commando's chest and digging its claws in a little over an inch. The cougar then opens its mouth wide, completely swallowing the commando's face, and digging its huge canines into his skull and jaw.

The muffled scream of the commando vibrates through the big cat's muscular body and along its ribs.

Shrike tries her hardest to pull the big cat back off of the paralyzed commando. The cougar slides down the commando's quivering body, and to his still semi-erect penis. The cougar puts the penis delicately between its teeth, and holds it in a frozen pose, panting.

The commando yells, "Noooooooo!"

Shrike says, "Tell me your mission or the cougar gets wiener for din din."

The cougar slightly bites down on his quickly shrinking member.

The commando winces and whines, "Oh. Mommy. Mommy. Where are you Mommy? Mommy. Mommy."

Shrike gets pissed, "Yes yes yes, you miss your mommy. You are going to be missing a lot more so stop dicking me around or you'll be a dickless Dick."

James adds, "Gee Shrike, aren't you being a little bit too *dickadent*?"

Everyone within earshot chuckles heartlessly at the wordplay.

The commando cries, "Okay, call him off."

Shrike yells, "Him? Him? How do you know it is a him? Pretty insulting, don't you think cougar?"

The cougar growls and sucks the commandos balls into its mouth as well.

The commando says, "I'm sorry. We are here to hijack the plane, and, and get a bunch of ransom for you."

Shrike says, "Who sent you?"

The commando says, "Some lady. I swear. I don't know anything. I was told to hijack the plane. I was following orders."

Shrike interrogates, "You just follow stupid orders, never asking why, or who gave them?"

Sara yells, "Orders for what? For money?"

The commando says, "Yeah. Money. For money. What do *YOU* work for?"

Shrike says, "So this is just a job for you?"

The commando thinks it better not to respond to that.

Shrike says, "How many people are coming for us now?"

The commando says nervously, "I have no idea. Believe me please."

Sara says, "Well what kind of resources does this lady have?"

The commando answers frankly, "Look at how well I'm equipped. She's got a lot of power, and political money and clout. I don't mean this as any disrespect, considering my current situation at hand, but seriously, all of you guys are screwed. They are going to find you soon, and track you down. You gotta give up and make it easy on yourselves."

Looking over the commando's state-of-the-art gear forces James to say ominously, "I bet this lady could front a little army."

They scan the commando's face to see if his eyes betray him. They conclude that he tells the truth.

Shrike pulls the cougar off with ease. It licks the rough roof of its mouth repeatedly and sticks its tongue out, trying to get the taste of yucky commando off of it, then the cougar gives hugs and lovingly licks to Shrike and Sara. The five guards, who had pretended so well to be scared, surround the cougar with big teddy bear hugs. The cougar loudly purrs with affection.

The commando says, "What the fuck! What the fuck? You tricked me. I was duped."

As Shrike releases the fake leash, and turns to leave with the cougar, she says, "No, no trick. I still may have it bite your dick off and swallow your friggin'' mercenary face."

The commando stares off at Shrike and the cougar as they vanish into pitch blackness. He then looks over at the sweet girls who had been so nice to him, and he smiles. They look at him with complete disgust. He was so sucked in by the foreplay before the cougar encounter that it's not until now that he realizes that none of those girls really like him.

Hesitating, and not really wanting to know the answer, the commando says with disappointment, "You mean we aren't goin to finish what we were, ya know, doin'?"

Tara picks up a sharp stick. She stabs him in the side of the neck, excavating a deep puncture, then stabs him again in the middle of the forehead. The already battered commando tilts his head back in pain, bleeding profusely.

The tiny gymnast Tara says, "You know how disgusted I feel after having touched you. Ewww. You are less than a person. You are less than human."

One of the synchronized swimmers says, "You are way less than that cougar, that's for sure."
All of the woman stare at him with despising eyes.

The commando closes his eyes in disbelief. In his mind, he still thinks he is going to be part of some big orgy. Physically, he is in excruciating pain, and now bleeding in a horrible nightmare of his own creation.

Moments later, reclining down for the night onto a comfortable bed of moss and lichen, and surrounded by furry animals, Shrike smiles and says, "It's starting to work," to James, who beds down right beside her.
Daniel leans up on his elbow to see how close James is to her. He doesn't like it one bit.

James responds, "I don't know. Even if he totally breaks, how much more info are we gonna get from this guy?"

Shrike puzzles, "Hmmm. Good point. The last thing we want to do is torture out of malice."

At that same moment, Jay still hikes way up above all of the goings on. He has been mostly in the alpine zone, and didn't want to bed down until he found the crash site. Sitting on a huge rock, he lights his pipe and takes a big hit of some fine herb. He holds it deep for a good 20 seconds, then lets out a nice bluish cloud into the moonlit night. He scans downward with his binoculars, knowing that the plane crashed somewhere below his vantage point, but he can't see anything. He knows nothing of the commandos, much further below. Suddenly, a herd of bighorn sheep and a pack of wolves appear. Jay stands up. They surround him, but since he doesn't flinch, they act non-aggressively. The herd of mostly rams melts in around him and presses up against his sides. They squish Jay, then start trotting down the mountain. They sweep Jay away, while the wolves shepherd along the perimeter, keeping a close eye on Jay and encircling the bighorns. They guide him (in a somewhat polite manner, for a prisoner), down the hill, and straight into Shrike's part of camp.

Having only fallen asleep moments earlier, Daniel says with uncomfortable surprise, "Where did this guy come from?"

As everybody sits up and the marten and owl jostle into alertness, Sara suggests under her breath, "He must be one of them."

Jay defends, "I'm a lounge singer."

The shot putter accuses, "He's a commando. Let's beat the shit out of him."

Shrike says, "Look at his gear, he can't be a spy."

Several people and animals rip through Jay's gear and pat him down for weapons or wires. The most dangerous things he has on him is a small Leatherman utility tool and his lighter. The marten lets Shrike know that he's clean.

Daniel, after hesitating for a moment, says, "Maybe that's exactly what he's supposed to look like?"

James eggs on the Trojan Horse scenario, "Maybe that's what we're supposed to think?"

Jay grows uneasy and states, "Maybe you people are entirely paranoid? What the hell are you doing up here dressed like this anyway? How do you get the animals to do what you say? And if you were in that plane crash below, why would you be heading up instead of down?"

Shrike says, "We can't tell you anything about anything right now, but you can tell us: Did you see any other people?"

Jay states truthfully, "All I saw was a plane quickly circle back around and crash. Then I saw a small cargo plane come up from deep in the clouds down in the valley. I swear that's all I saw and I don't know anything about the anything going on. I'm hiking. I'm looking at nature, trees ... birds."
Shrike, Daniel, and James glance at each other for a second, but maintain their poker faces.

Sara peppers, "What were you doing up here?"

Jay repeats, "I'm telling you, I was hiking. I'm just hiking man. How did you train these animals?"

Shrike says, "We will ask the questions. Sing us a lounge song singer, quick!"

He breaks into a Sade number, the notes languid and smooth, but solid and strong. His voice sounds great in the great outdoors, and one thing's for sure; Jay, without a doubt, spy or not, is a great singer. The nearby animals all prick up their ears. The wildlife definitely warms to the bliss of the *a cappella* serenade.

Colt says, "Sade is a lot harder to pull off than she sounds."

Sara gushes like a Beatles fan, solidifying the instant, "You've convinced us you can sing! He can't be with the commandos."

Shrike, angered at Sara's inappropriate disclosure, tries to clean up after her, "Yeah, you sure can sing very well. A natural. You're not *Search and Rescue*, *Ski Patrol*, or anything like that?"

Jay replies, "A lot of hard work though too, with years and years of training. It's a labor of love for me though. I love it. I love to sing."
The entire athletic squad begins to soften and the animals sense no sign of creepiness from Jay.

Shrike asks, "Plans for tonight?"

Jay says, "Just planning on pitching a tent, but I felt like I wanted to keep hiking until I made it to the plane site. Before I knew it, it's already the wee hours of the morning. I still have enough food for two more days. That's when I plan to loop back to the trailhead and out of the park."
Jay looks over at his huge bag and sees a much huger black bear toying with it like it's as light as a feather.

Jay stammers, "Bear! B-b-b. B-b bear. Bear eating!"

Shrike quells, "Don't worry. She's guarding it."
The bear gives off a Chewbacca-like groan.

Jay says with surprise, "Guarding it? That's like leaving the fox guarding the hens, isn't it?"

Shrike softly announces to those athletes that are still awake, "Jay will be crashing with us tonight. He seems to be okay, but keep five guards on him at all times, and no one gives him any kind of information at any time."

Two of the smartest animals, a coyote and a crow, as well as three of the female athletes, simultaneously move toward Jay and sit around him. Some stay a little further back, but they all have their eyes trained on him. Since this setup feels a little redundant to the coyote, it decides to get some shuteye while the others maintain focused attention into the early morning hours. A couple of the other athletes who can't sleep, and a raccoon who is wide awake anyway, go through all of Jay's gear even further. After a prolonged sniff and a whiff, the raccoon finds Jay's bag of weed, and hands it over to Shrike right before she starts nodding off. Other than that, it's clean. No transmitters. No sneaky commando stuff.

Shrike laughs and says, "I have the feeling this guy might be legit, so we gotta get him as far away from us as possible before the commandos arrive."

"How?" comes a faceless voice from the peanut gallery.

Shrike thinks and offers, "Any number of way. Strap him to an elk and send it off to the valley."

James worries, "You sure about that Shrike?"

Shrike reasons, "They killed the pilots without a second thought. You think they're going to keep a meddling hiker around?"

Jay lies silently in a bed of bighorn sheep, pretty far away from Shrike, but can still make out some of what they are saying. He feels very warm and snuggled in. Only his face pokes up into the night air. Jay sees vigilant guards fixed on him as the last vision before drifting off to sleep with the cozy sheep. He's obviously an animal lover, and he gives off a completely opposite vibe from the injured commando ----- of whom none of the animals like in the least.

Simultaneously, far below and pitch black under the thick gloomy fog layer, the commandos sit in the thorny dark uncomfortably.

Joaquin says, "Why can't we light a friggin'' fire? I'm freezing my ass off here."

Dumpy conjures with agreement, "Ever heard of hyperthermia?"

Lohan replies with disgust, "So they can't see us, moron."

Joaquin fights back, mimicking Lohan's voice, "What does that matter? They can't stop us or anything. Maybe if they see the fire, they will come to it for help."

Lohan says, "What did you get discharged for?"

Joaquin says with a weird badge of honor, "Contributing to the delinquency of a minor. Can you believe that? Pfft."

Lohan responds, "Yes. Yes I can. Specifically, what was the act?"

Joaquin says with a smarmy smirk, "Ah, c'mon, act! The act! Don't call it that. I was poking a fourteen year-old and getting' her drunk. You know how it is. Big fuckin'' deal. She *totally* wanted it. I was the best part of her teenage years man. I never had somebody cool like me when I was a kid. I didn't know she would be stupid enough to get herself pregnant. Any guy will do it if he can. She just happened to be very short, ah, very, very short for her age, so she got a lot more sympathy in court cause as the defense put it, she 'looked young' and put on 'the baby act' for the jury: Just like she does to entice and entrap men. I, I told the judge I had nothin' to do with her attempting suicide. That was a total cry for help if I've ever seen one. Not my fault though. I didn't tell her to do that. You know how kids are today, right? Right? Vindictive!"

Lohan rejects, "Oh, you were entrapped by a fourteen year-old? When this mission is over . . . remind me to castrate you." At that moment, Cruise paces over to them and calls everyone in.

He orders, "We will set up a camp here and a command tent. Eat as much as you can and get as much sleep as possible, and be ready to move out in ten minutes notice, in silence, with no lights, combat ready, and with the Lord our God on our side!"

Dumpy scoffs with Flaca, under her breath, "Ha! Combat ready, hee hee hee."

Flaca concurs, "I know Dumpy. This is more like a search and recovery mission, if anything."

Dumpy begs, "Flaca, as my only friend, I wish you would refrain from calling me "Dumpy".

Flaca orders, "Don't have feelings."

Dumpy defends, "Hey, I'm as tough-skinned as anybody."

Flaca argues, "No, you are soft and weak and that's why everyone calls you Dumpy.   You brought that name on yourself. No one calls me Dumpy."

Dumpy reels, "You suck."

Flaca states with firmness, "Don't blame me, *Dumpy*." Almost wanting to cry, Dumpy bites her lower lip, pulls it together, and scratches her insect welts until they bleed.

Suddenly, a large number of wolves give off blood-chilling howls. A high-pitch caterwaul goes off like a siren. The troops can't discern its origin. It could be from a bobcat. It could be something else. The men start to freak out a little; clutching some of their hardware and straining to see something, anything.

Dumpy reports, "They sound close!"

A few of the soldiers stand up and look around through their termite-covered night-vision goggles. They can see shadows moving just outside their visibility range.

"Crap!" Flaca mumbles as she slinks back down to the ground to lie on her uncomfortable bedding of detritus.

At the exact same time that all of this commando consternation takes place in the foothills, the athletes apparently sleep deeply in comfort near the peak, getting full rest and plenty of R.E.M. time. Shrike slips out from under the jacket she uses as a blanket, and out from under the cougar's arm, and stands on the edge of a jutting point of sharp rock, over a dizzying cliff. She closes her eyes and senses what the animals see and feel. She stands, frozen, sending a solid simple message, and shining like a lighthouse. The cougar and the owl watch her intently, but the cute marten is still fast asleep.

Not but a few moments later that evening, as the very last of the commandos bed down restlessly for a shot at some sleep; centipedes, ants, and beetles cover them. Many can feel ticks biting their groins. They call over the medic to start removing ticks from commandos' scrotal sacks, but it is hard to do in the dark, and with more biting bugs crawling everywhere, and moths filling the night air like fluffy, annoying snowflake smokescreens that just won't fall, all actions seem futile. The medic calls two commandos over and teaches them how to remove ticks as well, then gets them 'on the ball' to speed things up. Many of the soldiers are itching and scratching with agitation, and well beyond annoyed, their stress levels burst.

One yells, "DEET! Who brought DEET?"

Others hold flashlights during the tick removal, while they wait their turns to be groomed like gorillas.

Cruise's tent is basically a small, opaque, camouflaged, one-person dome tent, where he and others squish in to meet, and use red lights to view maps and plans. He unzips the tent with aggravation and yells, "Flashlights off assholes! What do you not understand about 'blackout'?"

Joaquin whines with the stub of a cigarette dancing in the corner of his mouth, "Sir, the men are infested with ticks and what not. They're, ah, grooming each other," he stammers awkwardly, recognizing just how animalistic the scene actually looks, with everyone hunched in the dark and grunting like big apes.

A voice from the peanut gallery carps, "So much fah don't ask don't tell, ha ha hah."

Cruise yells again, "Shut up *smart ass*." Then he says to Lohan and Joaquin redundantly, "Get this situation fixed fast. Pronto."

As Cruise stomps off, he can hear a commando off in the trees say, "Better than being a *dumb ass*."

Cruise pauses for a slight moment as if he is about to turn and attack, but instead, he lets out a gasp of exasperation and dives back toward the tent. Tons of insects fly into the frustrated commander's face and ears. Cruise turns in anger for a second, pauses to swipe insects away and see his company frantically doing the same, then reaches for his command tent zipper, with absolutely no sense of humor. Cruise is literally bugged. Once inside the command tent, Cruise quickly rubs the bugs and beetles off of his head, face, hair and shoulders. He zips the tent tightly behind him, serious as hell. Unlike Shrike and the athletes, who seem to do everything with a sense of lightness and bravado, Cruise does everything with heavy anger and fear in his soulless heart and underdeveloped mind.

One of the most undisciplined troops on guard, Flaca, sneaks up on an even less disciplined soldier, Dumpy, and suggests, "Let's wander back into camp. I'm out of butts and I got bugs crawling all over me."

Dumpy says, "We are on guard duty."

Flaca responds in a stressed whisper, "Guard duty from what? What the hell are we worried about fighting?"
Dumpy agrees and they start walking back to camp.

The flustered troops in the camp hear the two guards walking back down into camp and scramble for their weapons.

"Night vision! I hear somebody moving out there," they say over the comlinks and aloud to each other.

Cruise's men almost shoot their own guards in a 'friendly fire' incident, leveling their machine guns at them before the guards respond over their comlinks, "Hey, are you guys talking about us?"

Everyone breathes a sigh of relief, realizing that with the insane insect effect, they could easily start blowing each other away.

Wolves, along with what sounds like a bear, growl ferociously in the ink black night. Ravens and crows invisibly mock with ratchet-set screams from the concealment of the thick evergreens.

Dumpy calls out, "Medic. Medic!"
The medic comes running up.

Dumpy says, "I think I got something biting me."

The medic complains, "We all have something biting us right now."

Dumpy confesses sheepishly, "Ah, I think it's on my ass."

The medic says, "Okay, drop your pants."

Dumpy drops her pants and underwear, and bends over to spread her ample cheeks. There, two ticks have largely engorged themselves in her butt crack just above the anus.

The medic instructs, "Don't move. I'll have these off in a jiffy."

As the medic prepares to carefully remove the second tick, Flaca looks on, to the embarrassment of Dumpy. Suddenly, Dumpy lets a nasty fart rip.

The medic flinches back with utter repulsion "Don't make my job disgusting!"

The rest of the troops laugh at such a preposterous comment. *Now* it has finally become disgusting? Dumpy pulls her pants back up quickly.

The troops direct their energy to the insect battle, as more yells erupt. When Cruise leaves the planning tent to attend to the yelling troops, standing and wiping insects away from their faces and necks, a huge mixed colony of several bat species and nightjars come flying in and hit the commandos in their faces repeatedly. The commandos yell, and swat, but they can't really see anything coming in on them. Nighthawks and bats collide head on into the commandos' faces, with their jaws agape! Owls of every size blast into the camp silently and snatch GPS units, flashlights, loose ammo, and anything else they can carry. One nighthawk scoops up a commando's glow stick from a stump and drops it into a hairy woodpecker hole some thirty-two feet up. Following the disappearing glow stick by craning his neck up, the soldier can't see what he is doing, and stumbles over a log and a boulder into a thorny blackberry bush. A ringtail slips into Cruise's tent during the chaos by tearing a little hole in it with its teeth, and takes off with the map. A great-horned owl knocks over a camp stove and lights the underbrush on fire. A great gray owl snags a small ammo belt and drops it into the flames. Some of the commandos make the mistake of shooting into the air, not only wasting ammo, but giving the athletes high up near the mountain top an exact fix on the commandos' location miles below. Bats bite soldiers' cheeks and noses. Their screams echo in the massive canyon.

From miles away, rubbing their eyes in disbelief, the athletes crawl out from under the warm furry animals to see Shrike balanced on the edge of the precarious peak; almost in a trance. The athletes walk to the edge of the cliff to look down and watch the glowing melee ensue in the thick forest far below.

"What on God's Earth is going on down there?" James asks Shrike, looking compassionately into her moon-reflected eyes.

"I told you," Shrike replies robotically, "I told the animals in the area to kill as many of them as possible tonight." Tears well up in her eyes. "I told you, it's you or them. The animals understand they have no quarrel with the commandos, but the animals also all have a sense that good must win, and that evil is just wrong. There is no evil in nature; only in man."

The athletes and Sara continue to look at each other in disbelief, then look back down at the tiny, flickering, undeniable orangey glow, far, far below. How can the crazy shit she's saying not be true?

A single blood-curdling scream, louder than all of the rest and actually reaching all the way up to the athletes, rises up from the flicker in the blackness as a commando gets bit in the eye by a bat while he tries to remove another bat from his jugular vein.

James says in awe, "Oh my god. Oh my god."

Shrike says, "I have no choice. It's us or them. We don't even really know what they want from us, but it can't be anything but bad."
She caresses his black shinning face. He calms.

If only the commandos could experience such calm. Way back down in the bottom of the canyon, still well below snow line but with raw temperatures dropping into the thirties, rodents -- like mice, gophers, and rats; along with other secretive subterranean mammals like shrews and moles, appear ubiquitously from beneath the loose forest floor and peat; gnawing holes through every wire, lace, or strap they can find. With all of the chaos of the nocturnal avian and invertebrate attacks punching forward in full swing, it makes it impossible for the troops to hear or notice any of the gnawing rodents at work. Even the large beavers nearby go unnoticed as the four of them drop a tree onto Cruise's command tent, completely folding one side like a taco. Everywhere and out of nowhere, little varmints tear into packages of food and first aid kits; spilling and mixing mess with meds. A badger comes up from a burrow and bites a hole into a ten-gallon plastic water container, causing the precious drinking water to gush out. Two soldiers run over to the container to pick it up and dump it onto the fire. They find it empty as soon as they lift it, look at each other with surprise, and then one of them throws it back to the ground.

At the height of the camp chaos, bullets start exploding in the fire. A soldier is hit and goes down. Suddenly; in the blink of a blinded, bruised, and bloodied eye; a herd of 48 bison, 19 elk, 16 white-tailed deer, and a moose, come plowing through the camp shoulder-to-shoulder, like bulldozers on amphetamines; stomping troops to the ground. There is no foreshadowing whatsoever ----- no warning rumble. The bats, nightjars, moths, beetles, termites, and other creatures of night flight have been keeping the commandos so busy with hits from behind, from the sides, and from the front, that they never see the behemoths coming barreling down the slope at a good 33 miles per hour. Everything happens too fast, and out of the pitch black. Most of the commandos have no idea what hits them. Also, these massive herbivores are not trotting, or even galloping. It is a full sprint right through the troops' camp, the black silhouettes strobing past the fire glow. 48 bison make such a formidable force that it's almost as if the interspersed elk, deer, and moose don't even exist, though they stomp and skewer their fair share, and continue on down the mountain unimpeded.

Right behind the first stampede, and so close on their heels that the soldiers don't even get a moment to bounce back, comes the next wave: 21 wolves, interspersed with seven coyotes, six bobcats, three foxes, a cougar, a black bear, and a grizzly. It looks like every single animal that was in the territory showed up. They jump on the splayed-out commandos and maul them viciously, with some of the unconscious soldiers being quickly decapitated. One soldier has all six bobcats on him; one ripping his face and neck wide open, while the others bite each hand and leg. Reminiscent a pride of miniature lions, they uncharacteristically team up like a pack, with devastating effect.

Another trooper looks over, then down, but can't figure out exactly what he is looking at in the dark. It looks like a wriggling mass of maggots, but no, ... it's the bobcats, biting, twisting, ripping, and tearing at the commando on the ground. Before he can acknowledge what he sees and register it in his brain, the big tom bobcat springs off of the prone commando, and up into the other guy's face; knocking him backward over a big log.

While all of this insane animal action diverts the troops from any other duties, Shrike calls the American gold medal cyclist over to where the asphalt begins at the fire road.

Shrike explains clearly, "According to the info we got off of Jay's hiking maps, we believe this is the start of the fire road, which leads to the main road out of the park."

The world record-holding track cyclist protests, "I'm a track cyclist, not a road cyclist. This is a track bike. I can't go on the road with this."

Shrike counters, "We *don't happen to have* a road cyclist or a road bike*, we just happen to have* you. I think we're gonna need the mountain and BMX bikers on this terrain we are going to face. Your bike would be useless up there. The most important way you can save us is to race down the mountain and get the word out. Why do you think we lugged your bike all the way up here for?"

All sinew-and-bone, the track cyclist protests further, "But it's not designed for the road. I don't know how it's going to hold up. Most years I race *Team Pursuit*. Look at my helmet."

Sick of the whining, Shrike dismisses, "Good luck."

And with a push, the camouflaged track cyclist with her Kevlar racing bike heads down the steep road in stealthy silence, and in a matter of moments, slips past the commando's elevation position. For a millisecond she thinks she hears a couple of commandos screaming in pain. With branches attached all over her bike, she looks like a bush moving down the road and blends in well, as long as she hugs the brush along the edge. It doesn't matter because the commandos are so occupied that they are oblivious to the adjacent fire road and her passing presence. She reaches speeds of 61 mph on the steepest declines. Her bike rattles and wobbles in the darkness so she cautiously brings the speed down a little bit. Once well clear of the snow and ice line, and having traveled several miles beyond where the commandos could be, she pulls over and dumps the branches, then continues to pedal on into the night, as silent as a cloud. Her body quakes uncontrollably from the cold, but she rides on like a true hero.

High up above, Shrike barks, "Before we lose anymore precious sleep, everyone bed down. Move in tight to insulate your body heat. The animals will also lie on top of anyone who feels cold."

The BMX dude says, "I volunteer my services, if any of the girls want me to lie on them. Seriously."

A ripple of laughter percolates through the crowd where they lie under overhanging cave lips.

Shrike laughs, "Or you can take 'Mr. Studly' up on his generosity, . . . for a price."

The smallest, youngest, and most petite of the gymnastic gold medalists, Tara, pogoes forward like a pixie doll, and says to Shrike in a delightfully charming little voice, "I might take him up on that."

Several people look taken aback, including Colt, the oldest person present.

The gymnast says, "What?"

Colt says, "Aren't you a little young?"

She responds, "Oh god, I'm so sick of that. I'm 18! I'm a sophomore in college. I know I look like a baby to you, but I'm all grown up and whether you like hearing it in your puritanical ears or not, I think Mr. BMX boy over there looks like a tasty little bad ass, and I'm a hot little wild fantasy that's going to rock his little world, cause I know how to treat *my* man."

Everyone looks way more blown away now after that little revelation of TMI. She's at that overzealous age where her self-righteous rage spills out beyond control. A broad grin spreads across the BMXer's face. Tara, standing completely erect, isolates her right leg and puts it behind her neck like a contortion freak, in defiant display for all to see, and assuring that she is no longer the only one erect.

"Oh yeah!" The BMX biker says approvingly.

Tara smiles at him with shiny, bright, all-American teeth; a stark contrast to the BMXer's broken yellowed meth-teeth and ratty looking hair.

Sara jumps in sarcastically, "Okay. Thanks for giving me a job to do. Everyone drop it, shut up, and get to bed. I feel like we've been lulled into a false sense of security. We still have to save our lives!"

With the track cyclist off and running far down the mountainous road, Shrike decides that the time is right to test Jay. With her cadre of three animals, along with Sara, Daniel, James, Colt, and the black bear that has been hanging around the camp, she moves in on him, surrounds him tightly, and wakes him like an unbelievable nightmare.

Colt interrogates, "Why d'ya got the weed for, dope?"

Jay complains, "Oh god; you woke me and you're givin me shit for having weed, up in the mountains? Isn't there some kind of Geneva Convention against cruel and unusual torture?"

Colt feels so embarrassed that he reflexively jerks his arm up to level a backhander.

Everyone else breaks into laughter. Colt's face goes beet red and he drops his heavy hand again.

Jay corrects, "Don't get me wrong: I love the Olympics and support everything you do. I like to get baked high up in the mountains sometimes, on my long solo hikes. I know you aren't cool with that."

The BMX biker surprises Jay with knowing nod.

Jay says, "I never thought I'd be saying this as a defense, but it *is* legal you know?"

Colt says, "But the question was, why do you need it?"

Jay scoffs confidently, "I really don't. Go ahead and take it away right now. I don't care. I just like it sometimes for fun; just like you enjoy any leisure thing you do. They don't call it *Rocky Mountain High* for nothing. I'll tell you one thing though: You're a bunch of hypocrites because cigarettes suck. Fuckin'' hate cigs."

A few of the athletes can't help but laugh as Jay rails on against tobacco so vehemently.

Sara chuckles, "None of the athletes smoke. No smoking allowed."

Jay says, "Oh," with mild surprise and considerable deflation.

All of the athletes find themselves becoming completely endeared to Jay. They like Colt too, but more in a kind of "glad you're on our team" alpha Captain Kirk type of way. After getting snuggled in, many of the athletes still have a lot of energy and feel wide- awake, too nervous to dream about tomorrow; while others slumber like torpid bats. With the slightest hint of twilight beginning to caste the first shreds of light, Daniel notices a tight flock of longspurs huddling nearby. In examining the males, he determines them to be Lapland longspurs. He smiles at them, so they all come hopping over and jump into the zipper opening to his sweat top. They snuggle in for a quick nap on his chest as Daniel drifts off like a peaceful daddy bird.

Back in the chaos of the commando encampment, Cruise stands up and points his rifle at the grizzly, its fur glowing in the fire as it swats troops to the ground left and right. A flying squirrel zips down and scratches Cruise straight across the eyes before he can pull the lethal trigger. He stumbles backward against a huge log and five scorpions (yes five scorpions at once!), sting his left arm. The rifle falls from his paralyzed arm. Cruise pulls out his pistol with his right while he squeezes his agonizing left arm tightly against his body armor. Cruise randomly shoots off rounds into the dark towards the grizzly. He breathes heavily as he panics. He can't see the bear. Where did the bear go? He strains to look all around. The animals instantly disperse into the darkness and the camp snaps back to total silence. Cruise holds his breath and strains further to look through the blackness, as another bullet goes off in the spreading, climbing fire. Then ---- the groans of the injured begin to hum like a choir. With that, the buzzing of the relentless insect plague returns; adding insult to injury.

Inconceivable allies? Impossible occurrences? Unquestionable intent?

Chapter 4

Snow Line Site

As dawn reaches The Capital, an aide says "Mr. President, we finally got Gwen on the phone."

Another aide patches it through onto the wide screen in Air Force One, as the president's plane prepares to take off. The technologically advanced communication platform that is Air Force One, provides an excellent sanctuary for the president to work from.

The President says hastily, "Gwen, come on, really? Threatening to fire missiles, tipped with 'boogieman' warheads? A little cliché don't you think? I mean, even for you."

Gwen says, "I never claimed my idea was original. I guess I'm just a product of American television."

The Vice President leans into the President, "She's right. The more you watch, the more violent and insane you get."

The President says to Gwen, "You put us in a bit of a quandary. If we give you the ransom for the athletes, you fire the missiles. If we don't give you the money, you kill the athletes."

Gwen recites, "It's so elementary, MOST POWERFUL MAN IN THE FREE WORLD! Ha ha ha," she laughs like Phyllis Diller after two packs of Kents. "It's a no-brainer, even for someone like you," she rails on. "It's up to you: You can have a bunch of dead heroes or a bunch of dead losers, your choice, but remember, the voters will be watching, and either way, there's going to be a lot of dead people!"

The Vice President leans in again and whispers, "Sir, if we let her kill the athletes, we can save a billion dollars, but your political career will be ruined forever. If we pay the billion, the public will understand that we did the right thing, and Republicans will have to side with us or look like complete hypocrites."

The President snaps back, "I know what the choices are!", as a flight attendant brings him some celery.

Gwen says, "Make one fast, Mr. Presidiot. You're time bomb ticks. Tick. Tick. Tick." Her chin juts out like a rooster on every annoying 'Tick'.

Then the Vice President butts in, trying to be reasonable, and says to Gwen, "Don't you understand that you are trying to cut back on human population on a micro scale, but we are talking a macro level grand scale of a problem, and your missiles won't have any impact whatsoever."

Gwen says, "I know, this is just the start. People thought Hitler was a monster for killing a measly six million, … I'm talking about eventually killing six billion. Six billion of the lamest, weakest, most undesirable people on Earth. You know I'm right. About two billion of the good, smart, pious, and wealthy left on Earth to run things right and clear the squalor." Gwen hangs up. The wide screen blips to black.

The Vice President says, "The first thing we should do is send in Green Berets."

The President says, "Green Berets? Our top elite Special Forces against whatever sorry-ass mercenaries she's sunk her teeth into?"

The Vice President argues, "Sure, Green Berets versus mercenary commandos. I'd bet on our guys."

The President says, "I don't like those odds, this isn't a football game, and where, how?"

Everyone in the meeting room puzzles over the dilemma, then The President says, "Find out where Gwen is. Cut her power and communications. Use recon. Find out where the athletes are. Get the billion dollars ready for transport and get it on the jet."

The Vice President leans into the President confirming, "The Green Berets are the most adaptable. They are quiet. They know how to deliver direct action and they have the recon skills to find them and the counter-terrorism training to avoid getting the athletes blown to bits. I recommend three units plus an air-support craft."

The President acknowledges, "I know you are a big Green Berets fan. So be it. What is everyone waiting for?"

Five people split out of the high-level session in different directions. The President leans forward on his fists with great consternation as the VP stands behind him with his arms folded pensively. Stress sweat percolates and glistens on their faces.

As the dim traces of morning light begins to come up on the huddled, rattled commandos, they look about.

One says, "What the hell was that?"

Of the initial 120 commandos left on the ground to capture Shrike and her athletes, 70 remain alive. They make pointed demands of Cruise who ignores them as he searches for the map and a number of other apparently missing critical items.

Joaquin says, "That was every kind of animal; working all together. I saw buffalos, bats, birds, bugs, friggin'' bears, *BEARS*; all working together. Like a friggin'' unit!"

Cruise blusters courageously, "I could barely see my hand in front of my face so I don't know what the hell you think you saw."

"What?" Joaquin yells, "Are you in friggin'' denial? The animals teamed up on us. Are you blind, Sir? It was coordinated!"

Lohan says sarcastically, "Oh yeah, I'm sure all of the animals in the forest had a meeting and decided they should gang up on us. Did you see how the bear was chasing the other animals down the mountain? It was a stampede -- Big fish eating little fish. Okay? We just got caught in a nature stampede. Get a grip. It's over."

Joaquin complains, "You have gotta be kiddin' me. It's like the animals are totally out of control."

Cruise breaks in, mumbling, "It's like the animals are totally *in* control, or being controlled. That's enough. Joaquin, give me a full report on the wounded. Lohan, have two healthy fire teams set up a guard perimeter, then give me a full report on

everything *but* wounded. Ideally, I want everybody to be ready to hit the trail in twenty minutes. Go!"
The commandos groan with misery in the dawn light.

High on the mountain, Shrike and James, and several pairs of athletes awaken entwined in each other's arms; some for warmth, some for more. They awaken to find annoying hairs stuck to their lips. They rub their eyes and pull fine threads of animal fur from the sticky corners of their mouths. All of the warm and snuggled furry critters that had come to comfort the Olympians begin to stir and stretch in the cutest ways imaginable. Shrike gets up unceremoniously, then stands by the cliff as she looks, listens, and feels for what the creatures are up to. She moves slowly ---- her quads burning from the mountainous accent, as she eyes Colt standing over some athletes. He silently looks down upon them, sleeping with a bighorn sheep and the cougar. A tear comes to his eye as he thinks about his deceased horse. Right then, one of the athletes wakes to find grouse huddled tightly all over him. He gently pets the grouse, which seem to love him as they fluff out their downy feathers.

Colt says, "*And the lion shall lay down with the lamb.*"
Sara says with surprise, "I didn't know you were biblical."
Colt says, "Oh, is that from the bible? I thought it was something like that. I have no idea what it means."
Sara says, "It doesn't mean anything."
Colt admits, "I don't even know if I said it right. I know there is supposed to be like a wolf in there."
Shrike chimes in, "It just means some day we will have Eden again."
A little brown bird sits in a tree at head level. Each waking athlete that walks by sees it, and is stirred by its sweet, graceful song, mixed with a noodling warble. Only James and Daniel actually know it is an American tree sparrow; and only Shrike knows that the reason the sparrow is there is hers and hers alone. When they finally meet face-to-face, the sparrow and Shrike

stare into each other's pit-like eyes ... black and without reflection. They communicate mentally, then the tree sparrow flies of in a flicking flutter, to telepathically notify its avian brethren.

James watches this entire exchange, and then says, "This already is an Eden. Look at this place. The only thing that ever screws anything up is people and their fanatical, homocentric beliefs. The animals would be fine if we would just leave them the heck-in-a-hand basket alone."

Daniel nods his head in agreement. Everyone is silent.

Sara, having witnessed what appeared to be a number of hook ups over night, nuzzles up sideways to Shrike with serpentine questions.

Sara says, "Cast fidelity to the wind in cases of emergencies?"

Shrike says, "Whether guys find me attractive ..."

Sara cuts in, "...Oh, ah, or people think you're beautiful ..." nodding in strong agreement.

Shrike plows on, "... is irrelevant. I know I'm fuckin'' strange. Am I going to fight being strange?"

Sara self reflects. She feels as if Shrike is a dozen-and-a-half times less strange than herself. She takes a gulp, trying to be a good listener while self-monitoring and obsessing.

Shrike says, "I shit you not! I used to belt out songs on the top of my lungs from inside my screened-in porch as a kid; and the stuck-up neighbor girls would be like 'weird', or 'weirdo'."

Sara examines, "You didn't have a lot of friends as a kid?"

Shrike reveals painfully, "I had periods with friends and periods without. The periods without were very lonely."

Sara tries not to strike, but does, "Is that why you think you can talk with the animals now, ... that they are your friends?"

Sara and Shrike look about at the waking athletes who all pile out from under the calzone-shaped caves. They enjoyed deep slumber under the watchful eyes of their animal protectors. They look over at a huge pile of rabbits. Suddenly, a few of the athletes sit up from underneath their lagomorphic comforter.

Shrike and Sara's eyes meet again.

Sara swallows hard, then states, trying to maintain logic against everything she experiences, "Whether the animals slept calmly with the athletes last night or not does not explain why it's happening, or if you have magical powers."
Shrike smirks a little and chuckles silently to herself.

Sara says, "I wrestle with the reality of this."

Shrike chuckles aloud, "Believe me, I wouldn't buy this any more than you would, if it wasn't happening to me."

Shrike stands and waves everyone over to the edge of the cliff. The shot put champion, a heavy sleeper, does not awaken to the surrounding ruckus and snores on. Finally, his pillow wriggles to life, and slides out from under his fat head. The shot put medalist's head hits a rock, and he sits up with a start in pain. He looks over at his former, warm, fluffy pillow. The heavy-set adult raccoon looks back at him with a mischievous jeer, and then gives him one lick to the tip of his nose.

The shot put guy rubs his head and then smiles and laughs, "Thanks buddy. What a great idea for an alarm clock; … a pillow that gets up and leaves."
The hefty raccoon rolls itself into a ball and begins licking its genitals.
The weight man heavily rises to his feet and hastily joins the group gathered on the lip of the precipice, in the orangey glow of the dawn light.

Shrike and the athletes, now having fully awakened and adjusting their eyes to another stunningly glorious day, look down from the mountaintop with great attention.

"It's good that we got a solid night's rest," Shrike suggests to the athletes, "The commandos got absolutely no sleep; bitterly bickering about the attack while they prepared for a second wave of animals with their guns at the ready … and tended to the wounded. They also harvested supplies off of the dead."

Daniel says, "The dead?"

Shrike says, "Yes. Our animal friends did a real number on them last night. On top of that, many of them don't know that key pieces of their equipment are missing; carried off by owls and dropped miles away, or in most cases, brought to us."

The cougar sits, leaning against Shrike's hip. Shrike scratches the cougar behind the ears and down the neck. A number of the athletes smile and embrace each other over the good news, while others stand in suspended shock.

Shrike says, "The art of warfare comes down to logistics." Everyone looks at her with astonishment. What does she know about art, or warfare for that matter?

Shrike goes on, "Without food and water, their ascent will be that much worse."

Without further explanation, Shrike sits on a flat rock with her legs crossed, and then she tells her electrified mind to make broad contact with the animals.

Down in the gloominess of the commando's camp, almost instantaneously, a slew of different animals dart in and start to frisk through injured and dead troops' jackets and bags, liberating them of food snacks and drink packs. Jays, ravens, crows, nutcrackers, and other birds stealthily snatch all of the smaller items and bring them in a steady stream up to Shrike and the athletes. Chipmunks pull open snaps and zippers and rummage deeply into the pockets. Larger hawks carry off heavier items, including canteens full of water.

Near the sunny mountain peak, the athletes eagerly accept the spoils with broad grins until the supply line finally slows to a trickle. They open their canteens and gulp down the water. They rip open the candy bars and energy bars and relish the nutrient-rich carbs and sugars; their morale sky high.

Shrike stands and turns proudly but absent of hubris, stating "Let's get on to our defense plan. Firstly, see that narrow crescent above those tiers, way up near that tippity peak? That will be our fort!"

The athletes crane their necks high toward the brightening blue sky in awe.

"Wow!" several of the athletes murmur.

The pentathlete Matvey says, "What an awesome fort!"

Colt agrees, "It's totally defensible. Brilliant!"

Matvey asks, "You got a military background?"

Colt says, "I served. You?"

Matvey spits out, "My folks immigrated from Russia to the Richmond in California. Same place Natalie Wood grew up. I was mainly a hockey player, but I had this killer tutor who was like this singer, athlete, nature-guru ranger performer kid-at-heart kinda guy, and he inspired me so that when I hit college, I dove straight into ROTC and then straight into modern pentathlon even though technically I wasn't allowed to as a freshman."

Colt, feeling pretty old and outmanned by Matvey's energy and exuberance, wonders, "… and you've got a gold medal and you are like what, 20?"

Matvey counters with pride-filled indignation, "Two golds, … and 22!"

Sara breaks in, "Do you mind?" allowing Shrike to continue.

Shrike goes on for about 35 minutes, with great details about who will be where, and how the booby traps will be set, and how the athletes will use each of their skills as their weapons.

Once Shrike pauses after articulately revealing her complicated, contrived, and even cockamamie defense plan to the athletes; a mutinous chorus erupts:

"Are you nuts?"

"Throw our sports equipment at an elite special forces commando unit?"

" … armed with machine guns?"

Shrike rebuts, "Please, give me a better suggestion. They want to harvest your organs. I don't think reasoning is an option. I think even if we lose, we should take out as many of them as we can. I've thought about it. I've thought about it a lot. I've strained. If we disperse, hide; they will find us and pick us off one by one, or the elements will."

"She's right!" the BMX biker carps. "We need a unified front or we are screwed man."

Shrike, sounding like Patton, enthusiastically cheers, "With the right defenses, and superior numbers and agility, and with our coordinated teamwork and outstanding physical prowess; We Will Defeat Them."

An athlete doubts, "Superior agility?"

Shrike rebuts, "Quite! They are bogged down by ammo, food, and other supplies, not to mention flack vests; as well as by their frustrated, constrained viewpoints."

The uncomfortable athletes eventually all get onboard with Shrike, James, Daniel, Colt, Tara, and skeptical Sara.

The tall, thin, chocolate-skinned James jokes, "But it's too bad they couldn't have hijacked the winter Olympians."

Everyone laughs out loud as they shiver a little, holding their shoulders and looking around at the icy scene. Matvey chucks a snowball at him, inducing more laughter.

Back down the mountain and under the heavy cloud layer, without the topographic map, confounded Cruise has to guess on a lot of decisions as he plans into the gray morning light. He decides on an immediate ascent up the mountain, even with over a third of the commandos either dead or knocked out of commission.

Joaquin complains, "We need a medivac. Half of those injured guys are critical. I'll ride down with them to supervise."

Cruise says, "You'll do no such thing. We need every soldier now that we lost fifty troops. As soon as we catch these athletes we'll get a flight out of here for everyone."

Joaquin complains, "I'm not talking about the fifty dead, Sir. It will be too late for a lot of the wounded by then."

Cruise says, full of bravado, "Hey, I got stung by five scorpions last night. Whatever doesn't kill you makes you stronger. Those injured troops need to toughen up if they want to live and reap the rewards. Staying alive is all a matter of will. If they're right with god, they'll be just fine."

Joaquin does the sign of the cross to placate Cruise, and continues "But someone has to stay with the wounded and guard them from animals, and bury the dead."

Cruise barks, "NO I said! We need everyone. Lohan, tell the troops to take all the weapons and ammo off of the dead guys. ONLY weapons and ammo! Joaquin, tell the fire teams on point to do one final deep scout, then have them pull all of the wounded guys together in one area, and let them keep their pistols for protection."

As the commandos scour the bodies of their fallen comrades, many notice how the corpses have already been picked clean of anything of value.

Minutes later, 39 determined-to-be "fit commandos" start the trek up the jagged slope, over laden with extra guns and ammunition. Some of these troops have serious wounds, while all of them have at least bruises and scratches. When Cruise isn't looking, some of them start dropping ammo clips to lighten their load.

Joaquin fears and derides, "Sir, we need to reevaluate the scenario here. We started with a full company of 128. We gut eight guys tied up with the heli'copters, 50 dead, and 31 that have to be left behind. Are 39 of us enough to capture 117 athletes? And, Sir, why the hell are we gonna need all this ammo for? We are catchin' a bunch of athletes who don't even have guns, pfft. As soon as we say 'hands up', it's over. We could use empty guns and take over. They'd be none-the-wiser. We shoot one of them to show we're real and easy peasy, we're done."

One of the many commandos annoyed by Joaquin's blathering stops to take a leak over a precarious ledge, as the others continue up the treacherously steep terrain. A bighorn ram suddenly pounces and with two gaping bounds knocks him right off of the cliff before anyone can see it coming. Another animal ambush! As the man's body cartwheels in space, he is only able to zip his fly as his last living act, snagging his unwilling member painfully in the process. He vanishes hundreds of feet below. Several commandos level their weapons and release their safeties, but by the time they are ready to shoot, the ram is gone. The crew now becomes even more pissed and antsy.

"Make that *38 commandos!* We gotta repel back down and save him. We leave no man behind," says Joaquin as a delaying tactic much more than out of concern for anyone else, especially another commando.

Cruise replies perturbed, "Anyone who repels down after him will also be left behind intentionally. Everybody has just got to start trusting me. I know what I'm doing. I have been studying the bible for like 15 years and I know a lot of stuff that I know and you don't know a lot of stuff that you don't know. We are going to get those motherfuckers now, animals or not! And we need to do it in silence."

Cruise turns with commitment, and the disgruntled Special Forces soldiers fall in line as the steep trek continues and intensifies. Cold driving squalls hamper their footing, causing the troops to slip and fall frequently in the gale-force winds.

After the rain subsides and the wind dissipates, the troops chafe from their wet, hypothermic uniforms, and the insects return with more biting and stinging, focusing specifically on the soldiers' eyes. Many soldiers don goggles, but the insects simply wallpaper them, making it impossible to see anything. The terrain is really slimy, with the help of the slugs, snails, and worms that have come out in force and aggregated along the paths, coating them with a thick slime layer. Imagine dancing on Vaseline. Struggling with burdensome gear, they straddle and climb over razor-like rocks and gargantuan fallen logs; exhausting and injuring themselves further.

Doubting the validity of their quest, Joaquin whines more "How many people could have even survived a crash up here?"

Lohan responds, "Dump the negativity and keep your mouth shut."

Fatigued and demoralized by the lack of progress, Dumpy, still walking next to Flaca, carries the company's bazooka slung high over her shoulder as she balances on some narrow rocks in a broad, steep, hazard-prone clearing created by a massive boulder slide. A golden eagle soars 1723 feet directly above. It scans each individual, then narrows its sharp eyes as it fixes on the long bazooka; an ample target. The eagle folds its wings and drops into an insane stoop. Blasting toward the Earth like an intercontinental ballistic missile, it comes in from behind and snatches the strap with all eight of its talons. Bombing past at 72 mph, the strap holds, allowing the 11 pounds of blistering fury the momentum to rip the bazooka right off over the commando's helmet. Dumpy feels as if David Ortiz has just smashed her with a Louisville Slugger and she tumbles hard to the rocks, snapping her right wrist and damaging her night-vision goggles beyond use. A few of the soldiers fire at the eagle in futility, then lower their weapons to watch helplessly as the eagle drops the cumbersome bazooka into a massive ravine 2.1 miles away and thousands of feet down. The eagle breaks into a soar again, and rides the thermals on outstretched wings in perfectly spiraling circles, regaining its position high above the troops again. As the shadow of the raptor teases the Earth-bound troops, another commando takes a few more desperate shots with his M60. At this point, Cruise and the soldiers feel as if the eagle is laughing at them ----- taunting, demoralizing them.

"Cruise?" Joaquin whines over the comlink.

Cruise responds reflexively, "Go."

Joaquin complains with deflation, "That was our only bazooka."

Lohan snaps with ferocity, "Will you shut up?"

"That's it!" Cruise yells into his radio link, "Stop it! From now on I want two scout units on point at all times, your safeties off. Shoot and kill any animal that moves!" Having just rescinded his earlier command for silence, the commandos shrug their puzzled shoulders.

Lohan pesters with general bitchiness, "Sir, do you want us to be quiet or shoot animals?"

Cruise simmers, "Follow my last command. You follow? Shoot any animal you see and otherwise stay quiet."

Dumpy looks over at Flaca. Flaca dumps her pack with all of the bazooka ammo, and walks away discreetly without a hint of a murmur.

Dumpy looks at the pile of bazooka shells, then spins back to look up into the sky where the eagle was. She carefully pulls herself back up off of the rocks, holding her wrist, and then follows Flaca and the rest up slope.

Ravens start out mildly at first; a squawk here, a guttural grunt there: then begin to come in with more frequency. At first, it's not a big deal; but within several minutes, the constant teasing and toying with the commandos' eardrums; and the diving, twirling, yelling, cawing; basically, it starts to drive the troops nuts. Each time they try to point their rifles in the general direction of the ravens, they quickly disappear behind a trunk like elusive gray squirrels that twist around a tree.

Joaquin complains, "What the hell are all these blackbirds hanging around here for?"

Lohan corrects, yelling over the caws, "Ravens. These are ravens."

Dumpy states, "Maybe they're after our food or something?"

An obstreperous raven dives down and startles Joaquin.

Flaca weakly speculates, "Maybe they can smell blood … or know we are going to die?"

Lohan scoffs, "Yeah, maybe *Damien, Omen III* sent them, you cowards."

Joaquin can't take it anymore. It's not just the ravens: It's Lohan!

Joaquin turns back to the other troops and complains, "I hate Lohan. What the fuck does she think she is? Doesn't she realize, to me, she's just a vagina to stick my dick into. Givin' me commands. Fuck her ----- no, I really mean it like really."

Even the most hardened misogynists among the court-martialed ex-convicts recoil at Joaquin's disgusting tidal wave of hate; not only against women, but against everyone; including and especially ... HIMSELF! They all shake their heads and continue to trample down the flora on their nightmare trek.

The golden sunlight caresses Shrike's face as it rises over distant peaks. She waves at the eagle with a broad smile and gives it a thumbs-up.

She looks up at all the athletes working feverishly near the mountaintop, and pulls the headset down from her ear to notify, "It's beginning to crackle a bit."

Daniel goes through the bag of one of the dead commando hijackers and finds another headset. They switch off the first headset and switch on the new one. He hands it to Shrike, who immediately listens in for a second.

She says, "The battery on this one seems to be at full strength."

They smile at each other warmly, Shrike twinkling at stunning Daniel.

Shrike listens for another moment and then proudly says to the Olympians, "The animals have already put themselves in enough danger, ... and the commandos are on to them, so it's our turn to shine. I can't ask the animals to further sacrifice their lives over stupid greedy human shit. Perform well. You are the best athletes in the world. The commandos are no match for us on any level. We hold both the moral and literal high ground. Let's get to the specifics of defending the rock fortress. Know that the animals will help us when they can, as long as it is deemed safe. It may end up being only non-combative support and recon. And with all of that said: Don't ever underestimate the commandos' abilities. They've made it through ranger school or whatever, so they are going to be tenacious no matter how hungry, tired, or beaten they are. Treat each soldier as an elite killing machine and you'll survive."

The rest of the athletes come running over to Shrike enthusiastically, like a football huddle in a two-minute drill. Shrike uses a stick to point at the incredibly intricate battle diagram drawn in the packed soil. The athletes, encircling her tightly, with their arms draped over each other like a rugby scrum, kneel on rock, ice, snow, and windswept lichen, as the brilliant plan unfolds. They nod at each other with confident smiles.

At the end of the strategic session, Shrike finishes confidently "I know there are no questions or comments, so let's get cracking."

Jay factually states, "Are, are you kidding? Ha, um, you are going to throw rocks and sticks at commandos with machine guns? This park has the largest concentration of mammals in the United States, except Alaska. Can't we harness more animal help?"

Sara, in a rare show of support for Shrike and the remarkably insane occurrences that have been going down, cuts Jay to the quick "You ready to start hiking down the mountain by yourself granola head?"

Jay looks into her eyes for a second. She is dead serious. He is surprised.

Jay stammers, "Ah, no."

Sara leans her body forward a few inches, "Then button it spy."

Everyone looks over at Jay with suspicion again.

Jay swallows hard and looks at Sara, "Sorry."

Sara smiles warmly, finally looking a little human, as she finds herself attracted to Jay and his outdoorsy charisma. Little does she know, Jay would drop it for her in 2.3 seconds. Of course he has already found Shrike and a number of the female athletes to be an incredibly attractive surprise on his long solo hiking trek; but Sara, oh yeah Sara; she is the kind of woman he could really fall for and have a nice, long-term love life with.

Jay smiles at Sara and corrects for the record, "Not a spy."

In the depressing gray fog below, the irritated and uncomfortable commandos finally make it to snow line, and then, look up through a gap in the cloud layer to see the aircraft still intact, high above in the deep powder. They press on over a sharp pass and toward the crash site; still another four-hour climb away. While the peak-inhabiting athletes use this time to prepare a myriad of weapons and booby traps, the commandos finally reach the crash site. Their immediate search produces two dead commandos and the few scattered remains of the horse; but absolutely nothing else of any use.

Joaquin cries like a baby, "Find food. Find some water. Hurry up and find something!"
The subordinate troops search hard, long and far, but can't even find a crumb. A mouse would even starve on this plane.

Lohan barks efficiently, "Sir, we got tracks heading up slope. Lots of them."

Cruise puzzles, "That's odd. Why the hell would they head up?"

Dumpy puzzles on, "Confused?"

Cruise wisely says, "Let's not go underestimating everybody's smarts right away here."

Joaquin happens upon the case of champagne left behind a tree by the athletes. He looks around and then slips a bottle under his flack vest. He sneaks off behind another tree, just a bit further away, coughs to hide the sound of the cork popping, and then starts chugging the bottle alone like a fiend.

In the denser part of the forest, another commando stumbles upon the other loosely discarded champagne bottles.

He yelps over the comlink, "Hey, booze! Let's party."
He pops the cork and gulps down a few swigs. Others come over and grab their own bottles. It's a party!

Cruise comes over at the end of his rope, "Do I have to baby sit all of you fuckers?"
He pulls out his .45 caliber and shoots the bottles out of the soldiers' hands. He shoots the ones left on the ground too; wasting precious ammo like a macho man, instead of simply smashing the bottles by hand. It's funny to see how gun nuts tend to lean on their weapons as tools inappropriately.

Cruise screams like a psychotic middle-school teacher, "There will be no celebrating until our quarry is captured. CLEAR?"

Still behind the tree, Joaquin chugs his bottle down. He dangles the empty bottle out from behind the tree, and slurs with a mocking voice, "Oh Cruise … you forgot diss one."

Cruise's reactionary anger bursts. He aims quickly, then fires, taking off Joaquin's ring finger at the hand.

"Arrhagg!!" he screams in pain.

Cruise spouts, "Sorry! I didn't mean that." His voice lacks any form of remorse.

The commandos stare at Cruise with despising eyes. Cruise feels insecure for the first time and realizes that he is starting to freak out! He's never felt like this on a mission before. He has always been in complete control.

Up above on the mountain peak with her face shining in the sun, Shrike chuckles for a second and utters to James, "Everything's working great so far. The animals performed spectacularly."

James says, enjoying the moment of solitude from the intrusive athletes "Ya know, all my life I've been so absorbed about my single-minded hurdling goal, that that has become my entire identity. I am a hurdler. That's it. A runner. A racer. I never spent any time thinking about mammals at all, and now, here they are saving our lives."

Shrike asks with mild incredulity, "You saying you never thought about mammals ever in your whole life?"

James says, "Nope. Never."

Shrike presses, "Didn't you think, as a hurdler, you were like a pronghorn or deer, or like a cougar?"
The always-nearby cougar growls at the insult.

"What? I don't even know what that first thing you named is. I grew up in the city, the inner city. I didn't know no animals except the birds in the parks and on the river," he says.

Shrike shudders, "You have got to be kidding me. What about nature shows; documentaries?"

James says, "Never watched that crap. We barely had a working TV when I was growing up and we didn't have cable, though one of my friend's dads stole it so we would watch it over his house, … but I remember trying to find track meets to watch, and watchin' football of course."

Shrike says, "Okay, I get the idea that you are a mega jock, but you eat mammals, right?"

James responds, "Well first off, one thing a lot of people don't know about me, and I'd like it to stay out of the limelight, is that I'm practically vegan now. I'm getting into nature a lot too now, in my own way, but I don't go around lettin' anybody know about that."

Intrigued, Shrike leads "… because …".

James quickly answers with a clever dodge, "Because of Carl Lewis. He was vegan and still kicked ass. And then I found out that Alicia Silverstone is vegan, when I saw her naked PETA ad, and even though I'm way younger than her, I totally creamed my shorties."

Shrike can't help but quickly look down. The last thing she imagines him having is a "shortie".

She quickly saves herself, "A ha, so you consciously thought of NOT eating meat."

James puzzles, "Yeah, I guess I did. Those aren't really animals to me. What the hell is a chicken patty, or bacon, or a sausage. To me, there is no association with any kind of animal. Just like with tofu, I can't really picture a plant or a bean. It's just tofu in my mind. Hey, you can't harsh on me for growing up in the city, impoverished of wildlife. Why the hell would I have to worry about a bear or a snake?"

Shrike questions, "What do you think the most important animal to humans has ever been?"

James darts around the spaces of his mind for a second, not trusting his first instinct, then going back to it. "Dog. Definitely the dog."

Shrike states, "I'd put horse and cow before dog."

James argues, "No way. No one had a horse where I grew up, but there sure was a shitload of dogs, and for a lot of guys, it was all about their pit bull."

Shrike says, "You are looking strictly at your own experience. Small states like Vermont and Wisconsin are defined by cheese. Pizza is like the number one food in America, next to cheeseburgers and cheesy fries."

James laughs, "That reminds me, have you ever heard that song *Speedy Little Pizza Man*?"

Shrike laughs loudly, "Yes! I love that song and agree whole-heartedly with the sentiment."

James concurs, "You're hip to that? Me too. It's funny because it's true. But anyway, so what, we get cheese from cows. But yah, you are right, cows probably have the biggest impact on people, if you look at feeding them and water and stuff."

Shrike counters, "But horses were ridden into battle and opened up conquest of The West and the subjugation of tribes and animals."

James thinks with a pause, then throws out "Well a hell of a lot of people got cats."

Shrike says, "Cats! No way. I love cats, but I don't even see them on the list. I think you have it narrowed down to horses, cows, or dogs as being the most important animal, to people that is, of all time."

James says, "I wonder, now that I have competed so much internationally, what the top three animals in other countries would be?"

Impressed, Shrike continues, "Would goats or camels or guinea pigs make the list?"

Shrike nestles up under James's arm and starts to hug and caress him.

Slipping her hand under his sweats, she runs her soft, warm, sexy hand over his bare thighs, squeezing his quads and gently fluffy over his genitalia. Her nicely painted nails make her fingers look even longer and more delicate. He achieves half a loaf with zero effort.

Shrike says, "You are so distant from mammals, and yet, you are one. You're an animal."
She looks deeply into his eyes.

James goes instantly hard.

He can't break off from her gaze.

His spine juts out like a razorback hog.

He looks like a freakin' panther.

Their eyes burn.

Burn.

Flames burn in their eyes.

They lean into each other.

Shrike slides his pants down to his ankles. James bends so low that his knee almost scrapes the naked poison oak twigs.

She softly runs her flat palm and long fingernails horizontally along the back of his hairline and squeezes his taut neck muscles with a fury. He cups her shoulder blades in his beavertail hands and brings her body in.

Their lips meet.

Two tears quickly roll down Shrike's right cheek.

Shrike and James collapse back into a vertical crack in the granite, just big enough for an intimately entwined duo. They have awesome sex together.

A true sensualist, Shrike's animalism awakens.

Not for money.

Not for gain.

Shrike simply, unapologetically, loves sex and loves to love and be loved. She gives it ---- she takes it. No one could ever call Shrike a whore. She never prostitutes herself. She does it because *she loves it*.

In the calming after-bliss, Shrike and James daydream with her head nestled into his bicep and armpit. They both feel warm, connected, ... fine. James feels so comfortable that he smoothly goes right back into conversation. He doesn't want the most incredibly irresistible loving he has ever had to get awkward or ruined or ANYTHING!

James wonders, "If this animal communication is possible, … what about time travel and stuff like that?"

Shrike says, "I don't know the first thing about time travel, other than it's just as impossible as communicating with animals is."

James gives a chuckle and then postulates, "If I could control time travel, I would have everyone go 30 years into the future to see what they would be like, and then when they return to the present, they get the choice to kill themselves or live that existence."

Shrike thinks for a moment, "Hmmm. I guess minimally it's another tool for lowering human population."
They both look at each other and then laugh at their callousness.

Now that the erotic fun has ended, Shrike and James reappear at the mouth of the narrow granite crack --- after-glow disheveled. Sara comes walking by and recognizes the implications of the scene immediately.

Sara anally analyzes, "What is up with you and sex Shrike? Where are the hidden cameras? Is someone shooting a porn flick or a reality show?"

Shrike replies plainly, "What," like a demand for an answer, not a question.

Sara states like it's fact, "If that birder guy you are dating cheated on you, you would be pissed and break up with him."

James slips around the rocks and vanishes down the slope before Sara can even notice he's gone. He passes Daniel on the way down the trail and mumbles over his elongated, silent strides, "Fuck that", obviously referring to Sara, not Shrike. Daniel looks around confused, climbs to the summit, and stops to listen to the women, staying out of sight.

Shrike explains deliberately, "There is a big difference: I love sex and 'that birder guy' as you call him does not like it at all. I like to have sex like every other day. Every other day, or every three days would be nice. Not every day usually. My last few boyfriends on the other hand, think sex is overrated, and they only want to have sex like twice a month! Can you believe that? Twice a month is enough for them. They don't think about sex, or have a sex drive. It is like they are more evolved than the cavemen I used to date who would hound me for sex three or more times a night."

Sara empathizes, "I've had my share of Neanderthals as well, almost the whole way through college actually. That can be good though," she reminisces gleefully about some of the testosterone-laden goons she romped with in the dorm-room bunk beds.

Shrike replies, "Yah, five times a day! If I let them, my boyfriends would do me over and over again. I've moderated, but I would still feel comfortable about having it a good four times a week when I have time, with the occasional second go around here or there. So I've said to my boyfriend that I want it more and he says he wants it less or is disinterested. Then I suggest that I hook up with some other guy to fulfill my sexual side, and then he rebuts that he will have sex with somebody else if I do!"

Sara says, "Well, it sounds like he wants it to be fair."

Shrike says, "NO! That's not fair. That's petty. Either he really wants to do it with me or he doesn't. If he says he lacks interest in sex then why would he want somebody else if he doesn't even want me? I want to have sex, with him, period."

After some thought Sara considers, "He says he doesn't want it, so you can't force it on him."

Shrike says, "Right. Oh god, it makes my stomach ache thinking about it. He doesn't want it, but I want it. If I go get it elsewhere, then he says he will too. Why? I don't get it!"

Sara asks, "Bottom line?"

Shrike gasps with exasperation, "Bottom line is that I love him and want to be with him and stay with him, but I also want to have sex more frequently in my life, and I don't want to sneak around, cheat or lie, and I don't want to have an open relationship, and I don't want my boyfriend to have sex with someone else."

Sara says, "Do you need to have sex?"

Shrike frowns, "Don't go down that path. I am fine and normal and I just like to have sex. Some people treat that like a crime. It's not."

Sara laughs, lightning the mood like a teen, "So, ---- tell me more, tell me more. Was it nice?"

Behind the boulder, Daniel's eyes widen and he crouches down further.

Shrike's little buddy, the screech-owl, zings over and lands on Daniel's shoulder. He looks up with a brief startle, and then relaxes. The owl digs its talons deep into Daniel's shoulder. Daniel almost lets out a grunt from the sharp pain. He strains to listen for the answer.

Shrike takes a deep breath and rolls her eyes, "Mmm, very." A soft, gentle, warm glowing smile scrolls across her face, "Mm. Nice." Then she says as she begins to march off, "And by the way, Number One: None of your business. Number Two: We might be dead in the next couple of hours so you better think about that, Mizzz High and Mighty Sweetheart!"

Sara looks at Shrike, taken aback.

Shrike stops in her tracks like she's been hit in the head by a Canada goose. She receives a strong animal signal in her brain.

Sara freezes, examining her every move, and skeptical as ever.

Shrike says, "Wow, scavengers are back in action."

Sara looks around suspiciously.

Shrike is right! Wherever commandos are not, scavengers of every style and design silently slip in and start to pick the forest clean. This time, the animals find the abandoned bazooka shells too, and with the help of a few red-tailed hawks and an osprey, shuttle the discarded shells up to the rock fortress. The large raptors delicately place the shells at Shrike's feet, right in front of doubting Sara, who shakes her head in unconvinced bemusement.

The athletes can't figure any way to use them. They try throwing them as hard as they can against the granite, but the velocity isn't high enough to make them explode. The strongest thrower from the water polo team, as well as the javelin thrower, try with all their might, but the shells just bounce off of the distant granite walls, eight meters below. Since the only real ex-military guy they've got is Colt, and he knows nothing of their fusing, Shrike decides that the best option would be to have eagles drop the bombs from as high as possible in the hopes that some of them will detonate under the shear force of gravity, and that the others will at least scare and distract the commandos.

Colt favors, "Let's just bomb them right now to see if they work and be done with it."

Shrike counters, based on her superior animal info, "No. They are in thick cover under conifers right now and a lot of the shells would be cushioned by the tree limbs. We will hit them when they are exposed in the open."

After the bazooka shell tests are done, Sara snidely asks Shrike, "What is the next nonsexual maneuver?"

Shrike, way above acknowledging that comment, continues on down the narrow trail. She passes Daniel, who shrinks into the bushes to avoid notice. Shrike actually senses his presence, but has more pressing matters to deal with at this time and remains too pissed at Sara to play nice with Daniel right now.

Daniel pauses, puts his hands on his knees and drops his head in thought, then steps out of the bushes right into a black bear. Daniel panics at first and hyperventilates, but the bear stands, pulls Daniel in gently, and gives him a hug and a big lick in the face. The bear drops back down to all fours to lovingly stroke its massive cheek and muzzle up and down along Daniel's knee, then trots off.

Daniel stands frozen in shock for a second, then stammers, "What the fuck?!"

Sara turns the corner to see an emotionally charged Daniel.

She crassly puts, "What are you trolling for sloppy seconds?"

She notices sticky, gooey bear saliva all over his face, and has no idea what to make of it.

She says, "Oh god. You have got a problem. We need to talk."

Daniel turns and runs down the slope away from her.

Sara yells, "Can't run away from your problems. Go chase Shrike's tail. Ain't gonna do you no good, only harm. You should come back and talk to me."

At that moment the bear loops back around and stands up right behind Sara's back. With none of the athletes nearby, Sara figures Shrike, James, and Daniel, to be off somewhere, or alone ... so who is this behind her? He sniffs her a few times, then repelled, he runs off at breakneck speed. Sara turns around with sudden suspicion to find nothing, so she shrugs her shoulders and starts to stroll down to the main fort, in the glorious daylight.

In the heart of the fortress, Shrike finishes delegating duties and rifling out orders, all of which are followed to the letter with an efficiency that makes the commandos look like mere toddlers in comparison. Shrike whips her gorgeous head around in the sunlight to fluff out her hair, then sees Daniel, who averts her look. Shrike does not suspect: Shrike knows Daniel must know about James, so she tries to break the ice a little as she follows him down a path.

Shrike hypothetically ponders, "Hey Daniel. If we hike on say a three-day trek into the park, and we find a dead body, would you leave it?"

Daniel understands simply, "You mean, ignore it so not to ruin my trip? Would anyone do that? That was somebody's life and their family might be looking for them."

Shrike consternates, "Hm."

Daniel suspects, "Wrong answer?"

Shrike admits guiltily, "No, probably right answer."

Daniel looks at her, bewildered.

Shrike reveals with hesitation and embarrassment, "While hiking with my last obsessive birder boyfriend, we found a freshly dead person, ah, corpse, in the forest on the trail near a dirt road … in some third world Latin American country which I'm not going to name. He said we should ignore it because they were already dead and there was nothing we could do for them. He really didn't want to ruin his bird trip. He didn't get the bird he was after. More importantly, he tainted me. I can never let anyone coerce or corrupt me like that again. I need to stand up and do exactly what I think is right and take responsibility for everything, right?"

Dejected-looking Daniel answers glumly, "Right. I can see why he would want to leave the body, but I don't think I could care that little about somebody else."

Shrike says gently, "Oh, it's a quandary alright. Daniel, what is it?"

Daniel says, "I have to admit, I thought I was falling in love with you, but I see you are with someone else. It feels bad."

Shrike says, "First of all, you knew I was already with someone else and you fell for me before I got involved with another someone else. You like me or not?"

With his beautifully deep eyes shining against the sunny backdrop, Daniel confesses softly, "Like, ya, I, I like you a lot. A real lot."
Tongue-tied, he feels an overwhelming rush of heat race over him.

Shrike says, "I don't know if it's the animal coming out of me or what, but I want you right now."

She grabs him and pulls him in.

He tenses.

She runs a soothing hand down the back of his neck and shoulder.

They look into each other's eyes and kiss passionately. Shrike and Daniel move between the rocks effortlessly, as if dancing a Viennese waltz, and slip into a concealed crevice to have sex.

The pale and bark-like western screech-owl looks over at the watchful marten and rolls its eyes as if to say 'Here we go again'. The marten snickers --- as best a mustelid can. But it's not really like that. In the least gratuitous way imaginable: miles from the sullying brush of brutes like Quentin Tarantino: ----- They make love.

The bond with Daniel is strong for Shrike; . . . at least as strong as it is with James, but not close to as strong as it feels with the animals.

The passion subsides as they lie in post-coital bliss and Shrike says to Daniel, as she straightens up and prepares to get back to work, "I need to spend a couple of minutes to check in with and explore my animal communication powers. I'll try not to be distant, but if I am, it's not personal, and you know that."

Daniel says, "Okay, go for it. I'll watch."

Shrike smiles humbly, "Okay... Don't be too under whelmed."

Shrike thinks hard about a bison as she stands in a meditative stance. She wants it to call even though it is a mile away down inside the gargantuan canyon. The bison gives out a trombone-like blast almost immediately.

Daniel hears the sound coming from way off and questions, raising his perfect eyebrows "That you?"

Shrike nods with a mild smile.

Unbeknownst to the two secret lovers, James comes walking down the slope looking for Shrike. The marten jumps up and down with alarm.

Shrike says to both James and Daniel, "Try this on for size, four in a row."

Suddenly, in rapid fire succession, they hear a moose, elk, wolf, and eagle, all sound off.

Daniel smiles broadly, his teeth shining in the sun, and with a congratulatory thumbs up, interjects, "Bravo, ah, but don't abuse your power."

Shrike says, "No problem. We have a number of willing allies."

James steps forward, sensing what has occurred between Shrike and Daniel, and moans deeply in painful heartache, "Who is abusing power ... and alienating allies?"

Shrike strongly jumps straight to the point, "I want you men to decide that you don't care."

James flips out and can't handle the sheer unconventionalism of this love situation, raising his voice, "Why are we crazy for you? Are you playing animal mind fuck games on me?! ON US?!"

The cougar stares James down with a glare that would make any lesser man lose bowel constitution. James brings his emotions back in check.

Shrike feels conflicted over her love for both men, but at the same time feels a more powerful love pulling her toward the animals, due to the constant messages bombarding her mind. She feels the animals' urgency. She senses their simple, direct, egoless intentions. It is a completely non-sexual love with the animals of course, but more akin to deep friendship and mutual appreciation, admiration, and respect; some of the best kinds of love there are!

James doesn't know what to say, and now feels embarrassed about losing his ultimately cool temper. He feels really hurt by Shrike, because he too also likes her a lot. Shrike grabs his arm and spins him around.

She looks deep down into the bottomless blackness of his eyes, and says, "Kiss me if you love me."

They lean in. He can't say 'No'. They share a long and lasting kiss.

Daniel complains, "What the fuck?" with disappointment and hurt.

The cougar snarls at Daniel, as does the marten. Daniel takes a step back from both of them.

Shrike says, "I've been wanting to talk with you, and you, about this. I'm in love with both of you. I want to be with both of you."

James knows that both he and Daniel barely know Shrike and that this whole thing is moving way too fast, so he blurts, "What are you like crazy, I'm not gonna share you whit 'notha guy."

Shrike judges, "Geez, that's a little possessive don'tcha ya think?"

James returns, "I can't believe any of us is even thinking about sex with the sitch we are in."

Shrike laughs, "Really? Why not? Why the hell not?" Daniel and James look at each other again. Her logic stands ------ -- impenetrable.

After a silence, Shrike urges, "Why shouldn't we have sex? Name one thing wrong with it."

It feels way too confrontational now so everyone takes a deep breath and sits down to talk calmly. The marten takes the opportunity to bound over and curl up in the triangular gap in Shrike's lap, nuzzling against her marshmallow thighs and bonding to her warm musky under region. Nobody wants to initiate at this point.

Finally, Shrike calmly breaks the tension by saying, "Everyone just needs to chill the fuck out. If we were back at my place, safe and sound, I'd suggest that we all get nicely baked." Both of the men laugh, chewing the chunk of surprise, glazed with relief. They thought she was kind of militantly anti drug but realize now it was more of a way to keep Sara's domineering antidotes at bay, and to manage the emergency situation they found themselves in.

Daniel offers, "One thing that's great about being a diver: I can smoke a little now and then and it's not going to hurt my medal chances. I wouldn't do it if I were a runner or swimmer."

James pipes in, "What? I can party it up once in a while. I have been known to, but mostly I stay off it cause I want to get one more gold baby."
Everyone smiles and shakes their heads like they are at a Ziggy Marley concert.

James wonders, "Where does an uptight girl like you get her stuff? I can't picture that."

Shrike evades, "Certainly not from a black guy."

James reflexes, "What? Why?"

Shrike replies as she lovingly massages the cougar's brow, "Every time I try to score weed off a black dude, they try to go rip me off. Every time I get it from a white dude, they don't."

Daniel proclaims, "That's the most racist thing I've ever heard in my life."

James defends, "Well now let's hold on a minute. She's got a point. White people just want to sell you the weed honestly and maintain good relations for repeat business. Not to sound like Chris Rock, but black dudes want to make some extra money. They are always hurting for money and they will always try to make extra on every sale, any way they can think of, without concern about their karma or anything. When you are brought up poor you are more likely to do desperate things to avoid goin hungry."

Shrike verifies, "Right. On the nose," gesturing at James. Then Shrike says, "Once they figure out you are a girl and you are alone, then they really try to put the screws to you, and the screw to you. As a matter of fact, though I never went through with it, they will give you the weed for free if you fool around with them."

Daniel iterates, "Are you kidding. I would too ... with you."

James agrees, "Any day, any play, any way bay bay."

Shrike surmises, "Well look, that digression seems to have steamed things off. This is what I have to say, calmly: I've been in love before and it's never been like this but I am in love with both of you and can love both of you in my life. I understand if neither of you want to be with me but I want both. I know this is sudden. I know this is abrupt. I know I have been struck by lightning and can communicate with animals. I don't care and none of that matters. I know how I feel in my heart."

James objects, "That's unheard of. I don't want to be a part of that."

The dandy diver Daniel leaps, "Good. If you could, then just decline, . . . and I'll be with her."

James defends, "No way."

Shrike convinces, "Come here both of you. I love both of you."

She grabs for them both, kissing them at the same time, and caressing them sensuously. The men, visibly uncomfortable, somehow get into it; overcome by Shrikes powerful sexual aura and charisma. Both men look at her in disbelief. These guys aren't virgins at all by any measure, but Shrike has that whole Scarlet Johansson thing going on. She bends over and pulls down her pants. She leads them both into her at the same time and gives out a low, pleasing moan: One of them smoothly undulates from behind while she sucks the other one into her perky mouth. They coil back and forth like an inchworm until Shrike and both of the men climax together in ecstasy. The men feel completely oblivious to each other; their total focus on Shrike. They feel weird and remorseful; but either one of them would do it again in a millisecond.

Shrike unloads "Look, I want you to talk this out, because if this is to become some kind of competition between the two of you and you are not big enough men to deal with this sitch, then I think I would rather have neither of you."
Shrike walks off with the cougar, and the men are left alone in a long silence.
With their backs to each other, still several feet apart, they adjust their underwear, etc.

James declares to Daniel, "I'm not gay."

Daniel rebuffs the accusation, "Look, I'm even a diver and I'm not gay; not that there is anything gay going on here."

James looks at him incredulously at first but then decides to believe him, not that he even really cares. Both of these men are very mature for their young ages and very secure in their sexuality. The owl slips in unnoticed and watches silently as they deliberate for a few minutes, each trying to take the higher road.

"Look, this could work but I'm not interested in ever seeing you naked again," says the diver.

"Me neither," the hurdler agrees with added emphasis. "For now on, it's sex with Shrike alone."

Daniel clarifies more, "In private."

They give each other masculine handshakes at first, then go into a big hug. There is not even the slightest hint of homosexual attraction or allure. If anything, they feel silly, for they are men and know what (and who) they want. Her name just happens to be Shrike. They instantly strike a balance: unusual among dudes of lesser caliber. They simultaneously avoid hostility and bromance with one another. They are strong, solid, individual men, and alpha athletes at the top of their game; who have fallen in love with the same girl at the same time! A girl … who just happens to have some kind of freaky animal mind power!

They split; with Daniel climbing up a tree to get a look around for anything unusual, and to think in the silence for a moment while James takes his long strides back down to camp to gulp down an energy bar with some water, filling his panging stomach.

Shrike brushes past Sara on the narrow trail in what appears to be almost a huff.

Sara turns gently and says, "Shrike. We can't let the pressure get to us."

Shrike keeps walking, apparently unphased, then freezes, and turns to look at Sara.

Shrike asks, "How much do you like sex? Like, really like it?"

Sara replies quickly off the cuff, "Honestly, like I would be anything but honest with you my dear, I'm not your average girl. I like it maybe once or more a week, and at other times I'd get more satisfaction out of it if I were on line shopping for dresses and looking at shoes while he does me and gets it over with. Why?"

Shrike contemplates, "I don't know. I just like it. I really like it. It feels good. That's all."

Sara replies, "Good for you honey."

Shrike presses, "As a psychologist…that's it?"

Sara curtly quips, "Yeh"

Shrike protests, "No comment or prescriptions?"

121

Sara again, "Nope. You sound normal."

Shrike laughs out loud, "My god. For once in my life I'm normal! I'm normal! Were your parents nuts?"

Sara responds, taken aback, "What? My parents. Well, no, they weren't *nuts* per se."

Long pause.

Longer pause.

Finally, Sara almost doesn't want to ask, but utters ... "Why?"

Shrike casually turns the tables, the cougar licking her left hand, "I don't know. You're the shrink. Just seems like if both of your parents are messed up, how do you expect to turn out normal."

Sara defends, "You're so sure my parents were messed up?"

Shrike smiles broadly, "Oh yah. I shit you not."

James rapidly strides over with the comlink in hand.

He reports, "Shrike, the chatter has picked up considerably. You better listen to this."

As the preparations hastily continue around the rock fortress, Shrike grabs the comlink and listens intently; the bridge of her nose red from lack of UV protection.

After listening quietly for a minute and 44 seconds, Shrike announces to Sara and the boys, "I don't know how close they are getting to us, but they are making progress so I think it's time we offer up a red herring. It will buy us more fortress building prep time and give Search & Rescue a chance to find us first."

Sara says, "We have no way of knowing if Search & Rescue is even looking for us."

Daniel says, "Even better reason to buy some time. What do you have in mind, Shrike?"

Sara, James, and Daniel huddle with Shrike in secret, out of view of the injured commando.

When they break, Shrike says, "I'm morally against this too, but this is life or death."

Sara nods with reluctant agreement.

Shrike silently asks the owl and marten to join her, then they approach the captive commando.

On Shrike's mental command; without word nor warning, the owl lands on the commando's eyes. Showing incredible restraint and precision, the little owl starts to dig its talons through the outer skin of his eyelids, as if to fly off with both eyeballs. Just as precariously, the marten holds the commando's testicles in its sharp teeth, and growls just like the cougar had done. The vibration crawls right up the injured commando's spine and completely unnerves him. He thinks he's tripping badly. How can these animals be doing this to him?

The commando screams, "GOD! What is it you want? WHAT?"

Shrike calmly secures the comlink to the commando's head.

Shrike warns, "A single, minor error; a slip up … will cost you your eyes and your balls... for starters."

The commando stammers, "Okay. Roger that."

Shrike forces her instructions onto the commando, who calls Cruise on the headset.

Cruise gives the signal and the entire company hunkers down in the heavy sleet storm, silently waiting.

Cruise commands, "Report!"

The owl gingerly steps off of the horizontal commando's eyes, but holds on tight to his forehead, ready to pounce back onto his eyes at the first sign of slip up. Sara holds cue cards above the commandos injured eyes. The marten growls again.

The commando reads carefully, "I am okay, but our comlinks were damaged in the crash. The athletes have been picked up by a search and rescue team. Repeat, all of the athletes are off the mountain. I am walking down the mountain alone. Wait for me in the pick up zone. Get transport ready. Mission over."

Cruise feels very unsettled and suspicious about this sudden, surprise transmission.

Cruise yells over the comlink, "Turn on your transponder. Turn on your unit."

The commando cleverly improvises under remarkable pressure, "Negatory Sir. Lost it. Repeat, no transponder." Cruise does not respond. He sits, grinding his teeth. He does not like this one bit.

Shrike takes the comlink away from the commando, and the owl and marten release his delicate parts.

Cruise thinks and strains and puzzles, knowing something is rotten.

Cruise's company, on the other hand, act elated and relieved by the sound of the commando's voice, and lie down, kick back, and chill; waiting for the order to bug out. Since almost all of the commandos have cigarettes, many light up. They don't have food; they don't have water; but the wildlife (per Shrike's subtle design) assured that the commandos would have plenty of butts. Of course, just like when leaving the champagne behind, Shrike thought ahead. Let them smoke their brains out at this high altitude, and let them keep struggling to stop and light them under mountain conditions. Let them have the psychological anxiety of coming down to the last cig in the last pack ... and then, the heartbreak of coming down to none, and throwing the back away ... and then, really feeling the hunger, not only for a cigarette, but now for food and water too, which the butts had been magically staving off somehow. Many of those who had been straining to keep up feel as if a burden has been lifted off of their shoulders.

In contrast, up at the fortress of stone, not a single athlete has cigarettes. During the next five hours, instead of kicking back and smoking butts, the athletes work at an insane pace: setting the final booby trap, foraging for the last food item, sharpening the last makeshift spear.

Finally, Cruise looks down at his watch for the fifth time in six minutes, then pissed, calls the injured commando back on the comlink.

With the owl back on his eye sockets, and the marten on sausage duty, the hurt commando explains to Cruise that someone must have made an orienteering error.

"I am at position 34.27650, 17. 88662" the commando states, reading directly from Sara's cue cards.

Cruise makes a quick hand gesture, and has his communications guy roll it up on the only GPS they have left.

A navigational expert, he reports to Cruise in fear, "Sir, he is about three and a half miles below us to the northwest, on the other side of the glacier."

"Fuck!" Cruise blurts out impulsively.

As low, black clouds roll right over Cruise's evil head, he stares with a blank, thoughtless expression; a vacant resemblance to a Gila monster of all things. Vapid. Vapid eyes: His mind one million billion miles away, about primed to snap.

He cracks, "That's not a glacier!" then calms himself again, and redefines, "It's just an ice sheet, okay? Damn, we've got to head down fast and smooth. I want to intercept that commando before dark. Let's go."

Cruise and the rest of the bitten, tired, beaten, injured, stung, hungry, punctured, and bruised commandos break into long strides as they drag themselves back down the hillside. They hoot with excitement, thankful that they don't have to keep climbing up the arduous slope.

Flaca lags behind his fire team. Still sore from several injuries, she suffers from the ticks biting her groin. A raven flies down into Flaca's face. She raises her arm to protect her dull eyes. A flicker comes blasting out from a massive diagonal fissure in a deteriorating old snag. The piercing bill of the pecker penetrates about an inch into Flaca's muscular neck. She screams in pain. The raven bites her finger, but Flaca shakes the raven off while holding her bleeding neck, and falls forward onto the ground.

"What happened?" Dumpy asks.

Flaca struggles, "Something stabbed me in the neck."

A soldier guesses, "Blow-dart gun?"

Another soldier reports, "It was a woodpecker. I saw it. Hit him smack in the neck right after the big black crow was in his face."

Joaquin mocks, "Hardy har har, you got taken down by Woody Woodpecker? Ha ha ha."

None of the men are laughing. They look around as the raucous din of screaming jays and buzzing wrens dominates the soundscape. They turn to join the other commandos, now far ahead of them. Though Joaquin lacks the perception to sense it, Dumpy, Flaca, and a number of the other troops are freaked out. Some of the troops kind of almost ski or slide down the steeper parts. Behind Cruise's back, one fire team decides to dump some of their extra winter gear.

One rationalizes, "We will be out of here soon and don't need all this heavy shit."

The idea catches on like wildfire and most of the soldiers drop all kinds of "disposable" gear into the woods as they go: mostly hats, gloves, flack vests, and jackets. They keep their helmets though. If Cruise (or Lohan for that matter) noticed a helmet missing, they would flip out.

High in the mountain fortress, Shrike laughs and says, "Hah ha ha. Good one."
She high fives Sara.

Sara laughs, "They are running in the exact opposite direction from us. Ha ha ha."

The commando, tied tightly to his stretcher, says, "You bitches."

Shrike says to Sara, "You think we are done with this guy yet?"

Sara, assuming Shrike must be joking, replies, "Yup. He is no more use to us now. Off with his head!"
Shrike points the commando's pistol at his head.

She says, "Do you have one more little morsel of information that would make it worth saving your sorry-ass life?"

126

The commando says, "You already got everything out of me."

Shrike says, "That's what I thought."

The commando says, "You said you were going to let me walk."

Shrike drops the Colt .45. The commando smiles with relief. Shrike snatches and jerks the duffle bag out from under the commando. His head smacks hard back onto the rock beneath the stretcher.

Shrike says to Sara, "Certainly not wasting a good bullet on this sellout. Couldn't even hijack a plane."

With that, she starts to suffocate him.

At first Sara watches and laughs, but then she realizes Shrike's intent, so she struggles to pull her off, pleading "No, that's enough. Stop it!"

Shrike bears down harder. Sara can't pull her off. Shrike is possessed, and holds the bag down hard until the commando goes limp.

Sara cries, "Oh my god. You sick, sick person."

Shrike says, "You wouldn't be saying that if he was raping you."

Sara bellows at the top of her lungs. Shrike jumps over and puts the bag over Sara's mouth.

Shrike hushes warily, "Shut up."

The muffled Sara pushes the bag away, "Oh, now you are going to murder me in cold blood?"

The women stare at each other with pinned-wide goshawk eyes, as the suffocated commando chokes up a breath and comes to.

Down below Cruise stops dead in his tracks. He turns and listens to the echo of Sara's howl from above. None of the other women or men hear it, as they keep stumble down the hill with hoots and hollers. Cruise has doubts as he hears the eerie calls of wolves skirting the edge of his company, blending with the deceptive sound of the sleet storm. Per Shrike's commands, wildlife around the region tenses and perks up to alert mode;

giving calls, screeches, and many other animal sounds. The befuddled Cruise looks around like a poser.

Cruise rails, "This is the loudest forest I have ever seen. Fuck these animals! I'm not suffering another attack, no matter what-the-hell kind of witchdoctor shit is going down around here with these critters."

Cruise gets on the comlink headset and calls for the heli'copters to come back for extraction.

Joaquin badgers, "Givin' up Sir? Wise choice. Wise beyond your years Sir."

Cruise responds dry and callus, "Regrouping to assure victory!"

The 'copter commandos state that the weather is too dangerous and unsettled at the lower elevations. They also report that they saw 'some rescue 'copters heading up toward the mountains an hour ago, and heard on the radio that other aircraft join the search in hopes that the weather will clear, or that the athletes are actually stranded high above the foul weather.'

Cruise yells in breathless desperation, "Stop them."

The 'copter commando worries, "How?"

Cruise serves up an instant scheme, "Fly up after them and shoot them down. They have no armor."

The commando reacts, "Our ''copters are too weak for violent weather."

Cruise casts doubt, "Are you sure those pilots aren't just being pussies? Get them up in the air and try to skirt the worst of the storm. What else can you do?"

The commando makes a totally wild suggestion, "We saw a Warthog on the tarmac by the National Guard base. They are pretty stable in bad weather."

Cruise eurekas "Yes! Snag that Hog, make sure it's armed, and get it in the air! We must get to the athlete's before Search & Rescue does or Gwen will have my nuts on her pancakes!"

In the dark of the sleet storm, the eight choppers fly over to the airport like dragonflies and the commandos shoot the place up; killing all three National Guard MPs on duty. They swarm around the plane, but none of the chopper pilots are of any help because they have no idea how to fly it, so the one commando with some flight experience, a dishonorably-discharged lieutenant colonel named Krayawn, decides he needs to be the one to try to fly it.

A second commando says, "I'm coming with you," and then crams into the cockpit. "As a team, we should be able to fly, navigate, and shoot."

The ranking commando climbs up on the plane and says, "No Way. We are already going to be down to seven choppers. We can't go down to six."

He pulls the disappointed commando out of the cockpit. It takes Krayawn a few minutes to figure out the instruments, then he flies off.

In the lumbering A-10 Warthog, the anxious commando hunts for the rescue choppers and planes for what feels to him like a long time. Nervously rechecking the controls again, Krayawn confirms that he is heading right for the drop meadow. Then, finally, he sees the lights of aircraft blinking in the distance. Coming up on it way to fast, he nearly collides into a Cessna search plane, causing the pilot to veer drop altitude.

Krayawn can barely make out flashing helicopter lights strobing in the distance through the horrible visibility. He fires two missiles at the rescue heli'copters but misses, and then he chases down a Piper Cherokee. Krayawn can't know that this plane has nothing to do with the Search and Rescue. It just happens to be a private plane flown by a retired couple returning from an enjoyable predawn flight to watch the sunrise over the Rockies. Krayawn swerves at them, then lines up a position behind the little aircraft and fires a burst from the machinegun-like cannon in the nose. The retiree instinctively dives in panic, vanishes into the low clouds.

Krayawn looks all around but can't find the plane as he circles in broad loops. He can't hit the rescue aircraft with the heavy Gatling Gun, which is really designed as a tank-killing ground-assault tool, and he has already fired his missiles. But worse, unbeknownst to the Warthog commando, the old pilot of the Cherokee calls in the A-10's exact location, as they safely follow it from below the tail. The old timer watches helplessly as the A-10 commando has fun trying out the Gatling Gun. Once the helicopter pilots realize that the A-10 fires upon them, they split off in different directions at full speed, and vanish into black cloudbanks.

Krayawn radios Cruise, with Shrike faithfully listening in from the mountain fortress, "Cruise, Commander, come in."

Cruise quickly switches on his mic to order, "Go ahead."

He reports to Cruise, "Sir, I've driven two heli'copters and two planes from the area. All clear. Awaiting further instruction."

Cruise says, "Are you sure the aircraft have left the vicinity?

Krayawn affirms, "Roger that."

Cruise says, "Have you been able to find the commando near the glacier?""

He replies, "Negative. I can't see anything over in the glacier area. Horrible visibility."

Cruise forces, "Find him. That's your next mission."

Over on the sunny mountaintop, the athletes can hear the aircraft engines, especially the sounds of the heavy Gatling gun in the nose of the attack craft. One of the errant missiles hits a granite spire 432 meters from the fort, causing the athletes to scramble like chipmunks and hide well into the deepest cracks and crevices. Many deer and elk cringe, and duck up against heavy tree trunks for cover as shards of rock rain down.

The Warthog pilot happens past the mountain fortress at slow enough speed and low enough to the angled rock and steeps to see a large number of the athletes' tracks going right into the cover caves. He loops back around and lines up the big noisy nose gun. He fires a short burst, then two shorter bursts. He comes back around for a second strafing run, aiming from a straighter approach.

Within the caves, the athletes scatter like pool balls on a fast break: deeper, lower, into better cover in tight pockets. The devastating bullets rip into the ancient rock; the intense lethality obvious to all of the forest's creatures that witness this murderous terror. Luckily, the athletes only suffered what amount to scrapes so far.

In all of the commotion, it suddenly occurs to Krayawn that this heavily armored, large lumbering beast, is actually pretty darn easy to fly. Though he flies slowly at 217mph, the plane seems to float and hang effortlessly. The commando wiggles the nose of the plane back and forth, not knowing where to focus fire, and then he just holds down the trigger and takes a random shot.

Granite splits.

Trees collapse.

Avalanches erupt, but in all cases the athletes hide safely in their cracks and caves.

Sara urges Shrike, "We won't be able to sustain too many more of those bursts. Somebody's gonna get hit."

Shrike uses her mind to send Peregrines to dive in at 217 miles per hour, practically landing on the windshield of the well-armored Warthog.

Krayawn tries to jerk the plane back and forth, and yells for the raptors to, "Get off. Get off!"

Though he yells repeatedly, the birds can't hear him at all.

He hears a warning beep from his instruments and finally finds it to be the Lock On Warning. It takes him almost another full minute to realize that a weapon is locking onto him! It's too late. While distracted with the heli'copters, and now with the Peregrines, the A-10 has been stalked by an Air National Guard F-16, scrambled out of Montana and armed to the teeth. After the guard base was attacked and the A-10 stolen, the pilot took it upon himself to take to the air before his captain had even called the orders down. The seasoned pilot doesn't even mess with the

Warthog and the unlucky commando. As soon as the F-16 gets within range and locks on for a definite kill, the Guardsman doesn't hesitate.

Poossshhh! The missiles take off!

Right before the rockets hit the Warthog, the Peregrines bail out. Krayawn looks down at the beeping controls. "What?" He reads MISSILES on his equipment, but he has no idea what kind of evasive action to take. Krayawn looks around the cockpit quickly for an eject button, and then decides to take a steep turn down and sharply to the right into the thick cloud layer. The controls beep louder and faster and he can't see anything, so he decides to climb. He climbs up and up, and finally, he breaks out of the sleet and cloud layer; high back into the beautiful blue thin air. The athletes dare to peek out from hiding to watch the climbing Warthog in awe, when, **Booooom!** The first of the missiles hits and the 'Hog' explodes in a massive cluster ball of molten metal. The second rocket rolls through the fireball unscathed; then lacking a target signal, shuts off its engine and falls into the forest with its warhead disarmed.

The cheering athletes come running out from under cover. They try to signal the National Guard fighter going over in the F-16 but he is blasting by so fast and focused on the Warthog debris that he can't see them at all; He doesn't even look in their direction. The pilot calls in the wreckage of the A-10 Warthog attack plane, takes reconnaissance photos as evidence, then peels off for home; putting miles and mountaintops between the stranded athletes and his jet in the blink of an eye.

Sara says, "Let's try to call them on the radio."
She picks up the comlink and hits the button, but the screech owl comes blasting in and snatches it from Sara's hand.

"What the fuck? Not all military are bad, obviously!" Sara carps.

Shrike accuses, "Are you out of your friggin' mind? You want the commandos to hear us?"

Sara counters, "But we're saved. The pilot is right there."

Shrike scolds, "We aren't saved yet."

Back down the mountainside, far below, Cruise interrogates, "Who was just on the comlink?"

There is silence on the comlink headset. The commandos freeze in position and listen intently, their eyes ever widening with each moment of anticipation. Some of the male and female troops begin hallucinating; their ears playing tricks on them over the sound of the incessant bird hollering.

Up at the summit, the small owl hovers back over to gently drop the comlink into Shrike's supple palm, then lands on her shoulder again in loyal position. Shrike, Sara, James, Daniel, and others all stand frozen in complete silence as well. Everyone's eyes shift about with fear as they hold their breaths. Have they been discovered? Is the jig up?

The hurt commando, tied and bound tightly, yells, "Ha ha ha, you fucked up. They caught you now motherfuckers. Ha ha ah, they caught you . . . they know you are alive. They know you have a comlink and been listenin' in."

Before he can finish, the cougar launches itself over several athletes and onto the commando. It covers his loud mouth with its massive, sharp paw, and does its best to swallow as much of the miscreant's head as possible, digging its teeth in deeply. The commando groans at first, then freezes in submissive compliance, silent as a cottontail in a bush. If the cougar penetrates another centimeter, it will crack the commando's skull. He agonizes under the pressure, but knows not to make another peep.

Joaquin says, "Sir, if I may, that must have been Krayawn's comlink that went down with the A-10, sir. It probably caught on fire and burned up."
Cruise thinks for a moment. He does not trust that instinct.

Joaquin says, "Sir, sir? There's no point in going back up."
The angry crowd of surviving commandos who aren't too wounded or exhausted to stand, pin down Cruise once and for

all. They surround him, with their weapons still at full compliment, though with sparse amounts of ammunition. Cruise, Lohan, and Joaquin stand together to face them. As the commandos pull in tighter, Joaquin (still smarting from the loss of a digit) slimily squirms over to their line, as to blend in with the greater numbers. Lohan doesn't flinch, and Cruise just laughs at Joaquin's cowardice.

Cruise yells with power, "What is this? You want to shoot me or something? Go ahead and shoot me. You're big boys. You can find your way out of here and tell Gwen what happened. Because, you know, you are going to have to tell Gwen what happened, or whatever version of what happened you want; but either way, you are gonna have to tell her. Just like you, I'm her property; and Gwen goes after her property... and will track every one of you mutinous motherfuckers down. Even if you go clean and civilian ... she will use her resources to find every last one of you. What would you rather deal with, her or me?"

A number of the commandos weigh their options. None of the female soldiers trust or believe in Cruise anymore, but a couple of the more weaker-minded male buffoons remain loyal.

One of the commandos says, "Sir, we want to know what really happened and we want a straight answer."
Ravens grunt loudly from the surrounding pine trees.

Lohan says with incredulity, "What happened? What are you talking about? You were there ... with us!"

The commando yells back, with his gun raised and sweat pouring down his face, even in the relentless sleet, "Cruise. You. I want to hear it from you."

Pelted hard by sharp ice lets, Cruise asks, "What? What do you want to hear?"

The commandos yell in disorganized volleys:
"What the hell happened?"
"Are we up against something we don't know?"
"What was that?"
"What happened?"
"Are you telling us everything?"

Cruise tries to convince, "Look, look, I don't know any more than you do and I know that is unsettling. I'm not an environmentalist guy, but I would say it looked like some kind of natural phenomena that was maybe triggered by our choppers. It could have something to do with the Lord our God. We all need to pray to him for ultimate victory."

Lohan yells, "Maybe the plane crash caused an avalanche that drove the animals down the mountain? What ever happened, it has to be something real ... and rational."

A commando says with impatient confusion, "Phenomena? What are you talking about?"
Coyotes howl nearby but stay out of sight, jarring the troops' nerves.

Cruise says, "You know, like stuff that happens once in a blue moon."
Several of the superstitious and mentally vulnerable troops scan the thick fog for a hint of the burning sun above the storm layer, but it's ghostly, ghastly dark for day time; like a spell has been cast over the mountain by a powerful, wicked witch.

A commando yells, "Like what sir?"

Cruise thinks for a moment, then takes a try at being clever, "Ya know, like the moths all came out last night for the first time in the season, and that lured a bunch of those birds and bats out and about trying to nab a meal. That scared the big animals, which ran like hell into a stampede, and ah, it just kinda snowballed from there. Yah, that's what happened."

Lohan jumps in, rationalizing, "And ya, that's why the predators were awoken and tried to chase down an easy meal."

Flaca's voice squeaks and cracks when she says, "I thought you said you were there! Those animals weren't running from us or anything. They were attacking us and killing us."

Cruise yells, "Pipe down! That's all we need is hysterics at this point. Everyone keep your head on straight. Stay sharp!"
The commandos look at each other with dissatisfaction, but unable to prove or disprove anything.

Jays make raucous screams that ricochet off of the high-tech helmets.

Joaquin complains under the assaulting nerve damage, "God, these squawkers are givin' me a headache."

Dumpy, quite possibly the most ignorant of the commandos, stands up straight and says, "Well Sir, let's hope the phenomenons are over for this trip."

"Phenomena," Joaquin corrects, "Phenomena."

Dumpy looks at Joaquin with a cursed stare, spits on the ground, and walks off. Her sweat burns like Mongolian fire oil mixed with the freshly squirted eye blood of the infamous horned lizard.

Cruise changes the subject, "More importantly; I think someone else on this mountain has a comlink ---- and we should be heading up hill, not down!"

Back on the sunny mountaintop, Shrike has the cougar release the commando. They listen intently, but the commandos are not using their comlinks right now. This worries Shrike, Daniel, and James.
The injured commando watches the cougar saunter back over to Shrike, and roll its head in her lap, between her soft thighs.

He manages to say, "Arh, are you a god?"
Shrike, Sara, and two nearby female athletes break into laughter.

Shrike replies in surprised disbelief, "What?"

The injured commando, always lying flat as a board, adds "How do you boss the animals?"

Sara states, "She doesn't master or control them. She loves them. They cooperate. Maybe ever think of trying love instead of hate?"
The commando lies perplexed. To his dim mind, he's convinced that Shrike must have some kind of 'god power'.

Shrike insults, "Funny that you jump to the conclusion of "god", or some other paranormal bullshit. I got hit by lightning and can connect with the animals."

Sara joins, "Yah, call that god if you want."

Shrike explains, "I say it's an electromagnetic disruption, ... that's been beneficial."

The commando's eyes widen. "Spooky."
Religious fear washes over him like a wave of primitive ignorance.

The cougar threatens the commando with a growl, then Shrike states, "Right now, I might as well be god to you. I'm all the god you got right now and heaven or hell is up to you and your actions."

The commando quakes with demoralization. He questions his faith. Has he been praying to the wrong god? To no god?

Meanwhile, way down below snow line at the site of the first stampede, where so many still lie wounded; the suffering mercenaries notice vultures kettling up above them; first a dozen, and then forty or more, until around midday. Now they roost in the trees directly above, on the highest branches ... and wait.

One of the most seriously wounded troops says with delirium, "I'm going to take a shot at one of those buzzards. They ain't goona eat me."

"You are stupid," a legless soldier complains, "They are way out of range."

Suddenly, the vultures defecate all at once, sending caustic streams of infected guano down on the injured. With stunning accuracy, they whitewash the helpless invalids. Open insect bites and stings, puncture wounds and lacerations: All of the commandos' raw and exposed skin on their faces and necks enflames beyond belief. It's practically a cross between biological and chemical warfare.

"Owh, that stings!" a female commando howls.
The medic comes running over.

He orders, "We gotta wash this off and disinfect this right away!"

Another injured commando cries, "It burns. It burns like acid!"

The medic works fast, but unfortunately they are out of water. The precious few drops left must be saved for drinking, not for washing off a slimy layer of penetrating turkey vulture shit. The insects return with a vengeance. Some of the troops suffer multiple hornet stings, and one goes into shock.

A coyote slips over to one of the dead men. The coyote, carefully keeping its eye on the other commandos, slips the helmet strap from off of the corpse's chin, then gently grabs the night vision goggles in its stalactite canines and silently pulls them off of the dead man's neck.

Over the endless groans of the injured, the vigorous medic vigilantly observes the coyote and yells a short "Hey!"

The coyote darts away with the goggles to a nearby promontory and stands tall with its head raised. A heron swoops in and delicately takes the goggles in its spear like bill without contacting the coyote's muzzle. The spectacular great blue heron flies off into the noonday sky.

As part of Shrike's established routine operations, the little elf Tara attentively mans her observation post in the top of the tallest spruce. For a gymnast of her caliber, a climb up this type of evergreen is child's play. As signaler, high up on the needle-coated branches, she also keeps her eyes peeled for rescue craft. She hears a 'gwalkk' and looks up. The heron comes in and delicately drops the night vision goggles into her tiny hands. She puts them around her neck and tries them on even though they won't be needed for hours. Not only will she be able to see light reflect off of their metallic gun barrels and gear when the commandos move; but just as importantly, from her perch, she can see where all of the athletes are moving as well. She feels emboldened that this is yet another advantage that the commandos know nothing about. The athletes have eyes in the sky, and silent, visual signals that can't be intercepted.

Back at the lower elevations with the injured stampede victims, the medic calls Cruise and asks for a medivac out, explaining how unsanitary the guano situation is.

Up to his waist in snow and with his toes frozen in his boots, Cruise forces his version of reality onto his medic, "We can't wait for shit like this. Sit tight until we come back down with the prisoners. Come on. Let's go!"

As they start to move faster, the birds intensify their calls when their camouflaged targets become much more revealed against the pristine snowdrifts.

For many of the wounded troops down in the foothills, the bright white caustic guano covers their eyes, glasses, and goggles. Some of the commandos who can move get up and seek cover in the young aspens. Some roll onto their stomachs to hide under their helmets. The animals know to take advantage of this. Kingfishers, woodpeckers, and raptors come in after the last of the guano screen has been laid and do as much face-pecking and eardrum-puncturing as possible. The medic and one other mobile commando decide to abandon the others to save their own lives and begin to run. It's too late. The large predators and other animals come rolling back in and decimate what's left of the wounded before anyone can fire a shot. Like a silent wave: cougar, bear, wolf, buck, and bobcat dispatch the wounded. The medic tries to call Cruise, but is killed by a bear before he can press his comlink to transmit.

In the distance, Cruise and what's left of the commando company can hear the faint screams of the wounded, several miles below, echoing in the pitch-black canyon. Their blood curdles as they look back and forth at each other in horror, and as the nearby wolves howl along with the coyotes, and the elk bugle in animal victory.

A commando excitedly discovers, "Antlers. I see antlers." He gets up and runs toward the thick river of brush tumbling down the 46-degree slope.

Cruise yells, forgoing the comlink, "Stop. Get down. Get back here."

The commando ducks and looks around, then runs back to the company with his tail between his legs.

"I thought we should get it," he reports sheepishly.

Cruise forebodes, "Watch out for traps."

The troops look about with paranoia overload.

High in the mountaintop fort, Shrike hears one of the wrestlers yell and grunt, then some breaking and cracking rocks. She stands to see a dozen or so athletes clumsily experimenting with a rudimentary catapult design. After some humorous mistrials, they finally give up on the idea.

One brawny athlete admits with a hearty laugh, "I think this thing would kill more of *us* than them."

Instead of it being a complete waste of time, imaginative Shrike, cougar dutifully by her side, concocts, "Let's use it as a decoy. Keep in set up over there, poised to fire and in plain sight of our parapets, and leave it loaded. Rig it to collapse and cause a landslide if anyone touches it, and I'll let the animals know to stay far away from it."

The beefy wrestler chuckles, "THAT ... we *can* do!"

The athletes laugh at Shrike's witty ways, and follow her orders to a T.

Sick motivations? Indomitable love? Confusing orders?

Chapter 5

Ascent to the Tier Battles

During another calm and beautiful sunset, the athletes; high in elevation, high on exaltation; bring their process up to factory level under the mild conditions. They believe in Shrike, no matter how insane she seems to be; and with that they believe in themselves and that they can win this battle! America hasn't seen this kind of war production since the military industrial complex took on the Nazi war machine in WWII!

While the commandos still suffer under perpetual sleet, with occasional hail beneath the cloud layer, the athletes bask in the life-giving sunlight.

While the commandos battle to cope with the elements, the fortunate athletes can work at full speed with weather impunity.

While the commandos have incessant wildlife harassing and haranguing them, the mountain creatures continue to help Shrike and the athletes.

Daniel looks around. Nobody really watches, so he spins Shrike around and tells her, "I know you have a lot of feelings for James. I don't care and I can't stop. Shrike, I want to make love to you. It is sweet, precious love: Like the kind of love no one should ever take for granted."

Shrike perceives, "Like the kind of love Kestrel feels for Chelonia in the insane adventure memoir **Humans Need Three Hands**?"

Daniel replies, "Yes."

She pulls him in hard by his clothes without a word.

Not awkward.

Nothing needs to be said.

They enjoy the silence together as they deeply coil in bliss.

Shrike steps back, turns, and organizes an old-fashioned bucket brigade, but instead of hauling water to a fire, the athletes haul "weapons-grade" stones into the top tier of the fort, like a conveyor belt. No obstruction hinders their progress.

With the commandos facing the steepest cliffs and still quite some time away, Shrike calls a meeting, bringing ever single soul in (even Tara from high in the evergreen), to explain every element of the details again; thorough to a fault.

They make hundreds of pine and aspen spikes, sharp as needles, with the help of dozens of chewing rodents; from beavers to mice, and work well into the early evening. Ribs from carcasses are collected along with antlers, and the athletes mount many of these sharpened stakes throughout the fort, bristling out like thousands of little daggers and just waiting for the company of commandos to try to scale them.

At that moment, they look up to see a light moving across the rich blue sky.

"It's a plane," yells Daniel.

Shrike says, "That's way too high to do us any good," peering up from under the overhanging rocks, "I shit you not! Keep working."

Many crane their necks up in hope, continuing to track it across the now visible Milky Way. A number of athletes discuss how to contact the plane, whether it searches for them, and the risk of revealing their position to the commandos. Most of the athletes get back to work on their weapons.

Shrike laughs, and says to Sara, James, and Daniel, "If you think I'm crazy or gonna get us all killed, that's up to you. But do you realize the massive advantage we have?"

They look at her in silent confusion, as more athletes crawl forward over the slumbering bighorn sheep to get within earshot.

Someone from the peanut gallery says, "Advantage? They got a friggin'' army."

Shrike laughs again, and says frankly, "Cruise, their commander, lacks situational awareness. Does anyone know what that means?"

Colt, who had been a major in The Marines, states bluntly, "Yaah. It's basically knowing where all the pieces are in the theater of war."

Shrike applauds earnestly, "Exactly! We know who is coming for us. We know where they are and have a good idea of their numbers and weapons."

Sara realizes, "That's why we came all the way up here?"

James, bristling full of hope says, "They don't know how many we are. They don't know our weapons, our strengths."

Daniel says, "They have no idea what they are in for, but neither do we. We do have the element of surprise, and the elevation and kind-of-like fortress thing going for us."

Sara adds, "As long as we have their headset comlink, and the animals, we will maintain situational awareness --- Tom Brady-like awareness. That *is* a huge advantage, isn't it?"

Shrike says, "We will *all* be prepared. They won't be." Sitting up on a big rock, taking in all the action, Jay takes another hit off of his pipe. Most of the athletes just smile and shake their heads at him in feigned disapproval. Some of the athletes begin to think that maybe the commandos won't find them by dark and instead will bivouac for the night down on the cliffs, so they prepare to bed down with the warm furry animals again, just in case.

Jay is like, "What?"

Sara crawls up onto the rock and sits next to him to say, "Why are you smoking that?"

Jay looks at her, puzzled, "Why not? You always seem to be prescribing things for people to take. Want a hit?"

Sara shakes her head with a soft smirk and says warmly, letting him know that she's falling for his sweetness, "You don't need that," as if to say, 'you need me'.

Jay says, in full awareness, "I know." He takes a huge hit and puffs out a massive cloud like the exhaust from a factory stack.

Sara desperately wants to reach Jay. She wants to reach out to him, but also reach him on many, deep levels. She wants what Shrike has, or at least half of what Shrike has. She wants that love. She wants that passion. She wants to be born again as an Italian, or a Brazilian, or a Japanese/Brazilian/Italian from Rio.

She wants a lot more than she's ever been able to admit to herself until now, and Jay (that lucky bastard) is the idol of her eye.

Sara suddenly feels like she could just reach out and take a hit, or lean over and kiss Jay right on the mouth, but she thinks it better to get off the subject, and jokes, "Well, why don't you make yourself useful and sing us a song?"

Jay says nonchalantly, "Okay."

He stands up high on the rock, takes a relaxing, deep breath, and sings some generic love ballad from the 60's or 70's. It sounds good, but totally kills the mood.

Sara suggests, "Couldn't you sing something with a little pep? We *are* about to go into battle after all."

"Okay", Jay giggles.

Jay rips into an old **Foreigner** song, *Juke Box Hero*, even doing the guitar solo and drum parts with his manic mouth. It is like fight song/psyche music and the Olympians begin wiggling to the groove, inspired. After the big crescendo, the Olympians clap and hoot like nuts.

Shrike comes running over with the cougar protectively heeling to her hip and says, "Hey, keep it down. We don't know if the commandos can hear us."

Jay wonders ignorantly, "Who cares if they hear us?"

Shrike can't be bothered with explaining, "I don't know. Just better to be safe than sorry."

Jay is like, "Whatever dude."

Meanwhile, the commandos, thousands of feet below and beginning to suffer from hypothermia, transverse the ridge over to the north side of the mountain. The wind howls and the snow violently blows off the mountain in blinding sheets. Almost all of the men, and the few women left, look around in a panic. Cruise tries to call back on the comlink to verify the coordinates from the hijack commando, but no one can hear anything over the screaming wind. Shrike however, listens intently to every desperate word.

Cruise signals the troops to follow their path back to the warmer side of the mountain and into the shelter of a low, tight stand of white pines. Many of the commandos take personal inventory to find almost all of their food and water gone.

One exhausted and parched commando stumbles and slips down into a deep crevasse. He is able to stop his descent by wedging himself in against the rocks about six feet down, but could fall 70 or 80 feet if he slips. A few of the other commandos dive onto the ice, and after some struggle, pull him out with cracked ribs and a lacerated face.

Cruise looks him over quickly and then says to Lohan, "Have the medic patch him up fast. We need every body who can fight."

A huge mixed flock of birds gush into the commandos, hitting them directly in their faces. No one can see anything so they just blindly punch and swipe at the birds. At the height of the chaos, rabbits charge in with a lightning assault. From under the snow drifts and tangled in the thick, low brush, the furry little critters remain invisible to the troops. Speedy little rabbits and hares plunge into the troops like swarming mosquitoes. Every commando suffers at least one sharp bite to the calf or lower thigh. The unlucky ones get bitten five or six times. While thousands of birds focus on the commandos' faces, thrushes, robins, wrens, thrashers, nutcrackers and other skulkers, as well as grouse, come blasting in noisily, low at about waist level, and fly in and around the commandos. The commandos can't see the rabbits and hares at all. A jackrabbit darts by a soldier's leg at 31 mph. As the jack rubs past his leg, the commando pulls his pistol and fires two shots. The bullets ricochet off the rocks and back towards the ragged company. A fragment strikes a commando about an inch deep into his calf, stopped only by the shinbone.
"Ow!"
"Ah!"
"Oh!"
"Ah!"
"Damn!" "Aaah!!" the soldiers squeal.

The soldiers stand in disarray with rabbit bites and bird punctures deep into their calves and Achilles, ----- their necks and cheeks.

Cruise, for the first time semi-panicked, screams "Climb what little trees there are!"

Like a pride of lionesses treed by hyena, the troops scurry up the small number of trees and thick shrubs scattered about; most of which are dead, and only two feet off of the ground, but it forces the small percentage of rabbits left to desist instantly; the vast majority have already delivered their sharp, stinging incisor bites.

Clutching a tree as the flock of birds flies away, Flaca prays "Oh god. Help get me out of here alive. I didn't expect this to be a survival mission."

Lohan carps, "You mean that figuratively, right?" Dumpy and Flaca both look at her perplexed.

Lohan clarifies, "You really asking god for help right now? You are trying to steal peoples' organs. I don't think you've stayed off the naughty list."

Flaca says, "Oh yeh. Guess it's kind of dumb to pray to god when you're doin kinda evil things."

Lohan replies coldly, "It's dumb to pray to god anytime." Flaca appears hurt by these comments.

An emotionally disturbed Dumpy weakly defends, "Hey, that's her prerogative."

Lohan fires back like a rat trap, "Pray to god to get your heads out of your asses!"

Deep in other thoughts, Cruise turns to them and wonders, "Lohan, I know this sounds cold, so don't pass this on to any of the other troops, but first off, it's a blessing from the lord almighty our creator that those 50 soldiers, heroes, are all resting in pieces, ah, I mean peace, right now. With no injured surviving now logistically for us, that is a huge headache we can forget about. Secondly, but more important; how could the athletes be over there? Something is wrong here. Look at where we found the plane wreck."

Cruise thinks about it again. Then he says over the comlink, "Troop, they can't be over there. That is friggin'' impossible. If the coordinates he gave us are right, he sent us on a wild goose chase, which must mean, as you know, that they are back up on the friggin'' summit where I thought they were!"

Practically all of the troops groan from amongst the trees, many bleeding and in pain and psychologically devastated.

The troops fall out of the trees like walnuts and accelerate the pace and urgency of their ascent up the steep slopes. Each hidden grouse buzzes as their territorial zone is violated, giving the athletes audio cues to the exact distance of the commandos' positions in the canyons below. Wolves follow the last limp commandos in line at they struggle up the almost vertical rubble and ice goulash. The wolves stay just out of sight but growl repeatedly. The troops keep turning and looking, but never see where the growls emanate from as they blend in with the gray monochrome and gloomy landscape.

A frazzled commando requests via the comlink, "Sir, permission to fire?"

Cruise says, "Fire at what?"

The commando says, "We got wolves back here."

Cruise says, "No. We don't want to give away our location. Only fire if attacked."

The commando defends, "It's necessary. They are right behind us. I can hear them."

Cruise turns to Lohan, "Go back there and get him up into the middle of the unit!"

Lohan obediently says, "Roger that," and turns to go back down the slippery, treacherous slope.

Up in the cozy cave by comparison, the athletes comfortably enjoy their food rations, made mostly from confiscated commando Ready-to-Eat meals.

Shrike turns to Sara and her command group, "Our distance runners are stationed at intervals throughout the forest, and a few of the gymnasts are high in the trees. When the gymnasts spot the terrorists, they will wave to the runners, who will run back to the fortress to give us firsthand reports."

Sara thinks, "What's the point of this?"

Shrike offers frankly, "This is just plain old-fashioned intelligence gathering, pure and simple."

Sara begins to understand, "They have no idea that we know exactly where they are."

A voice of a random athlete rings out, "When they get close, we will spot them, prepare the defenses, and spring the traps."

Shrike stands and announces to everyone, "Excuse me. Don't forget, eat and drink everything. Once the battle starts you won't be able to take a break."

Sara looks at Shrike, "Really?"

Shrike says, "Yes, and also, if we do get caught or killed, the commandos won't get any life-sustaining nourishment from our supplies!"

Sara is totally impressed with Shrike's deep strategic thinking and attention to every detail.

Shrike says, "Let's heave to and help set that booby trap." Sara and Shrike join 21 guys and bend a large limb back.

From the shiny green thickness of a cluster of firs, a mile below the Athletes' hulking makeshift fortress, the troops come back up the slope with a vengeance. Pissed, ornery, irritated, and annoyed from all of the deaths, setbacks, hassles, and nagging injuries: Now add *incredibly angry* to the list. Many of the commandos have a new, hardened drive to capture the athletes. To add more frustration to the troops plight; many of them search around for the supplies they dumped, knowing they will need them for the long ascent ahead of them. The men start to bicker, suspecting the first fire team of hording the supplies.

"Hey!" Dumpy says, "I'm sure I left a backpack of chow right against this tree."

She looks around for tracks on the ground.

Flaca says, "Bear probably got it. C'mon."

Dumpy freaks, "Bear!?" She looks about.
Now the commandos are starving. They are thirsty too. Some of them resort to eating snow.

In stark contrast on the pointed peak, the athletes have extra food left over, and on top of that, a number of animals have been bringing in nuts, berries, and edible plants for the athletes; so it will be a challenge for them to finish every bit of food before the commandos get there.

Far below in the valley, ravens and raptors snag even more food off of the tables down in the picnic areas, and drop drinks in on the athletes. A goshawk drops in a bottle of Gatorade. The athletes pass it around, never touching their lips to the bottle, and taking big gulps without wasting a precious drop. Remarkably, 17 athletes get a swig before the bottle goes dry. Unlike Cruise's troops below, there is no in fighting. Instead, there is totally unselfish cooperation. Shrike dumps the remains of a confiscated canteen into the empty Gatorade bottle, shakes it vigorously, and passes it on. The athletes continue to pass around the Gatorade-tainted water, smacking their lips with the remnant tanginess.

Shrike wears a beaming smile as she looks across the natural fortifications of massive granite formations, 11 meters thick in places. The scout athletes can see the first commandos emerging from the cover of the trees. The grouse burst from the trees like an explosion, then glides down the mountain and into cover, safe from battle fury.

Cruise spits sarcastically at the grouse, "Damn it! Way to announce our friggin'' presence."

Joaquin answers, "I'm tellin' ya, these animals got it in for us."

Shrike chuckles as she listens in over the comlink, but many of the athletes feel chills run down their spines. This is the first moment any of them see the ominous commando unit. Even from this distance, the starving, injured, swollen, limping, broken platoon looks scary formidable. Their particularly intimidating weapons shine against the camouflage uniforms of these death merchants.

Both a rifle and an archery medalist, prone and frozen, muster every ounce of their nerve and concentration. Neither of them has ever imagined killing anyone. The instant the archer hears the rifle shot ring out, she fires a single, lethal shot. Immediately they both retreat before the soldiers hit the ground. Every commando hits the dirt and frozen rocks, except for Cruise. Cruise stands like a statue in place, to view everything. A swollen wasp welt by his eye makes him wince. He sees his first guy go down on the left and the second way over to his right, almost simultaneously, then catches just the top of the archer's head for a millisecond. Sprinters run quickly through the stone and tree labyrinth, distracting the commandos' attention. Completely under cover, rabbits and hares stomp the frozen ground furiously. The sound causes the troops to look around in disarray. Some feel as if another stampede may be coming. The rifle and archery medalists nestle into position to prepare for targeting their next victims. A few of the closest commandos open fire on the sprinters, but they weave and vanish out of sight. The sprinters' identical Team USA uniforms makes it that much more confusing for the commandos, who can't tell if they see the same sprinter or not.

A couple of soldiers crawl up the hillside on their bellies, trying to outflank the snipers. One of the commandos has hornet welts all over his puffed-out eyes and cheeks, and pauses to take an antihistamine.

"What the hell are you doing? C'mon!" his comrade prods with agitation and nervousness.

He gulps down the pill and says, "You go ahead without me. The altitude and the stings ----- I can't breathe."

The second says, "Come on. I need you covering my back."

The first one pants, "Okay. I'll catch up. Go. Go."

The second commando darts up the steep slope for some rocky cover, then looks back down along the mountain side. He can't see anyone in the unit. Friendly fire paranoia set in. He doesn't trust his own unit at this point, so he wisely continues to bow the right flank way out.

The first soldier slings his weapon over his back awkwardly with a clank and scrambles up the mountain after his partner. They both stop at the same time about 42 meters apart, to take notice of a beautiful waterfall.

Over the sound of the crashing water they hear a thin wail beg, "Help me. Help me please. I'm trapped!"

The soldiers scan the cliffs until they spot a young woman clinging precariously to the slimy rocks. The two soldiers quickly run up the narrow path through the mist, over a long and slippery log bridge created by a fallen tree, and up to the little diver. They pass a series of thick bushes, which conceal the rest of the diving team.

The second soldier with the stung eye raises his assault rifle and points it at the square of her back. The first commando runs up next to him and slams the weapon down just in time.

"Why the hell would you shoot *that*?" he questions with a tone of sexuality. Then he shouts to the girl, "Be careful. Look girl, you are gonna be okay."

She pretends to slip, but instead, executes a perfect dive down into the pool some 71 feet below.

"What the fuck!" the puffy-eyed soldier says.

He wipes his face then tries to find her down below.

The soggy soldiers can't find her because of the mist so they turn back down the treacherous trail. A bald eagle and a great-horned owl grab onto the branches of the log bridge with their talons and lift with as much vertical thrust as possible. The diving team, sitting in the brush, push with their legs in unison, helping the large birds of prey to dislodge the log bridge, which tumbles down into the river with a splash, some 97 feet below. The divers slide down the muddy gravel slope, wave 'so long' to the bird helpers, and then dive over some sharp boulders and into a deep section of river, to swim away completely unnoticed by the two commandos shuffling down the trail.

The second commando complains, "Ya know, there's a fine line between commitment and stupidity. I think I've had just about enough of this fool's errand."

When the two soldiers get to where the natural log bridge had rested for almost 98 years, they find that they are moments too late. The first one can't stop his momentum and slides down the muddy slipway and off onto the rocks below with a smash ---- missing the river by a good 22 feet. The second soldier slides to a safe stop, but before he can call for help, the great horned owl glides up silently behind him and tilts his helmet forward forcefully. Like mythical furies, three bald eagles come wheeling in and smash and thrash and rip the commando horrifically hard. The large owl pulls the comlink from his ear and vanishes straight up into the mist, and that's when the eagles disperse at full speed. The shattered commando's rifle goes off accidentally. Cruise and the other commandos hear the shot and pause to listen for another.

The trapped commando paces back and forth, searching for escape options. He can't see any commandos. He can't see any athletes. He looks down to see the twisted body of his fallen comrade on the rocks far below. Drenched in heavy mist and spray under the roar of the waterfall, he waits. His boots sink into the clay-like mud. He hears wolves: first howling, then growling, closely nearby; then he hears the deafening scream of a cougar, even closer.

He holds his rifle tightly against his chest, desperately looking for a way out.

He moans, "Oh."

He looks around for his comlink again, to no avail. Yup. It's gone. He debates trying to clear the rocks by making a treacherous jump for the raging water. He thinks about firing some signal shots, but fears wasting ammunition with all of the predators so close by.

In the meantime, Shrike alerts a group of athletes, "If I were Cruise, I would try to move a sniper or two to high ground on our outer flanks."

Shrike decides to recruit a little animal support, but, at the same time, she is incredibly conscious about assuring that the animals will be in minimal peril. Instead of frontal assaults with the chance of high casualties, she devises more clever ways to safely incorporate the wildlife into her defense schemes.

The sailors rig up a boat with a dozen sticks, balls, and shirts, to create makeshift dummies; sitting them up against the aft gunwale. The crew rigs-up the sail and the tiller, then send it speeding across the glassy alpine lake on a gusting reach.

Cruise turns to his soldiers with hope, "Company, we have almost made it above cloud cover. I want a sniper on the outer flank. Get in a position where you can scan for them and inform us, but don't pick any off unless they are firing on us."

The commandos, finally clawing their way above the dismal cloud cover for the first time, watch with their binoculars for a second, in stunned silence.

Over the din of honking geese and grunting ravens, Flaca says to Cruise, "I can't tell if they are hunkered down or what, but it looks like there actually isn't anyone on that boat but dummies."

Lohan says to Cruise, "A trick?"

They strain their exhausted eyeballs as the boat moves into black shadows cast by the ebbing remains of twinkling sunset. They believe the boat to be a ruse. The light plays tricks on all but the owl's eyes, and the alpine lake is big and pretty far away.

Cruise says, "What? Why? What's the point of that?"

At that instant, river otters slip aboard and move about under a heavy sail bag. A few large cutthroat trout in the lake hit their entire two-pound bodies against the centerboard and rudder, slightly correcting the direction.

The commandos detect the jerking, unnatural movements, and snap to their feet.

"Get em!" some of them mumble.

Cruise foolishly sends a fire team all the way around the lake to intercept the boat. The rest of the commandos scan the rocks for ambush. The otters slip overboard before the commandos descend on the abandoned little sailboat, now scraping along the rocks on the pristine lakeshore. The commandos approach with caution. One wades out to his hips to grab the boat.

"Nothing," he says as he turns back to the boat.

He looks at the corpse-like dummies and says "Hey, what's in here?"

Another member of the fire team whispers, "Leave it for now. Let's get back to the unit."

In defiance, the first commando lifts up one of the dummies to expose a commandeered grenade. The commando only sees the grenade for one second as it rattles onto the fiberglass deck and slides down to the drain plug by the transom.

The fire team leader yells, "Watch it, GRENADE!"

BOOM!

Cruise and his troops train their binoculars and scopes onto the far side of the lake.

The commandos fall, crashing into the bushes by the lakeside, thrown by the blast. They pull their guns up and prepare to return fire. They wait, but hear nothing but the ringing in their ears. They realize it was a single grenade booby trap. The fire team leader has two of the guys go into the water to pull the unconscious commando out. Though his gear protected his head and torso, his face is blown off. Remarkably, somehow he lives. The little sailboat on the other hand, sinks as the snapping turtle-sized hole lets the lake gush right in.

One of the commandos looks at the fire team leader and says, "Only to find a fake," as he dejectedly looks back over at what's left of the smoldering sailboat.

The fire team leader says, "Let's head back. Double time. Go, go."

The three remaining team members, their ears still ringing from the grenade, take off running back up the trail to rejoin what is now a 34-person company. The fire team leader looks at the commando's *nonexistent* face, and pulls out his pistol.

He says, "Look man. I'm doing you a huge favor. You are a fuckin' living scab man."

The commando with his face blown off grunts an unintelligible, "Do it."
The fire team leader quickly shoots him in the head, devoid of human emotion.

The rest of the fire team stops in their tracks. They look back and forth at each other with confusion.

One of the fire team members calls with hesitation, "Captain? That you?"

The fire team leader comes onto the comlink and says, "It's all good. We have to travel another exhausting hour, bushwhacking back to join the forces high up the mountain ahead of us, so we better get crackin'."

He takes a few ammo clips and a grenade off of the commando's corpse, but decides it's too heavy to carry anything else, so he runs after the others. As he moves carefully along the slippery rocks, he hears a funny sound. The otters pop their heads up from out in the middle of the lake, with mocking, squawky barks. The three other commandos look at each other in utter frustration, then move at double-time, exhausting themselves before they get to the actual battle. A plague of frogs, newts, and slugs slime ubiquitously over the angled slate, causing all four commandos to slip and fall at least twice on the layer of slime.

Cruise orders the rest of the commando units to wait at a flat crest for the sailboat unit to rejoin them. Shrike gives the cue, which sends a woman casually jogging past the two scouts on the outer right flank, and down through some short trees and bushes.
Bournstien, the front scout, throws his pack and assault rifle off.

"I'm getting this one. She ain't gettin away," he yells, pulling out his .45 and sprinting to chase her down.

Though a former track star himself, Bournstien unknowingly takes off after a world record-holding long jumper. The second scout follows, but can't keep up with the high-speed runners. The long jumper had practiced this route three times earlier in the day, but now with the sun dropping behind the highest peaks, it looks a lot scarier and hairier. Still, she keeps her cool and gradually slows down enough to suck him right in. Just as he gains on her, his hopes rise and he begins to salivate. Unable to take a clear shot, he reholsters his side arm and leans into his run with more determination. This is the moment the long jumper had hoped for.

She passes her mark, accelerates to a sprint, counts her steps and jumps 17 feet over a treacherous ravine. Her launch trajectory perfect, her feet hit first, and hard, causing her to flip onto her back on the other side of the deadly gap. She summersaults back onto her feet and breaks into another sprint. Scratched and bleeding, but on the run again, she just keeps on flying and out of sight. Bournstien has no choice but to try to clear the ravine. If he tries to slow or stop, or even shows a moment's hesitation, he won't clear it.

The testosterone-amped Bournstien instantaneously convinces his mind, 'Hey, if that little chick can clear this ravine, so can an impenetrably fit commando in his prime, right?' Wrong!

Instead, he leaps only to find himself kissing the shear-rock cliff face as he hangs eight feet below the lip. Dangling by his fingertips, he feels grip slipping.

Silent Tara, high in the treetops, signals runners with her arms. These guys are in incredible cardiovascular shape. Three of them are quarter-milers. That's one whole lap around the track, just like in James' hurdle race. There's also an 800m runner, a miler, and other guys who can basically run at full speed all day long. The runners scurry in like ghost crabs to pick up Bournstien's commando pack and weapon. The 800-meter runner stays on the lookout, while the others are in and out with the gear in a matter of seconds.

The rear scout arrives up at the steep ravine, out of breath. He looks around, but can't see the girl, then looks down to see the Bournstien slipping and losing his grip. He looks around quickly for a way to save his comrade.

He thinks of different strategies, then offers, "I'm gonna knock over a large tree to make a bridge, then I'm going to hand another large branch down to you. Hold tight."
The commando stops in his tracks for a second and then decides to call in on the comlink for help.

After a moment of consternation, Cruise replies, "We have no way to help him. We have no ropes. Do what you can for him."
Lohan looks as Cruise with complete disappointment.

Cruise goes back on the comlink, "Fire team C, go up and assist at the ravine."
Cruise looks back over at Lohan with aggravation, while Lohan nods her head in approval without a smile.

Bull elk give off sensational bugles. The foghorn-like blasts rattle the soldiers like audible mortar fire. The commandos raise their rifles on the first few bugles, but the elk lay too well hidden and they give up.

After 15 minutes, and even with the help of six guys, Bournstien finally slips and falls to his death. The rear soldier pauses for a second in despair, then turns and starts back to return to the unit. On the way back, he looks to retrieve his partner's gear, but the middle-distance runners have already taken it and vanished.
The fatigued fire team and the commando stand casually in a stupefied line.

The Fire Team C leader asks, "What are you looking for?"

The rear commando says, "That's weird. I thought Bournstien dropped his pack and rifle right here ..."
BANG BANG BANG BANG BANG BNAGG!!! BOOM!
AAAHHHHH!

One of the runners, a quarter man infamous for anchoring the mile relay, who had hung behind in ambush, on his own volition and unbeknownst to Shrike, unloads the fallen-Bournstien's rifle and the grenade launcher into the rear commando and Fire Team C from about eight meters away. They go down fast and hard into cover, but all suffer serious wounds. The runner sprints over to the nearest commando as he falls in a slump. He rolls him onto his chest, pulls off and then puts on his pack, and grabs his grenades and guns over his subconscious groans. He pulls the pin on one of the grenades, wedges it under the commando's body (just like the trap in the sailboat), and then yells, "Help. Help me. Over here. I'm shot. Help."

The injured commando, unable to move, gurgles, "No. Don't come over," but it is very weak and muffled.

Cruise, the leader of 27 commandos now, says, "Did you hear that? Fire Team B, go check it out. Fire Team C. Fire Team C! Fire Team C, come in!"

The four-hundred-meter specialist says, "I ain't wasting another bullet on you."

He pulls out the commando's own knife and stabs him hard yet mercifully in the center of the throat. The commando tenses, then collapses motionless in a quick death. The runner quickly slides the knife back into the commando's sheath, while the other wounded commandos begin to rustle in the brush. The middle-distance man sprints back up toward the fortress with the spoils of his risky escapade dangling awkwardly from his neck and shoulders. Halfway there, three of his fresh teammates meet him (including the 800-meter runner), and relive him of his entire haul. They race each other in full sprint up to the fortress from there, with the lightened but still exhausted four-hundred-meter anchorman trying to keep up and beaming with accomplishment.

Cruise tries to contact the dead guys on the comlink, "Bournstien? Bournstien report. Fire Team C? Fire Team B?"

American robins, jays, and a number of smaller wrens and such, scream and blare at the tops of their little throats. The sound is deafening and causes the commandos' eardrums to vibrate painfully.

Joaquin yells over the din, "Sir, we got guys gettin' picked off, like dropping like flies."

Lohan adds analytically, "They do seem to be outmaneuvering us somehow. They're unencumbered by weapons, food and water for one."

Cruise puzzles for a second, pissed and frustrated, then he commands, "All units, listen up. Another strategy adjustment." A number of the commandos roll their eyes at each other, having lost faith in the commander.

Dumpy mumbles to Flaca in a disgruntled tone, "He was to lead us on what was to be a pretty cake mission."

Flaca concurs, "Ya with maybe the outside chance of one commando getting killed."

This comment points to the fact that none of Gwen's force, including Gwen, even have a grip on just how many commandos have already bit the dust, not to mention the fact that the athletes are listening in on the comlink, have confiscated some pretty mean firepower themselves, and, oh yeah, Shrike can control the friggin'' animals!! None of these commandos can even imagine what they are really about to be up against and what the body count is going to look like when all is said and done. People enter into war situations blindly like this; year after year, century upon century. Somehow, humans continue to survive. Some humans, that is.

Cruise continues, "Stay in five-man fire teams from now on. We will have no scouts on point. Stay in tight, defensive fire teams, but keep it spread out from the other teams. Cover your backs. Let's move."

The commandos snap into formations and run up the slope at a good clip. They look like a well-oiled machine for the first minute or so, when a rhythmic gymnast throws a ball and hoop straight up into the thin air from behind a monolithic boulder.

The soldiers freeze when they see the colorful equipment appear and vanish in a flicker. They raise their guns.

Wolves growl nearby. The troops spin back around and switch the safeties off on their assault rifles, but they can't find a target down slope. At this point, the commandos want to shoot. They are dying to shoot. Unlike the athletes and their eternal calm, the trigger-happy commandos' patience and discipline has broken down.

Peering down from the all-encompassing view of the rock perch above, Shrike gives the signal.

Daniel, doing his best impression of Cruise, yells over the comlink, "Open fire! Open fire now!"

With a total of four working M16s in their hands, Colt and three of the other athletes lay down a swath of machinegun fire and then slide down behind the rocks, and run for it. Their fire wounds three commandos and kills one.

Typical of American military tactics, the commandos react with an incredible barrage of heavy fire; like killing a butterfly with a bazooka. Most of them unload their clips … their last clips! The echo of bullets rings through the air, along with the sounds of clips being jettisoned.
Everything is suddenly quiet again. The animals restart their cacophony.

The four athletes pop up from the rocks with fresh clips and spray automatic weapons fire at the commandos. Eight more commandos get hit and another dies, as the rest twist out of the trees like gypsy moths to take cover and return fire. The athletes quickly turn and make a concealed retreat back to their next ambush points, as the commandos waste more precious ammo.

Once Cruise sees that everyone has taken cover behind the boulders, he orders, "Let's hunker down here for a while and reassess our approach. Lohan, how many soldiers we got in commission now?"

Lohan, having already done a quick analysis, reports "Including the three of us, we have 25 total."

Cruise screams like a magpie, "What? 25? I thought we were still up around 30?"

"No sir," Lohan verifies.

Looking down from the magnificent granite walls, Shrike says quietly, "Looks like the hares did their deal, and without the loss of a one. Now the assault-rifle fire should hold them for a while."

Sara says, "They're just rabbits. Aren't they expendable?"

Shrike, James, and Daniel stare at Sara in utter disappointment.

Sara says, "Never mind. Looks like *you're all* possessed by the animals now."

Daniel says, before the words can burst from Shrike's mouth, "As should you."

Shrike defends emotionally, tears building in her eyes with every word, "I'm not one of those arrogant commanders who charges her brigade into the teeth of death. Fuck that shit. My goal is zero casualties on our side when possible. Zero! I didn't ask toads and salamanders to wake from their torpid states to sacrifice themselves, their squished bodies and limbs and brains, for us. I have zero tolerance for the death of any of us, including the animals. If we start dying, then we surrender. We are not fighting to the last person, or animal, or any of that shit. Instead, we are just going to wipe them out! I shit you not!"

Sara swallows hard, her eyes as big as a ringtail's, glowing in the dark pre-dusk shadows.

The cougar, heeling by Shrike's curvaceous hip, lets out a vicious snarl.

Shrike calms herself, gathers her composure, and says, "Too bad we are at the wrong latitude to add some poison dart frog venom to the ends of our spears."

Daniel and James, then finally Sara, all chuckle.

James says, "Girl, I like how your mind works; animals or no animals, but preferably animals."

Daniel says, "Me too."

The three of them hug. Sara crosses her arms in front of her chest. It almost looks as if subconsciously Sara tries to hug herself.

They look over at Sara and Shrike says, "Hugs must be shared or they lose their power, silly shrink."

The men laugh heartily with Shrike. Sara can't bring herself to go over to them for a hug. She feels as if it's wrong somehow. She wishes she could.

Sara snarks back, "Hugs are drugs you know, … just as bad as any other crutch: Physical, chemical, spiritual, emotional, or otherwise."

Daniel and James dismiss, "Ya ya, what evah!"

Sara gets mad and turns away, only to see Jay, her love interest, staring down on her with disparaging disappointment. He was starting to really like her, but who wants to be with an emotional robot?
Jay turns and walks off discouraged.

Sara snaps her head back around at Shrike, "Well I guess you've proven I'm less human than everybody else. Can't wait to see the encore."
Sara goes off down the slope in the opposite direction of Jay. Daniel, James, and Shrike look at each other, but no one knows what to say.

Cruise, still frozen in position, breathes heavily as he listens. A few of the troops groan in severe pain, making it difficult to hear anything up ahead of them, like the movements of the four guys with the M16s, or anything else.
Birds screech and caw, yell and scream – all around the commandos.

Joaquin, limp and practically genuflecting asks, "Want me to get you a new causality report, sir?"

Cruise laughs, "Don't waste your time. We know we're hurt. Yuhd have to be a moron not to see that."

A large pack of wolves erupt into howls within feet of the commandos. Some take their safeties off, while others check their empty clips for bullets. Some lower their night vision, in an attempt to pierce the shadowy brush and boulders. Shrike picked such a perfectly wicked location because of its insanely extreme terrain; and it's working brilliantly. With they're ability to maintain alertness waning, well before the real battle has ever begun, and still having a lot of backbreaking work ahead of them, the sore, beaten, thirsty, and exhausted commandos fight to hold onto everything they learned back in basic training. They know they are losing.

Joaquin whines, "Fuck. Where are they? I hate when they are just out of sight like this. Can I hit'em up with a phosphorus flare so we can daylight them and put some heat on their furry little asses?"

Cruise looks over at Lohan for acknowledgement.

Lohan says, "Scare the fuck out of them."

Cruise nonchalantly permits, "Sure. Go for it."

Joaquin gets the flare gun from one of the other commandos and points it into the dark cloud cover that has been building up the mountain since sunset, aiming it carefully through a hole in the branches.

Suddenly, Lohan yells, "Hey, don't fire that!"

Joaquin says, "Commander's orders."

Lohan scans the rocks, detecting movement. It could be animal. It could be human. Either way, she's not taking any chances.

Lohan says, "You will give away our positions and light *us* up."

Lohan looks over at Cruise with incredulity.

Cruise says, "Oh yeah. What was I thinking? Don't fire that Joaquin."

Joaquin pulls the gun down like a disappointed tween with illegal fireworks. He empties out the thick shell and hands them back to the other commando.

Cruise admits, "Wow. That was a bad call on my part. I think we need to take a break."

Owls hoot, bark, and screech with eardrum-splitting effect.

Joaquin agrees idiotically, "We don't want to make any fatal errors sir. We should rest here tonight. Let them rot. We'll get them in the morning. A morning assault. They will be hungry, freezing."

Lohan confronts, "Am I the only one who isn't mad around here? Last time we camped, we were eaten alive, then pulverized by a friggin' stampede! Tonight, we gut some little evil gremlin things biting us so badly that we were actually treed! Let's push on, get up the mountain and above this miserable cloud cover, and get the athletes. Once we have them we can use their bodies for warmth. Then we can get the hell out of here as soon as day breaks, fast! We are getting our asses handed to us!"

Snapping himself out of it, Cruise stands with rejuvenated power and looks to Joaquin, "Ya can't argue with that. If you had Jesus on your side, you'd feel more at ease."

Joaquin protests, "Whad'ya mean? I'm born again. I follow Jesus."
Lohan, Cruise, and all of the nearby commandos raise their eyebrows in complete shock and disbelief, and at this point don't trust anything coming out of Joaquin.

Lohan directs over her comlink, practically assuming control, "Troops, let's go! We will push on at Blitzkrieg speed for one hour to see if we can intercept the athletes, then we will assess whether or not we should have shift breaks. Everyone can hold on for one more hour!"

Joaquin counters, "Sir, everyone is in a lot of pain. We're already hours past what we can handle."

With Shrike intently hanging on every word, Cruise says over the comlink, "Later isn't as good as sooner I gather, so let's do shift breaks. Fire Team B sleeps while everyone else continues up the mountain as fast as possible. After 20 minutes, Fire Team D, and then in turn, Fire Team E sleeps."

A number of the men, completely exhausted, mumble:
"Great."
"Sounds great."

"As long as I just get a few minutes to lie down with my eyes closed, ..."

"... without being bit, or bitten,..."

"... or stung."

"With no friggin'' ants crawlin' on me."

While Fire Team B sleeps, the other commandos cluster together to form a unified battlefront. They start their accent at high speed for the first few moments, only to run into incredible natural terrain and Shrike-designed barriers. Cruise looks about with disapproval. A pack of wolves howl from a peak on the adjacent ridge. Great horned owls hoot with repeated eeriness. The commandos huff and puff as the cold darkness of night closes in fast.

Cruise realizes, "This ain't working. We are all getting exhausted, and need more of a break, and it is getting too late."

Lohan pushes, "What if we try one more hour, then call it a night?"

Cruise puts his foot down, "No, this is how we will do it."

Cruise grabs for his comlink, still unaware that Shrike hears each word uttered, and relays his orders, "Under god's great graces, here's the plan. Everyone take a one-hour sleep break except for a two-fire team night watch. You guys alternate half hour breaks. After an hour, we are going to blast up the slope for one more hour to see if we can raid them sleeping. If again, we can't find them, we will make camp right there, and rotate the last of the guard fire teams."

Lohan adds, "And we'll set Claymore mines around the perimeter to stop any stampedes dead in their tracks."

Without even as much as a cigarette, many of the commandos pass out against and among the trees in which they sit, including the medic -- dead ragged.

High above, nestled in the rock fortress, and bathed in the ambient twinkle of the last twilight of day, the busy foils bump into each other. Sara looks a little weak and dazed.

Shrike says, "What's up with you?"

Sara says, "Oh, well, no big deal. I can't find my meds. I think I'm out."

Shrike counters, "You're dependent on those then?"

Sara straightens, "No, of course not. I function a little differently without them, but I can still function."

Shrike says with air quotes, "Junkie. And you've been trying to prescribe to me this whole trip, ... to "fix" my "problems"."

Sara defends, "That's unfair. What about when you're on your period. You function okay?"

Shrike argues, "Yes. I function fine."

Sara says, "Well, in my experience, you're one of the only women who does."

Shrike says with anger, "I'm on it right now!"

Sara raises her eyebrow, "I see."

Sara knows Shrike is not menstruating but she lets it hang.

Shrike calms her tone, "I'm not on my period right now, and you should do two things: Lay off the meds, and lay off telling me to get on them."

Sara smiles with final agreement, "Deal. Who would want a totally balanced Shrike any way . . . "

Shrike returns, " . . . or Sara?"

The marten runs up Shrike's back and curls itself around her supple neck. They snuggle and feel warm against each other.

Sara looks on with amazement. Since her scientific side still can't reconcile with everything else she experiences, she decides to rifle through gear and look under things for her meds. A pill bottle rolls out from under a bag. In her frenetic craze she doesn't notice it, but the marten does and pounces on it; bringing them straight to Shrike.

Shaking the pills like a maraca, Shrike hurls, "Looking for these?" as if she's calling pigs in for a once-a-day feeding.

Sara says, "Oh. Thank you."

Daniel and James come walking over.

Sara reaches for the pills, but Shrike pulls them back.

Shrike says, "Not so fast. I'll give them back to you if you absolutely promise you won't take them."

Sara pauses for a second, and then finally relents, "Okay." Sara reaches for the pills, but Shrike drops them on the rocky ice and smashes them hard beneath the heel of her boot.

Sara screams, "Nooooo. Nooo!"

Shrike laughs, "Ha! I knew it you liar."

The boys look at each other in total confusion.

James questions carefully, "Ah, what kind of relationship you two have anyway?"

Sara grabs Shrike by the jacket with both hands and yanks her into her face.

Sara yells, "We have a hate-hate relationship. Hate-hate!" Sara breaks into tears and stomps off pissed. Shrike sees that those drugs really were holding her together.

Shrike, following her down the hill with her eyes, says softly, "She'll get over it. Or, we'll all be dead. Either way." James and Daniel laugh their asses off.

Shrike brings her finger to her lips, "Shhhhh. Let's get back on the commandos."

Creeping ever closer to Shrike and her crew, the commandos continue their treacherous ascent. Shrike tells Sara, James, Daniel, and Jay how funny it is to hear how the commandos struggle, one by one, solo individuals, alone. Each soldier struggles with each obstacle. Whereas the athletes just made this same ascent and they worked like ants; helping each other up, holding each other's gear, grabbing each other's arms and boosting each other's footing. It was as if the athletes were a smooth conveyor belt, because they wanted to work together. On the other hand, the macho-ninny commandos can 'do everything themselves' and are Rambo independent. This myth falls on its face yet again; and in these commandos' cases, literally and repeatedly.

Joaquin wrenches his ankle on a boulder and reaches down to grab it in pain. When he looks up, he sees three or four coyotes moving around right in front of him. They bare their toothy, macabre grins. Joaquin wants to yell, but stays frozen.

Some deer bound by, startling Joaquin who whines and flinches, and when he looks again, and the coyotes are gone. Four commandos appear from behind the lip of the rock ledge and take shots at the scurrying mammals, but don't even come close.

Cruise yells in a panic over the comlink, "Stop! Stop! Cease Fire! Cease Fire!"

A few errant shots ring out.

Cruise pauses to assure they really have stopped, then yells, "Who gave the order to fire? Who gave the order to fire?!"

Before anyone can answer, Colt and the other three athletes lay down yet another swath of machinegun fire, unloading their clips.

The commandos blindly fire back with everything they've got.

Cruise yells for them to stop again, but Daniel keeps yelling 'Fire! Commence Firing. Fire at will!' on the commandeered comlink, over Cruises commands, so the commandos keep firing.

When the smoke clears, Cruise looks about, shifty and puzzled.

Cruise calmly transmits, "Okay. Listen to me. I don't know who said to fire, but it wasn't me."

The perplexed commandos look at each other as the few with remaining clips reload for the last time.

Joaquin erroneously reports, "Not to worry sir. We still have plenty of ammo."

Lohan rebuts, "For now."

Suddenly, the tiny rhythmic gymnast reappears, hucking her bright hoop in plain sight of what's left of the company of Special Forces commandos. Many of the men point their guns, but no one fires. Cruise thinks for a moment.

Cruise says, "Go after her and get her alive. We need to beat the information out of somebody for Christ's sake."

A fire team goes after her in tight, fast formation, but she turns a corner and quickly falls out of sight among the black moon shadows. She jumps onto the back of a waiting BMX bike, putting her feet on the BMXer's hips and holding onto his shoulders like a spider monkey in a circus act. They make a jump down an icy dirt slope, bounce over some large rocks, smash through a shallow snow bank, and turn behind some dense brush and out of sight again; covering 84 meters of insane terrain in a matter of 11 seconds.

The commandos climb to the top and look over rocks to find nothing. One commando yells in frustration and fires a grenade into the rocks. The explosion does no harm.

The leader of the fire team turns to the tantrum guy and says, "How many more of those have you got left to launch?"

The commando bows his head sheepishly, "Two more."

The fire team leader shakes his head, "Fuckin' idiot."

Cruise calls in over the comlink, "Fire Team, REPORT!"

The fire team leader says, "Negative. She got away. Repeat, she vanished."

Cruise responds with spitting anger, "How the hell did that little girl out run you?"

The team leader responds, "We don't know sir. It's impossible for her to cover that much ground. She must have ducked into a fox hole."

Cruise hesitates for a second, then says, "Get back here." The commandos turn and run back to join the other units when they notice the catapult. They call in to Cruise.

Cruise repeats, "A catapult? You sure?"

The fire team leader verifies, "Roger. An old, Roman-looking thing, and it's huge, and it looks loaded. If they launch that while we cross the exposed escarpment above the glen, we would come under decimating fire."

Cruise thinks for a second, then orders "Take your team back around and below to the west."

The exhausted, hungry fire team commando gasps, "Sir, the men, that's at least 200 vertical meters back down slope, . . . to get out from underneath the trajectory, and come up on the other side."

Cruise says, "Move fast and you will be out of its range right away."

This little detour costs the commandos an extra hour of effort. When they finally surround the catapult, they use their knives and other tools to dismantle as much as possible; wasting another 20 minutes on another diversion.

"Ingenious" one of the commandos spouts, not understanding the physics behind why this lame design could never work.

Suddenly, one of the load bearing arms snaps and the boulders bounce out of the concave cup and down the steep slope and pinning a soldier, who lets out a scream.

High above, like vigilant condors, Shrike and James hang out over a massive ledge in a quiet, sheltered crack-like cave; relaxing while they await the return of the runners. They can hear everything from their vantage point, including the yell from the injured catapult commando. James notices a red crossbill sleeping on a branch, and stops just long enough to simply enjoy the exotic beauty of this bird and its twisted beak.

He says to Shrike, "You have a kind ass girl."

Shrike responds gratefully, "Thank you."

They smile warmly at each other.

James changes gears, "How long do you estimate it will take them to get up here to us?"

Shrike answers, "At this rate, and with everything we have in store for them, I'd say they are gonna make it all the way up here, but it's going to be two or three hours of hell for them, easy." She thinks for a minute, then adds, "Unless they bed down and try to hit us at dawn. That's what I would do, but they have mental-munchkin egos, so they will probably come straight for us at night, like fools."

James says, "Not long enough."

When the rhythmic gymnast, the BMXer, and the runners return, Shrike sees to it that the runners go through the soldier's pack for useful items. She instructs another runner to sprint the newly acquired assault rifle over to one of the volleyball players who had former ROTC training in college.

As he fondles the weapon Shrike says, "You ever fire one of these?"

The ex-Army volleyball spiker says, "I can explode and reassemble this weapon blindfolded."

Shrike says, "Awesome. The gun has a grenade in the launcher, and we've been able to scrounge three clips. If you add that with the three hand guns we got off of the first three hijackers, plus all of the guns the runner could carry off the fire team, we now have a little more to shoot back with. Remember though: We don't play *their* game. We make them play *ours*!" Everyone within earshot nods with agreement and breaks off to their assignments in Shrike's well-choreographed "theater of operations."

The ROTC guy takes the rifle and moves serpentine down the slope until he can see the other armed athletes. He hides, straining to see any of the commandos. Then a minute later, he snipes a soldier and takes off. The gash from the bullet wound bleeds profusely. The medic moves in and tries to control the bleeding.

The devastating mental abusive starts to take hold. The troops show fear in their eyes. Screeching owls add an eerie soundtrack to the nightmare unfolding. The soldiers had no idea that real weapons would be used against them, so many of them are in psychological shock. They bog down for an hour bracing for more M16 fire, while the bleeding commando finally expires. Cruise talks over strategy with Lohan in a low, depressed-sounding voice. A badger comes up from its den near Cruise and Lohan and gives off a frightening growl and bluff charge. Lohan and Cruise jump up and back with shock but can't get a weapon trained on it before the badger is back underground and bulletproof. The commando leaders look at each other for a second in disbelief, and then get back to planning.

Back up top, with shooting stars dashing across the crystal sky and between the jagged peaks, Shrike turns to Daniel.

She says softly, "Ha ha ha, it looks like it's going to take them a lot longer to get up here than they thought."

Daniel and Shrike smile at each other. Without another word, Shrike reaches over and gives Daniel a passionate kiss on the lips. Lightning shoots down his spine and coagulates in his ganglia. Then, they turn back to the struggle at hand, skillfully pulling the marionette strings of her multi-fold scheme.

Though Lohan feels that the situation is too dangerous, Cruise finally decides that the commandos need to start moving again. The ROTC volley guy patiently snipes another commando as soon as he appears visible in the moonlight, and is gone. The troops hunker down again as they watch the wounded commando tumble down the steep rocks and ice.

Cruise says, "C'mon guys. On my command let's move, and let's move fast. We will overwhelm them by sheer strength and force."

"No way," a number of the commandos respond over the comlinks defiantly.

Cruise stands up boldly, "Follow me." He runs up the slope quickly, covering a little over 34 meters, then ducks behind a large, dead stump with a spiky top.

Owls, nightjars, and other fast flyers dart by at varying elevations, calling only when they see soldiers begin to move or stir. Some annoyed troops take a few pot shots at the silhouettes overhead, in vain. Weasels and ground squirrels bounce back and forth behind the rattled soldiers, making as much distraction noise as possible, and bluffing fake charges.

"Knock it off!" screams the impatient Cruise.

"I thought you said pick off any animal that moves," replies Lohan, confused.

"That's for when they were attacking us. Now they are obviously just trying to get us to waste our ammo. Save your ammo for kill shots. Don't take waste shots."

Joaquin whispers to Lohan, "Now he thinks the animals are trying to get us to waste ammo on purpose? Obviously?" Pointing at his own helmet, he wiggles his finger in a crazy oval.

Lohan puts up a front, "Shut the fuck up," but she too doubts Cruise's sanity.

Shrike overhears this on the comlink, and has runners spread the word throughout the athlete network.

As dozens of the athletes join in simultaneously from the nearby shelters, Shrike says in a hushed and excited meeting voice, "Since they won't shoot at what they can't see anymore, it's time to go on the offensive."

Two athletes in the peanut gallery blurt out, "Yes!" and "Finally" with relief.

Shrike takes one of the few grenades they have and hands it to a goshawk flying by. The hawk quickly flies it to Tara, sitting like the diminutive little gymnast thing that she is. A freak. A freak of nature really. As much a freak as Wilt the Stilt or Joni Mitchell, Usain Bolt or Nadia Comaneci, Vince Wilfork or Sade Adu. You know: Not like the rest of us. Not like Shrike and Daniel and Sara and Jay; almost a different species you could say --- A step above the Olympians themselves! One of those rare creatures that almost shouldn't really exist, except in Greek myths or fairy tails. That's the kind of delicate Earth angel Tara evokes, planted daintily in the top of a tree. BMX boy is so sweet on her. Why wouldn't he be? A moment later, the grayish looking hawk with bold eyes, drops the grenade to Tara. When she sees two soldiers in the right spot passing underneath her, she pulls the pin and drops it right in on them.

BOOM!

Soldiers rush over to consider possible scenarios. Some think it was a mine.

A soldier suggests, "Maybe they dropped one of their own grenades?"

One of the soldiers just happens to look up to the heavens with an anguished sigh, and spots the girl peering down and silhouetted against the emerging star belt.

"Sniper!"

Commandos fire at the treetop. Tara scrambles quickly to the safe side of the trunk.

"Two can play at that game," Lohan says like a psychopath. She grabs two grenades, pulls the pins, and throws them at the foot of the tree. The tree shakes, but still stands.

"Fuck!" yells the frustrated Lohan, as she pulls another grenade off of an adjacent commando. A dozen troops lay fire into the lowest part of the trunk.

"Cease! Knock it off," yells Cruise.

"That's what I'm trying to do," replies Lohan like a wise ass as she defiantly throws her third grenade, breaking the trunk and causing it to fall.

As the behemoth evergreen falls, nimble Tara jumps to the next tree as it scrapes by, loops around a limb, and hangs on like she is on the uneven parallel bars apparatus. The soldiers run to the tip of the fallen tree, but find nothing. Scanning the treetops, they can't find her hiding in the dense canopy.

"She must be under the tree," one of the commandos surmises.

Joaquin says in a frantic panic, "What the hell is going on here? I didn't have to sign on for this. I thought this was going to be an easy hijacking and ransom deal. I could have just kept collecting unemployment and food stamps. I thought there was gonna be some rapin'! Where's the motherfuckin' rapin' motherfucker?!"

A few of the other men stand angry by the fallen tree, directly looking at Cruise for answers and instigated by the raving sadist Joaquin.

Cruise rants, "You guys have been here the whole time. You want to blame me for freak animal and bug attacks? And organized counter strikes?! Lethal strikes! You saw that shit with your own eyes. A fuckin' ram rammed Maxwall off a cliff while he took a wizz!"

The prospective mutineers stop to reflect on the impossibility of it all.

"Then it's settled," Lohan states. "We take no more casualties. We watch out for crazy animals, and watch each others' backs, and we balls-out kill any of those dumbass jocks that don't surrender."

Joaquin kisses major ass, "Sir, I think a lot of us have had enough of this. No disrespect, but we are down to 19 combatants at 100% Sir … About 20 more soldiers are partial. They can lay cover fire. We gut wounded guys behind us Sir. We just left 'em for the wolves, Sir," he breaks into tears.

"Shut up you fuckin' pussy," screams Cruise like an out-of-control wife beater. "Don't look back. Don't think back! We are moving forward and we are going to get every single one of those athletes, dead or alive, animals or not! And hear this; when I get my hands on that world record-holding 400-meter hurdler James, he is mine. I'm going to have his super heart transplanted for my inferior heart, at Gwen's rejection-proof lab, where every organ always takes. That will just be my first major improvement. I watched him kick it in the Olympics last month and his abnormally-massive heart will be mine."

Lohan then spouts, "Good, and fuck the forest."

With that, she throws an incendiary bomb at the foot of the trees and turns up the hill. Smoke and fire quickly climbs the trees toward the hopeless gymnast Tara, who feels forced to jump. Just as she prepares to take a suicidal leap of faith, a bald eagle appears through the black and gray smoke and snatches her wrists. Even she is too heavy, so the eagle struggles and flaps vigorously. Together in a death spiral, they descend toward the ground at about 31 mph. It beats terminal velocity, but still looks to be a rough, semi-controlled landing. The eagle tries and strains with all of its might, but it finds that it must drop Tara into a snow bank. She completely vanishes seven-feet down into the freezing powder but she remains unobserved by the commandos and relatively unharmed.

From their concealed positions in the peak fortress, the athletes watch the destruction caused by the massive fire in sorrow and trepidation, as the flames light up the night.

Cruise nervously fumbles for a cigarette and struggles to ignite it, takes a few addict-like puffs, and looks up the slope. The trees become thick, with straight trunks spaced about a foot to a meter apart. Suddenly, he hears a peculiar sound. Cruise barks, "Silence!" over the comlink.

Everyone freezes, and sure enough, wafting up from the valley as if it were traveling up a massive, Earth-made megaphone, Cruise hears what might as well have been The Who's down in Whoville.

People.

People of all things, are singing far below in the valley. There is a festival, and the sound carries up like in *The Sound of Music*. The commandos pull their comlinks out of their ears and tilt their helmets back. Everyone stops and listens. At first, it sounds jarring, almost chaotic and demonic; but then, it blends together like a massive swarm of blackbirds wriggling through the purple and auburn sky. Even the ubiquitous wolves and coyotes give it a rest, as the entire mountainside suddenly becomes nothing less than a sacred cathedral: A natural, perfectly designed amphitheater of sheer wonder.

The mercenaries look at Cruise as he stares down the mountainside for a long moment. Even in the darkness, everyone can see it as clear as day. No one, including him, wants to fight anymore. They are sick of it. They have already lost, even if they win. They have had their asses handed to them. Cruise can't get over the ridiculousness of the entire escapade.

Instead, like his father, and like his father before him, he takes a few long, hard drags off of the end of his cancer stick and buries it into an ice bank, then bites back hard on his pain and emotions, turns up slope, and says proudly over the comlink, "Let's end this thing now!"

Even though the commandos finally get high enough to see the athletes' cliff fortress, they fail at detecting their well-choreographed movements. Like in all protracted warfare, the well-trained troops still face an incredible challenge. Basically, they can't pin the athletes down. Part of Shrike's plan is to use the athletes' physical stamina as an advantage over the equipment-laden troops. The cat and mouse game goes on for several minutes, and frustrates and exhausts the commandos further.

Concealed under slate slabs in a large patch of scrub, a wolverine gives off a startling snarl, causing the shell-shock troops to jump.

The commandos' throats burn with thirst as some feel dehydration setting in. By order, none of them shoot, but instead they just try to inch closer; to no avail. The athletes feel fine in the high altitude air. They train at Colorado Springs.

Commandos see athletes pop up on rocky outcrops, left and right, so they go after them, but these guys are actually on mountain and BMX bikes, and just like before, by the time the panting troops make it to the location, the bikers are waving at the troops from the next hilltop over, and duck again before the soldiers can level their weapons. The troops finally begin to shoot in frustration, wasting more ammo, and against orders. They never actually hear or see the bikes themselves, just the riders. They can't imagine how the athletes are getting so far away from them so fast. It starts to freak them out. None of the troops are savvy enough to look down on the ground and see tire tracks in the mud and ice. They are too tired, and have been going for too long, and are in a lot of pain, and the light is too dim for their training to kick in.

Joaquin complains, "Cruise, a lot of the guys are having trouble breathing. We gotta turn back. We're too high."

Cruise belches over the comlink, "Medic."

The medic replies instantly, "Sir?"

Cruise says, "How much oxygen do we have?"

The medic says, "Enough to save someone if we need it. Why?"

Cruise ponders, "What if each troop took a hit of oxygen before we make the final assault and capture, -- ah, um ....up this icy cliff?"

The medic replies, "I think that would backfire Sir."

Cruise asks indignantly, "How's that?"

"Well," The medic continues carefully, "I believe there's not enough for every guy to get a hit, and the ones that do will have a head rush of good air and then crash when the thin air hits them again."

Cruise casts a stern eye in the medic's direction, "Is that scientific fact?"

The medic takes a gulp and wonders if Cruise suffers from altitude sickness or something else, "I would defend that statement in court, even without actual evidence."

The medic's academic reply softens Cruise's ire. He strains through his night-vision binoculars to see the two furthest fire teams ahead on the left near an outcrop. He pans over, but can't see the fire teams on the right. The Commandos must now pass into a relatively open glen in a basin. Cruise does not like the strategic topographical disadvantage one bit. At first he commands them to hug the tree-lined edges and stay near the shrubs, but eventually, the already shattered company has no choice but to move out toward the center of a frozen, barren savanna with a huge, steep rock escarpment. It looks like the area was cleared by a gigantic bulldozer but a massive rockslide is more likely.

Coyotes and wolves, as well as a black bear, growl out of sight in the dark woods without venturing into the clearing.

Instead of watching where they are going, the commandos keep turning back, staring into the unknown with their night-vision but only rarely catching eye shine for a moment.

Lohan notices that some of their nerves are getting frazzled, so she says, "Who's the toughest man here? I bet I can make it up into their fortress before *any man* does, except Cruise. He'll beat even the youngest man up in there."

The soldiers don't respond well to the challenge.

Lohan pushes, "C-mon."

Joaquin complains, "C-mon Lohan. A lot of us have ticks on us and stuff."

Lohan turns sharply, "Oh, boo hoo hoo. I have a tick right on my you-know-what; but I'd rather have that irritating thing suck my blood than let you try to help me with it, you letch."

Dumpy comments, "Ah, he's more of a pedophile than a letch."

Lohan smirks as she looks at Joaquin, "I stand corrected."

Shrike sits huddled in a sharp crack in the granite. Though she refuses to show it to the group, especially Sara, the stress crushes her. She feels a tight ball of pain in the center of her chest. She needs just a few moments to completely clear her head and relax, ... but she can't. She tries to settle herself and focus, but she keeps being reminded about how frozen she is every time Jack Frost gnashes on her nose; or into her fingertips and ear lobes. A black bear, maybe close to 293 pounds, strolls up to the crack and wedges itself in around Shrike. Shrike snuggles up under its arms and onto its chest and belly. After a moment, she stops shivering and a broad smile comes across her serene face as she looks as if she will finally get a second to drift off.

Instead, she starts singing in a soft, languid voice,

"I'm ready to leave, I want to be out of here
I'm ready to run away, I don't want to die in here
I'm ready to ride."

She doesn't sing the lyrics exactly right, but her voice sounds impressive within the rocks.

Daniel, who happens to be stretching nearby, hears the siren-like voice draw him to the rocks.

"What a beautiful song," Daniel says, "Did you write that?"

Shrike laughs, "No, that's an old *King Crimson* song from 1981."

She gives the bear a big kiss right on the muzzle, and squeezes her head against its face, then reaches demurely for Daniel. She pulls him down into the bear, and the three of them steal thirty winks in the furry hammock for 17 minutes. A quick but much-needed mini nap. When they awaken, warm and revived, Shrike feels relieved of her chest pain. Daniel magically flips up to his feet, being a limber diver and all, and gently pulls Shrike up out of the fluffy bear crack, like a delicate crystal rose, glazed with ice. They look deeply into each other's eyes.

Shrike says, "I know we don't have time to talk about this right now, but, I'm in love with you, and, I'm in love with James."

Daniel smiles, "That's the way it is. We better get back to the attack plan."

Shrike smiles and gives him a warm, soothing kiss. Shrike then bristles, and snaps back into aggressive action mode. She marches down the steep slope and up to the jagged parapet, past the stunning mountain ridges glistening in the night air.

A number of athletes run up to Shrike to report in, she looks at the assembled American heroes, fit and strong, and coaches "The final preparations have all been made. We are ready for them and will defeat them, without the animals. Once the battle starts, no talking unless it's necessary. Human voices carry well over far distances and we don't know if they have listening devices or surveillance overhead. Just follow the plan and do what you are supposed to. One stick can break, but a hundred sticks bound together can't be broken. We are a team, the Olympic Team. We are the best."
Many of the athletes grumble.

James pushes himself forward in the crowd. He grabs Daniel by the shoulder, who nods in agreement. They don't want to fight Shrike, but they question her true understanding of the commandos' power. True, up to now Shrike has been kicking commando ass, but the fact still remains that they haven't actually confronted any troops yet.

Daniel says, "Shrike, we need the animals to help us now or we are dead."

Shrike counters, "It's not their fight. We can't ask them to die for stupid humans. Don't you think we've already done enough to hurt animals?"

James thinks for a second. He knows she is right.

He adds what's on his mind, "What's flippin' me out is all this new bio-hacking crap that's going on. Making stuff glow that ain't suppose to."

Shrike looks at them both in earnest, "Now I know that these animals, all wildlife really, they all know somehow innately, and understand, that the strange animals (humans) have a science that needs to flow forward with nature, not against it in some ghastly Dr. Moreau shit!"

Daniel says, "And is that what's going on Shrike? They want our organs and their mastermind has some messed-up medical lab?"

Shrike boldly looks at them both with uncompromising seriousness.

Nobody moves.

Complete frozen silence on the mountain.

Shrike thinks for a second, then says, "Fight WITH Nature! We need to fight WITH Nature, not against it. They helped us, and they fought with us. Now we have to fight for us, just like when we get out of this, we need to fight for them, and help them."

While all of this has been going on, Jay has been slowly moving closer and closer towards Sara. It is almost as if he fears her, like a male black widow spider, and yet he's drawn to her anyway.

He leans over to Sara and says, with almost a plea, "Ah, Sara. Honey? If, I mean when we get out of this --- I don't know where you are living or how far away or anything, ya know, but, ah … I would like to call you or email, ah … more than email."

Sara feels floored by the flattered, and Shrike can tell by Sara's body language that she is just tickled pink.

Sara says, in the sweetest voice she has ever mustered, "I'll give you my card ok? It *would* be nice to talk with you again, under slightly less-stressful circumstances."

Jay exhales a sigh of relief, "Nice. Thank you."

Sara laughs coyly with pleased embarrassment, "Oh, you don't have to thank me or be thankful or anything."

She holds her hand out and he gently squeezes it. They are both sooooo excited.

James smiles, "There really is somebody for everybody."

Daniel corrects, referring to Shrike, "Or half a somebody."

Shrike laughs, "Oh don't you worry... you'll both be getting all of me and I'll be getting both of you, in your entirety."

The two men blush but neither understands why.

Not far below on the mountainside, Cruise says over the incessant howling of wolves and screaming jays, "Okay then; there is nothing that says we need to catch these fools quickly. Everyone stay low and move slow to conserve air. With the lord's blessin' we will surround them methodically. Let's all take a moment to say a good Christian prayer here. (There is an 11-second pause). Go from deep cover to deep cover."

The communications commando crackles over the head set, "Cruise, this is Comm."

Cruise answers, "You go Comm."

Comm adds quickly, "At this angle of the mountains, we can get radio signals. Do you want to contact Gwen?"

'Damn', Cruise thinks too himself. "Give her a call."

The Comm Guy patches Gwen through to Cruise's headset.

Gwen says, "Well?"

There is a pause.

Gwen says, "Report soldier!"

Cruise returns, "Haven't acquired target yet."

Gwen snorts, "Why the hell not? Do you not want to have your little warmongering mercenary army funded? Do you? Hmmm?"

Cruise says, "Yes Mam. We haven't found them yet."

Gwen snorts again, "Again I have to ask? Don't make me fuckin' ask again. The All- Mighty knows I don't like askin'. Why the hell not?"

Cruise answers in a straight, controlled monotone, but simmering with frustration, "They weren't at the plane. They didn't head down slope. There are no signs of any of them except for foot trails leading straight up the mountain into the alpine zone."

Gwen blathers accusations, "You mean to tell me you don't even know where they are yet!?!? Why do you think I want to go after athletes, for my health? Well yes, but too, I hate their self-righteous healthiness. Americans are on their way to chronic obesity and then every four years these numb nuts come along and remind people to 'Be healthy' and 'Eat right'. Fuck them. Luckily, so many lazy Americans are so occupied with their Fantasy leagues and video games, with the NBA and NASCAR to obsess over, they are too fat and sedated to give a rat's ass --- even about themselves. So, stay on it! Do you think you matter? There's soon to be eight billion people on this planet. As Drats said in his song *Hate Race* all those years ago:

Primal, stupid, hate-filled goons; never evolve beyond baboons!

You still hold faith in humanity? Only god can save you now, and I've got you covered because I speak to god and am god's messenger. God does his good work through me. Let me just get rid of about five or six billion scum and set the world free!" Livid Gwen hangs up.

Cruise, pulling his comlink down from his bleeding mouth, mumbles, "I hate Gwen."

Joaquin slimes over to Cruise, appearing like a little devil on his shoulder, to declare, "Not as much as I hate that bitch Lohan."

Cruise looks at Joaquin sternly, "That *'bitch'* is number two, and you are number three, and if you think you gonna be taken her out, you better make sure I'm out."

Joaquin taunts, "Ooooww. Something special going on between you two?"

Cruise says, enflamed, "Yeah! She is great, and you suck. That's what's goin' on. You suck on every level compared to her. The distance between second and third might as well be here to Mars. I just needed somebody who would be completely amoral, and heartlessly brutal. That's what I keep you around for. It's hard to find someone with NO conscience."

Joaquin turns and walks away without a word. Somehow, he actually feels bad for a moment, for not having a conscience, and not understanding why.

Cruise notices nothing in regards to Joaquin's mental or emotional state. He's too self-absorbed, as usual. Cruise hand signals a commando over toward his position.

Cruise orders, "Listen up. Take your fire team up through that tight gorge on the far left. Be careful. Move fast, but be careful. If it's clear, blow forward and we will file in behind you. If it's bad, pull out of there fast."

A moment later, the fire team enters a narrow path on the way to the gorge. Steep granite cliffs funnel the troops into a single file. The first one hugs the left wall. The second hugs the right. The third goes through the middle, steps on some loose branches and leaves, and falls eight feet down into a natural gash in the gorge. Unnatural though, are the punji sticks placed sharply at the bottom of this pitfall trap. Four different punji sticks pierce deeply into the commando as he screams. Luckily for him, he averted the other 17 punji sticks around him; stabbing out on all sides. The other members of the fire team look down into the nightmare hole in horror.

"What the fuck!" the fire team leader screams into the comlink.

On the sound of those words, the athletes shoot a volley of machinegun fire into the narrow gorge. The commandos don't know that both of these guns had been taken from their comrades, and now, are used in perfectly contrived ambush against them? Three of the four commandos get hit, with one of them falling head first into the punji crack and going unconscious. The last commando in the fire team, formerly a Navy SEAL, backs away quickly, with three fresh flesh wounds. He calls on the link, "Cruise, commander, they knew we were here. They knew!"

Cruise uses visual hand signals to call Joaquin, Lohan, Dumpy, and Flaca over to him, as well as a few others.

Cruise whispers, "We should have thought of this before. If they have some of our weapons, they probably have our friggin' comlinks and have been listening in this whole time!"
The other commandos bristle at the idea of what easy suckers they have been.

Cruise goes on with conviction, "From now on, play along with me. Even though everything I will be saying over the comlink will be a lie, it is for their ears, not ours!"
The other commandos concur, and spread the word verbally among the bakers-dozen of commandos left.

One of the injured fire team members calls from his pinned-down position in the gorge, "Sir. Sir? I got men down over here. Waiting for instructions."

Above the narrow gorge, a hulking weightlifter heaves a cleverly balanced mass of boulders over the edge. The boulders smash down into the gorge with the sound of thunder. The two commandos in the punji pit are sealed in by tons of rock. The conscious one screams, and can faintly be heard through the rock cluster. The two other injured fire team members are crushed. Alive? Who knows? Only they know, and will ever know: Their tomb sealed. It would take a crane to dislodge these rocks.

The SEAL, now the last surviving fire team member, yells desperately, "Sir? Sir?"

Cruise replies cautiously, "Go ahead team member."

The commando pauses, looking at the boulders, then says dejected, "Forget it."

Cruise replies insistently now, "What!? Go ahead soldier."

The commando says with a gulp, "Returning to main unit... alone."
He turns and runs down slope to collapse next to the medic, who starts on his wounds.

Cruise says with a wink to the others within sight of him, "Good, cause we are heading back down the mountain. Let's go men. Good job. Mission accomplished. Let's get out of here."

Of course, all of the soldiers stay put, lying in their prone, concealed positions.

Back up in the mountaintop fortress, Shrike simply laughs at the ridiculous ruse, and then continues to orient a large group of the athletes, who listen intently to each of her words with frozen anticipation; like at the start of a race. Like a maestro, she flails her hands about descriptively under the light of the rising moon.

Shrike says, "Now that you know the entire plan with every detail rehearsed, let's get back to some fundamentals. The athletes are team players, selfless, and disciplined. The commandos are rogue, rugged individualists and selfish, self-minded hero wannabes. The athletes display the best in human behavior: Kindness, altruism, trustworthiness, and moral correctness; while the commandos demonstrate all of the worst aspects of both human behavior in general, and more significantly and specifically, American superiority by brawn-mentality, and all of its conservative trappings. We all hate bullies. That's what they are."

The athletes drink down the metaphorical Kool-Aid by the gallons. With maws gaping wide, they eat it up. Every articulation seems 100% right! Shrike is on fire! Who wouldn't fall in love with her, even if she was already in love with someone else? Who wouldn't follow her into battle?
A coyote comes rushing up to Shrike with a Claymore mine in its jaws.

Shrike says, "Good girl."

She takes the Claymore and says, "One little detail I forgot to add. Sorry. The animals will be bringing us equipment when they can, safely. She got this off of one of the dead guys out there. Colt, set it up in the lower crotch of the gorge, quickly, before their next assault."

Shrike tosses the mine to Colt, who adeptly snags it and takes Matvey and four others with him as his own little fire team.

Shrike continues, "If any other animals bring you ammo or anything; take it, thank them, and use it."
Many of the athletes smile with cool nods.

Shrike says, "No more waiting. Let's take them out methodically. Everybody do exactly what you are trained to do, and we should come out of this unscathed."

"But Shrike, I can't even see these guys. Their camouflage is incredible," Sara worries.

Shrike commands wisely, "Close your eyes tightly. Do it for 10 seconds."
All of the athletes within earshot comply. When they open their eyes, they can see miraculously better. That athletes puzzle over how Shrike knows all of these things.

Sara says, "I don't know why I'm surprised that worked, knowing what an Eagle Scout you are."
The comlink crackles, and Shrike freezes to listen in again.

Cruise lies, "It was a worthwhile mission men. Let's get back down to the pick up site."
She smiles as she hears the transmission and signals her different group leaders.

Shrike whispers to the athletes as they race past her into their prescribed positions, "Stay incredibly synchronized and organized. Every member helps. Table tennis and rowers supply ammunition to the shooters and throwers."

As the troops get to about 80 meters away, the athletes take their well-planned positions completely out of sight. Peeking from the dense leafless bushes, high on the cliff, Shrike can see the moonlight reflecting off of the soldiers weapons as they slowly move into the broad open alpine meadow area, which the athletes had spent hours clearing industriously. All of the spots with fluffy banks of powder are compacted down, with nothing left to hide behind. Right in front of the commandos stands a sheer, polished ice slope; impossible to scale. When the troops finally see the land beginning to slope sharply to the cliff, they start shitting their pants, ---- Joaquin literally. The cliff is terraced; with the first tier at about four meters above, the second another ten meters up, and the last peaky-top of the mountain another five meters up. The mercenaries can see why Shrike chose this spot specifically because the only real way to get from terrace one to terrace two is through the narrow gorge of rock, carved by an ancient, now extinct waterfall, … and now the tomb of the two punji-punctured soldiers.

Cruise orders, "Send a commando climbing high into one of those trees to gather intelligence."

The soldier agilely scurries up the tree to get to a decent vantage point. Slipping on his night vision, he begins to scan about. He happens to look over at the tree next to him and sees a gymnast looking back at him with the confiscated night-vision goggles she dons, scavenged by the critters. He reaches for his comlink when suddenly; a squirrel attacks his face viciously, knocking him right out of the tree. The soldier hangs for a second from his safety rope, and yells for help, but now a couple of tree squirrel gnaw through the rope with their molars, while owls dart by his head. The soldier falls hard to his death before he can report the tiny gymnast spy.

Cruise scans the terrain with his binoculars and then swallows hard. He's got no saliva. Before Cruise can devise the proper approach, a runner bursts from the bushes near the commandos, as a diversion. No one can get a clear shot off in the darkness. They watch him with rifles raised, but they just watch. A soldier named Cumarek throws down his rifle and pack, determined to catch the athlete, and takes off after him. The athlete runs around the corner of a boulder. Little does Cumarek know (a track athlete himself), but he pursues a steeplechase runner, who hurdles over a skylight to a mammoth cave. Cumarek hurdles the long horizontal rock while in tight pursuit over the deceiving shadows of the night, only to plummet 761 feet to the cave floor. This is almost an exact replay of the move the female long jumper used on those two commandos earlier, but the troops don't have the benefit of that knowledge, so the same plan works like a charm again.

Cruise realizes that he can trap the athletes near the peak, so he sends troops to circumnavigate and cut off all exits down the mountain; thinning his frontal attack force even more. Cruise's crusaders take one more step, and then another, until finally they hit the subtle marker left behind by Shrike on a dead stump, earlier this afternoon. The friendly screech-owl flies to Shrike to confirm the intelligence, for this *is* an important moment.

"Now!" Shrike signals from hidden silence.

Cruise flinches his head up like a spastic nuthatch. First, the commandos hear, then see, javelins and hammers randomly crashing through the branches like an ancient nocturnal artillery barrage. Four tiny gymnasts scissor-hold large branches with their lobster-claw legs while they use their pale, swan-neck arms to silently telegraph coordinates back to ground-athletes from the highest treetops; signaling the throwers as to where to adjust their aim. Still, practically all of these volleys fall to no harm because the tiny number of commandos are pretty thinned out by now.

Dumpy blurts with a chuckle, "Javelins and discuses."

Cruise responds briskly, "I can see."

Dumpy chuckles, "They are trying to hit us with javelins and discuses. Ha, ... and hammers," over the comlink.

Cruise commands, "Keep it down. No more mistakes from now on."

Cruise burns with anger, not at the loss of the troops themselves, because as he has put it to Lohan more than once, he could *"really give a shit about them"* and sees himself apart from, superior to, and therefore, better than the scum he commands. NO. What pisses off Cruise is that his intensely aggressive record, up until this mission, has been pretty damn spotless. He had never lost a battle, a soldier, or anything else. He always has been, and probably would have always been, a winner, until as far as he is concerned, insecure generals and other commanders out to get him, fearing not only usurpation but also fearing Cruise's combination of great intellect and his absence of human empathy, tried to ruin him. Cruise feels that he should not have been knocked from the ranks. Some people's luck just runs out sometimes. Cruise is determined to finish the quest without another commando casualty, but again he displays how much that he doesn't really understand what he does and doesn't have power over.

Cruise commands in a whisper with his hand carefully muting the comlink, "On 'five' we move. Stay low ---- and lighting fast."

Shrike cues the throwers to cock their arms. She looks for a signal from a moonlit kayaker poised on a jutting rocky peak.

Cruise silently counts down on his fingers, and the troops start scrambling up the steep terrain quickly. The gymnasts, looking almost straight down from their precarious perches, stretch their dainty arms into arrows, pointing steeply down at the best targets. The kayaker waves his paddle, which reflects and shines a moonbeam over to Shrike and the throwers. They fire instantly.

Finally, one discus grazes a soldier's arm, for a bad laceration, but the medic is able to tape it up quickly, while the rest of the hungry, stung commandos fall behind some scattered low trees and rocks.

Cruise looks back to see that he is the only one still charging up the slope, so he ducks into a little scrape of a cave and says, "What happened to the charge? I thought no one was afraid of athletic gear? You were just laughing at them a second ago."

No one replies and everyone stays hunkered down for the moment. Many of them have moonscape faces from all of the insect bites and stings, ... and everything else they have suffered.

A team handball player pulls the pin on a confiscated grenade and throws it so far that it blows up in the air behind the furthest group of troops, knocking one of them out of combat. Cruise and the other 11 commandos take deep cover, concentrating in the few pockets of refuge among the area of sparse boulders.

Once the ringing in their ears settles, Cruise barks, "What the fuck was that?"

A commando near the rear assesses the damage, "Grenade sir."

Cruise puzzles, "One of ours?"

Lohan says, "No way to know sir. One of our guys could have popped a grenade, or they could have hit a booby trap."

Joaquin pipes in, "Sir, they have a mortar. We are getting shelled by mortars."

Cruise says, "Did you see a mortar?"

Joaquin replies, "No, but no one can throw a grenade that far."

Cruise thinks for a second, then says, forgetting that Shrike listens in silently holding her breath high above, "Nobody move a muscle. Everyone take a grenade inventory right now."

There is a quiet pause as they sit covered in nature's crannies and crooks.

"Well?" Cruise presses.

Lohan reports, "It looks like everyone who had one still has their grenades Sir."

Cruise stops and thinks again. He looks up into the trees and wonders what's going on.

Joaquin asks nervously, "Sir? Sir? Should we be doing something or what? These, these guys gutt bombs? Whad are we gettin into here?"

Cruise says, "Shut up!" and goes back to his deep consternation.

A moment later, Lohan breaks the silence, "Sir, we are missing another commando."

She has just realized that Cumarek, the soldier who fell 761 feet, is gone!

Cruise does not reply, but instead sits in dejection. He knows that even if everything goes right from here on in, this is still by far the worst mission he has ever lead, and he seriously begins to consider whether this should be his last.

Lohan says, "Sir?"

Cruise does not respond.

Lohan plays with the frequency on her comlink, and then says, "Cumarek, this is Lohan. Cumarek, can you read me?"

The comlink still crackles, undamaged at the bottom of the cave; but Cumarek lies motionless, with every bone and organ shattered and splattered inside his bruised skin. Lohan lowers her head in silence.

Joaquin crawls over to Cruise on his belly, then puts his hand over his comlink, creating a little feedback on the system.

He whispers, "Sir, what are we gonna do? This was supposed to be a simple kidnapping. We gotta get the hell out of here. We are dropping like flies and we don't know how, or why, or who by. I'm getting the fuck out of here."

Thought completely dark now, several of the athletes in the fortress can make out where the commandos have dropped down onto their bellies and crawl like crayfish. Brilliantly hidden and completely unseen by the commandos, a rifle shot from the far northeast edge of the cliff rings out in the cold, crisp air. The Olympic gold-medalist markswoman's bullet hits a soldier in the face. An arrow comes whistling in from the southeast first tier, about 90 degrees from were the rifle shot had come from, and ends up stuck through a soldier's neck. The commandos may only barely be able to see each other, but they can certainly hear what is happening to their miscreant compadres.

Another arrow whistles in and hits a soldier through the middle of his neck. Another precision sharp shooter sniper shot hits a crouched soldier in the balls. The night air is cracked yet again when one of the few female commandos left has her knee shot out intentionally. She goes down with horrible screaming and wailing, like Melissa Etheridge on her second encore, for all of the soldiers to hear over and over again; completely psyching them out.

Cruise yells, "Where are these shots coming from? Find them and pin them down."

Joaquin whines, "They have us pinned down."

Lohan orders two scouts, Dumpy and Flaca, to move forward quickly and to find the snipers. Dumpy stops so Flaca turns back to look at her.

Dumpy says, "My targeting is compromised. I will have to lay down cover fire and you will have to take'em out precisely."

Flaca says, "Why?"

Dumpy looks up and tilts her helmet back, revealing her wound. "That's my aiming eye."

Dumpy's eyes are swollen from 97 insect stings, with her right eye clenched closed like a clam.

Flaca says, having no choice but to accept the situation, "Okay, let's move."

They run low and quick through the alpine terrain, staying near any little bit of cover.

The Olympic shooting medalist, now a sniper, hits Flaca, and Dumpy sees the smoke from the gun and returns fire, spraying shots over a concentrated area.

Dumpy says over the comlink, "The sniper is on the far north end of the cliff. Flaca is down."

Cruise states, "And the arrows are coming from the far right. Save your ammo. Don't shoot until you can see something."

Dumpy hunkers down; her eyes in horrible shape, and clutches her weapon. She toys with the idea of taking a peek or trying to look around, but then crumbles down into the fetal position next to Flaca to cover up to stay warm; basically surrendering at this point.

"Flaca? Flaca?" Dumpy begs.

For the first time ever, Flaca doesn't respond to Dumpy.

After sweating profusely since first dropping down into Yellowstone, and with nothing to drink for hours, the commandos are parched. They lick their lips. They run their tongues over the front of their teeth. They can't think straight.

One of the commandos asks, "Anybody got any water?"

Cruise broadcasts over the comlink, "Nobody has any water. If anybody does, drink it. Put a little snow in your mouth and let it melt."

Lohan chimes, "Suck on a stone, or a cough drop if you've got one."

Dumpy slowly reaches over Flaca's body for her canteen, shakes it, then unscrews the cap and takes the final swig.

With her teeth chattering, she says to her unresponsive partner, "You would'a wanted me to have it."

As the enemy approaches, each layer of Shrike's ingenuous strategy unfolds, with distance throwers hurling what's left of their barrage. The last of the javelins, hammers, and sharpened discuses come whistling in as the commandos follow Cruise on the charge up the steep, slippery, sharp slope. A javelin comes whistling in like a missile, it hits some rocky outcrops, then bounces down the slope as it splinters and shatters into long shards. A hammer smashes into an adjacent rocky outcrop like a cannonball, sending rock-fragment shrapnel exploding about. Team handball and water polo players hurl rocks with tremendous accuracy, and weight lifters launch boulders down the cliff to instigate mini avalanches. When the javelins, hammers, and discuses run out, they switch over to sticks and stones. These all serve a purpose: Psychologically, no one likes being bombarded; and, it gives the troops something to worry about while the real assassins, the archer and the shooter, take their macabre toll. As the troops crawl closer to the base of the cliff, some scurry in quick jaunts and jags forward while others fire at where they believe the barrage emanates from. Much to their chagrin, spears and boulders still pelt down on them, relentlessly. Joaquin looks about, frazzled and nervous.

Cruise says, "What are you worried about? Remember, sticks and stones will never hurt me."

Lohan says, "Ah, I think it says 'sticks and stones shall break my bones'."

Cruise says, "Oh yeah. Well, I ain't afraid of no sticks and stones. Let's go."
On that less-than-profound order, the commandos charge up the slope to the edge of the first tier.

Sara (who has been listening in on the commandos' comlink) psychoanalyzes Cruise, but like with the Shrike/animals situation, she finds the wall of cognitive dissonance deafening; mainly because she can't figure what motivates individuals to be *as bad* as Cruise.

Shrike reads Sara's face, then states as if replying, "If this were a well-written novel or movie, they would give us a bunch of background on Cruise to round out his character and make him more three-dimensional. This is reality. In real battle you'd be extremely fortunate to barely even get a two-dimensional look at the freak, so how are we to sympathize with his upbringing or understand what this means to society in the bigger picture? Just like a dragonfly or a minnow, all we know is 'bastards want to catch us.' That's all anyone in battle ever understands about their faceless and one-dimensional enemy. They have to remain anonymous or nobody could go about antiseptically killing people they actually know and like."

Sara counters, "You of all people telling me to give up? From a psychological perspective, I see it's worth a try."

Shrike smirks sharply, "Focus on your role in the battle. Soldiers shouldn't think too much."

Sara worries, "But if we're captured. . ."

Shrike affirms, "We won't get captured!"

Sara feels convinced by Shrike's resolve, but Shrike has her own doubts and does feel that capture is likely. Of course, just like a good coach, she can't let the team know that.

Over 123 miles away, the lone track cyclist finally encounters someone: An ignorant rancher taking a leak by the side of his barn. He was just about ready to nod off, after drinking himself to sleep with cheap, generic booze, but instead had decided to take a look at the stars. He wonders about the distant gunfire and explosions high on the mountain peak, and the military aircraft activity earlier in the day.

When she arrives behind him on the racer, she stops to let him shake it off and zip up. When he turns to lay eyes on her, he feels as if an angel from heaven has been sent down upon him. Without so much as a word, he paws her like an animal.

Instead of loosing her cool, she tells him with a funny drawling accent, "I wants to get drunk with you too. Get on down to your cellar to retrieve some bottles so you can show me what you got and I have a couple of different choices of liquor in which we can imbibe."

She cleverly locks him below, gets to his kitchen phone, and alerts 911. Finally, for the first time, the authorities know that the plane was hijacked, that it crashed in Yellowstone, and that insanely psychopathic killing machines are on their way up after America's heroes. The 911 operator does not believe her, and thinks it's a prank, so she grills the petite, wiry cycle champion, who fumbles nervously as she hears the farmer stumbling back up the stairs. He begins to pound on the door and that rattles the track cyclist even more.

He slurs, "Hey youngin'. Yah don't know how to close a door proper? Yah let it a'latch. Come on over and open it up little lady."

The cyclist implores to the 911 operator quietly, "Look me up by name. I'm telling you, I've traveled 100 miles to get to a phone, my life is in danger, and I don't know when or if I'll get a chance at another phone. If you do nothing, you will be responsible for the death of our Olympic team. Is that what you want?"

The 911 operator answers curtly, "Oh, you almost had me there, but, that's laying it on a little thick don't you think honey?"

The cyclist yells, "You idiot!"

The farmer, from behind the door squeals, "Little pig, little pig, I'll blow your house down. Aahh, my house down."

Suddenly, a shotgun blast is heard, and pieces of the old-wooden cellar door fly into the kitchen and hall.

The cyclist says sharply, "Gotta go," and leaves the landline phone hanging.

The operator clearly heard the shotgun blast, so she promptly starts real emergency procedures on her end. As the cyclist sprints down the hall, she notices two sets of car keys on the hooks. She grabs them and throws the keys for the pick up truck and the station wagon out into the tall grass. As she goes to get on her bike, she sees a Harley. She didn't notice any Harley key, so just to be safe, she runs over to the '49 pan head and pulls two fuel lines out of it, spilling gas on the ground. Then she steps back and 'Kung Fu's' the bike over onto its side. Then ... she gets on her bike and hauls-ass out of sight before the rancher knows she left. One would think, 'wouldn't she have been better off taking the truck or wagon?' In her mind, 'no.' She's not a thief, she's an Olympian; and secondly, she had no idea if they would run or how much gas they have, whereas she knows she can go practically forever on her twenty-nine thousand dollar, silent bicycle.

He stumbles around the house with the shotgun, calling for her, then slumps onto a beaten recliner, and goes unconscious, never even looking out at his flopped Harley or knowing that his car keys are lost in four feet of grass. In the morning, he will think the whole encounter was a dream.

Under the thick gray cloud layer, the cyclist blasts ahead until she comes to a broad, open crossroads, 21 miles from the drunken farmer's place. This is the only open place nearby with enough room for a rescue helicopter pick up. She ditches her bike in the bushes, and hides in vigilant expectation while she copes with the bone-chilling night.

Meanwhile, still under bombardment, the communications guy calls Cruise over.

"It's Gwen again," he reports, as he hands the phone to Cruise.

Cruise doesn't want to, but he knows he has to report to Gwen.

"You lost more men?" Gwen grinds her teeth in surprise. "How many?"

"29," he replies with an embarrassing gulp.

Gwen jumps down his throat, "29! You lost 29 commandos! The top trained commandos, and you lost 29; a freakin' platoon!?!"

"No," Cruise stammers, "We have 29 troops left."

Gwen hits the roof, lambasting him, "YOU said a platoon would be enough, and I insisted on a company, and now I think I should have spent my loot on a frickin' battalion! 99 troops. You lost 99 troops!" She spits, "I'm not unrealistic, I just expect immediate results. When I say something, do it, and get it done, period!"

Cruise says, "You don't understand what's been happening here, and why we've incurred losses. You weren't on the ground."

Gwen returns, "Losses in the first place. That's what you really mean to say. You had this all planned out. You had all the top friggin' mercenary rejects money could buy. You have the best Russian and American made weaponry; ... exactly what you wanted. I don't even understand how the plane went down in the first place! Oh God Bless me! God Bless America!"

Cruise butts in, "Gwen, let's stay focused here, . . ."

Gwen rails, "Fuck You! *Let's stay focused!* How much have you lost already on this little excursion? How much have you gained, huh?! You haven't done anything you were suppose to yet."

Cruise, losing the little veneer of cool he fronted, slides into a tone of bitchiness, "Gwen, we are about to now, we are poised to ... the animals, the bugs, ..."

Gwen explodes, "Oh, nature? Nature did you in? My big, strong, hard, tough boys and girls. Oh, you are so hard and deserving of the athletes' organs. Pffft! You can't handle being out in nature? Don't people go out and hike and camp in that park for fun?"

Cruise wants to interrupt, but he lacks explanation.

Gwen exhausts, "What about Parris Island and all that shit. I thought you were fearless of snakes and tigers and bears?" Cruise has no response. There is a rare moment of silence.

Runners continue to dart about out of range on the far wings, causing the commandos to waste more ammo, while the bombardiers jostle to more secure throwing positions and continue the battery.

Gwen can hear the gunfire in the background, "Well at least you've made contact. Don't damage any of my spoils!" She hangs up.

Sara reminds the throwers, "Remember what Shrike said, 'No Grunting'. We don't want them to pinpoint where we launch from."

A young doe, stomps the ground near a fire team member.

"What's that?" Joaquin cries in panic.

The men jump up and say, "It's a deer!"

Four turn and fire at the deer, which bounds off and behind some rocks. The men drop back down to the hard rocks, prone.

"I think I got it," one of them brags.

Another argues, "I think we all missed."

The last fire team makes a panicked dash for the safety of the overhanging cliff.

Finally within range of the anxious and super-testosterone-filled shot putter, he starts lobbing shot puts onto them with much relish. A soldier looks up, sees the shot put dropping straight for his head, and steps to the side cleverly to watch the shot put smash some brittle rocks. He accidentally steps on a broad piece of ice and slides 30 meters down slope. Bruised and injured with at least one broken bone, he stands to shake it off. The rest of the company looks down at him.

"I'm okay," he waves with assurance in the darkness.

An arrow hits him in the forehead of his helmet and shatters into a billion fragments. The impact knocks him backwards and upside down onto the ice with a concussion.

Owls hoot, chirp, and bark at an ever-increasing decibel level. Demoralized, the rest of the company turn back to the battle.

Flaca comes to and reaches into her backpack and pulls out a bottle. She twists off the cap and downs three or four pills, then looks for her last gulp of water.

"What the hell are those?" Dumpy puzzles; always wanting some of what everyone else has.

Flaca belches back, "Roids! But, I, I need some water."

Dumpy stutters as she crams snow into Flaca's mouth, "What? Say what?"

Flaca groans louder, "Roids man, ROIDS!! I always said, 'If I'm ever going back into battle again, I'm going to be on steroids the whole way."

"I'll try some," Dumpy begs.

"No way! I'm not wasting them on you. You'd probably blow through half a dozen before you felt anything anyway," Flaca states with defiant conviction (plus, the fact that she holds a finite supply).

Joaquin slimes over like an eel in the muck, "Give me two of those."
He snatches them from Flaca, and downs them together without any water.

"Keep movin'!" Joaquin commands as he struts up the challenging, pathless terrain to press himself against the cliff ledge with what's left of the company.
With their backs against the cliff, the commandos search for handholds and spots to boost each other up.

The rowing crew, basketball, volleyball, water polo and swimmers, soccer, racquet sports, field hockey and team handball players line up with their backs against the sloping ground, right above the commandos. On a silent arm signal hardly visible from high in the dark trees, the teammates heave. 70 athletes in all push in unison with their powerful quads. 140 legs move like a single unit. Before the thousands of pounds of carefully piled boulders can come tumbling down onto the

commandos, the teams spin up to their feet and retreat up through the narrow gorge to the second tier of the cliff.
A long moment of dead silence ensues once the rocks settle.

The surviving troops begin to stir. They remove the dust and rubble from themselves. No athletes remain on the first tier now. Instead, they wait patiently at their next assignments; with every athlete unselfishly doing their job. Once the soldiers recover from the completely contrived landslide, they shake themselves off and get their bearings.

Cruise orders a scout, "See what's going on up there."
The scout peaks his head up over the ledge to the next tier, and the sharp-shooter gold medalist beans him right in the head, from the second tier. The scout falls backward onto the hard ice, dead.

Cruise yells with vengeful anger, "Grenades."
The men grab for their grenades and pull the pins.

Shrike stands and screams, "TAKE COVER!!"

Cruise pauses for a second with a puzzled expression, and then says, "Now!"

11 troops lob grenades onto the first and second tiers, devastating some of the athletes who moan from the concussive shock. Colt can't stand seeing the injured athletes writhing in pain and in an unplanned fit of rage flies down the gorge to the first tier. He then slides over the lip of the first tier and down to the ground-level slope, and behind some rocks. The commandos see him, but it's too late. He sprays bullets all over the troops, who duck for cover. He then fires the grenade from the launcher, right at the center of the line of troops amongst the landslide rubble. Once the shrapnel blows past his head, he fires at more of the troops closest to him, keeping low against the frigid granite. Lohan launches her last grenade from the far end of the cliff and blows Colt away. The athletes suffer their first human fatality! Shrike had said she'd accept no causalities, but here, now, it's gone too far. No one can control every aspect of war.

Two more soldiers lay down withering cover fire as the rest of the troops pull themselves up to the first tier and run for the gorge. A fire team goes running into the opening at the end of the icy, rocky gorge, only to be hit by soccer balls and hand balls; right in the face, repeatedly. The basketball players launch their balls high in the air on huge arcs, so they come straight down heavily on the tops of the soldiers' helmets, bringing rocks down with them as well, and breaking off gigantic icicles.

The lead fire team point soldier crawls up between a narrow gap and into a slice of rock near the mouth to the gorge. He lies prone, and scans for targets with his night scope.

High above, a skinny 'Olive Oyl' of a rhythmic gymnast, wedged in a tight cleft in a massive pine, screams with all of her 97 pounds "NOW!"

The soldier in the slice of rock feels the projectiles raining in on him as everything from field hockey balls, rocks, and chunks of ice are hurled against his helmet and gun. It's so constant that he has to slide backward and behind the sliver of rock. The commando collects himself, takes a gulp of air, and then rolls out to the right side of the rock this time, to start slithering up to a firing position. Before he even gets to a decent spot, the barrage ensues. Hit over and over again in rapid-fire succession, the soldier falls into a backward summersault and rolls behind the rock spire again; bloodied, bruised, and dazed. He adjusts his helmet and then readjusts it. He grabs his collar and pulls it far from his neck, thrusts his tongue out, and then adjusts his ammo and uniform. He looks down at his scope. It's ruined. He tries to bend it back with his smashed hand, but it's no good. With his back against the monolithic wall he searches around for his comlink in frustration. His hands shaking, he feels around until he finally finds the wire.

He pulls it up to his ear and calls, "Commander. Commander. Come in."
Nothing.
He wiggles his tongue and opens his lips to let a broken piece of tooth fall out.

He repeats, fumbling, "May cay, May day! Who can hear me?"

He traces the wire with his hand and sees that it's mangled. He looks back down the gorge to see the rest of his fire team slowly, methodically, creeping forward, toward him. He pulls a grenade off of his chest, waves his team to come forward, and pulls the pin. From an awkward angle, he twists his shoulders against the stone pillar and then throws the grenade spastically.

Observing from on high, the Olive Oyl-esque girl cries, "Grenade! Short."

The athletes take cover in unison, like the well-oiled machine they are.

Another wasted grenade.

When the rest of the first fire team reaches their tenderized point man, they realize their predicament and call up a second team.

The second fire team comes blasting in and also ends up mired in a pile of rubble and balls at the gorge exit. Stalemate! Everyone hunkers down. The commandos have no way to take any shots due to the barrages, and the athletes have no way of making an offensive move. They simply have to hope that the commandos will give up.

High on the tip of the mountain peak, Jay leans into Sara with alarm, "That's Shrike's strategy? Hope they give up?"

Sara realizes, "Isn't that funny, because Shrike for one, and pretty much all of the athletes, and even me, also, would never give up."

But Shrike still has other aces up her sleeves. A group of athletes release the canoe, filled with boulders, and with a straight ramming trunk tied forward like a Cyclops spear.

"Ramming speed!" One of the hulky athletes declares.

The little canoe flies straight down the icy slope, reaching 43 mph when it enters the gorge. The ten commandos duck the spear, diving and squeezing to the walls, but four of them get hit and injured, and one is pinned under the boulder-laden vessel.

Sara quips, "Gee, who woulda thunk a little canoe like that could carry 3000 pounds of boulders?"

Daniel and James look at Sara.

James says, "Shrike woulda."

Sara says, feigning apology, "Oh, okay, alright; … She's good, but none of this proves she isn't mental."

The men laugh, then everyone turns their focus back to their cue in the battle.

As each sport of athletes runs out of balls, they seamlessly switch to rocks, with the occasional spear; and Matvey, the pentathlon medalist, makes every pistol shot count by repeatedly firing his laser into the soldiers' riflescopes; temporarily blinding them.

Two of the most injured commandos come limping quickly back down and out of the gorge, while the others stay to fight or remain pinned.

Cruise says, "I told you guys not to hang around in there. It's a death trap. You gotta push straight through."

One of the injured commandos says, "Sir, we got eight men piled and stuck at the end of the gorge."

Joaquin whimpers in amazement, "They got boats, Sir. They got boats!"

Cruise yells, "Grenades!"

He fires a grenade down the gorge, over the heads of his prone troops, and into the athletes hidden behind the rocks and tree stumps. The other troops fire off their last three grenades.

Three of the rugby players get blown apart, but the volleyball players react in time.

The last several troops left surge forward, with some of those in the front taking shrapnel spray from their own grenades. For the first time, Shrike sees how evident their drive is. This isn't about anything else anymore: Not about anything else,

…but winning! Flaca, Dumpy, Joaquin, Lohan, and Cruise, and just a few other soldiers, intend to find a way to capture over 100 athletes.

Shrike yells, "Draw some fire!" to what is left of the team handball guys hunched behind a long log.

Two of them jump up and start moving around erratically, then drop behind the log again. A table tennis player joins in, popping up and down like a jack-in-the-box. With no other visible targets, the commandos keep wasting shots on them, as the rest of the commandos charge up through the narrow ravine.

Shrike mentally signals a ground squirrel, which instantly appears from the safety of its deep subterranean tunnel network. It grabs the string for the Claymore mine and pulls it tightly down its hole. Within another second, --- BAAAAMMMM!!!!

The mine blows up right in the faces of one the fire teams. Now only three of those five soldiers remain fully operational.

Cruise looks around. He can't believe the devastating casualties he is taking. Like a long, horrible nightmare; the more he fights, the worse it gets!

Cruise drops his head like a drooping willow, then makes rare eye contact with Lohan and admits, "Right when I think we're on the verge, I'm on the verge…"
Lohan looks at him with despair.

Rabbits, rodents, and other small critters and birds appear again out of nowhere, and move about in dazzlingly-distracting chaos. The troops struggle to focus on the humans with all of the other movement about in the dark.

Shrike yells, "Keep up the mortar barrage!"
Field hockey players feed stone after stone to the seven-foot ebony giants, who continue to launch what would be equivalent to full-court bombs. The height, arc, and accuracy of this bombardment astonishes the commandos and athletes alike, but it's still not effective enough.

Shrike says, "Shooter, archer: Single out some good shots."

The shooter immediately sees a commando looking up to avoid a falling stone and an icicle the size of a luge sled, and rifles a bullet into his chin; breaking his jaw in half and shattering it and his teeth in several places. The commando kneels up onto his knees in a daze. Another commando grabs him by the back of his flak vest and pulls him with a hard thud and a moan of sheer agony. A large stone from the high arching basketball barrage hits the helping commando in the middle of the back and bounces off. It hurts, like a heavy-fisted punch, but the commando is only bruised. Another of the archer's arrows whistles right by his neck and shoulder, but misses.

The archer yells back to Shrike, "I'm out."

Shrike has the screech-owl give a vocal signal to the archer, who surveys, then retreats under distractive cover. A stray bullet from one of the commandos does graze the lethal archer's right shoulder, chipping the collarbone, but she continues on without missing a beat and vanishes into a large crack.

First a bear roars, then a large wolf pack appears below the commandos.

One commando screams, "Wolves!"

Several of the commandos turn to shoot, but the animals split off in an instant, and the commandos only get more frustrated.

Resembling The Battle of Iwo Jima in some respects, the commandos struggle upward and forward, slowly. The fighting now becomes even closer, as the commandos see they can pin the athletes against the top. Most of the commandos have discarded their rifles by now because they have run out of ammo. Some switch to their .45s.

Suddenly the gunfire quickly trails off, diminishing to a few stray shots, and then, silence.

Cruise belches over the comlink, "What happened? Why isn't anyone firing? Fire. Fire!"

Several commandos step on each other's transmissions,

"Out of Ammo"

"Out"

"No Ammo"!!

Cruise says, "Shittt!!"

Cruise pulls up his Colt .45. He looks at the clip. He only has three bullets left.

Cruise says, "Switch to pistols."

There is a long silence.

Cruise rephrases, "Does anyone have any ammo left of any kind?"

Only one commando responds, "I have one bullet left in my clip, and one chambered, so that's ahh, two."

Cruise says to himself, "I don't care."

As Cruise is just about to order another all-out assault, do or die, he hears something crackle over the comlink.

It's Shrike, who, at the most appropriate of times, alerts Cruise of his folly by seducing, in the most sincere and credible voice imaginable, "Come into our kill box Cruise. Don't worry. As you can see from recent experience, we aren't ready for you at all. You have the upper hand, even if you are out of ammo. Come on in. Come play."

The commandos freeze in a petrified silence. For the first time, they hear the voice of the enemy. For the first time, they realize just how suckered-in they have been. Commando after commando look around at each other. No one says a word as their eyes widen. No one knows what to do, but they know one thing: Following Cruise and Lohan up that mountain now is sure suicide.

Cruise feels like he wants to cry. Everything he has done up to this point has been wrong, and stupid, and futile. He has lost a hundred women and men. He doesn't even have one commando who isn't seriously hurt at this point. His ammo and weapons are practically gone, and his provisions *are* gone.

Cruise surveys his thirsty troops as best he can in the darkness. Everyone has blood coming out of them from one place or another. None remain unscathed.

Shrike continues, her calmness chilling, "You can give up to us if you wish. We just want to get off the mountain, just like you do. Shame to waste everybody."

Like a slimy slug, Joaquin slithers over to Cruise on his belly.

He whispers, "Sir? Time to live to fight another day. All of the troops want to retreat down slope, at least, at least to get a rest, and make a plan, and get provisions dropped. You know Sir? No face lost in a tactical retreat."

Cruise looks at Lohan first. Her eyes narrow as she shakes her head with a derisive 'no'.

Cruise then looks over at a number of the beaten soldiers. A pack of coyotes howl loudly nearby. The troops look dead. They have no fight left in them. They want to quit. They look weak.

Joaquin tries to convince again, "She used your name. She called you by name. Sir, she knows what a kill box is. How the hell does that bitch know that?"

Lohan snaps like a wounded fox, "I'm *a bitch* who knows that."

Joaquin looks over at Lohan sharply, and takes a deep gulp.

Cruise, with full, repulsive disgust, says to Joaquin, "Are you out of your mind? Retreat?"

Cruise pulls the comlink up to his mouth with a defiant, "Fuck you!"

Shrike laughs and states confidently, "Expected as little from you. You'll never surprise us, that's for sure, with that predictable behavior."

The commandos look at Cruise for his devastating comeback. Instead, his face goes beet red. He looks like a friggin' fool.

Making it ten times worse; Joaquin whimpers with a whisper, "Sir, we gotta back down the mountain. We ain't gut nothin. We can call Gwen for another air drop."

Cruise gristles, "Call Gwen again? She'd have our heads, and maybe even literally. How the hell did we run out of ammo? Where the hell is all the back up ammo? I thought we had guys specifically dedicated to carrying extra ammo supplies!!!"

Frustrated, Lohan barks, "We don't need no ammo. We are commandos. Let's draw bayonets and mop up this job like real soldiers."

Joaquin cowers at the idea. Cruise thinks it's a poor strategy, but feels 'out-manned' by Lohan ---- his ego tugging at his balls.

Cruise pushes the comlink to his lips, not caring anymore that the athletes hear everything, and says, "Listen up. Fix bayonets. We are going to go up there and take every last one of them, dead or alive!"

Lohan grunts, "Finally!"

She whips her bayonet out and takes off up the hill and through the narrow gauntlet gorge: Scrambling over boulders like Spiderman, or Spiderwoman if there is one.

Cruise looks at Joaquin and threatens forcefully, "Let's go."

Joaquin hesitates. He knows he is going to get killed, but if he doesn't budge in the next second, he knows Cruise won't hesitate to take him out now. Joaquin swallows hard, then reaches back, shaking, and pulls out his bayonet. An instant impulse tells him to quickly stab Cruise in the neck and run away down the mountainside, to live a free coward.
Joaquin stares forward, frozen, like he's having a panic attack.

Cruise pulls out his deadly commando knife (more like a bayonet, with a blood groove and everything) and displays it nicely to Joaquin with another threat, "I never give an order twice. With honor, or with cowardice? You can fight by the knife later ... or you can die by the knife now."

Joaquin struggles to get on his feet with a whimper, then turns and heads up slope. Cruise falls into step right behind him, as if to use Joaquin as a human shield.

As they prepare to enter the gorge for the final time, the exhausted troops suffer with sticky, dry mouths, their throats burning, yearning for saliva. Most of them are in severe pain and have broken bones. They are at a huge physical disadvantage now, as well as the emotional, mental, and moral inferiority that hampers them. It finally comes down to hand-to-hand combat, as Shrike had prepared the athletes for as an absolute last resort before surrender.

First the commandos strip off practically all of the heavy gear they have left, with the exception of the encumbering heavy flak jackets, their helmets, and their knives. A few mount bayonets onto the end of their empty rifles. Then, in a blitz assault, they run full speed up through the gorge with Lohan in the lead. They quickly fracture into cover before the athletes can manage any critical blows. The commandos start up past a narrow stand of trees. When they reach a certain point the fencer uses her sword to cut the volleyball net. This allows the bent back tree branch to come flying across horizontally, at knee level. Four out of the five soldiers hit go down hard. Two struggle to their feet, while the other two can't. The rest of the commandos continue on.

At the narrowest part of the gorge, large rocks plummet 48 feet down onto the commandos. Shrike had the weightlifters balance dozens of large rocks on the most precarious of ledges, teetering. Now, emerging from their safe stone tunnels, cute pikas push the stones over with their hind legs from endearing little handstands. Each rock only needs a pika push, and then it's bombs away. For tiny little guys, the pikas pack a powerful punch! The troops are forced to look up while they try to scramble over jutting boulders. One gets hit in the shoulder; another has his hand smashed.

At the mouth of the gorge, a spinning Herculean appears and launches. The shot putter nails a soldier in the face from 53 feet away with a 16-pound shot put he had held in reserve. The effect is similar to a cannon ball hitting an overripe pumpkin. The commandos look at each other incredulously, as they watch their dead comrade fall into a limp mass. After a few aimless shots at the quickly vanishing shot putter, some commandos drop their empty side arms and go for their butcher knifes.

Every conceivable Olympic weapon is used, from field hockey sticks to foils, epee, and sabers. The rugby team finds two commandos cornered in a panic, so they scrum in on them in a rush, pressing them back against the hard walls of the gorge. The two commandos try to run like scared rats on a sinking ship. Even the synchronized swimming team startles them back into the scrum, where the rugby players sort it out hand-to-hand.

The boxers and martial arts medalists kick ass as they spring out from behind rocks in synchronous attack. A wrestler, disguised as a spruce, reaches out his long limbs and strangles a soldier who had the misfortune of brushing by. Once the dead commando collapses, the wrestler goes right back into his tree pose. As the brutal battle ensues, Shrike detects that four athletes bleed from getting shot by what little ammo the commandos have left. This causes her concern, but then she sees a kayaker pop up from behind a tree and thrash a commando with his paddle 15 times in 4.2 seconds. The commando collapses unconsciously like an invertebrate slim mold. A taekwondo medalist spins and kicks a soldier in the face. As the soldier falls backwards toward the ground, he shoots the medalist with the last shot in his pistol. Blood soaks into the white taekwondo gi. Fencers slip out from behind cover and skewer the commando through his neck, right where he sits, then plunge back into thick cover. Blood splatters over the granite and ice, as the commando falls onto his back, convulsing. One by one, the commandos get picked off, but not without cost to the athletes.

Previously fearless, the terrified commandos doubt the survivability of this mission, but fight on. A couple of them think about what Joaquin has been saying all along: 'Bolt when no one watches and live to fight another day'. It's mutiny, or desertion, or whatever, but it beats getting hosed by a bunch of jocks. With morale at an all-time low for even this malevolent bunch, and thirst, hunger, and pain at all-time highs, a percentage of the troops seriously consider running back down the hill and getting the hell out of there alive.

Lohan senses the mutinous tension, and like a Gatling gun says, "Those pussies who just want to panic and die; go ahead. Curl up in a fetal ball right up against those trees and wait to die like the pathetic cowards you are. For any of you who want to live, and want the glory, … come with me."
The stunned commandos look at each other.

Cruise pops his head up from behind a large log and quips at Joaquin, "That's why she's superior to you."

Cruise starts to bark out commands, moving the troops into perfect position, "See if there is anyway to repel the cliffs and bypass the gorge."

Most of the time, Cruise finds he has to repeat his commands twice, just because the cacophonous caws of the ravens overhead never stops. Cruise doesn't even realize that they have no climbing gear now. The troops haven't been carrying any of that stuff since the bison stampede; and the rodents ruined most ropes and ties anyway.

Lohan looks up with wonder at the ominous black silhouettes against the stars while she takes a quick count, "What the hell? I don't think I've ever seen 50, 90, 170 ravens like this before."

Joaquin responds with a delirious chill, "Yeah, spooky."

Since drinking the whole bottle of champagne, losing a lot of blood from the finger Cruise shot off, the altitude sickness, the complete lack of food or water for over eleven hours now, and the swelling all over his face from the stinging insect stings and miscellaneous animal hits; Joaquin starts hallucinating. Looking down at the rocks he thinks he sees Coke cans.

More than that, they call to him, "Drink me. Drink. Mmm. Drink. Drink me down good. Mmm."

Joaquin bends down to grab a can and stumbles forward onto the rocks and unforgiving ice. His helmet protects him from any damage.

Lohan rolls her eyes, having no fear of a Hitchcockian rebirth, but instead worrying much more about Joaquin and the state of what's left of the company. If any of them are half as bad as Joaquin, the company is doomed.

Lohan says to Cruise, "We are going to find out right now what the last of our troops are made of. The U.S. government would never let me lead soldiers into battle. Now, I will!"

Lacking anything intelligent to add at this point, Cruise parrots, "Roger that!"

As they charge up over the lip of the top tier and onto the higher ground, a commando gets separated from the rest and becomes overwhelmed by sneak attacks. He sees an athlete running away from him, so he raises his .45 to take careful aim. Suddenly, a large rock hits him in the back of the helmet. He wheels around, only to be hit in the back of the helmet with another large rock. He has no idea that he has stepped into the middle of a thinking, breathing, living, well-coordinated booby trap. Four team handball players surround him. Each hides behind a large rock, has piles of cantaloupe-sized stones, and moves their position under concealment after every throw, to pop up at a totally different spot. They only throw when they see the back of the helmet. The commando's helmet starts to ring like a pinball machine. Bong, bong, bong bong, bong, bong bong bong, bong bing. After the ninth strike in seven seconds, the commando gets dizzy. He spins with frustration; getting peripheral glimpses but never being able to fire a shot. Nine more stones ring the helmet in eight seconds. The soldier drops to one knee, inviting three simultaneous stones to hit from the sides and rear. He falls flat on his face like a tree being timbered; dazed. They rush him from behind the boulders with stones cocked. One kneels on his back as the others take his pistol and bayonet. Another commando suddenly appears from the darkness, and ominously approaches.

Magnificent restraint? Impossible odds? Unacceptable aggression?

Chapter 6

Evil Gets Its Way

"Look out!" screams one of the team handball players who emerges from the pitch darkness of a cave.

They dive off in different directions to avoid being mowed down, but two of them take superficial wounds. One of the team handball players tries to fire a pistol, but the other commando is too fast and shoots the pistol-wielding sportsman, forcing him to drop the sidearm. The other three, including the wounded handball players, make a scattered run for it. The commando quickly whips around in a 180, looking up into the black jutting peaks and back down into the icy cracks and craggily caves. He leans over to check the other commando's neck for a pulse, then looks around quickly again. He doesn't see anything but he can hear the battle continuing on the other side of the boulders. He pulls the clip out of his .45 to see that he has only two rounds left. He straddles the dazed commando and rolls him onto his back, unable to find anything of use on him, he loops back to where he shot the athletes. He picks up the pistol that the athlete dropped when he got shot, to see that the clip cradles only a single round. He loads the bullet into his own magazine and takes a handgun and a grenade from two other fresh corpses. He turns to rejoin the battle when, POWW! A water polo player hurls a three-pound stone square into his nose, knocking him unconscious. A daredevil mountain biker careens down the slope, rushing up on the comatose commando. The mountain biker quickly rifles through the corpses, returning to the main chaos with two empty pistols and a grenade.

The battle takes on an incredibly medieval brutality. Most of the commandos hold knives now, menacing and fierce. James and Daniel see one of the last commandos with a pistol. He points it at them so they turn and run full speed down into the gorge. A second commando steps up to the end of the gorge, blocking their way. The first commando doesn't shoot, because they are way too far away to hit in the darkness and he has only one round left. James, without breaking stride, hurdles directly into the second commando's face. James's lead foot comes up perfectly into the commando's nose and chin. James runs straight through him as he falls backward. Daniel does a high flip, landing on the commando's flack vest knees first! Daniel hears three ribs crack as he springs up and follows James into cover. The commando writhes in pain on the frozen ground.

With anguish and death surrounding her, she can't take it anymore. Shrike goes back on her vow and begs the animals to return. Without hesitation, falcons show up first, then swifts and swallows, all flying in front of and into the soldiers' eyes. Gophers dig up under a soldier lying prone with an M16, and bite him with their big yellow teeth. A pair of wrens fly into the end of the commando's scope. He shoos away the birds repeatedly but they will not allow him to aim. Two minks and a weasel sneak over to a dead commando and remove a grenade from his vest. A raccoon picks it up in its slender black fingers and hands it into a red fox's mouth. The fox squeezes the handle and the raccoon pulls the pin with its dexterous fingers. The fox sprints off at full speed toward Cruise. Lohan launches their last grenade from her gun. It blows up the fox. The fox's mouth pops open and the grenade bounces forward and detonates. The commandos duck and take superficial wounds. Shrike feels a sharp pain in her head when the fox expires. Birds are getting shot. Athletes are dying fast. Though Shrike feels nothing but sorrow when people die, when animals die, she feels a physiological pain, right in her skull; a stabbing pain for every animal's death. The severe pain is unbearable.

Shrike says to Sara with worry, "We need to implement Plan 92."

Sara confirms, "The hijacker?"

Shrike says, "Yes."

James and Daniel spring into action. They lift the injured commando and his improvised stretcher and quickly whisk him away down the path.

The hijacker complains, "I told you they were gonna get to me sooner or later. I told you. What are you going to do with me?"

James and Daniel enter a well-hidden cave, stocked with supplies and guarded by a black bear, among other threatening predators.

Daniel says, "Put him down here."

James says, "Gag him and leave the note."

Making it difficult for him to call out, James and Daniel run back out of the cave. The bear stares down on the commando's frightened face, gnashing its ferocious fangs. A bit of the bear's drool smudges a portion of the letter, hand-written by Shrike:

Attention Authorities,

This vile creature is a terrorist against the USA! He is a confirmed hijacker and killer of innocent pilots. Prosecute him at the fullest level!

Shrike Tomial and the US Olympic Team

Out on the front, for all of the barrage and shooting and grenade throwing they do, the athletes can injure only one more commando, but loose three more of their teammates. Shrike, a shrewd strategic mind, sees there is no way to win a fair firefight and has no element of surprise left. The booby traps have all been sprung so Shrike decides to put up a white flag and call off the wildlife.

Shrike says over the comlink, "Cruise, listen up. There's no point in fighting to the death. We surrender, lay down our arms, and expect reasonable treatment for everyone."

Thick black clouds block the moon and stars, the wind heavily picks up to a howl, and the temperature drops by a murderous twenty degrees. The commandos and athletes all shiver in the severe cold. The commandos find ways to get a few fires lit in the shelter of shallow caves and crevices, but the warming and cuddling animals are absent. Many of the athletes wonder where the animals are.

Some animals rest; others feed or lick their wounds. Most of the animals are still part of the army of scavengers; collecting and transporting everything the commandos have so graciously left behind in their scramble down hill and whatnot. Since the commandos have the athletes captured, the animals stockpile the supplies in a nearby bear's den for safekeeping. One of the items the animals scrounge for just happens to be Tara, who a pack of wolves dig from the powder. She's blue, but okay. She climbs onto the back of an adult billy mountain goat, and grips the fur tightly with her tiny frozen fingers.

From indiscernible origins, the several commandos jump when they hear the big tom cougar growl and roar from the late blackness.

The athletes suspect that the troops are almost out of ammo, and hurting. They counted over and over again and most of the Olympians come to a silent consensus: There are still 88 athletes at full strength, and only eight commandos. If one subtracts the track cyclist who went for help, Colt the equestrian, and Tara on the mountain goat, along with all of the other injured or dead sports stars, only 88 of the original 117 remain to fight the blood-thirsty commandos; but that is 80 more than Cruise has, not counting Sara, Shrike, and most of all, Jay. A few of the commandos who still have .45s have one bullet left. They are still lethal killers; and demented, pathological time bombs, so the athletes have to play their cards right and follow Shrike's lead loyally.

Cruise laments, "I've got to figure out what's going on here. How can so many things in one operation go so wrong? How can such an inferior group of civilians thwart such an intensely powerful unit as ours, …my unit?"

Shrike says, "Hey, even the raptors have to deal with the ravens!"

"Yeah, and the raven have to deal with the raptors!" Cruise snipes back, not getting it at all.

Shrike laughs, "You'll never get it."

Cruise lunges over, "What's that? What's that you say? I get what I want. I take everything I want. You get that?"

Shrike laughs again, "Take whatever you want. Steal it. Still, you are never gonna get it."

Cruise's perspiring face blisters with bulging fury as he walks off into the bitter night air to think.

Sara gives Shrike a sly wink. She approves of her psychological technique. It is actually ridiculous to think that Shrike could have the upper hand in this situation, and yet, Cruise and the rest of his ilk let their weak minds dominate their unbridled emotions, and therefore, their moronically violent, primitive actions.

Shrike and Sara sit tied on the floor of a narrow cave and close enough to talk with each other. As one of the guards moves off to get closer to the fire, they take the opportunity to connect.

Sara asks softly in a shivering whisper, "You all right?"

Shrike chuckles, "Pfft. They caused me pain, and it hurt. So what. I can take it. Mind over matter."

Sara says, "Do you understand now why we need psychologists?"

Shrike says, "No, I don't. I certainly don't need one."

Sara replies, "Really? Everyone, everyone is sick and needs some kind of help. If these commandos don't prove it, I don't know who does."

Shrike replies, "You can't use the worst, most extreme examples to justify the rule."

Sara explains, "I'm not. I'm just saying, anyone who goes around saying that they are normal and don't have a problem are the ones who need help the most. We all have problems deep down inside. We are all crazy."

A squirrel suddenly appears silently with some confiscated trail mix in its cheeks. It crawls up Shrike's chest to sit on her ample bosom, then passes several peanuts and other pieces of snack from its diminutive mouth into Shrike's. The furry dynamo leaps in one bound over onto Sara's flat chest, and gives her the rest of the trail mix, straight from its mouth to hers. A guard stirs and looks over, but the squirrel ducks behind Sara's back as it would duck around the back of an oak trunk. The girls freeze their mouth movements, so the guard doesn't see them chewing. The guard watches for a second, then looks away. The squirrel bails as quietly as it had arrived.

Shrike chews, swallows, and says without missing a beat, "Great. Let's psychoanalyze the psychos. I know they are psycho."

Sara says with spunk as she licks some pumpkin seed from between her teeth, "Now you're talking," not picking up on Shrike's sarcasm. "First, these troops must be under incredible stress right now. They should be grieving their exposure to combat. They have a number of risk factors, and we know they can harm others. The question is, …"

Shrike jumps in, "… can we get them to harm themselves?"

Sara says, "That would be a swift trick."

Shrike says, "You are right. I think we should focus on how to get out of this, but I will keep in mind that everyone is crazy."

Sara replies, "Thank you, … I think."

The freezing cold wind whistles and howls, pushing the soldiers off balance. The guards realize they've strayed too far away to get near the fire, so Dumpy and Flaca rumble back over to the bound maidens.

Dumpy queries Flaca, "You got any ciggs?"

Flaca rejects her flatly, "No way. I'm not giving you any of mine. You should have paced yourself."

Dumpy bends down to Sara's face sadistically, and says, "You ready to start crying yet?"

Sara replies in a dull tone, "Quite frankly, I don't see how ever putting anything in those terms can be beneficial."

Dumpy says with surprise, "Whad arh you a scientist of something?"

Sara starts assuredly, "No I just. . ."

Dumpy cuts her off due to her lack of impulse control and attention span, "Is it true about professors, like, ya know, they don't know how to have sex?"

Flaca jumps into the fray of the misinformed, "No you fool. Where'd ya get that? Professors and librarians are always the sleepers."

Dumpy questions like a dope, "Sleepers?"

Flaca explains, "I bet the brainiac is way hotter in bed than 'Miss Looks' over there," as she nods toward Shrike.

With subtle glances, Sara and Shrike roll their eyes and grin.

Sara baits, "Ut Oh. Someone likes you Shrike."

Shrike plays along perfectly, "Who? Which one? Oooohh. I'd like it to happen naturally."

Dumpy snaps over at Flaca with bitter betrayal and says "I see. You like her and you're trying to stick me with the egghead who you know is going to suck. Fuck you, 'sister'! I am pissed."

Dumpy marches off across the broad rock slope. Flaca hesitates, then calls in two other commandos to watch Shrike and Sara. Hurt, Flaca then leaves after the emotionally out-of-control Dumpy.

Sara reports with a whisper, "That gal has had emotional problems her whole life, since she was a little kid, I can tell you that," offering up her unsolicited analysis again.

Shrike can see that the new guards sit too far away to hear them over the wind. The bound women lean back to pretend they've fallen asleep, and begin to conspire.

Cruise sneaks up behind Shrike and Sara. He needs information; military intelligence. He lacks intelligence. He has to get it from somewhere. He holds his breath to listen, but thanks to the tell-tale barks from Shrike's western screech-owl friend, the girls know he's there.

Sara asks, "When you say 'nature's flaw' what do you mean?"

Shrike reiterates, "Nature's flaw. That's what it is."

Cruise listens more closely to try to get a handle on the subject.

Shrike reveals, "The period. The woman's period … what a flaw."

Cruise suddenly realizes what they are talking about. This banter is useless to him. He needs more info and he needs it now. He marches over to the two women in the most intimidating stance he can muster and signals Joaquin over to join them.

Shrike lectures, "Cruise, your men are starving and thirsty. Don't you know how to run a command? Have them cum in each other's mouths for Christ sake."

Joaquin nods because he is sick enough to like this idea, "At least they'll get some sodium and vitamin E."

Sara continues to badger and confuse Cruise with lies as she springs off of Joaquin's support, "Or you could have them urinate into each other's mouths. At least they would live. Why do you think we look like we have been doing so healthy and great? We've been up on this cold, exposed peak with no food or water for a lot longer than you have, and we look like spring daisies compared to your motley runts."

Right on cue, two of Cruise's sickest men cough off in the background, and one leaves his guard post to vomit.

Meanwhile, Shrike silently asks her feathered buddy to do her a little favor. When Cruise brings eight commandos together under a cluster of short trees and starts doling out orders, the screech-owl gives off a loud, long horse whinny every time it hears Cruise try to speak. Cruise looks up and right at the camouflaged bird of prey, but all he sees is bark. He tries to talk again, but the owl drowns him out. The soldiers are too tired, hurt, and beaten to laugh at Cruise's mocking embarrassment. Cruise speaks progressively louder, until he finds himself yelling over the diminutive western screech-owl. Shrike thinks this is a grand game, and urges the owl to push it to the limit. Cruise, straining his voice, stops in mid sentence and looks up in anger again. The screech-owl stops whinnying immediately, closes its eyes tightly, and presses itself against the trunk motionlessly. Cruise shines his flashlight exactly onto the invisible nagging nocturnal neighbor, and again, he can't locate it at all. He returns to talk with the troops when "e-e-e-e-e-e-e-e-e-e" the incessant ear-splitting horse neighs continue.

Joaquin whines again, "Not for nothin but, that thing is driving me crazy."

The frustrated Cruise yells on the top of his lungs, "God damn it all to hell!"

He pulls out his pistol. The screech-owl silently bails out. Cruise points his light at the tree and fires three shots into the trunk, right near where the owl had perched to annoy him. Cruise examines the area and then he relents and resumes talking to the commandos. As soon as he starts his second sentence, the owl flies through at full speed overhead and darting in broad zigzags: the whinny at full volume. A number of the men and women, rattled, raise their guns and swing their heads around.

Cruise rails, "Forget it. It's just a bark beetle or some little bird we disturbed."
Cruise leans into the huddle and quickly gives out concise direction.

In non sequitur, Shrike says, "You know, now that I can kind of think and feel the animals, I wish I could be one. I wish I could just say, 'Size of a moose,' or, 'Size of a deer mouse,' and blam, I could actually physically turn into it."

Sara smiles, "That would be really cool, huh?"

Cruise comes marching in all piss and vinegar, "Shut the fuck up! Who is letting these two talk to each other?"
Cruise latches down hard on the neckline of the on-duty commando, and pulls her into his face.

Cruise barks, "You watching this shit? Flaca? Dumpy?"
The sleepy commando looks puzzled and doesn't know how to respond.

Shrike yells, "Leave her alone, waron. She was just telling us the whole reason behind why you fools are pulling this shit."

Cruise looks at the commando, but doesn't buy it. "Stay sharp. Keep them apart." He then turns to Shrike and says, "waron?"

Shrike says, "Yeah. Cross between a warmonger and a moron."

Sara cackles, "Waron. Hey waron. Look at that stupid waron."

Cruise says, "You forgot one thing bitches: War is about who is strongest!"

The women laugh hysterically.

Shrike says, "War is about fuckin' with the enemy's mind. This is going to be a cakewalk because your mind is already so fucked!"

Cruise looks like he is about to explode, but instead, he sits down all Zen like, takes a breath and calms himself down; to prove to them, and to himself, that he maintains control. Cruise's men watch ever more closely from under their helmets.

Cruise lectures, "Every generation needs their heroes, its leaders."

Sara says, "What? Is that what you think you are?"

Shrike calls out, "You're just a psycho Nazi."

Cruise counters, "Nazi? I'm an American. I'm an American hero! More American than you. I risked my life for my country. My heart and soul for what?"

Sara cuts, "First of all, real heroes don't go around calling themselves heroes! And secondly, I see you as a Hitler, not a hero."

Joaquin belts, "Okay, we don't have to take this."

He raises a crooked stick up to strike Sara, when Cruise commands, "No. Don't hit her."

Cruise reflects on himself for a moment.

He says, "You are all wrong. I'm trying to make the world better for everyone."

He hesitates. He doesn't believe his own words. Maybe at one time in his life he did; maybe even right before this trip he did; but he certainly doesn't right now. Sara and Shrike can see what he is thinking, but none of his soldiers can.

Shrike says, "No. No. It can't be true. You are one of the bad guys. Oh my god. You are one of the bad guys."

Joaquin yells, "No shit Sherlock. We are bad. We are the badass guys. The bad dudes. That's why they call on us. You want bad?"

Cruise raises his hand piously, "Joaquin, please."
Joaquin backs down like a disgruntled badger.

Cruise says, "The first one who tells me what you two were talking about gets a punch in the face. The one who remains silent, gets stabbed with this knife. Punched or stabbed?" he offers like a side dish.
Cruise keeps his left arm pinned tightly against his ribs; the scorpion wounds still smarting.

The girls say, almost in unison, "Waron!"
Cruise's face goes totally goshawk, as he struts up to Sara, unzips his fly, and crams his dick into her face.

Sara gasps with belittling laughter, "Oh my god, you've got problems."

Cruise replies viciously, "God? You're way off lady. Way off. I'm about as far from god as you are ever gonna get."
With pride, Cruise grabs the back of her head in his hand as he forces her head onto him. She turns her head to the side, keeping everything shut tight.

Shrike fires, "Greatest Generation huh? I shit you not! You're a real John Wayne. Don't you represent some great line of fighting men? You are nothing but a Madoff! You are even worse than Madoff."

Cruise complains, "What?"

Shrike attacks, "You're a fuckin' Madoff."

Cruise jerks Sara's head back hard by her hair, hurting her neck. He says to Shrike, "How do you get that?"

Shrike looks at him with bitter distain, "You're a whore. You don't care how you get it, you just have to have money. You're a hollow, empty shell. No wonder your troops show absolutely no respect for you on any level."

Then Sara dares to say, gasping for breath, "They're just as disgusted in themselves for being greedy Madoffs like you. You hate yourselves."

Shrike strikes viciously, "No point in giving us your name 'commander': Waron and Madoff will suit us just fine. That's all you'll ever be to us."

Cruise steps back and pulls his zipper up with mortification. It's not working.

He says, "Don't give me that Greatest Generation crap. Hitler was from that generation. Stalin was from that 'Greatest Generation,'" he says with nagging frustration. "The friggen Lindbergh baby, the Ginsbergs, World War Two itself! Lots of horrible shit was happing in that generation too. Everybody's fucked up all the time."

Shrike yells, "That's the biggest copout. Everyone else is fucked up so I'll be."

Sara says, "It's okay to *be* fucked up, but it's not okay to *stay* fucked up. You gotta be able to find a way to fix yourself."

Shrike says, "Yeah, and they wouldn't act like you."

Sara says, "They were men."

Shrike says, "Real men."

Cruise goes ballistic, spins around and yells, "Gaarrrrrrrraaarrrrhhhhhhhgghhh!"

He grabs a handgun out of his holster and marches over to the girls like a spaz. The women maintain complete eye contact with him. He points the .45 to their heads alternately.

Cruise spits, "Go ahead. Say it again. Say some of your shit! Waron! Call me a fuckin' waron."

Cruise's troops look on in utter disrespect and disgust. Both of the women stare at Cruise. He looks like he is about to cry, then lowers the gun. He thinks, then holsters it. He looks about only to find that all of his troops turn away to avoid his eyes. Then he looks up at Lohan, who projects a complete look of wrong on her face.

Sara says, "You're not the type of person to make a lot of friends, are you now Cruise?"

Cruise answers, "What, what dya mean friends? Everyone has friends when they are kids. You don't need friends once you grow up."

Shrike laughs, knowing the truth; "Nobody wants to be friends with a guy like you."

Cruise defends, "So what. I could care less."

Sara analyzes, "Self-fulfilling prophecy: You could care less to have friends, and by that neglect, you have none because they also could care less about you. Beautiful world you've created around yourself huh?"

Cruise snaps again. He turns back to the girls and says, "Okay. We're gonna play a little game here. I gut the commandos lined up by serial number. They are going to come through one at a time, pick who they choose, and impregnate a bunch of these unprotected and ripe females."

Sara warily goads Cruise, "You don't think you're a fool?"

Cruise thinks for a second, "No."

Sara snickers, "Classic."

Cruise defends his honor, "What do you mean by that?"

Shrike announces, "Those who can't see their own foolishness... they are the biggest fools of all."
Cruise can't tell if he has just been insulted, but he doesn't like all the free running-of-the-mouth and whatnot.

Joaquin, at the front of the line, yells, "I'm fuckin' mine in the ass, thank you!"

Cruise continues with a dead-serious smirk, "I don't know what the female commandos have in mind, but if they're not into women, I'm sure they'll find a sodomistic way to take the men."

He stares at Shrike and Sara for a long time. They know he's not bluffing. The women look at each other for a second, trying to think of what to do.

Cruise says, "I don't think you know what I'm capable of." The women laugh again.

With a snicker, Shrike says, "We know what sick people are capable of."

Sara says, "Yeh, we're lucky animals aren't as brutal as humans."

Cruise scoffs, "Pfft. Hah! Not as brutal. Animals have been killing my men. Animals have been killing people since the time of Jesus and Daniel in the lion's den.   Animals have decimated my troops. I have stings, and bites, and cuts, and scratches from friggin' bugs all over the place. We have ticks sucking blood out of our groins! Not brutal? On our balls! You don't know nature lady! Nature sucks! We must have landed in a tick infestation breakout. Our job isn't to bend to Mother Nature; it's to rape her, to dominate."

Joaquin sputters "Me too!" with the excitement of a true bugger.

Shrike says, "So hypocritical, and you speak of strength and war."

Sara intensifies, "Who was talking war to begin with? This isn't war. This is a bunch of unarmed, untrained athletes, American heroes . . ."

Shrike adds quickly, " . . .real heroes . . ."

Sara says, " . . . going off for a photo shoot with The President. And you, a bunch of two-bit commando wannabes jump us. You call that war? You stopped us from seeing the leader of the free world, and somehow you are patriots because you know a little bit about a couple of amendments?"

Shrike convinces, "Believe me, I know: If the animals don't like you and know you are wrong, they can sense that, and they hurt you. It's mostly about a defense mechanism built in to protect the young."

Cruise says, "Dr. Doolittle bullshit."

Shrike says, "Really? Look at us."

Sara says delicately, "None of us have swollen up cheeks and ticks, ah, anywhere."

Cruise considers his wounds and losses, then says, "Bullshit. I'm not buying it. I'm not buying the supernatural gospel, but nice try though."

Cruise pulls down Shrike's jacket, then abrasively rips her shirt up to the armpit. He unbuttons Sara's top, exposing and examining both arms. Cruise stares at the girls' pristine arms in complete shock. In his head, a giant light bulb, like a compact fluorescent on a freezing cold night, slowly burns on and brightens.

Cruise turns sharply, "Lohan, go see how many animal injuries the athletes have and report back. What the fuck is going on here?"

Cruise looks at his infested arms covered in bleeding welts.

Shrike says, in a voice as soft and seductive as Sade, "You hate Nature, so Nature is going to put the hate back on you, naturally."

Cruise rejects, "Bullshit! I don't buy any of this."

Joaquin whimpers, "Sir, everything they have said so far confirms with what has happened, and what I think will happen. We gotta get out of here now Sir."

Cruise dismisses with bigotry, "Get the sex change over with already, ya pussy."

Sara goads Cruise, "Oooh, real mature."

Shrike says, "Yes, just tell the truth commando. What do you want with all of this stupid running around with guns? Respect? Ignorant gun nuts like you want respect Cruise, but can't get any without their big phallic guns, right?"

Cruise says, "I'll tell you what I *don't* think about. I don't think about killing the prisoners and refugees. You think I'm sick?"

Sara and Shrike quickly glance at each other with surprise.

Shrike says, "The refugees?"

Cruise says, "In Africa. In country after country. In the favelas outside Rio. She could bomb consolidated, concentrated pockets of poverty and wipe out millions of lives, suffering lives of squalor. Blow them up if you want or don't, I certainly don't care about that. That ain't my battle. I wasn't born there. Our boss is misguided."

Cruise licks his parched, chapped lips. He, like the rest of his troops, feels so much hunger and thirst that it almost disables him.

Shrike says, "Don't you feel like an idiot, working for an idiot?"

Cruise fights back, "I've worked for lots of idiots lots of times. I don't care."
The wind whistles past the spiky spires of granite and through the stalactites in the caves.

Shrike says, "You're such a fuckin' whore. Look at how stupid your master's plan is. She thinks blowing up a bunch of people is going to make the world better somehow. How can you work for someone that sick and stupid?"

Cruise says, "I've worked for stupid people all my life. Every boss I ever had was a fuckin' stupid ass. Who told you about Gwen's plan?"

Sara chides, "Ya think you're just surrounded by idiots, don't ya huh."

Cruise snaps his eyes over at her like a Rikki-Tikki-Tavi clone, "You know my ass bitch!"
Shrike frowns at Sara for bad tactics and Sara backs off wisely by simply not reacting.

Cruise states, confused beyond belief but steadfast in his fabricated convictions, "I don't know if there will ever be hope for the American military being really great again, but, God willing, at least we can make people see that some of us have gotten screwed over, and when you screw people with our kind of power *over*, well, then sir, we screw *you over*, double hard!"
Sara and Shrike both break out into embarrassing laughter at this creaky, John Wayne wannabe diatribe.

Cruise flares his nostrils. He thinks, 'How dare they?' but he doesn't know what they are laughing about or why, and he doesn't want to look like he cares by asking.

Shrike questions, "God willing? God willing? What kind of a freak of a god you got on your side buddy?"

Cruise feels like he will burst with insanity, "What? That's the part you were laughing at?"
Cruise doesn't know how to respond. He feels like he is in over his head intellectually.

Cruise betrays with anger and power in his voice, out of control as usual, "If I hadn't gone through that 12-step program, I wouldn't be half the man I be now!"

Sara's eyes dart over to Shrike. Broad smirks spread across their delicious lips.

Shrike facetiously utters, "Glad we didn't know you then."

Sara agrees, "It's hard to picture *even less* of a man."

Cruise percolates like the aquifer right beneath Old Faithful. He is so used to screaming orders and using brute force to bully his way through anything that he simply can't cope with being outsmarted by what he and his idol Donald Trump consider as 'inferior women' who are 'mainly just good fah fuckin' n cookin' as has been their mantra these long years. Cruise goes marching off into the bitter darkness to reconsider his approach and blow off a little steam. They got to him, but he doesn't want them to know it, so he simply runs away instead of facing any sort of personal, vulnerable truth.

At that moment, the injured, pissed commandos come and take different girls off behind the rocks to rape them. Shrike and Sara can hear the girls muffled screaming. Though beaten and exhausted, this is what most of the troops have been looking forward to, especially Joaquin, and they muster their strength.

Shrike says to Sara, "These fuckers are seriously going to pay for what they are doing. Mark my words."

Practically a dead ringer for Penelope Cruz, Sara looks deeply at her in earnest and whispers defiantly, "I believe you."

Shrike feels horrible and responsible about the women being raped, but comforts herself in the knowledge that she sent some of the youngest and most vulnerable of the girls to hide right before the tier battle went hand-to-hand. The smallest of gymnasts (except for Tara) still remain hidden high in the trees. The commandos don't know of their roosts, safe from assault. Shrike dares not glance up, for fear of giving them away. She thinks of ways she can still use them for signals, or rescue, or something. She racks her brain hard and thinks of contingencies for if the tables turn again.

Shrike confesses to Sara, "I can't think of another plan that would have worked better than this one."

Sara says, "After witnessing their brutality, in combination with you somehow acquiring animal power, you made the best choice there was. We would have done a lot worse if we headed down, and giving up would have just been suicide."

Shrike takes a stab at levity, "You lost my glasses, didn't you!"

Sara tangles back, "You mean MY glasses?"

Joaquin approaches Cruise, then pulls him off to the side and says, "Sir, from what we've been able to gather from the girls we raped is that Shrike is not only like their commander, but she has some kind of mental power that makes the animals protect her.

Cruise says, "Oh my god. I need that power. I wonder if Gwen has a way to add her brainpower to mine?"

Joaquin goes on, "Sir, also, the other non-athlete lady appears to be the team counselor; like a psychologist or something."

During this discussion, Flaca, Dumpy, and Lohan, the last of the female troops, have their own disgruntled discourse.

Lohan states, "We are women soldiers. We die on the battlefield just like them."

Flaca complains, "At Fort Benning, they said they wouldn't let women fight. I'll show the Army Rangers. They are double standard."

Dumpy adds her two cents, making sure Cruise can't hear, "All my life I wanted to be in the 75th. They told me I couldn't get in 'cause I didn't have a dick. They are the dicks!"

Lohan argues, "If we meet the standard of excellence, we should be allowed to fight in Special Ops. This mission will prove to the world that women can be rangers and women can fight alongside SEALS or whoever. That's why the three of us need to make it out of here, even if Cruise or nobody else does, if you know what I mean."

Many miles and states away, Gwen has her servant contact Cruise again. She takes a deep breath and tries to handle everything calmly for a change. Cruise explains the scenario completely while Gwen listens carefully.

Like a flamethrower, Gwen blasts, "Interrogate Shrike viciously. If she is controlling the animals, I want to know how. Force her to watch as the commandos rape the smallest and weakest of the female athletes, and kill a couple of the biggest and strongest whom you not only fear, but who have the harvest organs you desire. Chip away large hunks of ice and snow to pack the organs for transport."

Cruise takes the orders begrudgingly and hangs up. He begins to realize how much he really hates Gwen. On this alpine summit, the tension is the only thing thick about this air.

For the first time, Shrike and Sara get a taste of Gwen, and what might be behind all of this. They know it is a lot more complicated than a simple ransom-motivated hijacking. They worry. They worry a lot more than they already were.
Shrike snickers under her breath, self-satisfied.

Sara says, "God knows women love to turn men into monkeys."

Shrike puzzles, "How's that?" unable to come up with a mental image.

Sara semi lectures, "You know how women sometimes repeat certain behaviors, like feigning ignorance or helplessness to bluster his testosterone up, or withholding sex from him to get his drive heavier. The frustrated man starts jumping up and down like a spoiled child. You don't play those games?"

Shrike thinks with a pause, "I guess I kind have done things like that, on the fly."
They look over at the guard. He is too cold and tired to pay attention.

Sara continues, "Oh yeah. It doesn't have to be premeditated or contrived to happen all the time."

Shrike says, "Men have their behaviors and women have ours. It's like we are different animals. It stems all the way back through not only our early primate ancestors, but to all mammals."

Sara corrects, "All mammals? Try bird, and lizard and even fish behavior."

Shrike laughs, "I know. When I heard we had the 'lizard brain' still triggering our most base functions, I thought that was a stretch at first. When the whole 'fish brain' thing blew up, it helped me see human behavior for what it is."

Sara says with madness, "Oh god, you are so damn bipolar and you can't even see it. You should take . . ."

Shrike cuts her off shrilly, "Biplover? Tripolar? I am quadpolar, okay! I am some kind of so many polar that they haven't even invented my polar yet, okay!? So what! Being bipolar is great. It makes the world more extreme! Let bipoles be bipoles for crap's sake!"

Cruise assembles what's left of the commandos. The eight of them gather around Shrike and Sara. The other Olympians and the animals in the shadows watch with great concern.

Cruise presses Shrike on her animal communication techniques and she explodes, "You idiot! Do you think I know? Do you think I understand? The lightning bolt changed my brain. That's it. It's like a light bulb came on in my brain, or, more like, a light bulb came on in my head... shining on my brain. Something like that."

Cruise says, "I don't give a fuck how you are doin' it. If I can't use your power myself, I'll just have *you* use it *for me*."

Shrike explains sincerely, "Even if I could, I can't. The animals have this incredible moral compass and won't help anyone do wrong. It's like white magic in voodoo. They will only do good."

Cruise cries, "Bullshit. They killed a bunch of my troops."

Shrike explains as calm as Gandhi, "They know you are bad."

Cruise roils.

Sara explains, "There has been new research done on neuron stimulation, firing spikes in the brain with TDCS and that kind of thing. Some people who get shocked in the brain become incredibly sharp and focused; better than caffeine. Of course, nobody has ever been documented communicating with animals, but there are new discoveries in science every day."

For the next hour or so, Cruise continues to press Shrike on her powers with question after nagging question and a number of ferocious threats, but she refuses to bring any of the animals in or cooperate on any level, so he says, "Maybe your resolve is strong because you can take it, but can you take watching it happen to someone else?"

The mercenaries throw Sara roughly onto a flat slab of granite and rip her pants and Victoria Secrets panties. Sara braces. Two male commandos hold her arms and legs while Lohan holds her in a strangling choke hold that almost cuts the circulation to her brain. Two other commandos stroke themselves and move their penises into threatening postures. One of the commandos starts to penetrate Sara, right in front of Shrike. One of the other soldiers suddenly grabs Sara's arm violently and starts to bend it like a twig to snap. Jay and the athletes watch in horror, as do a large number of animals that have been amassing just out of sight. The animals can't believe the human brutality they witness, for they know that no animals anywhere are that brutal!

Cruise says sadistically "You might as well talk now because you're next!" with a cold, calculating dryness.

Sara looks at Shrike. A tear rolls down Shrike's beautiful, soft cheek.
Sara smiles with internal strength, while Jay continues to feel horrible and helpless.

A commando says to Cruise, "You sure you want us to do this one? She's older and not as fit and juicy. I think she might break, ha ha."

Joaquin, who has already raped two of the smallest, most fragile of the young female hostages, pushes the subordinate troops out of the way and says, "Three's the charm."
He punches Sara in the face with glee and her head bobs back.

Joaquin says to the soldiers and then Sara, "Make sure to hold her arms for me. Don't get any ideas about doing anything against me."

Sara says to her brutalizers, "Don't you think? Don't you think for even a moment? You are a warrior. You inflict war onto others. You create refugees, and amputees. You kill people and make rubble. You destroy families. You separate loved ones. Can you see any of this?"

Devoid of impact, Joaquin quips, "Wow, now I know what they mean on the radio when they are talkin bout bleedin' heart liberals. Jeezsh."

Sara grunts like a lowland gorilla at him, "Urh. Urh. URg Urh."

He grits his teeth and his eyes narrow at the mocking insult, "Watch it. I might like that."

Sara accuses correctly, "You are messing everything up. Stop everything that you are doing and change your course right now."

Joaquin responds like a baby, "I'm never changin'. I'm never goin back. I'm never goin straight or good. I am bad and I do mess shit up. That's what I do and what I am. I never been no damn good at anything except fuckin' shit up."

First Joaquin puts his finger up into her in a deviant, vile manner; then he unzips his uniform trousers and vulgarly, devoid of any form of respect, violently starts to rape her.

Sara just closes everything off psychologically and emotionally, and takes it. She hasn't had sex in a while, and she has never been taken this violently, or abused, though she has worked with hundreds of patients who have been. By considering the circumstances completely, she remains remarkably unfazed. This enrages Joaquin and makes him drive harder, but he might as well be doing a tree stump because Sara feels nothing; completely humiliating and emasculating Joaquin to the point that he can't even bring himself to ejaculation and instead starts going soft.

Shrike knows she must do something, but she doesn't know what, so she starts by simply saying, "Stop."

Cruise yells, "Stop. Stop. Freeze."

Remarkably, everyone stops.

Shrike says, "You're such a coward. A real man would take me on one-on-one without any of his little crony pawns helping out. Whose side are you on, your own? The bottom 50 percent of Americans (including all of the troops you command) possess two percent of the wealth, … and *you're* working for Gwen?"

Cruise says, "You don't understand me so good. I could give a shit about any of that. I'm a Libertarian. I only care about me and my own, and my shit."

Daniel notices a pair of evening grosbeaks. He focuses on their big yellow bills glistening in the moonlight. Odd sight for night. Are they strong enough to bite through zip ties? He tries to use his mind to send them a message. They look at him blankly. Then Daniel sees that Cruise and Lohan are watching him, so Daniel scoffs, "Wow, 'Libertarian', that's a big word for you, but it sounds like you don't know what that means either."

As the commandos turn to watch what is happening, Sara sits up and covers her body the best she can.

Shrike says, "You accept the situation because you don't understand what's going on."

Cruise looks at her, perplexed.

Shrike laughs heartily, "Like you and your gang of rapist losers hiding behind your guns like a bunch of pussy-ass NRA cowards? Okay. I'll take you on. I'll take you on bitch."

In his feeble state of mind and his weak physical state, the challenge leaves Cruise absolutely no choice. Of course, a smarter man would ignore Shrike's junior high psychology; but as has been established, like most bullies, Cruise is a stupid, vain man. The troops he has left are fixed on his face and he's gotta make a move. He knows he can beat Shrike easily, …but to what end?

Much to the chagrin of the athletes, Cruise cuts Shrike free and pulls her up to her feet so that *The Battle Royale* can begin.

Sara cuts like a knife, spitting with defiant anger, "Never had a friend Cruise, huh?"

Cruise knows they parry with his inferior mind, so he fights back, "Me? Ha! I have plenty of friends. You're the one with no friends."

Shrike says sharply, "I'm her friend."
Cruise looks over at Shrike with complete surprise.

Sara kneels, clutching her torso, and continues clinically, "It hurts to have no friends, doesn't it. To have no one you can call a friend. No one you can call. To be unable to put your finger on a name … a name of just one friend."

Cruise yells, "Shut the fuck up."

Shrike belts out an old rock song from The Who:
How many friends have a really got?
I can count 'em on one hand.
How many friends have a really got?
How many friends have a really got?

Cruise cuts her off, "You know gags are an option … or cutting your tongue out!"

Unfazed, undaunted; Shrike sings the song from well beyond her years:
That love me? That want me? That'll take me as I am?
Cruise shakes his head with frustration.

Sara hypothesizes, "That's why you had to join a brotherhood; a fraternity."

Shrike adds, "You just needed to be one of the boys. You wanted to be accepted, but nobody accepted you. That turns weak men bitter."

Sara spits up some blood, then digs in, "Yeah, you must be replaying blame-game scenarios over and over in your head right?
The government dicked me over!
My teacher in gym class was a jerk.
That guy who fired me once, and that chick that rejected me in front of the other guys.

You had something to prove and joining the military gave you the tools to prove it; and prove all of *them* wrong."

Cruise deeply contemplates how unbelievably on-the-nose every word appears to be.

Shrike says, "Let's go," and punches Cruise square in the face.

He doesn't' even feel it. He limps closer and lunges at Shrike but misses. She tries to hit him again but he grabs her and twists her down onto the ground and starts choking her. He could easily kill her if he wants to. The marten sprints over in hyper bounds and issues a hard bite to the back of his neck. Cruise reaches back for the marten with his wounded left arm, but it clamps down hard on his hand and won't let go. Cruise is forced to release Shrike, and as he tries to grab the marten it releases him from its toothy jaws and dodges his grasp. Shrike tries hitting and kicking him. No effect. She shakes her hands and wrists in pain. Commander Cruise grabs her and reaches back to punch her in the face, when the little owl darts in and sticks its talons into his eyes. He releases Shrike again to shoo the owl and protect his face. Cruise's women and men watch, but there is really no opportunity for those few with pistols to get a shot off at either of the speedy animals. The bark-like owl flies straight up and out of reach. Shrike breaks a stick over Cruise's shoulder and the soldiers laugh at her. He lunges toward Shrike again but before he can get his tainted hands on her, the gigantic cougar jumps from the shadows on Cruise and pins him to the ground. In shock, the commandos that still have .45s go for them, but the cougar bounds back off before anyone can take a shot and vanishes into the inky blackness.

Shrike looks down on Cruise and says, "Guns and bombs and hate can never win over animals and wildlife and love. Get up."

The cougar growls in the distance as the faces of the troops, even fearless Lohan's, all go pale. Cruise slowly crawls back onto his knees on the jagged rocks. The ruckus of animals at this late hour becomes unnerving to the corrupt criminals. Now, it sounds as if a chorus of a thousand animals from one hundred different species erupts in cacophonous noise.

Winded, his eyes bleeding as much as his other wounds, Cruise accuses "You a human being or what? Seems like you side more with animals. You a traitor?"

Shrike shakes her head in disbelief; "I trust animals over people, any day."

Cruise says, "You're sick in the head."

Shrike says, "Ha. You think I'd trust the likes of you over a cougar or a marten? They're not conniving or evil."

Cruise says, "That's the problem with animals. They are totally unpredictable."

Shrike falls over laughing, "Ha ha ha. Ha ha ha. Ha ha. That is so hysterical. Humans are one hundred times more unpredictable than sharks or coyotes or anything else. Imagine being a Canada goose and running into humans on a daily basis. One person wants to pet you and love you. One person wants to take your photo. One person takes a swing at you with a golf club 'cause they hate animals. One person wants to feed you disgusting, junky white bread, and one wants to shoot you --- and you don't know why … or what for ---- or which one. Humans are a mess. Would you have predicted that commandos would hijack our plane and hunt us down in Yellowstone?" Cruise seems overwhelmed for a second as he tries to absorb everything.

Sara jumps in, "And animals don't kill for no reason."

Cruise counters, "I kill for a reason. I kill for lots of reasons, called dollars."

Shrike looks strongly at Cruise, getting back on point, "Humans are a gigantic nuisance to animals!"

Cruise rebuts, "People don't think of it that way."

Shrike says, "I do, especially now. We are a giant pain in the ass to animals. That's what we are. With people gone; especially selfish, destructive, primal, stupid, hate-filled murderous people like you; the animals, fish, and plants, would be way way better off."

Cruise bristles with infuriation.

A pack of wolves moves in and surrounds Shrike. They affectionately rub their muzzles against her face and twist against her thighs with warming whines. She hugs and kisses each of them one at a time. The closest commando thinks to raise his pistol for an instant, when from out of nowhere ravens and raptors swirl about like shrieking tornados. Owls swoop in on silent wings with unnerving hoots while weasels run about the commandos' legs. The soldier hesitates, and then lowers his gun in fear of what might happen to him if he shoots. The wolves lick her like happy huskies and just as quickly dart off again into the darkness. The commandos all look around at each other in panic, then back at Cruise for leadership and answers. Shrike smiles as the wolves howl in hearty unison.

Lohan runs up to Cruise and reports at a level only Cruise and Joaquin can hear, "Sir, I just finished checking every athlete. None of them have any animal wounds."

Cruise says, "What?"

Joaquin puffs, "Seeeee?"

Lohan continues, "But I have a logical theory Sir, if I may." Cruise nods his permission as he glances over at the sniveling coward Joaquin.

Lohan postulates, "They crashed way above snow line and we landed way below. That's all. They had no bugs to bother them."

Neither Cruise nor Joaquin find hothead Lohan's theory plausible in the least, especially considering how the animals act right now.

Cruise, now at a complete loss, decides to retreat to a cave for a nap, "Lohan, Joaquin; with me! The rest of you, we've had enough for tonight and need to get some shut eye. Tie Shrike back up, and with all these animals around, stay on guard … all of you!"

The disappointed soldiers drop Sara at Shrike's feet in a half-naked mess. The bloodied Sara looks up at Shrike while they retie her arms behind her back.

Sara says, "I'm fine. Are you okay? Do you need anything?"

Shrike is shocked. She and the athletes had come to think of Sara as a bit of a quack. However, even though Sara just suffered a traumatic rape, she psychologically puts her own assault aside to counsel others. Shrike sits amazed at Sara's fortitude, and the inspiration sends a strong chill down her back. Shrike and the athletes respect her much more now and hold her closer to Shrike's level on the ethical ladder in their minds.

Sara has a revelation, "I was wrong about your animal telepathy, and I realize we don't need drugs or outside powers. We just need to be strong and believe in ourselves, and that humans can be good and overcome the evil that exists within each of us!"

Noting the mushy overstatement and the obvious understatement, Shrike agrees, "After communicating with the animals and understanding their intellect, I realize ... the only difference between us and them is that we have developed a bunch of tricky toys and gadgets; which obviously have made us worse, not better; and the fact that the animals lack a super-ego, or even an ego, makes them much better off than us! There is no such thing as a smart phone. There are just dumb people who use them and fool themselves that they are smart."

After all that has happened, Sara has no choice but to agree, "It's our big brains, and our out-of-control need to dominate, rule, possess, and reproduce unchecked that is destroying everything else . . . and us! We need to eliminate ego, not develop it. Ya know, Cruise and these guys appear to be religious nut jobs, clinically speaking of course."
Shrike listens intently.

Sara continues with remarkable focus, considering what she's just been through; but like Shrike, she's a fighter and theorizes, "We should be able to use that to our advantage somehow ... make them think they are seeing ghosts or something ---- the return of the messiah. Use their feeble caveman beliefs against them."

Shrike looks at Sara in disbelief, "What do you think I've been doing this whole time? I never expected any of these guys to be geniuses, but that's a slippery slope you want to go down. From what I've seen, even though all spiritual whack jobs are brainwashed, they're all programmed differently. The key thing though … they are sick and dangerous; they'd have to be to buy into such desperately-moronic shit."

The women continue to run scenarios.

Back on the trail by the mighty waterfall, the all-but-forgotten commando who had been duped by the divers and left without a log bridge to cross, finally decides that he has no choice but to try to climb down into the slippery blackness. As soon as he reaches for his second handhold, small and dark American dippers come out from under the waterfall itself. He slips from the shiny, slimy rocks he clings to, falls like a sack of pond turtles, and lands in the water awkwardly. He lies there in the freezing water paralyzed as the crystal stream carries him past the rocks and down the precipitous mountainside. Chunky dippers land on his face and peck at his eyes with their tack-like beaks. All he can do is squint in a vain attempt to protect his eyeballs, never to be heard from again.

Abominable cruelty? Mental munchkins? Moral and Morale disintegration?

Chapter 7

Down in Flames

After a few hours have past and as dawn approaches the absolutely paradisiacal Yellowstone landscape, with chickadees ratcheting up the rhetoric, Shrike awakens, reaching up with her injured right hand to wipe the water droplets and incrusted blood from her eyebrow and the outer edge of her lashes. She sees that a commando aims a .45 at her head as he straddles a rock several feet away. He looks flimsy and weak, like he can barely stay erect. It's amazing that no one perished from exposure.

"Commander. She's up," he relays over the headset.

Moments later, Cruise stomps over full of aggressive testosterone. Shrike gently closes her eyes again, like a garage door coming down.

He commands, "We're leaving soon. You are coming with us. All of you. You lost. That's the way it's gonna be. We will find out about this animal thing eventually at Gwen's lab, but bottom line is, animals can't compete with us. We've proved it over and over again. Name something great, the greatest achievement humans have ever done. Animals can't compare."

Daniel, James, Sara and Jay lie nearby. They sit up in the dim light. Some of them lean against boulders and dead trunks. Their shivering voices randomly ring out in the early morning air, but their faces remain unseen:

"Domesticate horses," one says.

Cruise fires back, "Invent the gun. I'll take a gun over a horse any day."

Another voice disagrees, "Fool."

Another athlete offers, "Language."

Cruise snickers, trying to maintain his cool, "The computer is way more important than language. With a computer, you don't need language."

Another voice retaliates, "A computer is a tool that uses a language --- and could never have been designed without language you fool."

Cruise flustered, blathers "The atlatl!"

"No way . . . not even close!" the voices chide. "Fire." "The hand ax," they suggest over each other.

Cruise looks like he is ready to go for his gun and just start popping people. He can't handle even minimal defiance.

Many of the athletes are thinking the same thing. There are so few commandos now, and they are so weak and tired compared to the athletes. How many Olympians would die in a mad rush? Three? Seven? Ten? It would still be worth it to save the other seventy-five. The only question is ... who will start the riot?

Once it's bright enough, the athletes steal subtle glances and shifty glares from each other. Shrike picks her head up off of the cold ground, her cheek filthy, and can see what's about to happen.

They look at her for nonverbal guidance, but instead and as usual, Shrike puts everyone else's ideas to shame, "Standing up. Standing up let us use our hands. That changed us. Most animals never learned how to stand up and walk like *Australopithecus* did."

Everyone stops in stunned contemplation. Shrike musters her strength and stands up tall and strong; a true biped; while Cruise and his exhausted commandos sway back and forth on wobbly legs – hallucinations springing from their beaten peripheries.

Shrike sings in graceful tones:
It won't do,
to dream of caramel,
to think of cinnamon,
and long for you.

It sounds like a bossa nova reminiscent of *The Girl from Ipanema*. The commandos, the athletes, even the animals off in the distance, prick up their ears and enjoy the sweet ephemeral serenade. Cruise looks around and realizes *he is* the bad guy, and everyone knows it. No one dares to interrupt this beautiful, soft,

minimalist rendition of an old Suzanne Vega song, but Jay
harmonizes, making the moment even more surreal:
It won't do,
to stir a deep desire,
to fan a hidden fire,
that will never burn true.

Shrike stops singing abruptly, then says strongly "Standing
up. The animals know that's what makes us different … and
makes birds fly and snakes slither. We stand up. That is all that
made us great. That is all that makes us different. We stand up,
just as we stand up against YOU!"

With those words, the first rays of the beaming sun shine
over the mountain peaks and straight into the commandos' eyes
like spotlights. The wilderness comes alive. All manner of
creature, furry and feathered, give off blood curdling roars and
shrieks. The Olympic athletes, even the severely injured ones, all
stand in unison as well, like compelled marionettes pulled by
Shrike's spontaneous strings. Cruise balances awkwardly on his
heels, jerking around like a Devo wannabe.

The commandos prick up their ears and go for their
weapons, even though almost all of them are empty. They listen
with anticipation, when suddenly they hear helicopters
approaching from out of the valley shadows, … and coming in to
take everyone to their doom. If the athletes and commandos look
over to the west now, they can see smoke billowing up from the
Warthog wreckage. With almost everyone on frazzled edge, a
transmission crackles over the comlink and a broad smile of
relief spreads across Cruise's smarmy face. Shrike looks around
quickly for a solution.

Shrike cleverly jabs at Cruise's conscience, "What is your
opinion on what is about to happen to all of these innocent
athletes?"

Cruise puzzles, "Opinion? Soldiers don't have opinions. We
just follow orders."

Shrike strikes, "Cut the crap Cruise. All the shit you've
been spouting so far, and you have no opinion? You are just a

mindless drone … a pawn? You must have some kind of inner feelings that help guide your course toward beauty and love, or to destroy it. The thing is, pushers like you are so self-righteous. There's tons of self-righteous opinionation out there."

Cruise doesn't follow what she's getting at, so he attempts to crack a feeble joke, "It's an opinionation nation … a nation of opinionation."

Shrike attacks vigorously, "Why do you even bother to make such statements? You're not my boss. You're not the boss of any of us – yet you think you're in charge. You're not! Where do you get off acting the way you do?"

Cruise snidely counters with his primitive understanding of the world, "The man with the gun is the man in charge."

Shrike ricochets, "That's what the man with the gun always thinks."
James and Daniel laugh. Cruise gives an eye cue to one of the commandos who kicks James in the stomach.

Shrike cries out, "Stop!"

Miraculously, Cruise finally senses the relationship, "So, you wanna get in this guy's pants huh?"

Shrike answers with complete directness, "Not *just* that guy's and *not just* get in his pants."

Cruise pushes forward with excitement, "Oh, you like another guy too?"

Shrike states frankly, "Love."

Cruise attempts to comprehend, "You can't love more than one person at once."

Shrike fires back, "*I* can."

Cruise accuses, "You're a mental case."

Shrike takes a breath and lowers her voice to a more reasonable sounding level "Why? Where is the rule? Why does one person have to be with only one other person, … out of fairness? What if two people fall in love with you, … only one is allowed to be happy and the other one must deal with it? Who made it this way and why does it have to stay this way? Can't anyone love anybody; anything?"

Cruise cynically snickers, "Love? You idiot. We don't even waste our time thinking about love. Lohan has never been in love. She don't know what love is; … and Joaquin, … c'mon. Obviously nobody has ever givin' a rat's ass about this loser." Lohan and Joaquin look at Cruise with silent resentment.

Meanwhile, back in Gwen's hideout, an unfortunate servant massages Gwen's corn-ridden feet as she listens to *Achy Breaky Heart* loudly. Occasionally, she turns down the volume to listen in on the commando operation, then back to the blaring, obnoxious music.

Gwen reports aloud, but mainly to herself, "Good, the choppers are flying in and the game is over."

The servant says, "Yes Mam." Averting her glare.

Gwen says, "Oh shut up."

Back on the spectacular-looking mountain, emboldened by the sound of the seven choppers, Cruise smirks with a George W. Bush kindergarten-chimp expression and snaps back with a severe sense of delayed reaction, "Wrong again. You're not going to be doin' much standin' against me when you're tied up in the back of a chopper. Standing, Pfff," he dismisses and disses.

Shrike yells, "When Australopithecines, and *Homo habilis*, *ergaster*, and *erectus* started to walk and run, that precipitated all of the other differences between us and them. Otherwise, we are just like them. Animals belong to this world as much as we do."

Cruise laughs with complete misunderstanding, "Ha. I ain't one of them. I didn't come from no baboon."

The other commandos standing about start laughing in unison, unintentionally sounding like cackling apes. The athletes look at each other and shake their heads with depression and disappointment in the lack of human evolution exhibited.

The starving, parched commandos crack smiles when they hear the helicopters coming in closer. More than medical treatment, most of them are looking forward to drinking water, and having something to eat inside their growling stomachs.

Shrike rips off the old cliché, "It's simple: Winners never cheat, and cheaters never win! When, in any scenario, in any book, or any flick you've seen, has there ever been a clearer line between good and evil?"
Cruise looks at her with a fixed glare, perplexities pounding his cranium walls.

Cruise bristles, "Hey, I'm a grown-up adult man. Don't tell me how I'm suppose tah believe just 'cause yah have some hoity-toity degree. You believe all the wrong stuff you want. I'll believe in what's right ... Jesus our Lord."

Sara laughs to herself again. Shrike was right! Shrike was right during her first big speech, when she said, 'The commandos think we will be heading down, so we will be heading up. They think we are weak, peaceful athletes, but we are the strongest foe they've ever challenged, for we have them beat.' Sara remembers how at first everyone scrutinized and doubted Shrike, and then how quickly she won everyone over.

One of the athletes asked, 'How do we have them beat?' fearing it to be baseless rhetoric.

And Shrike answered, 'We know they are trained commandos with guns, but they don't know what we are. They will be clinging to a precipitous slope, but we will be nestled and hidden in our granite fort. They think we will be easy to catch; we will be impossible to even find. We will have the moral edge, for they are the most impure of the most evil, and we are all good and righteous examples of the absolute best of incorruptible America. We have the psychological edge, because they will be tripping out!'
Sara remembers how righteous and even mushy that first speech struck her, and how the entire crowd seemed to warm and smile like a Hare Krishna cult.

Shrike blustered, 'Whatever they have, we will take from them. Whatever opportunity they expose to us, we will capitalize on to the fullest extent. Protracted war of attrition, surprise attack, mind games, an unpleasantly hostile environment filled with booby traps and tricks over every ledge! Keep in mind; commandos operate in a certain way and use specific protocols. We will operate to the opposite of those protocols.'

A tear rolls down Sara's reminiscing cheek as she brings herself back to the present and now looks over at marvelous Shrike; beaten and down, but still just as full of fight.

Shrike shivers as she levels another volley toward Cruise, "I can't believe even Rambo is smarter than you guys."

The athletes laugh, and one says "You guys are actually dumber than Chuck Norris."

"Shut up!" yells Cruise; Norris being one of his main idols, and one of the main reasons he's programmed so. He spurts, "That's it. Troops, get ready to load!"

A commando calls in landing instructions while another stands on a pointed cliff, giving hand signals. Another one of the soldiers remains on the ground, unable to move.

Lohan bends over him, "Put a spark in your step soldier, let's go."

She kicks him a little, but he won't budge. She leans over, pulls off her glove and examines his face with her fingers.

"He needs medic treatment!" Lohan yells.

Another commando runs over to find that he suffers from hypothermia and treats him with First Aid as quickly as possible.

Lohan snaps the exhausted mercenaries into action one last time, in the belief that the mission is finally over and that they are going back home. They herd the athletes, signal the choppers, collect and straighten gear, etc. While she has a moment when no one watches her, Shrike closes her eyes and calls the animals back one last time as well. In the stillness of the freezing dawn air, Shrike summons up all of her lightning-bolt powers. Her head crackling, her brain still hot, it first sounds like a beat. It sounds like ancient African bongos in a far off jungle. Shrike concentrates more deeply and falls into a trance like state. It's heartbeats! Animals' heartbeats! The heartbeats of all of the animals in Yellowstone. As she calls each animal, they resist her. It's as if they have seen enough of the sick humans and their destructive violence. Shrike begs, but each animal turns and heads away down the mountain to greener, safer pastures. After an anguish-filled six minutes of telepathing with them, and with the first chopper on the brink of touching down, she uses so much brainpower that she pops a vein in her head and goes unconscious. A commando medic and Sara examine her.

Cruise demands, "The prognosis?"

The soldier replies, "She may die if she doesn't get into a quality emergency room, stat! The altitude must be adding to the effect."

Cruise, can barely hear himself over the grumbling and tumbling of his empty stomach, and flippantly dismisses, "Don't worry; if she ain't fakin' it, Gwen's lab can fix her fine. Load her on my 'copter."

Cruise turns to Lohan and says under his breath, "Don't think we'll be needing any of her body parts anyway … except maybe the brain. She got a mighty pretty face though."

Joaquin jumps in, "Sir, if you're going to throw away the body anyway, ya think I could have it?"

Lohan barks, "God, YOU ARE SO DEPRAVED AND DEPRIVED!"

Jay looks on from twenty-seven feet away and wants to say something, but he can't. He is tied and beaten. He is angry. He feels bad for everyone and everything that has transpired and he wants to strike out at Cruise and Joaquin. Helpless, he knows he can't.

Once a few of the commandos move a little further away, Jay whispers, calling out to Shrike, "Sara, I, I mean, Shrike? Shrike, you okay?"

She doesn't respond. His head falls back against the unforgiving granite with sorrow.

The animals, one-by-one and then dozens-by-hundreds-by-thousands, try to contact Shrike, to no avail. A variety of species: elk and bear, fox and opossum; all stop, then begin lifting their feet up and down nervously. The animals get no brainwave signal from Shrike and this drives them ballistic, sacrificing their own lives wantonly and hitting the helicopters with everything they've got.

First, the eagles come in with the bazooka shells with astonishing accuracy. They drop them from over 10,000 feet, like B-17 bombers. Only one of the shells hits the main rotor of a helicopter, and explodes, taking down the chopper. The other shells hit random spots around the helicopter-landing zone, with three out of four of them exploding. A couple of the nearest helicopter pilots begin to panic, but their dominatrix-like masters keep them flying straight and level.

With no warning whatsoever, mammals and birds appear from throughout the mountaintop. Pikas appear from rocky holes and dart about at full speed, causing rock slides. A flock of several geese and swans fly into a helicopter cockpit. A lynx jumps from a rocky ledge and lands on a tail rotor. Animals of every kind flood in over the commandos like a tidal wave, and now the athletes fight toe-to-toe alongside wildlife in bloody combat. It's a fight WITH nature, not against it. A dozen bison and a few moose ram into 'copters when they land on the ground. The helicopters move, bend, buckle, and break in several places. Grouse, ducks, cranes, herons, and even massive white pelicans dive into the three helicopters still airborne above the melee, and they crash down onto the four 'copters on the ground and start a chain reaction of explosive fireballs! Fuel, munitions; everything goes up in mushroom clouds of flame!

Several ounces short of a pound and full of fury, a vicious, rust-orange weasel, rare for this elevation, comes blasting into the fray, with none other than an even rarer mammal, a wolverine, by its side. They hit the legs of the last two commandos standing guard, with deep, injurious bites into the ankles and lower shins. The commandos cry out in severe, burning pain --- the flame radiating up through the hamstring and into the sciatic nerve. From there, the pain jumps to their eyes; now just sockets full of dry red pain. The adorable assassins run up the men's backs, and with what could only be anthropomorphized as an overwhelming expression of "glee", bite hard on the spinal column; cracking vertebrae.

Still not signal from Shrike!

Another one of the few commandos left on the ground that hasn't either been engulfed in flame or killed by an athlete or an animal, pulls his .45 up to shoot an elk, its antlers tipped with red commando blood. Before he can squeeze the trigger, a magnificent adult bald eagle, its wings flexed like a bodybuilder, stoops down at full speed and nails him with both sets of talons in the face. As the soldier falls onto his back, the eagle clenches its feet into fists and lifts off with the man's face shredded beyond recognition. He wriggles for a second, then goes into shock. Two synchronized swimmers come over to the helpless commando, in perfect synch smash a boulder down onto his forehead. One of the girls grabs his pistol and then turns and shoots a slumped commando in the head. After all of the rapes, no one will be taking any chances, or giving mercy of any kind. The girls duck down flat by the body and look for other commandos to shoot. They see none, so they start rifling through the dead commando's gear. One girl finds his last Clif Bar. She hands it to the other girl, who quickly tears it open, breaks it in half, and sticks one piece in her mouth and the other in her teammate's, her hands busy frisking the corpse.

Cruise spins around to see Jay, of all people. Jay, surprised, puts up his dukes like he wants to take Cruise on in a display of mano a mano fisticuffs for what they did to Shrike and everyone else; but especially for what those creepy bastards did to his beloved Sara. Cruise, .45 in hand, strikes Jay hard across the forehead before he can even react. Jay goes down hard, and in harsh pain. Before anyone can get close enough to help him, the skid of one of the falling helicopters comes sliding down the mountainside and crushing down across his chest. Jay is pinned, but still conscious.

A dazed Lohan gets to her feet after the catastrophic blasts subside. She doesn't know she is fatally wounded, as she looks around for other commandos. She tries to say 'medic', but nothing really comes out, as she teeters like a cottonwood in a gale. Athletes, commandos, and especially tons of animals, slowly stir as they recover from the shockwave of the explosions, the heat, and the nerve-damaging sound. A massive tom turkey blasts into her head on, at full speed, knocking her over some rocks and down into a little gully, where she lands on a sharp stump and pointed rocks, bleeding out. She doesn't possess the strength to get up again.

As the sky darkens markedly from the smoke from the smoldering wreckage, Lohan looks over and sees Joaquin lying on the ground behind a tree, pretending to be dead.
He holds his finger to his lips in a mimed 'shhh'.

With her last ounce of strength, Lohan draws up her weapon and rests it on a knot on a log. She points her pistol's laser sight onto his fly. Joaquin sees the red light and slowly looks up at her.

"See ya in the next life, perv," she quips as she fires.

Joaquin screams like a little girl and grabs his crotch. An osprey comes down through the smoke and takes out Lohan's throat with a fluid sweep. Coyotes and the marten jump the screaming Joaquin and start ripping pieces of flesh off. He turns and falls over a beaver, face first into a porcupine, and goes into petrified shock. The animals continue to tear at him in a hellish nightmare only demons like Joaquin deserve.

When one of the last live commandos lifts his gun to take out an injured Olympian, six ravens dart down in short order, taking turns pecking at the soldier's face and pulling at his gear and straps. These large black birds aggressively stun the commando, who finds himself fighting in a blind panic. A stately bull moose trots up to the commando. The ravens, joined by some raucous robins and a couple of ill-tempered mourning doves, disperse at the very last second; like a firework exploding in all directions. The moose gives him a one-two ram with the head and a hook with the antlers. The battered commando falls to the rocks. The moose steps over his body and tramples him, resembling a macabre soft-shoe routine, but minus the "soft" part. The moose looks up to see Cruise rising to his feet, so he turns and silently vanishes back into the brown tree trunks at full speed.

Cruise stops to scan the dead soldiers, then questions to his God, "Oh man, what did this?"

He hears a peculiar gurgle. He leans in, thinking the noise may be coming from the dying trooper. Instead, Cruise looks up to see the six ravens that initiated the attack sitting smugly in the branches just above head level.

Cruise blurts with fury, "You bastards!"

He raises his weapon and starts taking potshots at the nimble ravens, which twist and dart out of trouble in an instant. His gun then goes 'click click'. Five dozen athletes stand around him along with a huge group of very large, very angry animals.

Strongly sensing the death of so many animals causes Shrike to stir and partially awaken to find everything destroyed and that the athletes have Cruise tied up and surrounded. The heavy guard is mainly made up of wolves and a black bear. A golden eagle and a merlin falcon fly high overhead as an umbrella of protection. Sara gently presses a damp cloth to Shrike's forehead. Shrike shakes off her malaise and goes to turn the tables on Cruise.

After an hour and forty-four minutes of profitless, grilling interrogation, Shrike's eyes narrow like a gyrfalcon as she says, "Look, we are not going to kill you … even after what you have done to me and everyone else, not to mention the hundreds of animals that have died because of you. Just tell us who sent you and why, ---- and walk away a free waron, or come back as our prisoner and rot in jail for life, for no purpose, like the rest."

The commando says, "You are going to have to kill me. You think I'm afraid of dying?"

Several of the girls who had been raped, along with a male gymnast who was also raped, march up and slap Cruise hard. He laughs as they relieve their fury across his despicable face.

Sara says to Shrike, "I thought that would be good therapy."

Shrike nods with disapproval and then pulls down Cruise's pants and grabs his penis in her hand firmly. One of the girls hands her Cruise's own knife.

"You not afraid of dying?" she questions as she presses the knife against his hog and it starts to bleed. She shows great self-control as she refrains from cutting it off.

"Aauuaarrhrr!" Cruise grunts like one of his own victims, then follows by giving out a bellowing howl. Shrike cuts his ropes free while the others brutally grab him and pull him outside of the rocky cave area.

Cruise grits his teeth and growls in pain, "I follow my orders."

Daniel yells, emotionally pained, "What about Jay. A friggin' lounge singer? What did you smash his head in for?"

Cruise snipes back, "He was one of you."

James and Daniel say, "No he wasn't."

Cruise puzzles, "He wasn't? Well, he wasn't one of us."

The cougar moves up to his side and Cruise stands up straight.

Cruise says, "Okay, you won."

He offers his hand to Shrike with honor ... but mainly to pacify the pugnacious pussy.

Shrike says, "You want to touch me? Show me your hands."

Cruise stands frozen like a granite monolith, his hand outstretched like a blade. The cougar stares straight into Cruise's eyes and licks its chops with circular sweeps of its cheese grater tongue.

Shrike calmly demands, "Take off what's left of your uniform."

Cruise strips to his underwear. One of the rape victims pulls his shorts down and off, as spitefully as she can. He stands there in the cold: naked, bleeding, and freezing. One of the athletes slips off her wet sneakers and puts on Cruise's boots. Others don his uniform over their sport suits for a little added warmth. Cruise takes these to be souvenirs of war; victors' trophies.

Shrike says, "Unlike you, I'm not a murderer or a rapist, but, we obviously can't let someone like you go, so I'll give you a fighting chance. Good bye."

James says, sounding a lot more like cautious Daniel, "Ah, you sure you wanna do that?"

Daniel looks on with concern, sounding a lot more like slang-ridden James, "Yeah, don't we gotta, ya know, *off this guy?*"

As Shrike prepares to banish Cruise to the elements, she realizes the folly of her decision.

Shrike says, "Just like those stupid Batman shows, the villains always give the hero a chance to escape. Whenever I have watched shows like that, I've always said 'God, why don't they just kill them to get it over with?' Of course, if they did that, there wouldn't be a show. In my case, I'm not a cold-blooded killer, nor do I believe that a human has the right to take a life; even an animal's life. This guy is no longer a combatant. He is a prisoner. You gonna kill a prisoner?"

A couple of the raped girls want him murdered, but none of them are willing to carry it out.

Cruise blusters, "I'm not worried."

There is a long, confused pause.

Cruise illuminates, "I'm covered. I've got God on my side."

Sara laughs, "You do?"

Shrike says, "How do you know that?" as she scans the carnage and debris smoldering all about; Cruise's entire team and all of his commandeered helicopters in ruins, their innocent pilots dead.

Cruise says with confirmation, "The Lord Jesus is my savior. I shall not want."

The athletes, many of them spiritual, roll their eyes at Cruise's pretzel logic.

Sara tries to clarify, "Wait a minute, God's on your side?"

Cruise parrots like a robot, "I shall not want."

Sara continues, "God's on *your* side, but not *our* side?"

Cruise smirks with self-assured confidence, "You're nonbelievers. I have a huge advantage over you."

Shrike snaps, "You think because you pray, God will help you kill people and animals, and commit vile acts, and let you steal peoples' organs, … because you have God on your side?!" Cruise looks over the incredulous crowd. He is so brainwashed that the thought never occurs to him that he could be wrong. Instead, he plows deeper.

Cruise states, almost in euphoria, "The Lord is my shepherd. You can accept Jesus into your hearts, and he can help you."

Sara says, "Holy shit. You are pretty messed up about religion, rapist."

Cruise laughs through his shivering, "Ha, what if you are wrong."

Sara fights back forcefully, "No, what if *you* are wrong?" They look at each other for a long time. Neither thinks they could be wrong.

Cruise argues minus any sense of rationale, "I have been studying the bible for like15 years! I know a lot of things I know and you don't know a lot of things you don't know. You gotta face reality. More than a billion people across the world have chosen to be saved by Jesus. You can get on board or miss the train."

Nobody bothers to respond at this point. It's too sad. After all that has transpired over the last three days, Cruise still thinks he has God on his side. Sara on the other hand, basically, doesn't really even believe in god; so for her, the whole discussion feels like a primitive digression during time that could be much better spent.

Shrike, completely annoyed now, scats "That's enough of that. Good luck waron."

Popping the religious discussion balloon, Cruise visibly deflates. He gives Shrike a deep, hate-filled stare, for he knows it's impossible to push or pedal any of his bogus mythology here. Then, he smirks and starts heading down the snowy mountain, naked and alone. He's trying to save face. He's trying to make it look like somehow he has won. Cruise climbs down over some boulders and past a bludgeoned commando corpse with remorselessness.

He chides with his back to them in disrespect, "You are letting me go? You idiot. Obviously the good Lord has me covered. You have no idea about my survival skills, my conditioning, *My* training. Do you?! Ha. You fools. I never forget Shrike. I never forget."

Sara mumbles under her breath, "Friggin' hypocrite!"

Daniel says, "Little harsh for a trained professional?"

Sara strikes, "I hate people who use religion for evil."

James opens his eyes widely, "Wow!"

Daniel agrees but takes a different approach, "I feel bad for people like that."

Sara counters, "Don't! The last thing they need is sympathy."

Shrike says perceptively, "People like that live in their own foggy world of confusion. Just imagine the hell he's lived in his whole life, within his own mind."

Daniel protests, "But ya still can't let him just get away?"

Shrike says with a totally straight, understated face, "He won't. I shit you not!"

Psychological jabbing? Blind Fanaticism? Bogus constructs?

Chapter 8

Who Gets Through?

As the bold sun rakes high into the visceral western sky, a giant sigh of relief in the form of a silent hush permeates the frigid air. For the first time since the discovery of the hijackers on the plane, the athletes feel like they can let their guards down. Every species of bird and mammal appears to be represented, as they lick, preen, and groom each other in a nurturing, medicinal way. The mountain goat appears with Tara clinging to its back. The healthy animals and athletes line up the dead: The few athlete and animal carcasses on one side, and the long line of dead commandos on the other. It's a morbid scene: Elegant swans and geese laid out next to dead volleyball and high jump heroes; the commando side looking like typical war zone footage from Nam, Guadalcanal, or wherever.

When the smoke from the smoldering wreckage finally starts to dissipate, everyone can see Sara on her knees, crying over Jay's dead body. He survived for a few minutes after the crippled helicopter fell upon him, but now lies expired. Wolves, coyotes, and a few deer nuzzle against her firmly and lick her tears with commitment. They force Sara up to her feet. She smiles at the loving animals and wipes their salivas from the top of her cheeks.

Sara mentions with a cry in her voice, "You really are loving animals, aren't you."
Shrike surveys the scene, in excruciating pain.
Sara puts her hand on Shrike's shoulder and says, "What a waste. What a waste of everything, … for nothing, … just like every war humans ever fought anywhere."
Sara allows herself to think of Jay again, just for a moment.
Shrike painfully stretches her arm over Sara's shoulder for a solid hug, "You said it sister."
Daniel and James come walking over; their body language reflecting relief.

Daniel says, "Oh, so if women ran the show there would be less of all of this?"

Sara says, "Indubitably!"

Daniel says, "What about Thatcher? Don't forget Thatcher. I wouldn't say Gwen sounds like a doll either."

James says, "There you go, like Shrike says, proving the rule with the exception."

Everyone laughs.

Suddenly, a harsh voice crackles over a helicopter radio that's still working. Everyone freezes to listen for a second.

"Cruise. Cruise. Goddamn you. I know you can hear me. Cruise! Over!"

No one knows what to make of the raspy chimney of a voice.

James jokes, "Oh Cruise … your grand mommy is calling for you."

Everyone laughs hysterically until Shrike shushes them down again.

"Cruise damn you. Jesus in heaven above – will you pick up? Are the choppers there yet?"

James says, "Let's answer her back and fuck with her. I can do a good Cruise voice."

Everybody snickers as they rest their tired bodies against the living furniture made of elk, black bear and plenty of canines. Foxes keep running around with their happy tails wagging, and licking every face they get a chance to.

Daniel says, "No, even better, let's use the 'copter radio to call for help."

Shrike says, "Yeah, let's try it right now."

Everyone springs into action, only to find that the fire has destroyed practically everything, and that there is no way to transmit. All they can do is listen to the painfully-sharp voice of Gwen.

Most of the athletes become annoyed with it, but James and the BMXer have a good laugh.

Gwen rambles, "Cruise, if you don't answer me, you, you, you know you are going to be more than fired!"

James spouts, "Oh man, I wish I could respond to some of this shit. This is golden."

The mischievous men high-five each other immaturely, while many of the other athletes and the river otters just chuckle. Jays and nutcrackers spring up about five feet off the ground and back down, over and over again. They look like they are just having fun.

Shrike says, "I wish we could let the animals run things. I shit you not! They really know how to strike a balance. We don't. We are too greedy and excessive. Animals will be decadent when they can, be we've made it so we can be decadent all the friggin' time."

Sara blurts, "And that's wrong!"

Shrike looks at James, then Daniel, with deep love in her eyes for both.

Sara says to Shrike, "Bit of a sadist there aren't you? You're going to break the birding guy's heart, and these two guys' hearts?"

Shrike flashes the lucky men with a beautiful, broad smile, then to everyone's surprise, says the opposite of what one would expect from reserved and serious Shrike, "I want to dominate and make you say 'please' and 'sorry' to me". Then she whispers, as an aside, "And make you cum."

Both men feel instantaneously sucked back into Shrike's "Venus Flytrap".

Sara is nothing less than amazed and can only utter with astonishment, "Wow. Wow."

Shrike laughs heartily in Sara's face and spews, "You either gotta stop pretending that you don't like it or start pretending that you do."

Suddenly, the athletes brace as they hear another helicopter echoing against the shear rock faces. Animals jump to their feet and many birds take to the air. The smoke from the burning helicopter wreckage acts as the perfect beacon. As the chopper turns the corner and drops into the smoke and wounded, everyone breathes sighs of relief at the sight of the Search &

Rescue team logo emblazoned along the fuselage, and with the female track cyclist on board, waving from the open door. The animals notice that they receive no warning signals from Shrike and return to their respective perches and bed-downs. Some of the wounded animals lift their heads up to look, then rest them gently back on the ground.

At last, the 70-odd surviving athletes are saved.

As a steady stream of rescue 'copters airlift the most wounded athletes and animals to local hospitals, Shrike turns to say goodbye and thanks to the animals in the forest. She stands silently like a statue. The cougar runs up and licks her face and then saunters off up the rocky slope. The owl kisses Shrike's nose with its dry little tongue, coughs up a pellet as a present, which drops to her boots, then flies straight up high into the evergreens for a nice view. The marten scurries down a tree, up Shrike's pant leg and into her arms. Shrike hugs the marten for a long time, up under her bruised, scratched chin. All of the animals in the park, near and far, feel as if Shrike hugs them with thanks. The animals rub against each other affectionately, lick each other's wounds, and give off loud calls throughout Yellowstone. She releases the marten, which scurries up a tree and into a hole.

Shrike bursts into tears, and climbs into the last helicopter. Everyone has taken off, except for the coroner's, FBI's, and Park Service's investigators. Military and National Guard helicopters arrive at the scene and monitor activities while they take some photos for the record. Finally, the Green Berets arrive. One of the choppers touches down while the rest hover.

The senior Green Beret yells over to the National Park Service Ranger, "Hey, too little too late?"

The Ranger responds with cliché, "Nothing to see here folks, except, … Shrike says there's a hijacker tied up in a cave back in there."

The Green Berets spring into action and find the cave in a matter of minutes. Before they get too close, the bear removes the gag with its knife-like claws and takes off out of the cave safely.

The hijacker calls out, "Hey. Hey, can somebody hear me?"

The Green Berets see the bear running up the slope and out of sight. They remove the injured hijacker from the cave and take him back to their chopper, and make a beeline for their base.

In the nearby towns and local cities, once cleared by medical staff, the athletes check into hotels for showers and some quick sleep. After less than three hours, the athletes are back on the move for their rendezvous with another C-17 to meet the President. Exhausted and with absolutely no fear of hijackers, the athletes sleep in each other's arms like babies; much closer and more connected than they were on their first flight experience.

Hours later, pacing back-and-forth in her dim loveless lair, Gwen takes a hard shot of whisky and sings along limply to a *Donny and Marie* song, then pounds her fist as she watches the Olympians' presidential photo shoot go off without a hitch on live network television. CNN, Al Jazeera; everyone is covering the miraculous story of pure good's triumph over incredibly horrific evil. It's like V Day in Europe in 1945. People celebrate all over the world. Bitter babble and grunting groans gush from Gwen's mouth in such twisted phrases that no one from any language could discern them, and yet, her body language speaks volumes. Only deep, psychotic pain twists one that violently.

She listens to the voice-over from the newscaster as she watches the flickering images in anger, '… and this joyous occasion may have never taken place. What a scathing indictment of humanity: Taking peoples' organs!'

The other commenter states, 'Nest parasitism is just as cruel; kicking out the young and raising somebody else's.'

The first commentator argues, 'Yah, but we are humans. We should know better.'

The second commentator responds, 'There are a lot of sick, mental people out there, … quick to beep their horns at you or call you a name. Who are the people on the street out there yelling 'dick' and 'learn how to drive' at each other? Certainly not me.'

The first commenter surmises, 'Bottom line is, just 'cause people might be filthy rich, they still got to be responsible and intelligent about what they do with it, because it effects society. It's like social responsibility.'

And the second blurts, kind of thinking aloud, "Yeah, maybe there is some way to get the sick and evil rich to give up their greed and take a vow of poverty, for the good of humanity, and I guess nature; by putting their money in the hands of people who can use it to do the most good, not evil."

Gwen can't take it and convulses like Joe Cocker, "Dratsss --- Foiled again!" she yells, smashing her beloved ceramic statue of Gene Simons (from *KISS*) onto a porcelain antique vanity top, marring it indelibly and instantly rendering it as worthless as her ideas. "The only fools to take a vow of poverty are those who can afford to do so!" She yells on the top of her lungs, "You hear me! YOU HEAR ME!"

Her voice echoes in the vacuously cavernous mansion of empty loneliness. Her servants are gone.
All gone.

Gwen looks around for a moment in her solitude, her words still ringing in her ears. No one is listening to her. No one cares what she has to say or what her plans or demands are. Shrike has two guys in love with her and Sara had a guy that she just met who was willing to die for her; but Gwen, … Gwen stands alone. A true, independent, rugged individual go-getter, self-proclaimed red-blooded American who doesn't need anybody or anything … or any love. She wants to live alone, if one calls that living. She wants to be alone.

Gwen says to herself in a low resolve, "Wait. Wait until my Teacup Micro Pigs come out on the market. I'll make billions by monopolizing the little porker market. Get it? Little porker?" She chuckles a little with a husky Joan Rivers haw.

With no servants to respond with their forced laughter, her ideas don't sound so funny or brilliant anymore.

Staring straight forward with intense anger, Gwen says, "I'm not done yet. I'm not done. Not by a long shot. The prom. Three boys. All rejected me. I had the gumption to ask three. Three! After being rejected by the first one, I, I just kept going, like an idiot ... to be embarrassed again and again. I demand attention. I will command attention. Cruise? Cruise? Get your ass back here fast Cruise. I'm going to get them back. I'm going to hurt, and get them all back. I'm gonna get those athletes ... especially Shrike!"

Legitimate transport? Overwhelming connection? Disgruntled depression?

Chapter 9

A Grizzly End

A ceremony with pomp, circumstance, and whatever else doesn't fall under either of those two headings, ensues, in which Shrike receives a medal from The President to the roar of the crowd. Shrike smiles. Everyone thinks it's so nice to see her smile, and really beam with joy and pride. She then boldly kisses her two boyfriends: The thin diver and the long-legged hurdler, whom, both in love with her, maintain that they will stay open to the current relationship situation.

When Shrike tries to step down from the podium, a reporter knocks Shrike ajar. The reporter looks remarkably like Gwen. Sara rushes to her aid and pushes the reporter aside.

The reporter stumbles, regains her balance, and probes forward with a question, "Are you trying to make some kind of profound statement about love?"

Everyone eyes the rambunctious reporter carefully, but it turns out to be coincidence. She really is just a reporter who looks a lot like Gwen.

Shrike laments, "Not trying. If you want to make a statement out of it, that's up to you. Though I love them both, I remain conflicted."

The reporter presses, "Do you feel like what you are doing is wrong?"

Shrike smiles and thinks for a moment, then says, "That my true love is wildlife?"

Shrike's former boyfriend, the birder who has returned from Peru, goes up like he wants to either confront or hug Shrike, but instead, he cowers and backs off like a bird nerd and sheepishly walks away. He looks like he is going to cry, but then he suddenly hears a bird, gets excited, forgets Shrike, and goes after the little warbler.

The President begins his speech: "*This is a day of triumph, and, a day of mourning. These brave athletes, with the undaunted leadership of just a regular person like you and me, a woman, ..."*

The President is forced to pause because of an explosive outburst of applause and cheers.

He continues, with a smirk, *"A, ... a woman."*

The crowd goes nuts again.

He says, *"An ordinary worker. Not a hero. Against insurmountable odds, and let me say this; let me say this: For every one or two crooked, twisted, bad commandos out there, there are a hundred good ones, who will fight for right, just like Shrike Tomial and the Olympians did. How you survived, no one will ever understand, but you did and you are here now. And we know there are some bad people out there, but it is a very small, minute percentage of a great population of great people and future Olympians, achieving and continuing to strive to do great things."*

The audience bursts into tears and cheers.

A chant builds, "Shrike. Shrike. Shrike. Shrike. Shrike!"

The President waves Shrike forward. She stands slowly, takes a step, then stops to look down at a newt wriggling along on the White House lawn. She smiles, senses it, but realizes that the connection doesn't work here. She shares her mind with those that shared the lightning with her. When Shrike steps to the microphone, many of the viewers watch in tears, including those personally at the event and those watching on all forms of media, everywhere. Like an assassination or spaceship disaster, everyone in America will remember where they were when they saw Shrike for the first time, in all her stunning radiance, visible wounds and all. Though she does not like the moniker, the media refers to her as QUEEN OF THE ANIMALS, and that's how The President introduces her.

Shrike stares out over the huge mass of people --- 'the anonymous flock,' she thinks for a second.

A crowd member yells, "Way to go. Way to go Shrike!"

The crowd chants, "Shrike, Shrike, Shrike! Sssssssshhhhhhhhhhhrrrrike."

Shrike looks around and says humbly, "Once you've ah, connected with the animals; you really see how much work needs to be done on humans. Lots. Lots and lots. Finally, I just want to say that some people may feel solemn, or depressed, or some other thing about all of what happened. I say, 'you have to be able to see the comedy in the tragedy!' How foolish. How ridiculous a figure Gwen represents: for trying to do things the way she does them, and for having those kinds of ideas in the first place; and secondly: The idea that even the top commandos with the best training and equipment can simply do whatever they want whenever they want. I call that Rambo-itis. Might usually doesn't make right. Think about it. What a foolish, arrogant, wasteful, and damaging enterprise to undertake. You have to laugh at the hubris of the whole idea from the beginning. Maybe super-rich people should be forced to take a test to see if they are smart or moral enough to keep their fortunes. If not, then they should study quickly and prove that they can handle it, or pass the dough on to someone who can do really great things with it, especially for the benefit of the other creatures on the planet. Our world can handle stupid poor people and smart rich people, but not stupid rich people. Stupid and rich is the worst combination on Earth. Also, all of this bullshit about computers and artificial intelligence has somehow duped us into thinking we don't need nature, and animals, and plants and trees. We don't need streams and butterflies. Keep thinking *that* fools. Peace, love, and wildlife will always triumph over war, hate, and weapons of destruction, because the Earth naturally strike a balance. If we take the next step and let computers take over, they will immediately see no value in any number of species on this planet, including and especially meaning humans."

Shrike tilts her head up and looks far off into the distant clouds. Tears start rolling down her face. Relief. Exhaustion. Everything and all, at once.

Daniel and James each take an arm and parade her off stage and out of sight. Sara approaches quickly with consternation, and a bit of jealousy.

She squawks, "Looks like you are gonna try to make it work, the three of you?"

Shrike nods yes. The men smile with confident approval.

Sara chuckles, "Well. Looks like you finally kicked the bird watcher thing."

Shrike says, "It's weird; for the first time in my life I feel like I am truly in love. We never even talked about him and he never came into the picture. I feel whole now and that's all a past that doesn't exist anymore."

Daniel says, "Hear that? I love that sweet song."

He refers to a bird in the top of an oak tree.

James says, "What, the purple finch?"

Daniel says, "Oh my god, you know which species that is? No way."

James says, "Yeah. I am a birder. I'm a lister. I have a life and a count list."

The men shake hands and walk ahead of Shrike and Sara.

James says, "I got my first Townsend Solitaire the other day outside of Boulder."

Daniel, "Nice."

James, "Yeh."

D, "In town?"

J, "No, out by The Flatirons."

Shrike quips, "I sure can pick 'em" and rolls her eyes as Sara laughs and the rapid-fire exchange accelerates, with everyone walking off joyfully into the bright moonlight.

A million miles away in the gloomy cold and raw darkness, crawling on his hands and knees down a sharp, loose precipice, Cruise, the last remaining commando, begins to hallucinate. First he feels a warm presence and the soft touch of a pious hand on his quivering shoulder. He turns to see none other than Jesus.

"Hello Jesus, my savior. I knew you wouldn't forsaken me," Cruise stumbles.

Jesus replies shamefully, "Oh no you don't Cruise. You've been a bad, bad person."

Cruise tries to ask 'wha …' when the image disintegrates like dandelion seeds flying off in the breeze. He thinks he hears Gwen's voice, but then no; it's Shrike's voice. Back in the unnamed peaks of Yellowstone, wolves howl in every direction, but down here in the lower elevations, Cruise is so alone in the desolation. Where are the snarling wolf packs? Cruise rustles up the energy to crane his body up to scan the skies. Not a raven. Not a raven. After their incessant badgering and blaring, Cruise doesn't even have the comfort of a corvid.

He crawls on, trying to make his way down to the lower elevations in the pitch-blackness. Frostbite and hypothermia dance about his hollow, soulless shell of a being. His head droops. His eyes? Practically closed. He crawls onto a flatter slope even though it would be easy for him to stand. He is losing the will to care. If a cougar jumped him right now, he would welcome the swift efficiency of the neck crush. But his desire to survive, to live on to hurt others, still persists somewhere in him somehow, and drives him onward. Most of his obsessive thoughts consist of how he will serve retribution on Shrike; like damnation's holy revenge on her for the dishonor she has caused him.

Cruise yells to the pointed peaks, "She even refused to shake my hand! No one, no one raised up right in The Carolinas would display such uncouth rudeness. Nope. Damn Yankee. I bet she's a damn-it-to-hell Yank."

He reaches a ledge with an overlook, when he suddenly feels overcome with warmth again. He stretches his aching body out on the freezing ground and rolls over to see Jesus kneeling above him like a shepherd tending a lamb.

"Jesus, I served you my whole life. Help me."

All knowing, Jesus calmly states the facts, "You've never served anyone but yourself and your own beliefs. You are a selfish man who screwed up."

Cruise cries, "No Jesus. NO! Heavenly father. Talk to your son. My soul is saved. I never hurt my brother. Why have you forsaken me?"

Jesus explains, "Cruise, forsaken you? You forsook yourself when you turned your back on your own brothers by becoming a violent religious zealot. You forsook yourself when you turned your back on nature, and animals, ... and love. You turned your back on everything I've ever stood for. Nothing but your own personal greedy gratification drives you, and Gwendolyn. Greedsters don't get into heaven, and you of all people should never be telling *anybody else* to pray. Thy will be done, and I shit you not."

For a second, Cruise feels the sensational heat coming off of the halo, then the Christ figure vanishes again.

Cruise begs, "No. No. Please come back."

The dejected commander brings himself up to stand, like a beaten mass of bones and sinew. After hours of suffering in freezing conditions and blistering wind, there, on the mountain, Cruise looks down to see tourists a few miles below, playing with flares as they wind down the grassy slope, serpentine. As the night sky descends into a deep black, the drunken loudmouths in the nearby lodge cheer and toast the beauty of the exhibition, while others regale over the news reports of the defeat of the commandos and the safe return of most of the Olympic heroes. Cruise, his arms frozen against his naked chest in a constricting, desperate self-hug, gazes down at the glowing trail mesmerized, but feels nothing but spite.

He thinks to himself, 'Who has ever hugged me? Really hugged me? I can't remember my mother hugging me. Nobody ever called me. My own brothers never even called me once their whole lives. Nobody ever cared about me, or talked to me.'

He holds his breath while he listens to the nimble hum of revelers; who unlike Cruise and Gwen, are people who enjoy, love, and embrace life, and All it has to offer; for the good of all. For the good of ALL! Cruise doesn't get it.

Cruise mutters to himself with quaking fury, "Love? You gotta be kiddin' me. There's no love you idiots. Love! Stupid people. I fuckin' hate people!"

Cruise suddenly feels a presence for the third time, as if someone stands next to him. A sort of being or spirit ---- a big, heavy, perceptible presence; and weighty; very weighty, sends a chill down his spine. This doesn't feel like Jesus this time. He feels heat. Cruise turns to see the same grizzly he had tried to shoot that first night, standing over him on its two Sequoia-like trunks for legs. At first he can't tell if it's another apparition, so he touches the fur under its arm and trembles in terror under a steamship-like horn of a roar. Like the pussy he really is, crap runs down his exposed, pale leg. In one merciful swipe, the bear takes him out with a right hook that cracks his skull and breaks his neck. It's too good of an instant end for a "human" like Cruise, but que sera sera. The deed is done and the wicked witch is dead.

The grizzly sniffs the carcass. That's all Cruise is now, just another carcass like all of the troops Cruise lead to their foolish deaths. The gargantuan bear stands on its massive hind legs again, and bellows an incredible roar of finality. Thousands of creatures from all over the park rain in with floods of calls, roars, squeaks, and howls.

Way back in D.C., Shrike feels a shiver go down her spine. She flinches, and both of her lovers look down to her from each side. She breathes to relieve her tension. Resolution! They don't know how or understand why, but the men know too, and also slouch back in their seats in contented relief. Cruise will never bother anyone ever again, . . . but what about Gwen?

Shrike mumbles in a low and contemplative hush, "Makes ya think though,... , if the animals did unite, could unite, how we could use them in a way that could change the world! I shit you not!"

The men nod, "Let's get a team going."

"What are we waiting for?"

Outrageous Waste? A Grizzly End? Unpredictable future?

Fin

****

Praise for Drats and his awesomely entertaining book:

"Nothing less than the dawning of a new age. Drats has created another deliciously dangerous character in Shrike."
-- Newsweak Mag.

"… high energy, enthusiasm and good humor."
-- Maximilian C. Executor of The Wired Magazine

"The least pretentious author ever!"
-- Peter Pennypiper, PhD, Occidontal College

" . . . a fine job." "well organized" "easygoing but highly informative …"
-- Ruth L. Park, Natural Kaypop Service Center

" . . . evoking images of schizophrenic sea monkeys on acid."
-- Libby Molin, Critic, Music Connection Magazine

Other works by Drats include:
Rudy the Red Bat *(a children's book that's not childish)*
Rudy the Red Bat *(the live participatory musical)*
Truth Love Extinction *(a screenplay and trippy film)*
Humans Need Three Hands *(an alternative fiction novel)*
Stoned Man: *Harder Than Normal (a surreal screenplay)*
Kapu Problem *(an epic period novel)*

Drats, B.A., M.S.
Exaggerist Edutainment
Auckland, NZ

JayaDrats@hotmail.com

About the Author

Drats created and fronted the Los Angeles avant-garde band **InsectAffect** and sung and wrote lyrics for the industrial progressive bands **Death and Taxes** and **Burning Circle**. While working full-time (usually graveyard shift), he put himself through college and grad school. He became an award-winning video producer, worked as a federal ranger and biologist, and as a naturalist and writer, for over a decade. He holds an MS from one of the top-ten communication schools in the U.S.

What is Fiction?
Join Shrike on her chaotic, quasi-metaphysical journey through our sometimes surreal world, navigating through commandos, friends, co-workers, enemies, nature, and ice and rocks; dodging dangerous bullets from guns, and arrows from Cupid, and most importantly; her search for a real true understanding of wildlife. Can she survive the hijacking, and remote Yellowstone Nation Park?
If she can't, can we?

JayaDrats@hotmail.com

www.ingramcontent.com/pod-product-compliance
Lightning Source LLC
Chambersburg PA
CBHW072224190626
46809CB00016B/464